Alice in Leatherland

Iolanda Zanfardino & Elisa Romboli

BLACK MASK

Created by Iolanda Zanfardino & Elisa Romboli
Written by Iolanda Zanfardino
Illustrated by Elisa Romboli
Covers by Elisa Romboli

Produced by Matt Pizzolo
Production Art by Phil Smith
Published by Black Mask Entertainment, Inc.

ALICE IN LEATHERLAND volume 1. First Printing. JULY 2021.
ALICE IN LEATHERLAND is © 2021 Iolanda Zanfardino & Elisa Romboli. All rights reserved. Produced by Black
Mask Entertainment, Inc. Office of publication: 254 N Lake Ave #853 Pasadena CA 91101. Originally published
in single magazine form as ALICE IN LEATHERLAND no. 1-5. No part of this publication may be reproduced or
transmitted, in any form or by any means (except for short excerpts for journalistic or review purposes) without
the express written permission of Iolanda Zanfardino. Elisa Romboli or Black Mask Entertainment, Inc. All names,
characters, events, and locales in this publication are entirely fictional. Any resemblances to actual persons (living or
dead), events, or places, without satiric intent, is coincidental. Printed in China.
www.blackmaskcontent.com

For licensing information, contact: licensing@blackmaskcontent.com

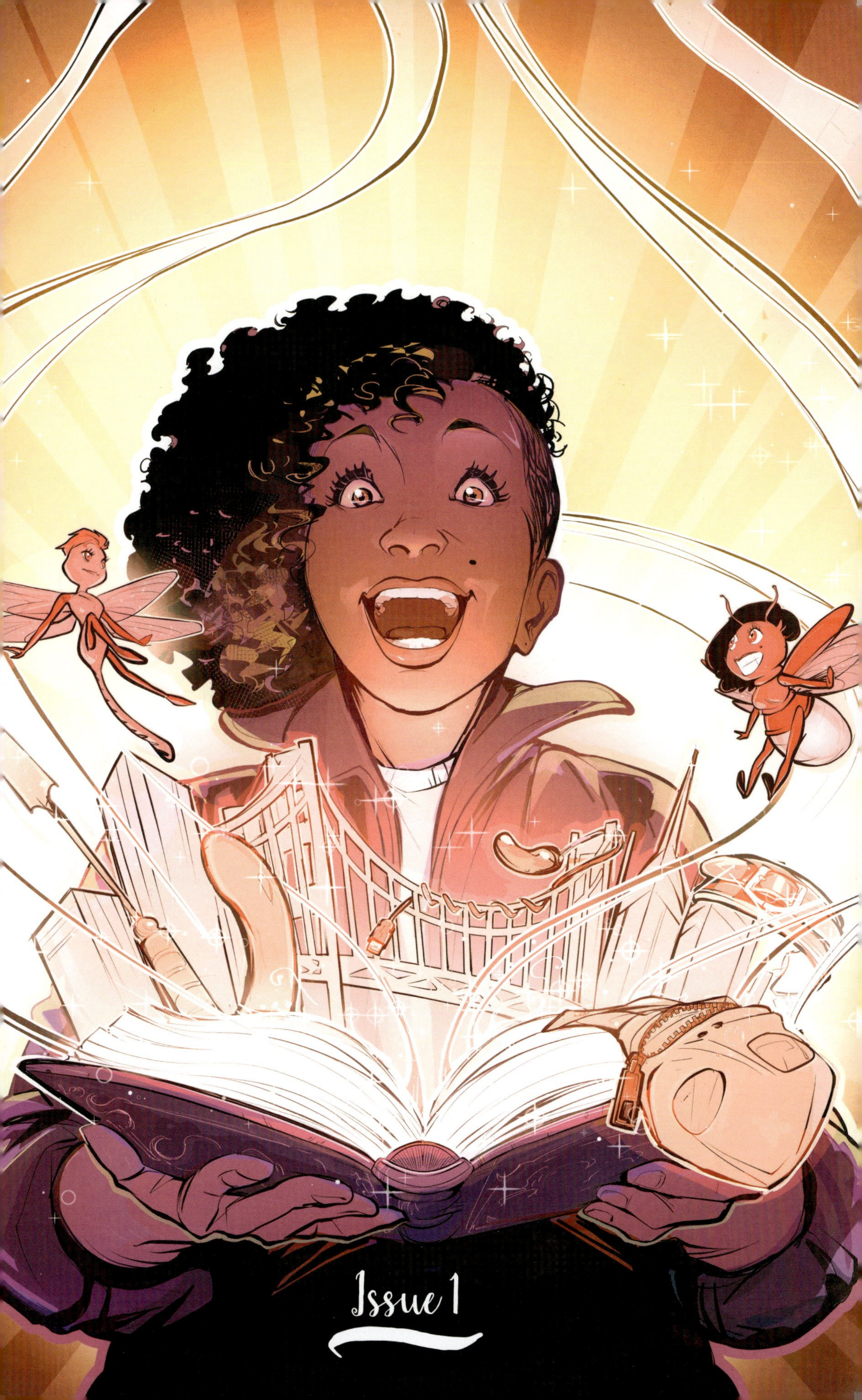
Issue 1

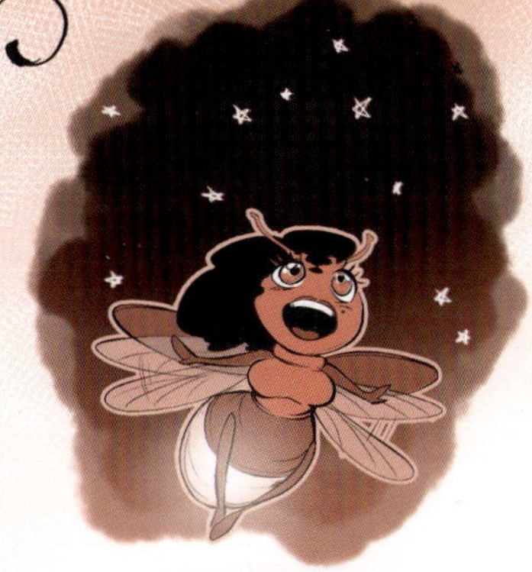

The sweet firefly LOVED the stars,
they looked so much like her!
Every night she used to fly around,
dancing and glowing as much as she could,
trying to get those pretty lights'
attention from so far away.

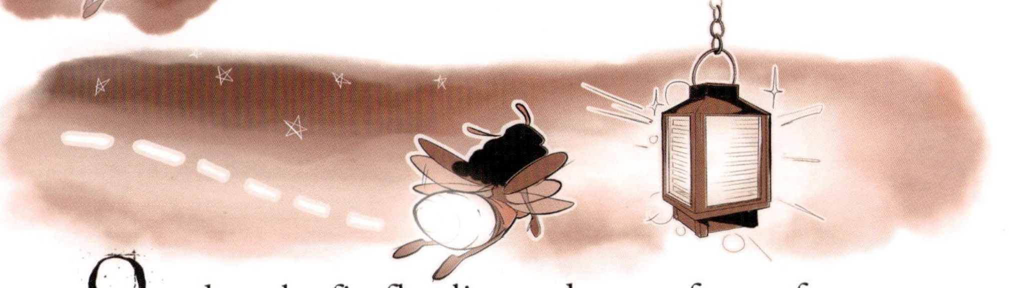

One day, the firefly glimpsed a star from afar
seemingly closer than the other! So big and beautiful!
She really needed to dance with her.

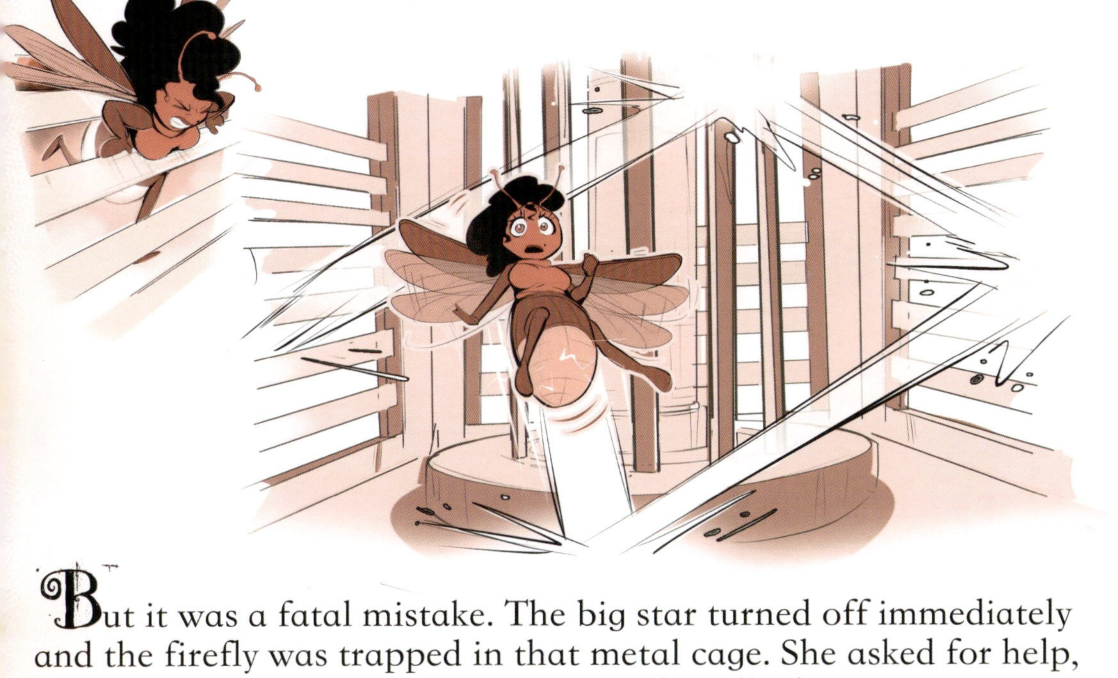

But it was a fatal mistake. The big star turned off immediately
and the firefly was trapped in that metal cage. She asked for help,
trying to get the attention of her friendly distant stars,
but she realized she could no longer glow.

She was alone. There was no way out,
no matter how hard she tried to throw herself
against those walls. No matter how loud
she screamed, there was no one there to save her.
And her light seemed to be off forever.

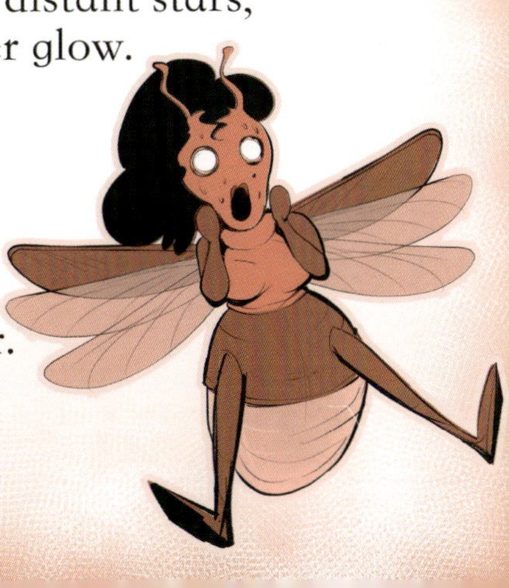

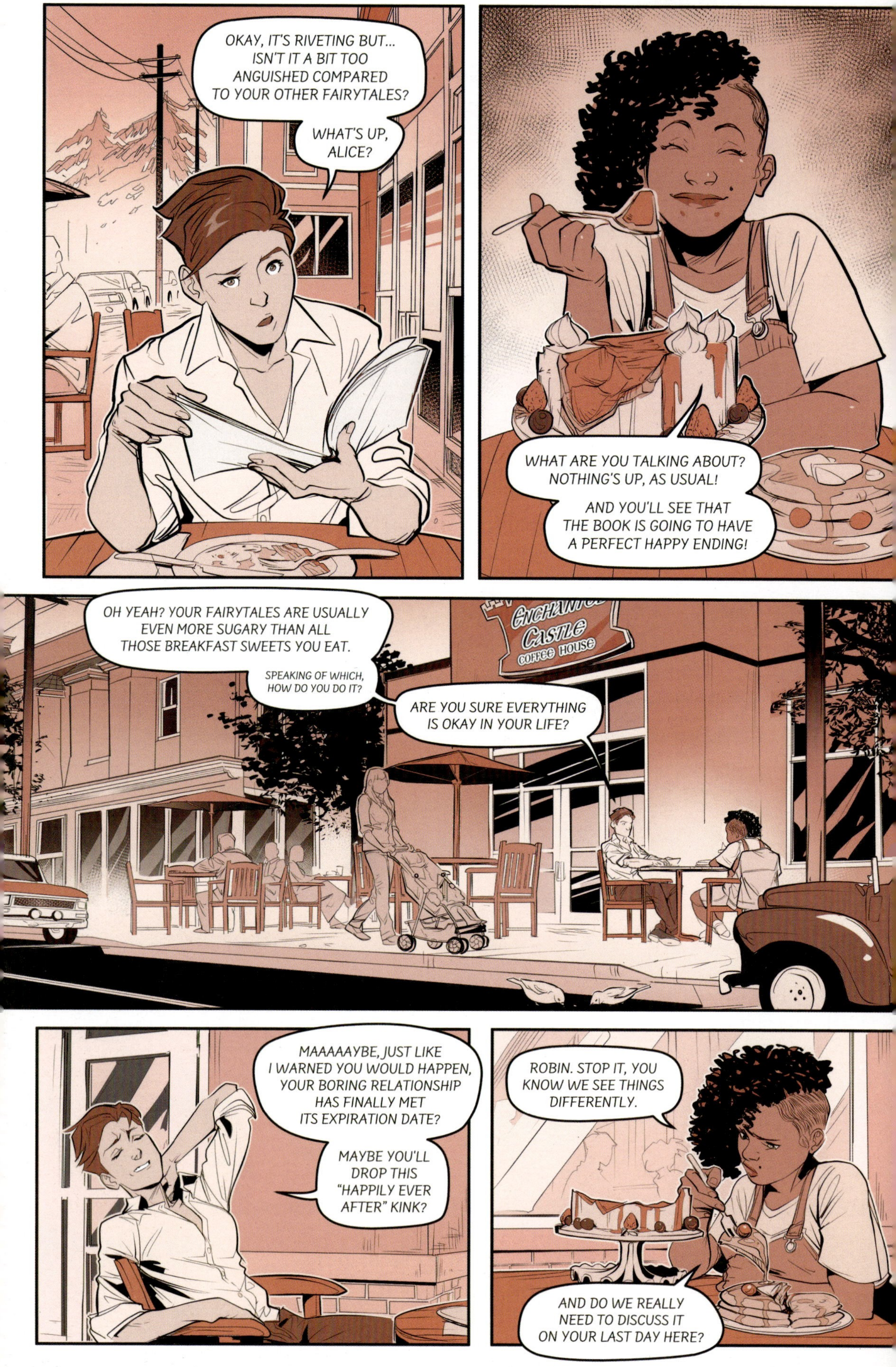
OKAY, IT'S RIVETING BUT... ISN'T IT A BIT TOO ANGUISHED COMPARED TO YOUR OTHER FAIRYTALES?
WHAT'S UP, ALICE?
WHAT ARE YOU TALKING ABOUT? NOTHING'S UP, AS USUAL!
AND YOU'LL SEE THAT THE BOOK IS GOING TO HAVE A PERFECT HAPPY ENDING!
OH YEAH? YOUR FAIRYTALES ARE USUALLY EVEN MORE SUGARY THAN ALL THOSE BREAKFAST SWEETS YOU EAT.
SPEAKING OF WHICH, HOW DO YOU DO IT?
ENCHANTED CASTLE COFFEE HOUSE
ARE YOU SURE EVERYTHING IS OKAY IN YOUR LIFE?
MAAAAAYBE, JUST LIKE I WARNED YOU WOULD HAPPEN, YOUR BORING RELATIONSHIP HAS FINALLY MET ITS EXPIRATION DATE?
MAYBE YOU'LL DROP THIS "HAPPILY EVER AFTER" KINK?
ROBIN. STOP IT, YOU KNOW WE SEE THINGS DIFFERENTLY.
AND DO WE REALLY NEED TO DISCUSS IT ON YOUR LAST DAY HERE?

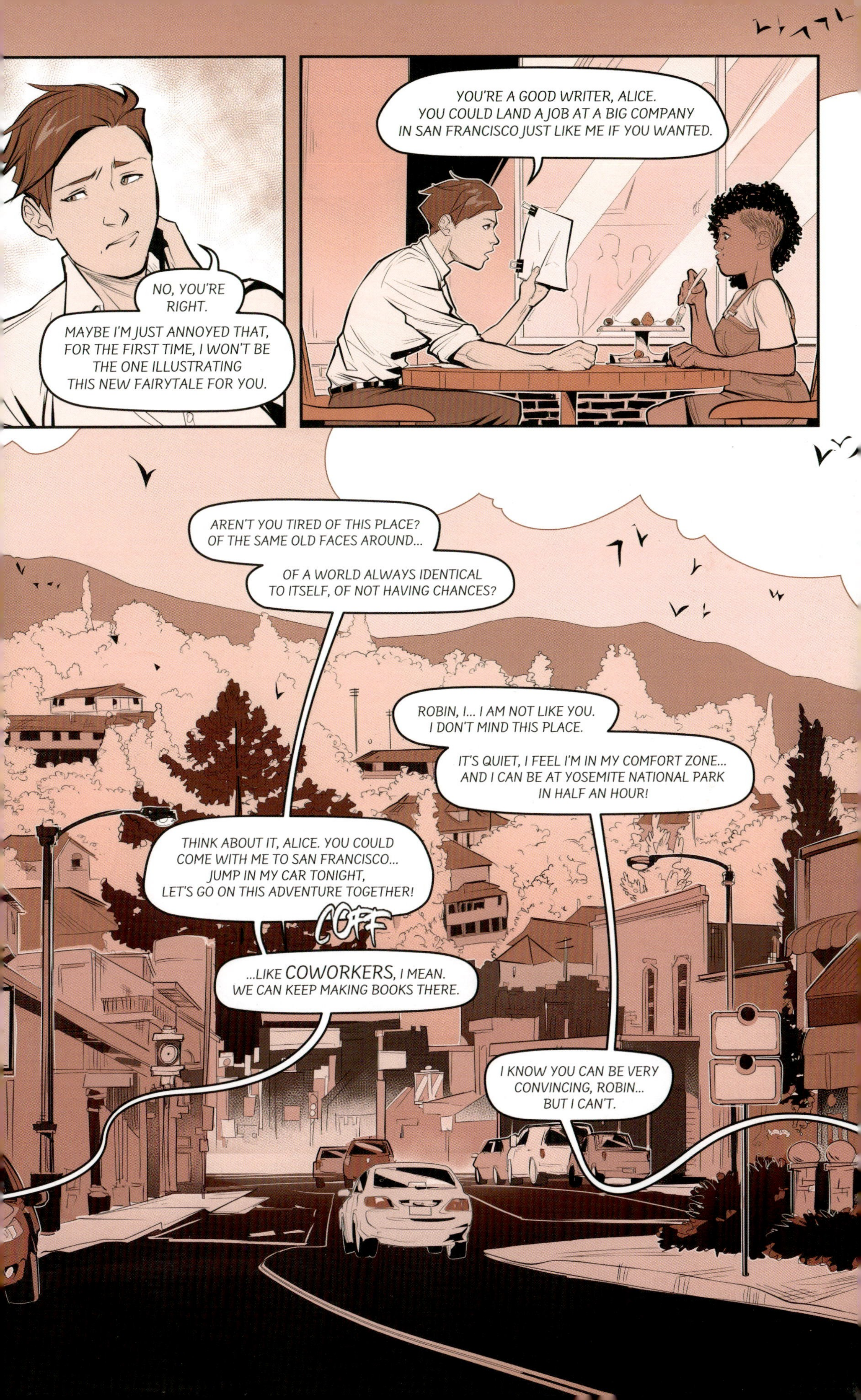
YOU'RE A GOOD WRITER, ALICE. YOU COULD LAND A JOB AT A BIG COMPANY IN SAN FRANCISCO JUST LIKE ME IF YOU WANTED.
NO, YOU'RE RIGHT.
MAYBE I'M JUST ANNOYED THAT, FOR THE FIRST TIME, I WON'T BE THE ONE ILLUSTRATING THIS NEW FAIRYTALE FOR YOU.
AREN'T YOU TIRED OF THIS PLACE? OF THE SAME OLD FACES AROUND...
OF A WORLD ALWAYS IDENTICAL TO ITSELF, OF NOT HAVING CHANCES?
ROBIN, I... I AM NOT LIKE YOU. I DON'T MIND THIS PLACE.
IT'S QUIET, I FEEL I'M IN MY COMFORT ZONE... AND I CAN BE AT YOSEMITE NATIONAL PARK IN HALF AN HOUR!
THINK ABOUT IT, ALICE. YOU COULD COME WITH ME TO SAN FRANCISCO... JUMP IN MY CAR TONIGHT, LET'S GO ON THIS ADVENTURE TOGETHER!
COFF
...LIKE COWORKERS, I MEAN. WE CAN KEEP MAKING BOOKS THERE.
I KNOW YOU CAN BE VERY CONVINCING, ROBIN... BUT I CAN'T.

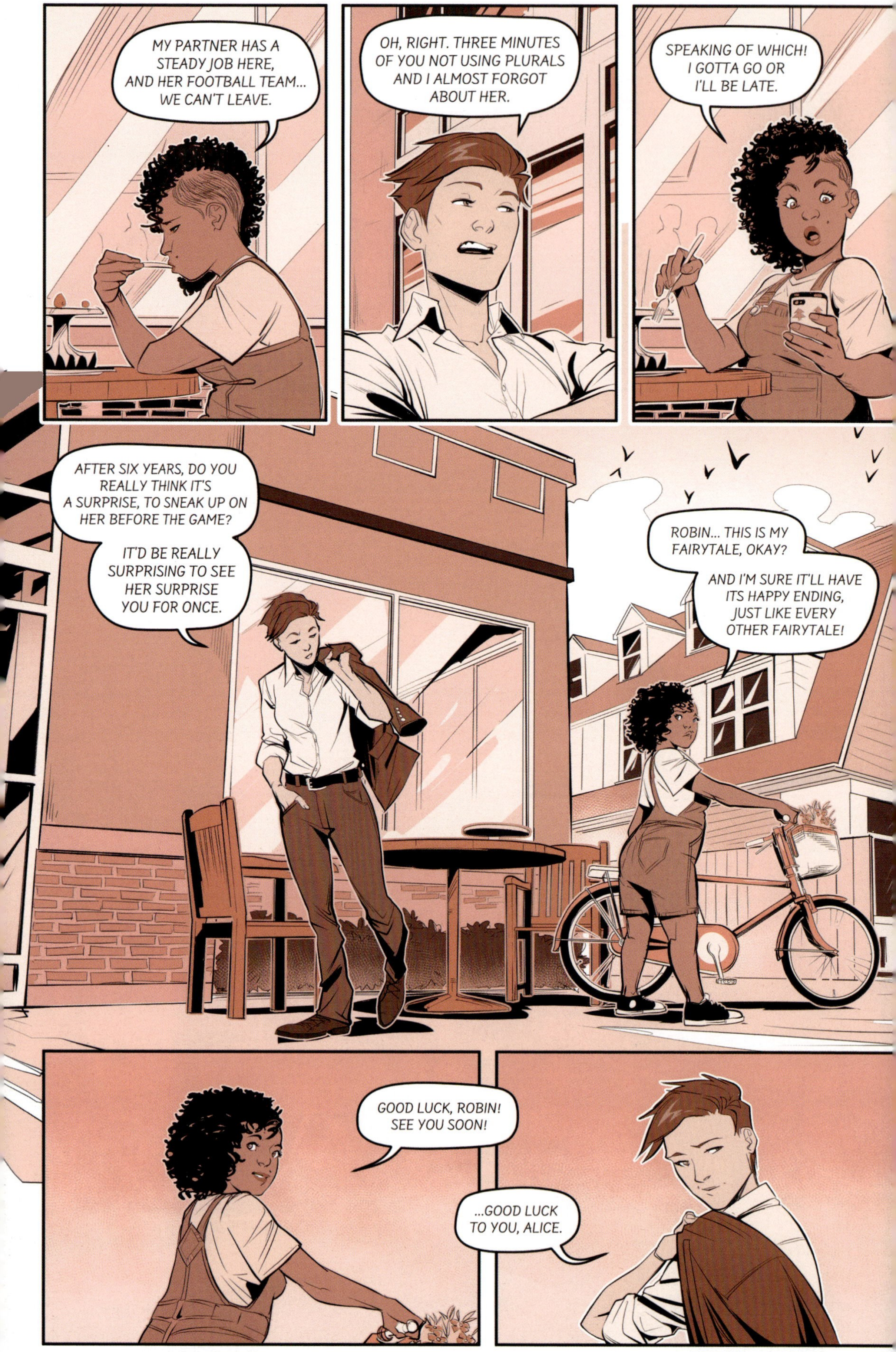

MY PARTNER HAS A STEADY JOB HERE, AND HER FOOTBALL TEAM... WE CAN'T LEAVE.
OH, RIGHT. THREE MINUTES OF YOU NOT USING PLURALS AND I ALMOST FORGOT ABOUT HER.
SPEAKING OF WHICH! I GOTTA GO OR I'LL BE LATE.
AFTER SIX YEARS, DO YOU REALLY THINK IT'S A SURPRISE, TO SNEAK UP ON HER BEFORE THE GAME?
IT'D BE REALLY SURPRISING TO SEE HER SURPRISE YOU FOR ONCE.
ROBIN... THIS IS MY FAIRYTALE, OKAY?
AND I'M SURE IT'LL HAVE ITS HAPPY ENDING, JUST LIKE EVERY OTHER FAIRYTALE!
GOOD LUCK, ROBIN! SEE YOU SOON!
...GOOD LUCK TO YOU, ALICE.

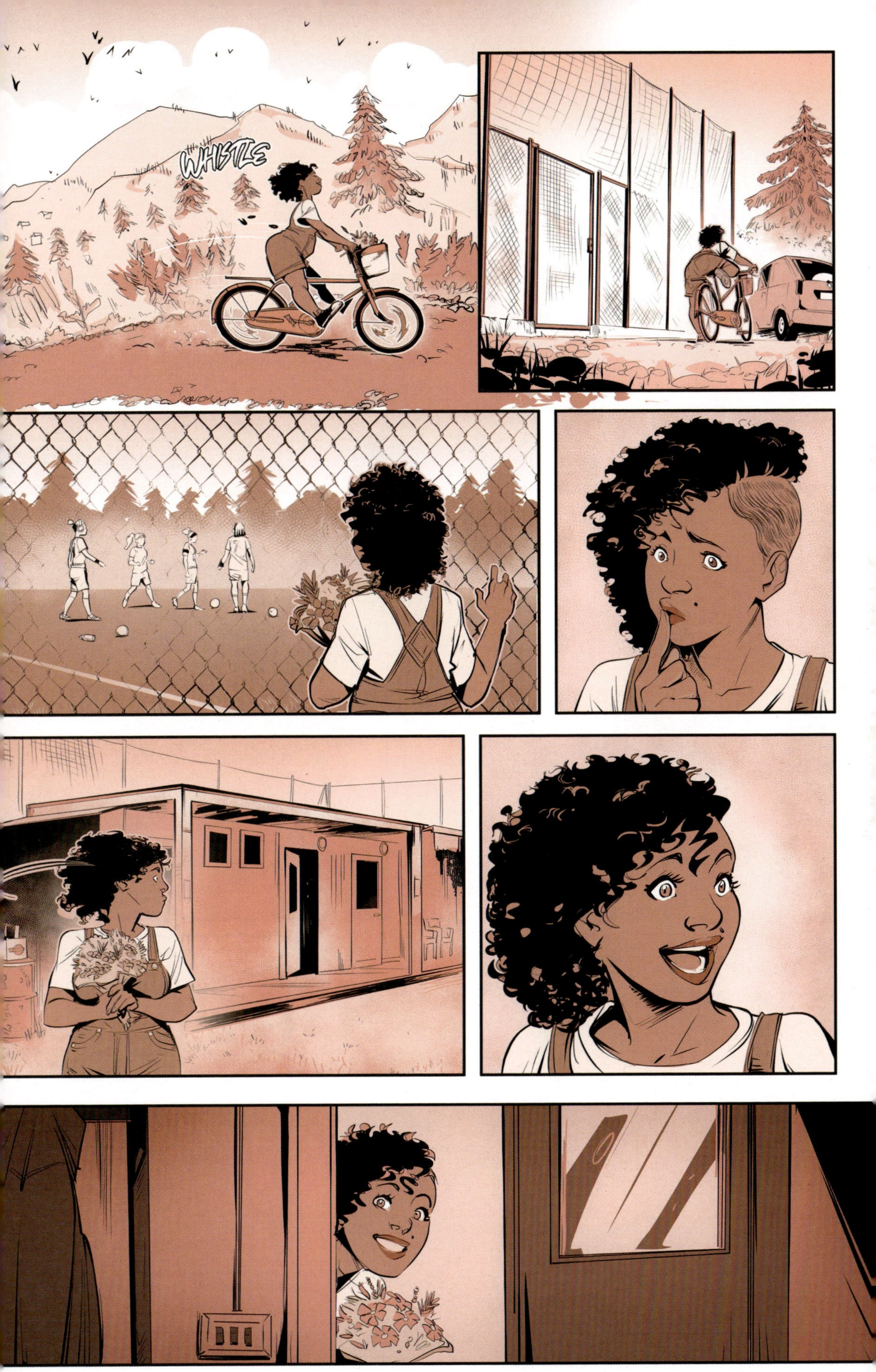
WHISTLE

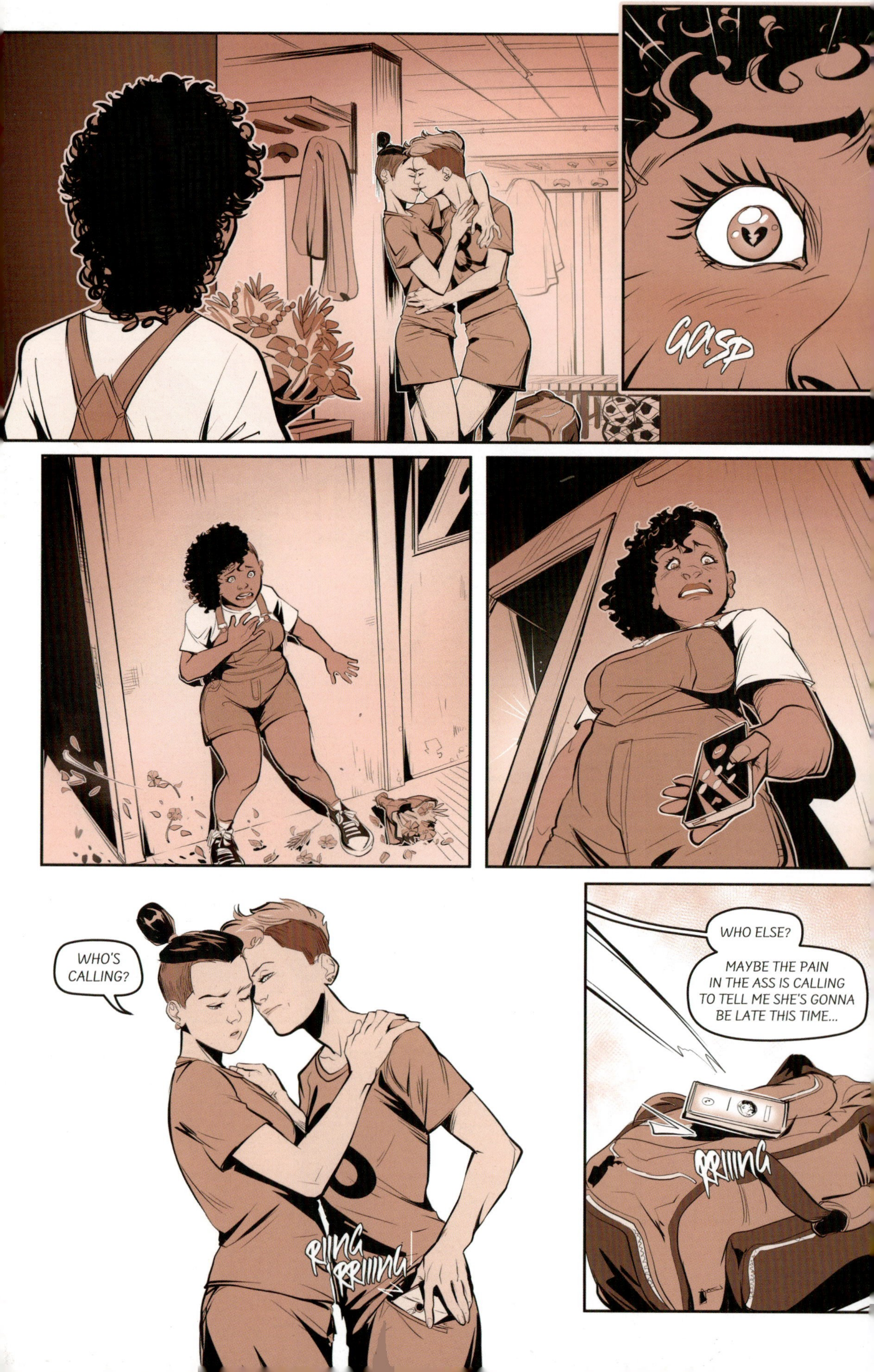
GASP
WHO'S CALLING?
RIING RRIIING
WHO ELSE?
MAYBE THE PAIN IN THE ASS IS CALLING TO TELL ME SHE'S GONNA BE LATE THIS TIME...
RRIIING

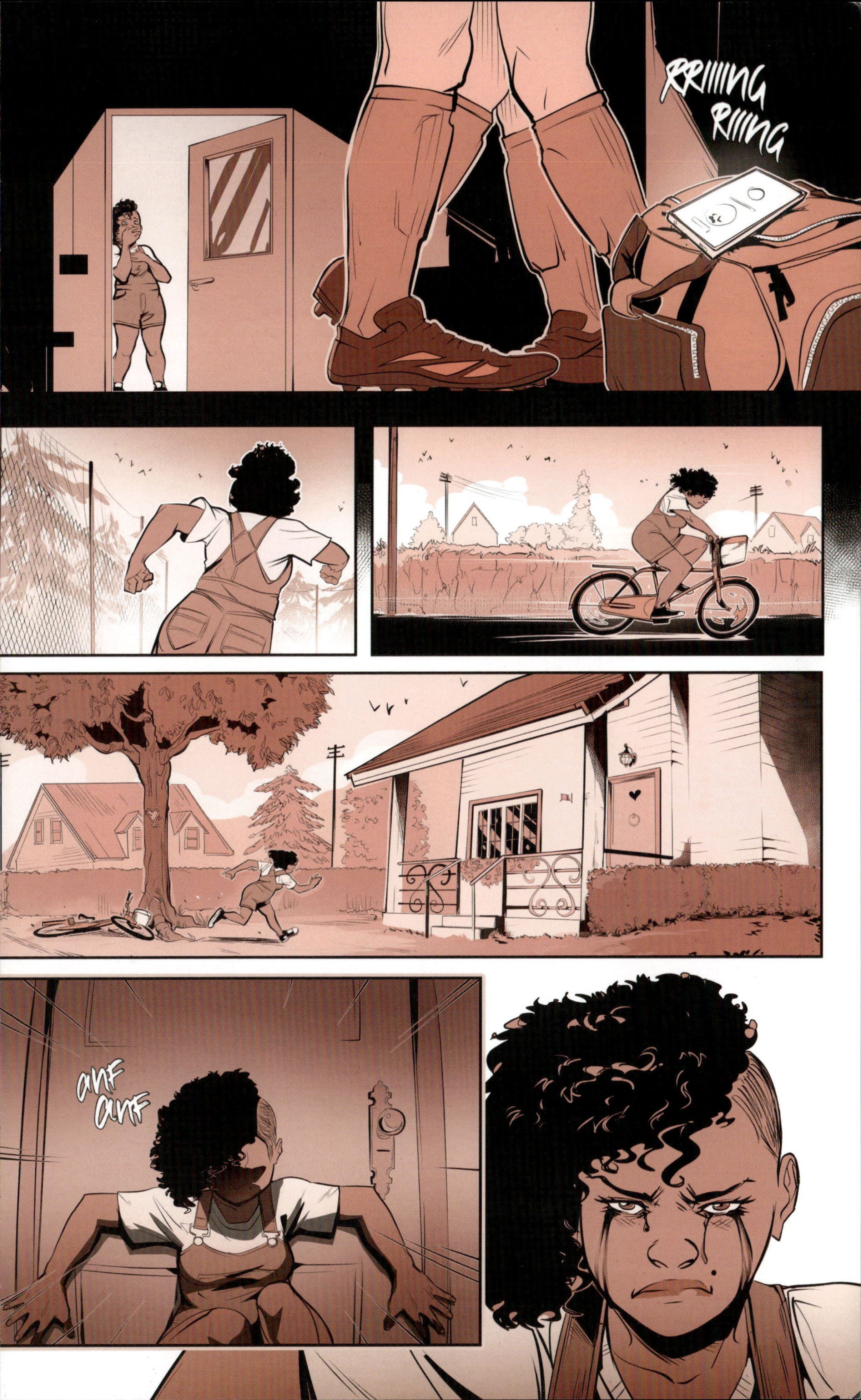
RRIIING
RIIING
anf
anf

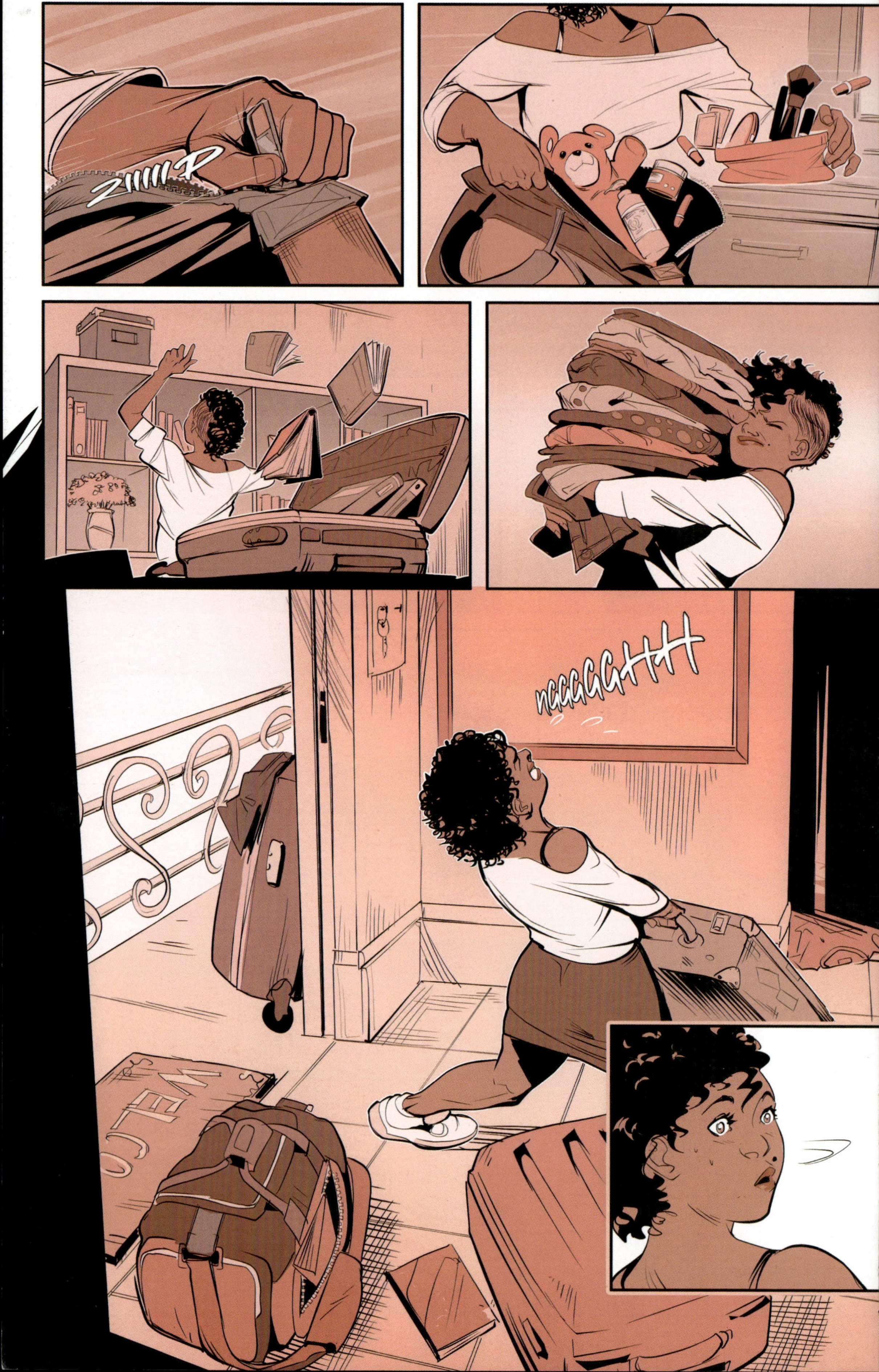
ZIIIIIP
nGGGGGHHH
WELCO

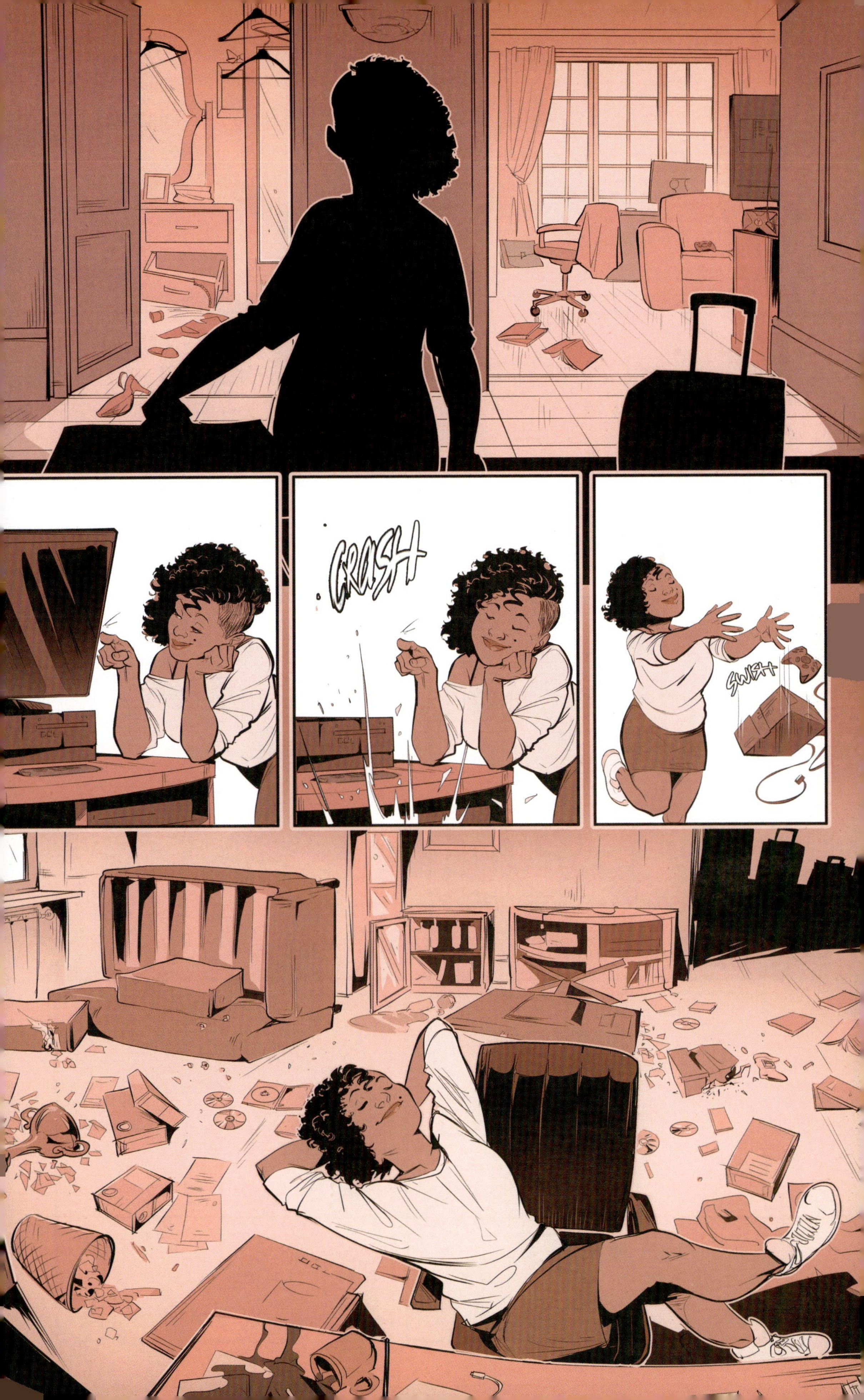
CRASH
SWISH

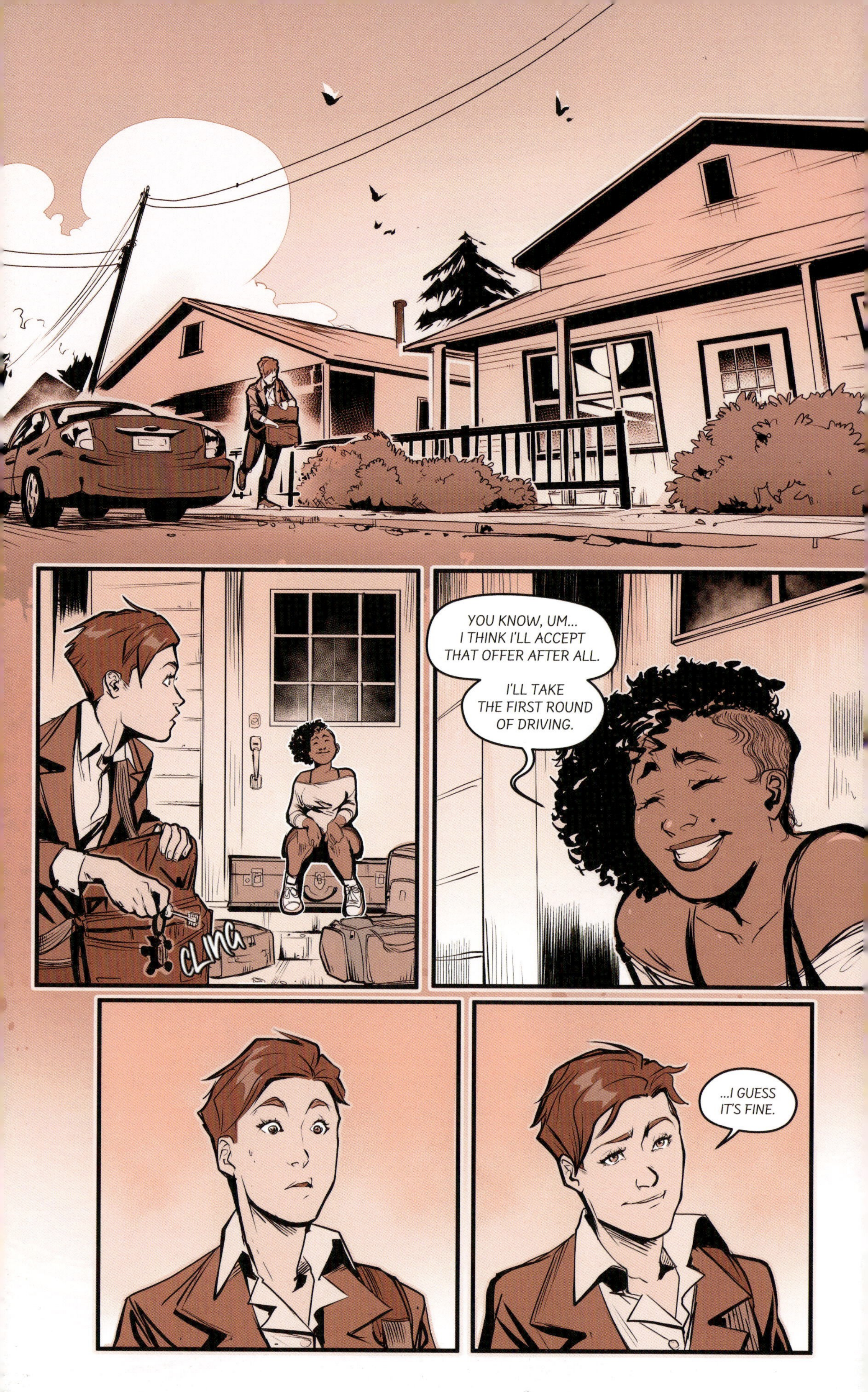
CLING
YOU KNOW, UM... I THINK I'LL ACCEPT THAT OFFER AFTER ALL.
I'LL TAKE THE FIRST ROUND OF DRIVING.
...I GUESS IT'S FINE.

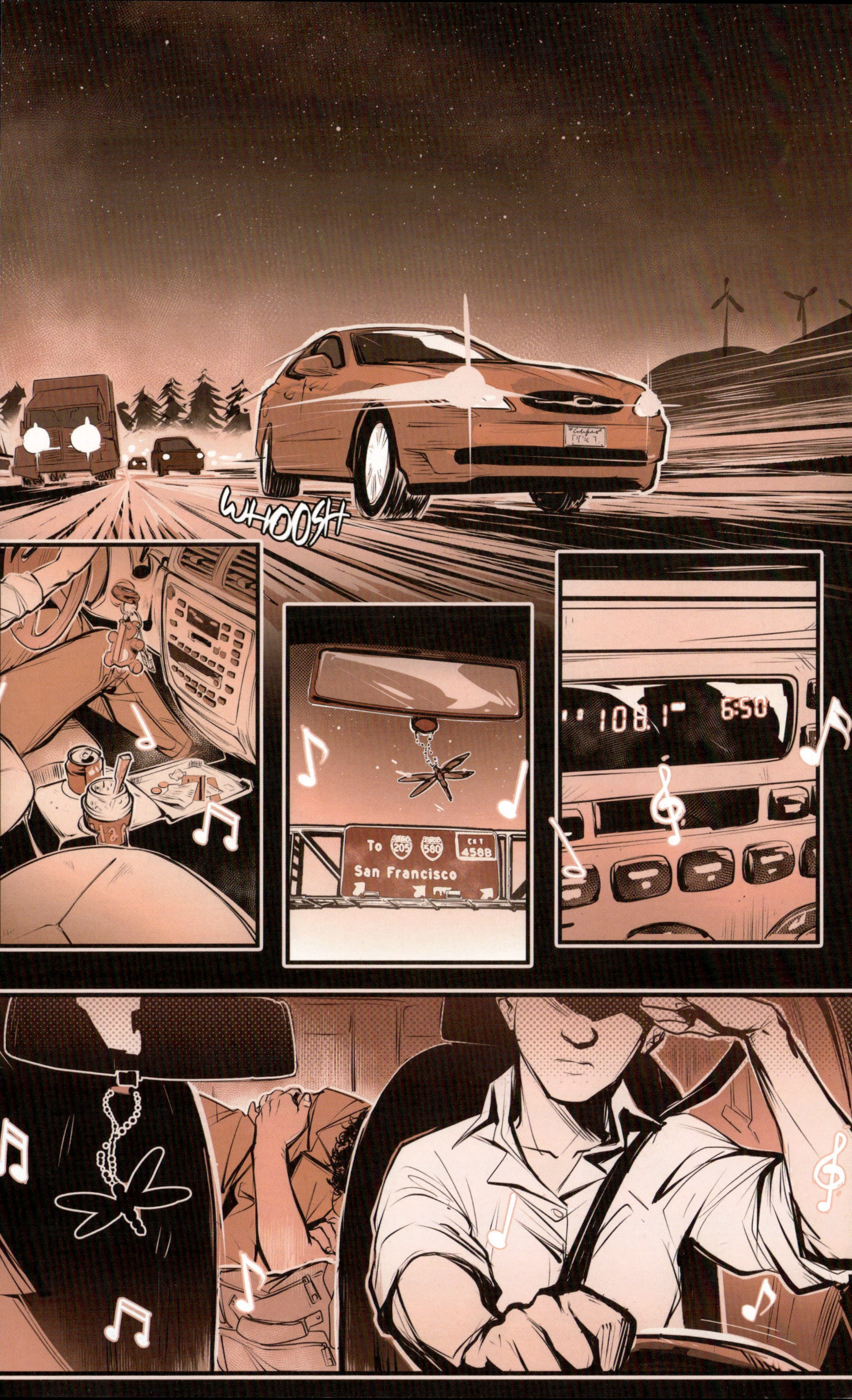
WHOOSH
To 205 580
EXIT 458B
San Francisco
108.1
6:50

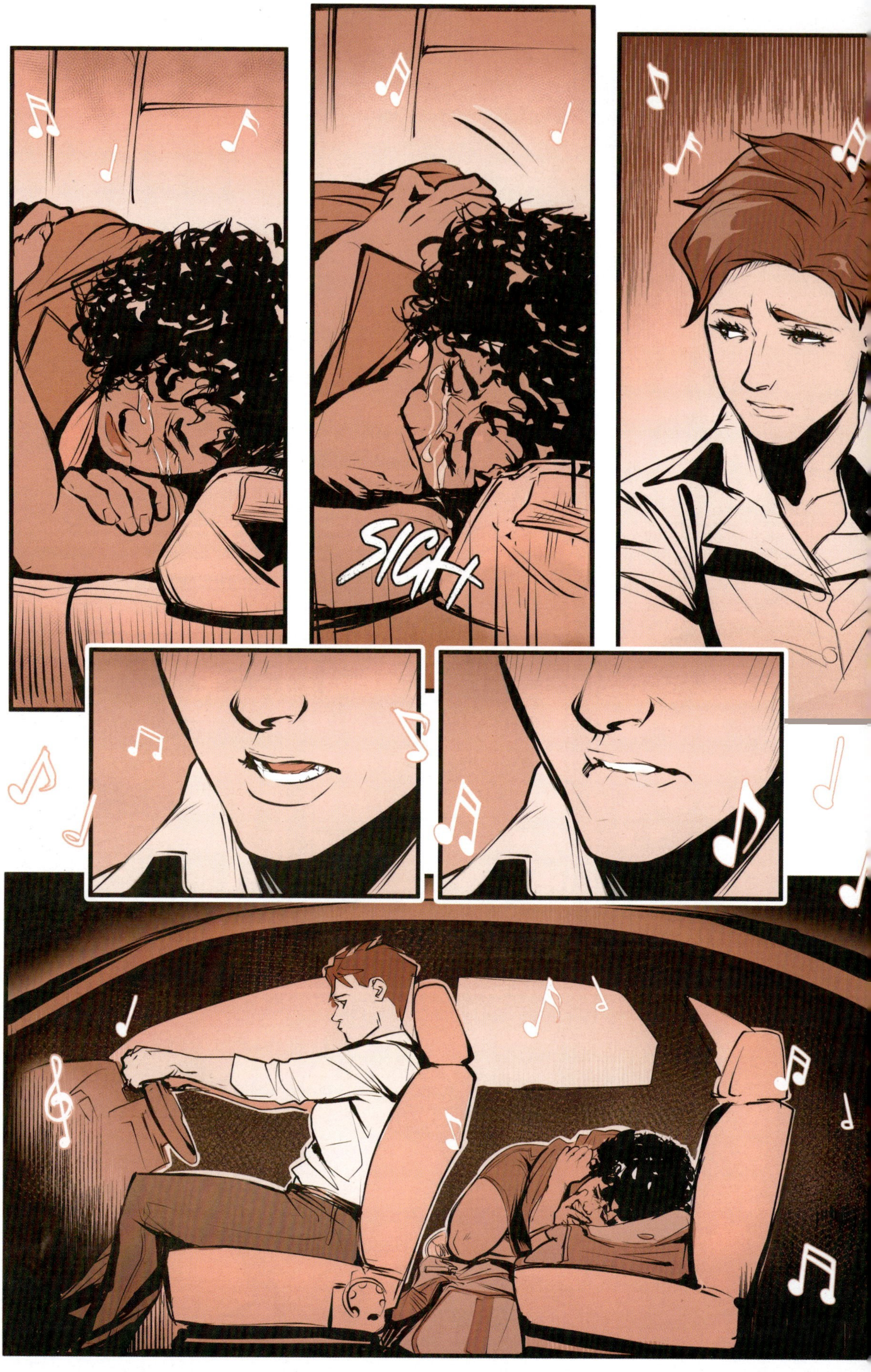
SIGH

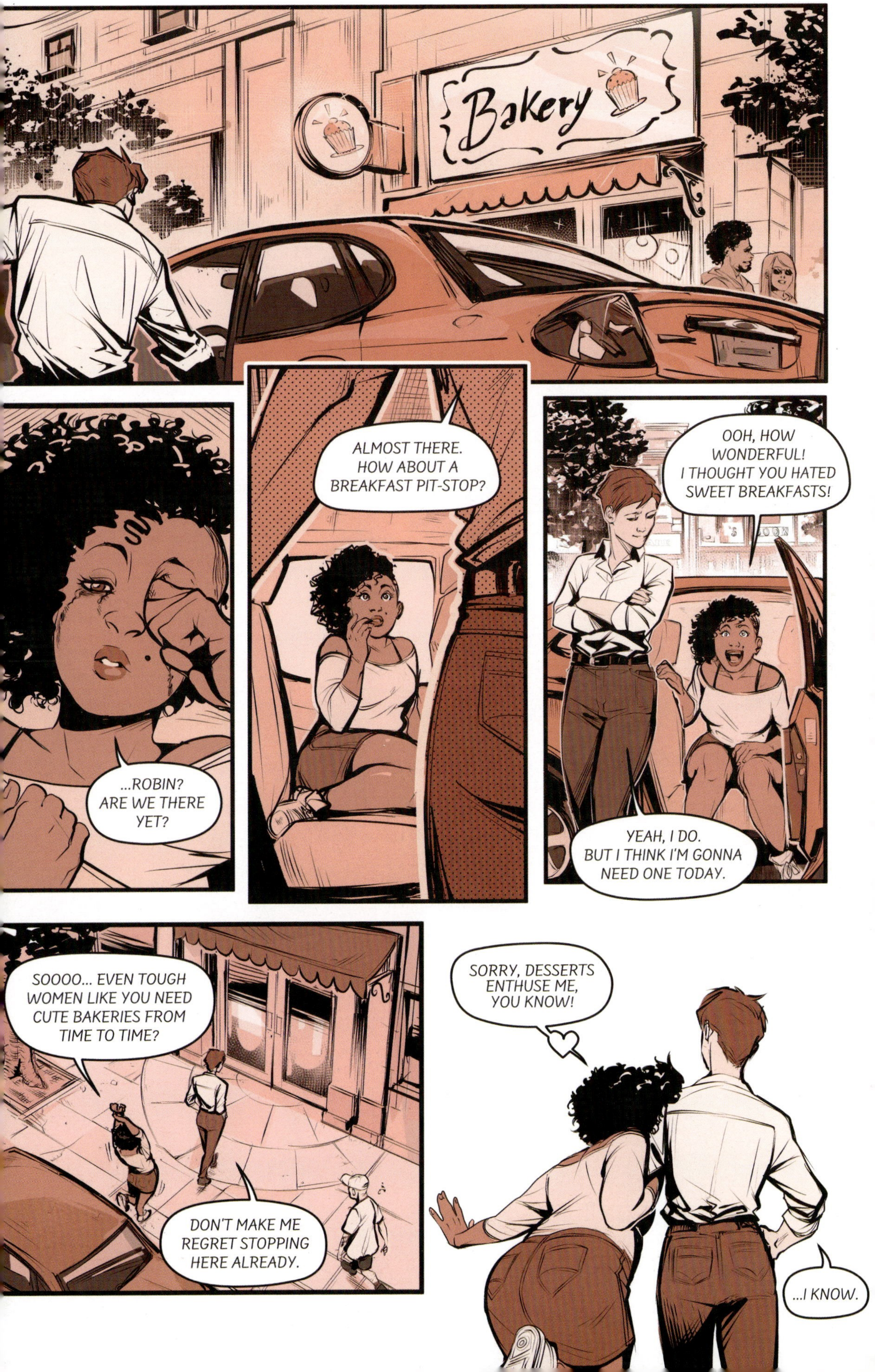
Bakery
...ROBIN? ARE WE THERE YET?
ALMOST THERE. HOW ABOUT A BREAKFAST PIT-STOP?
OOH, HOW WONDERFUL! I THOUGHT YOU HATED SWEET BREAKFASTS!
YEAH, I DO. BUT I THINK I'M GONNA NEED ONE TODAY.
SOOOO... EVEN TOUGH WOMEN LIKE YOU NEED CUTE BAKERIES FROM TIME TO TIME?
DON'T MAKE ME REGRET STOPPING HERE ALREADY.
SORRY, DESSERTS ENTHUSE ME, YOU KNOW!
...I KNOW.

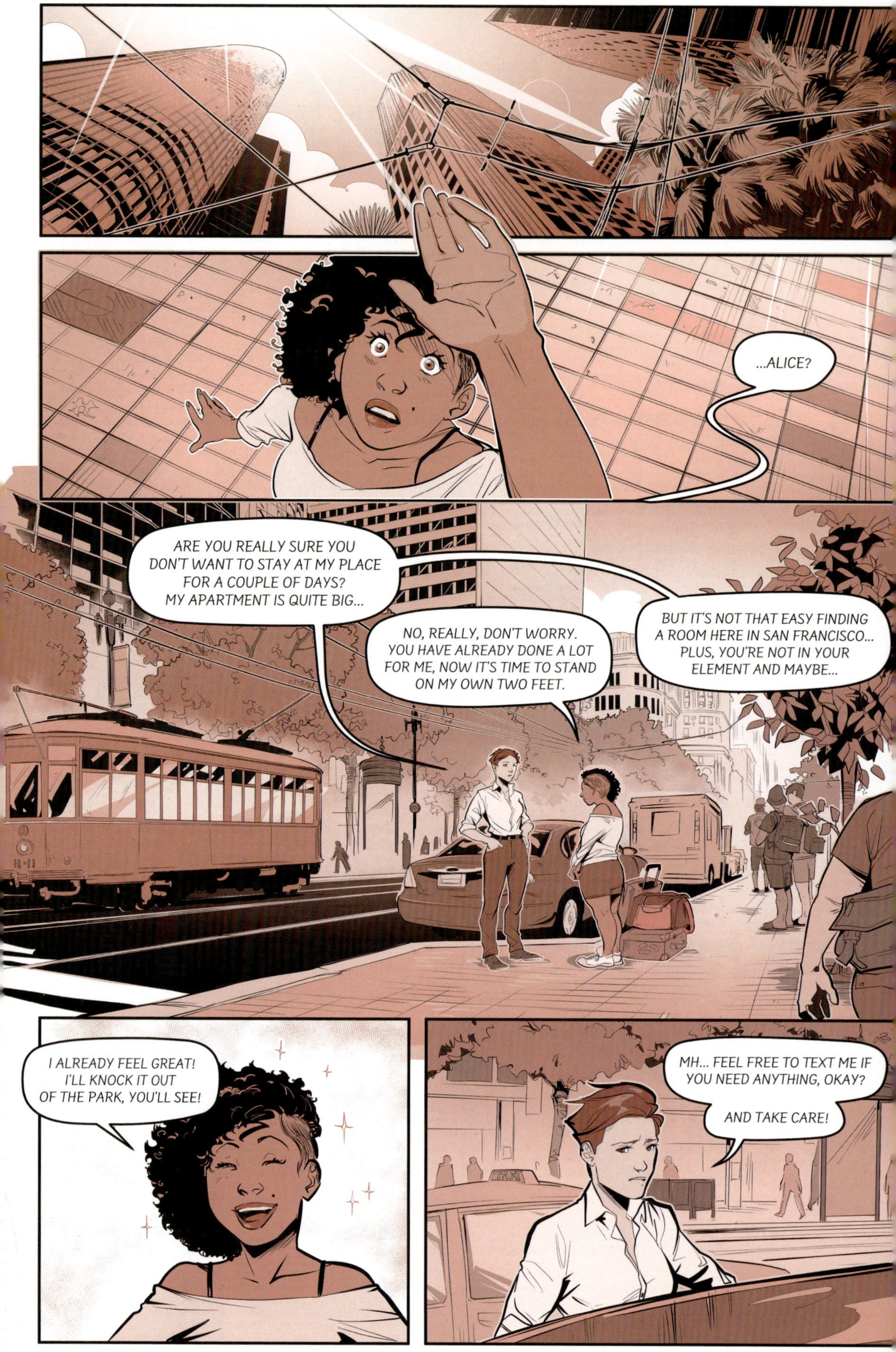
...ALICE?
ARE YOU REALLY SURE YOU DON'T WANT TO STAY AT MY PLACE FOR A COUPLE OF DAYS? MY APARTMENT IS QUITE BIG...
NO, REALLY, DON'T WORRY. YOU HAVE ALREADY DONE A LOT FOR ME, NOW IT'S TIME TO STAND ON MY OWN TWO FEET.
BUT IT'S NOT THAT EASY FINDING A ROOM HERE IN SAN FRANCISCO... PLUS, YOU'RE NOT IN YOUR ELEMENT AND MAYBE...
I ALREADY FEEL GREAT! I'LL KNOCK IT OUT OF THE PARK, YOU'LL SEE!
MH... FEEL FREE TO TEXT ME IF YOU NEED ANYTHING, OKAY?
AND TAKE CARE!

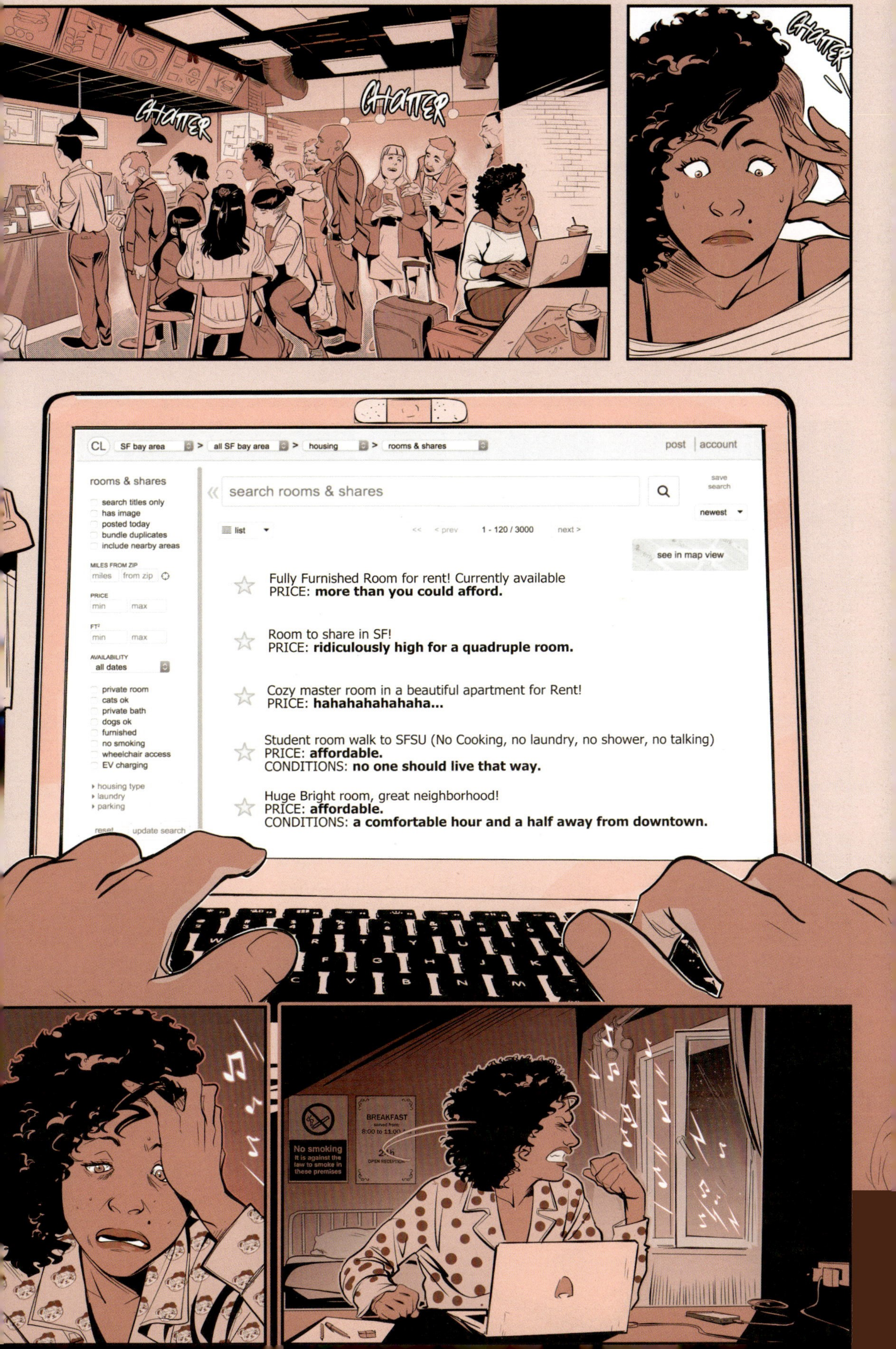
CHATTER
CHATTER
CHATTER
CL
SF bay area
all SF bay area
housing
rooms & shares
post
account
rooms & shares
search titles only
has image
posted today
bundle duplicates
include nearby areas
MILES FROM ZIP
miles
from zip
PRICE
min
max
FT²
min
max
AVAILABILITY
all dates
private room
cats ok
private bath
dogs ok
furnished
no smoking
wheelchair access
EV charging
housing type
laundry
parking
reset
update search
search rooms & shares
save search
newest
list
<< < prev 1 - 120 / 3000 next >
see in map view
Fully Furnished Room for rent! Currently available
PRICE: **more than you could afford.**
Room to share in SF!
PRICE: **ridiculously high for a quadruple room.**
Cozy master room in a beautiful apartment for Rent!
PRICE: **hahahahahahaha...**
Student room walk to SFSU (No Cooking, no laundry, no shower, no talking)
PRICE: **affordable.**
CONDITIONS: **no one should live that way.**
Huge Bright room, great neighborhood!
PRICE: **affordable.**
CONDITIONS: **a comfortable hour and a half away from downtown.**
No smoking
It is against the law to smoke in these premises
BREAKFAST
8:00 to 11:00
24h
OPEN RECEPTION

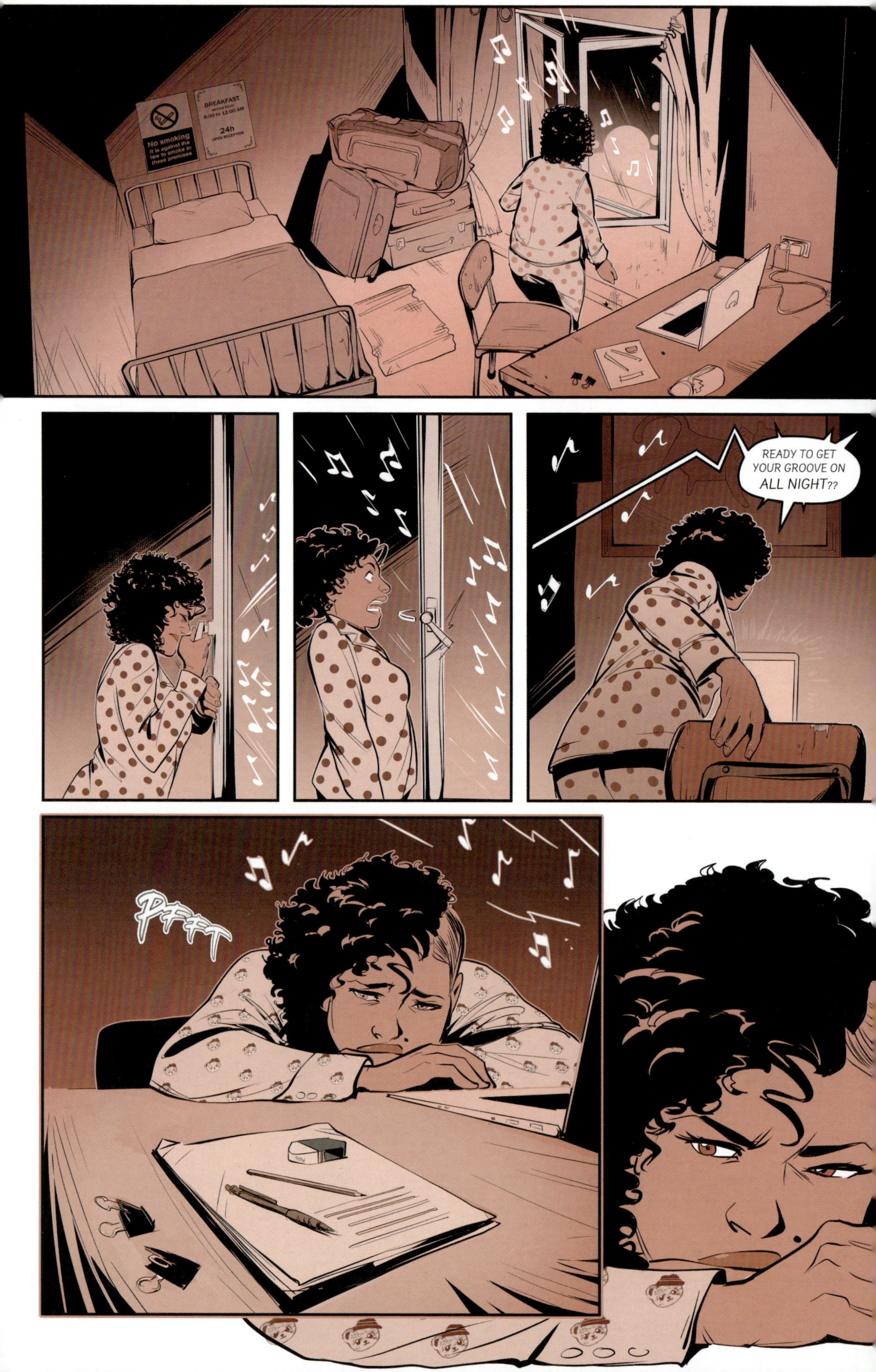
No smoking
It is against the law to smoke in these premises
BREAKFAST
served from
8.00 to 11.00 AM
24h
OPEN RECEPTION
READY TO GET YOUR GROOVE ON ALL NIGHT??
PFFT

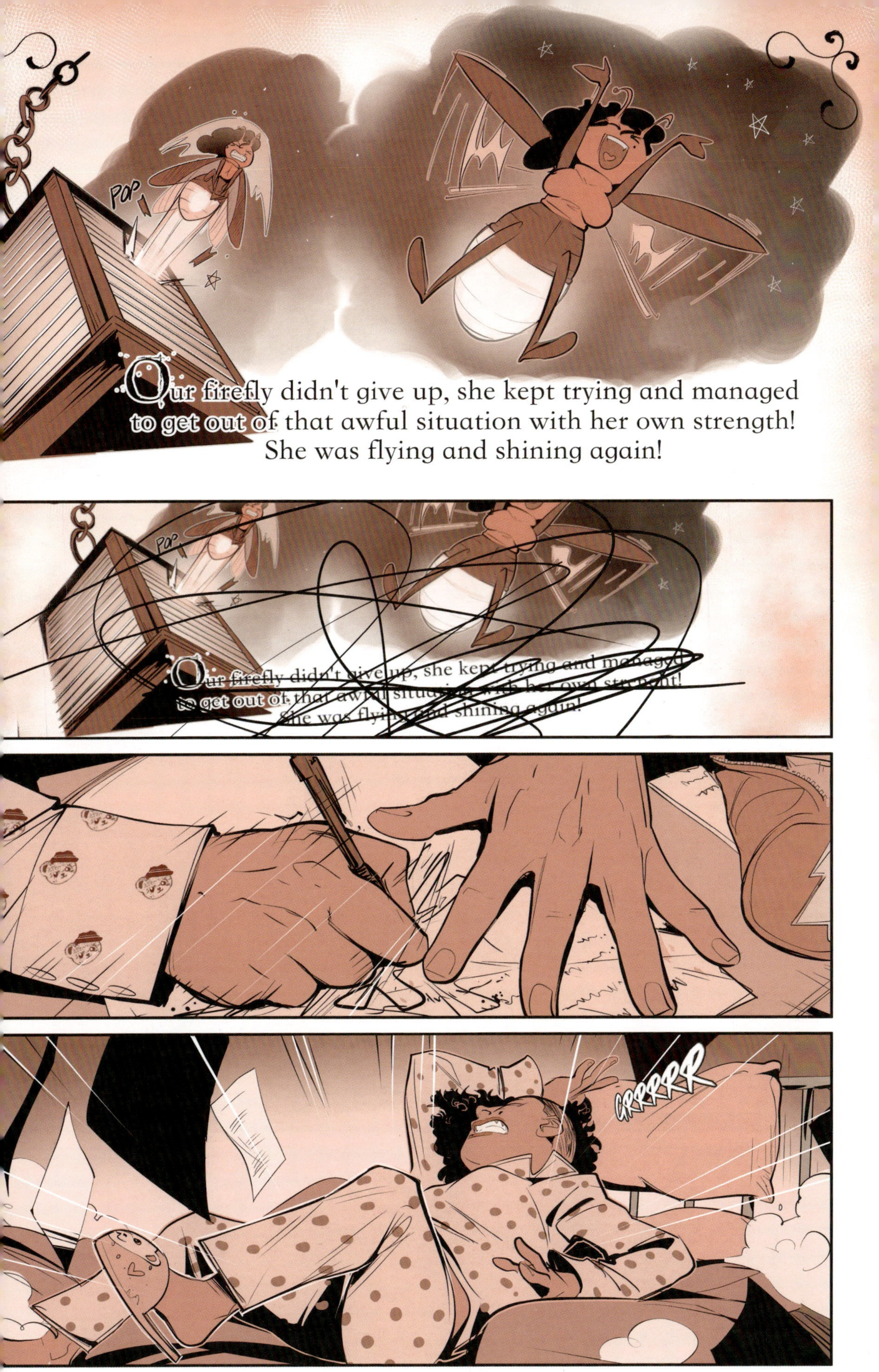
POP
Our firefly didn't give up, she kept trying and managed to get out of that awful situation with her own strength! She was flying and shining again!
POP
Our firefly didn't give up, she kept trying and managed to get out of that awful situation with her own strength! She was flying and shining again!
GRRRRR

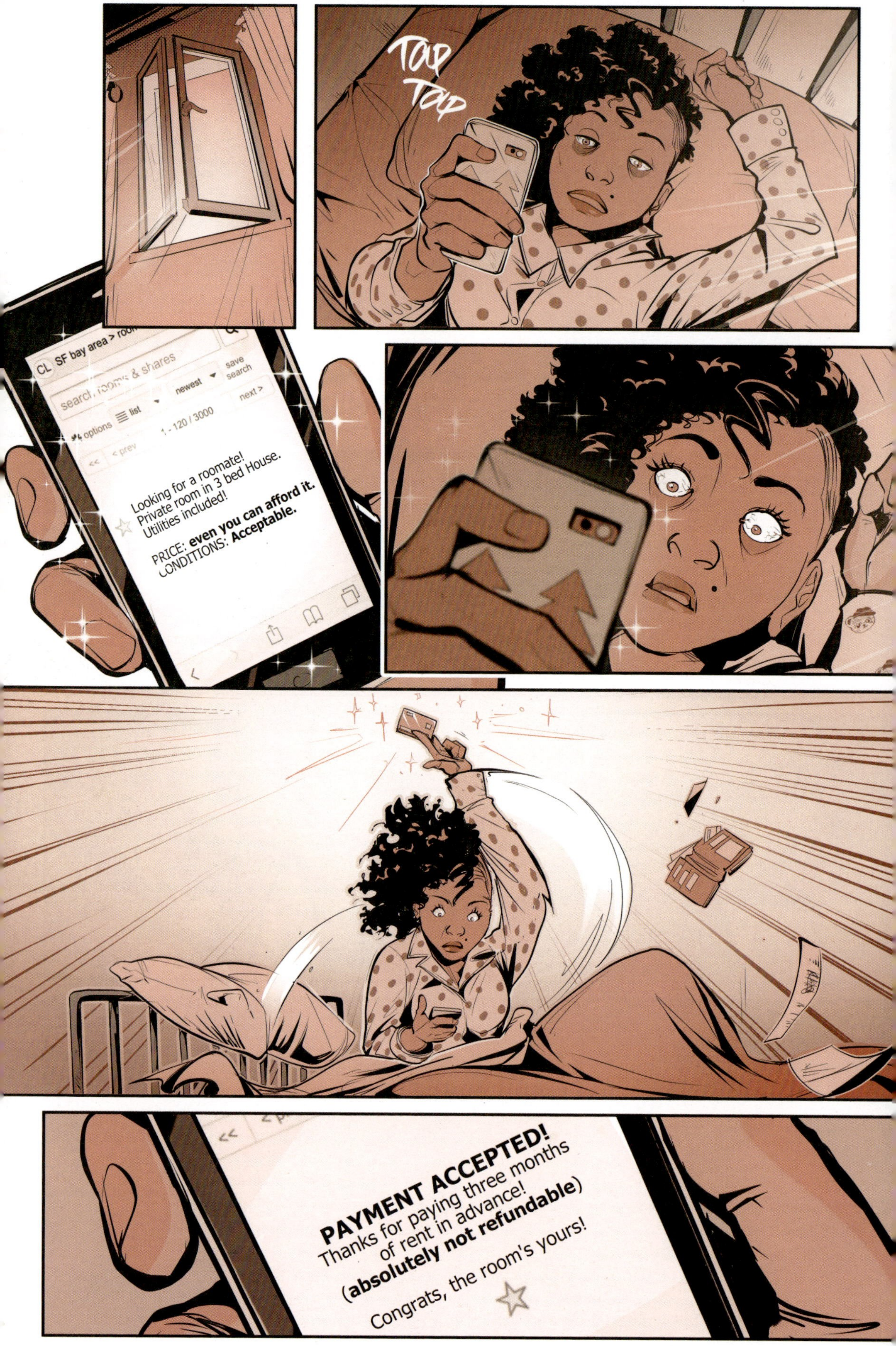
TAP TAP
SF bay area
search rooms & shares
newest
save search
list
options
1 - 120 / 3000
< prev
next >
Looking for a roomate!
Private room in 3 bed House.
Utilities included!
PRICE: **even you can afford it.**
CONDITIONS: **Acceptable.**
PAYMENT ACCEPTED!
Thanks for paying three months of rent in advance!
(**absolutely not refundable**)
Congrats, the room's yours!

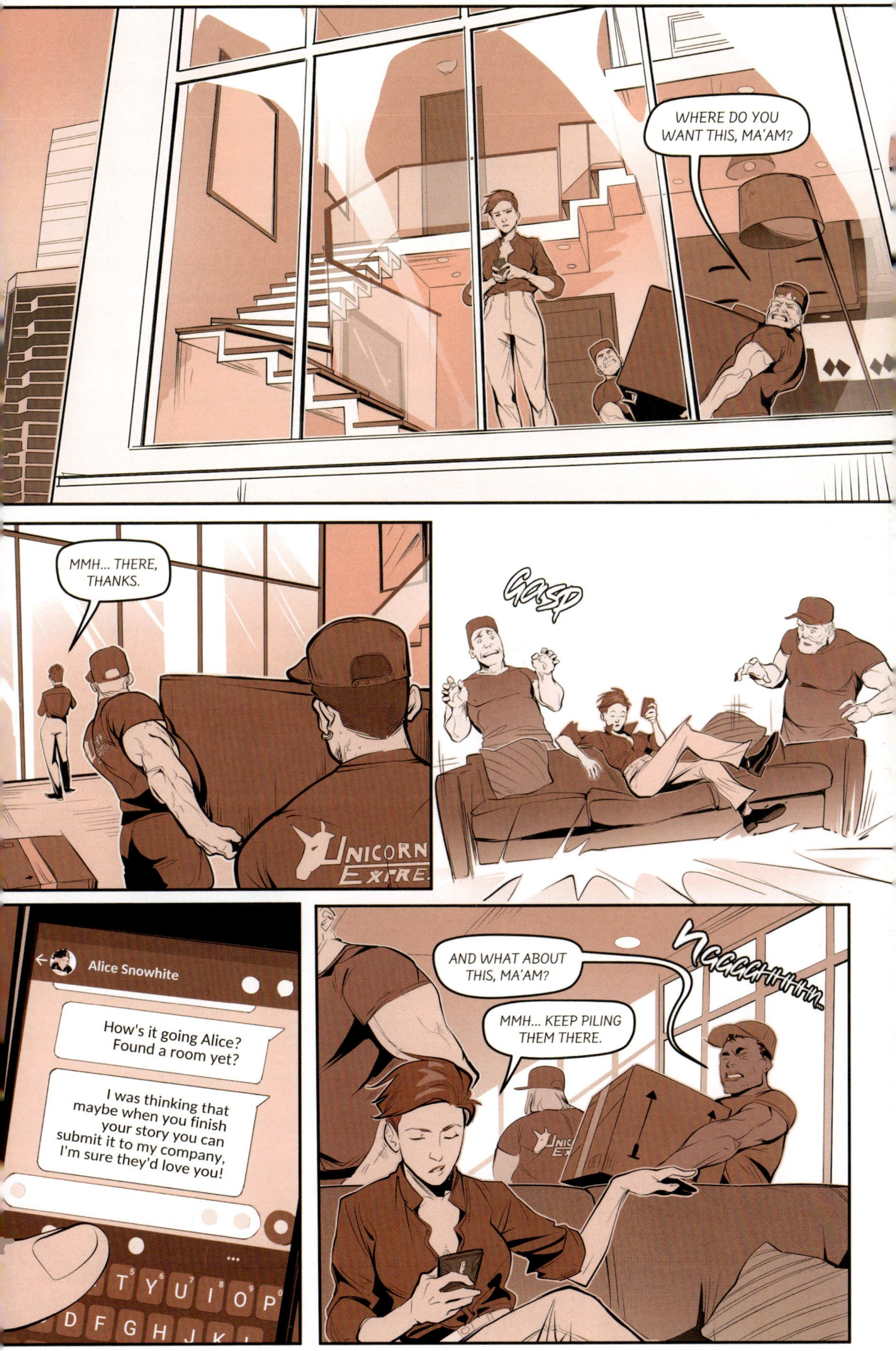
WHERE DO YOU WANT THIS, MA'AM?
MMH... THERE, THANKS.
UNICORN EXPRE
GASP
Alice Snowhite
How's it going Alice? Found a room yet?
I was thinking that maybe when you finish your story you can submit it to my company, I'm sure they'd love you!
AND WHAT ABOUT THIS, MA'AM?
MMH... KEEP PILING THEM THERE.
NGGGGHHHHN...

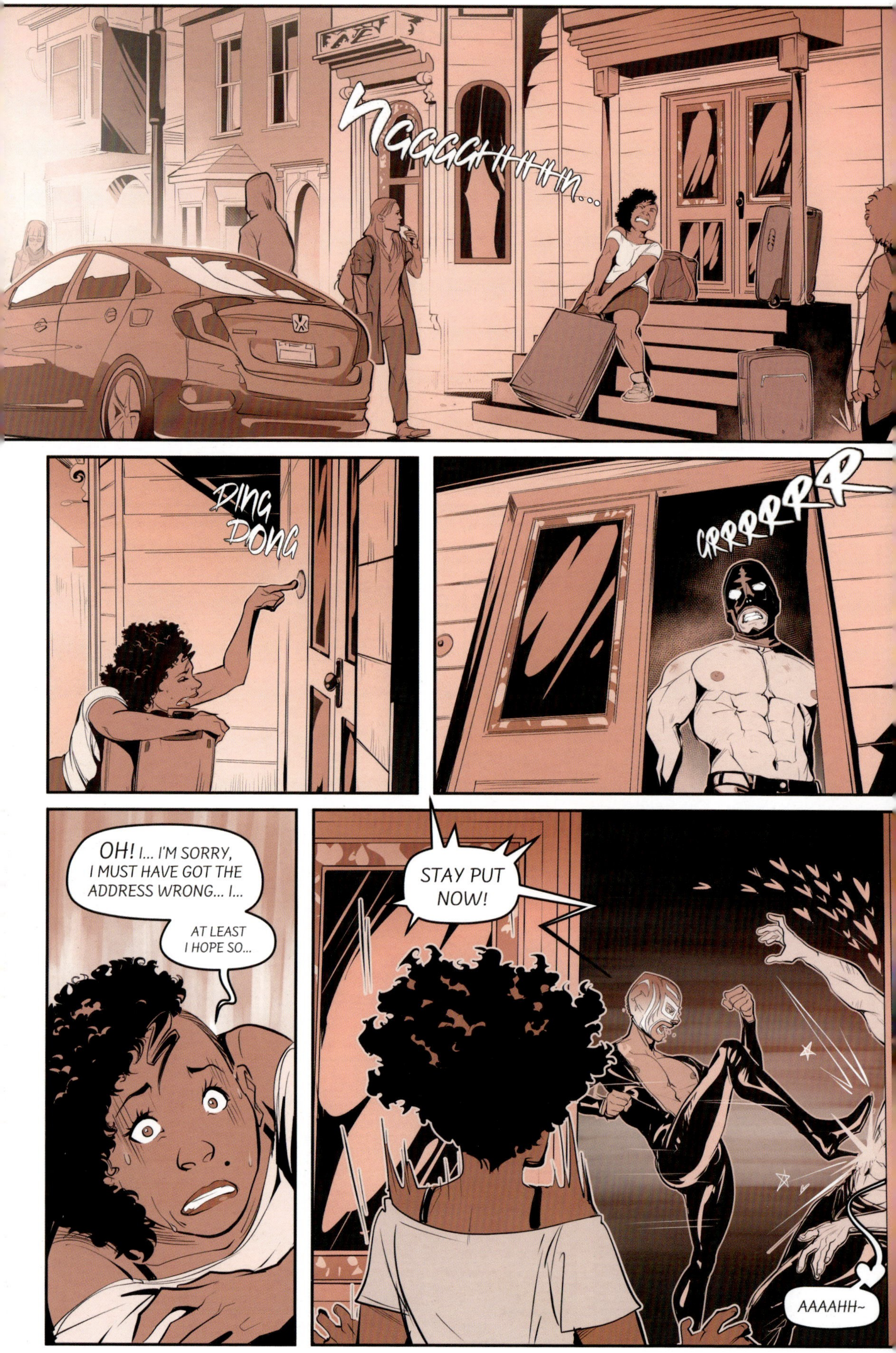

NGGGGHHHHN...
DING DONG
GRRRRRR
OH! I... I'M SORRY, I MUST HAVE GOT THE ADDRESS WRONG... I...
AT LEAST I HOPE SO...
STAY PUT NOW!
AAAAHH~

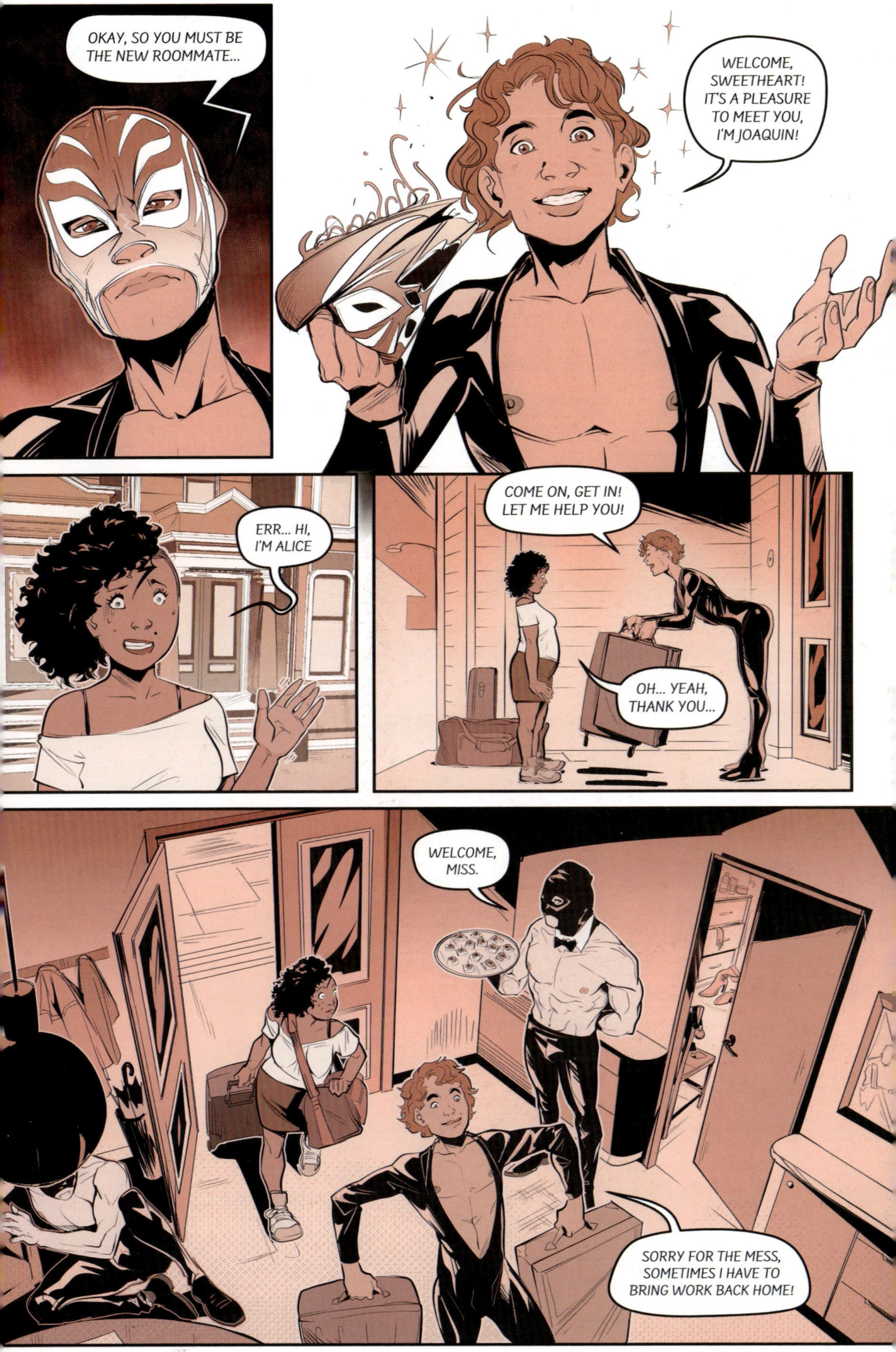
OKAY, SO YOU MUST BE THE NEW ROOMMATE...
WELCOME, SWEETHEART! IT'S A PLEASURE TO MEET YOU, I'M JOAQUIN!
ERR... HI, I'M ALICE
COME ON, GET IN! LET ME HELP YOU!
OH... YEAH, THANK YOU...
WELCOME, MISS.
SORRY FOR THE MESS, SOMETIMES I HAVE TO BRING WORK BACK HOME!

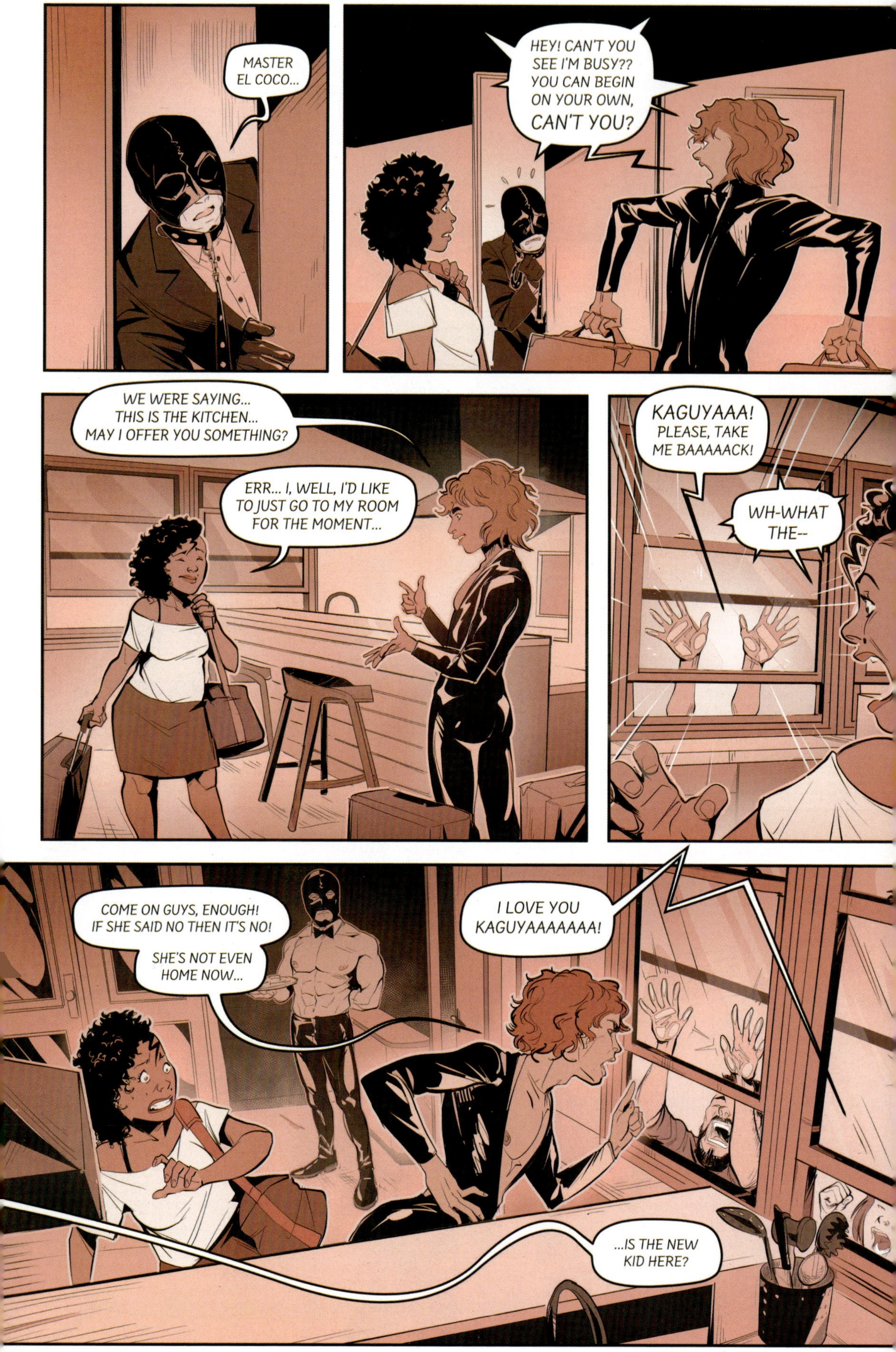
MASTER EL COCO...
HEY! CAN'T YOU SEE I'M BUSY?? YOU CAN BEGIN ON YOUR OWN, CAN'T YOU?
WE WERE SAYING... THIS IS THE KITCHEN... MAY I OFFER YOU SOMETHING?
ERR... I, WELL, I'D LIKE TO JUST GO TO MY ROOM FOR THE MOMENT...
KAGUYAAA! PLEASE, TAKE ME BAAAAACK!
WH-WHAT THE--
COME ON GUYS, ENOUGH! IF SHE SAID NO THEN IT'S NO!
SHE'S NOT EVEN HOME NOW...
I LOVE YOU KAGUYAAAAAAA!
...IS THE NEW KID HERE?

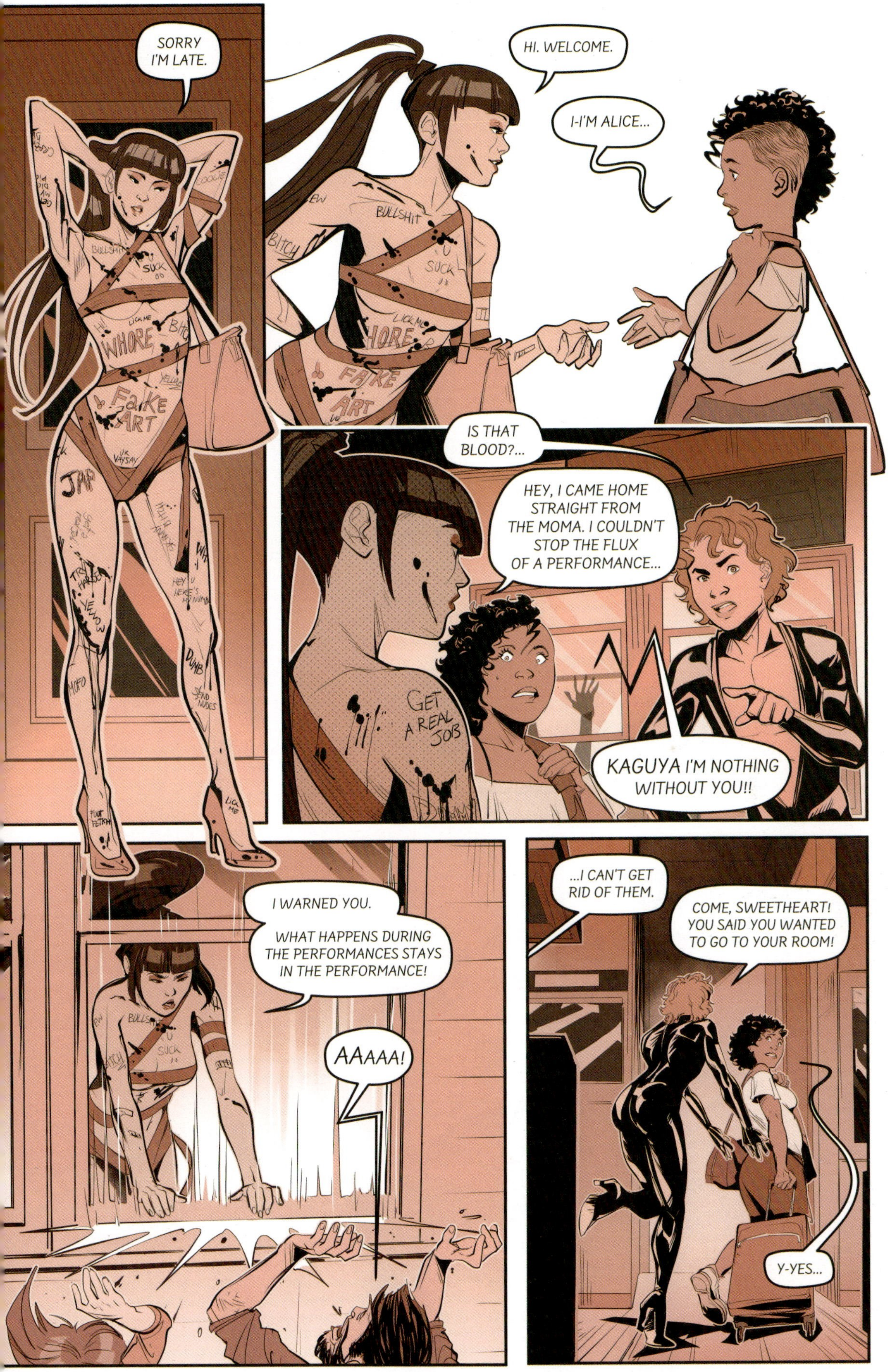
SORRY I'M LATE.
HI. WELCOME.
I-I'M ALICE...
IS THAT BLOOD?...
HEY, I CAME HOME STRAIGHT FROM THE MOMA. I COULDN'T STOP THE FLUX OF A PERFORMANCE...
KAGUYA I'M NOTHING WITHOUT YOU!!
I WARNED YOU.
WHAT HAPPENS DURING THE PERFORMANCES STAYS IN THE PERFORMANCE!
AAAAA!
...I CAN'T GET RID OF THEM.
COME, SWEETHEART! YOU SAID YOU WANTED TO GO TO YOUR ROOM!
Y-YES...

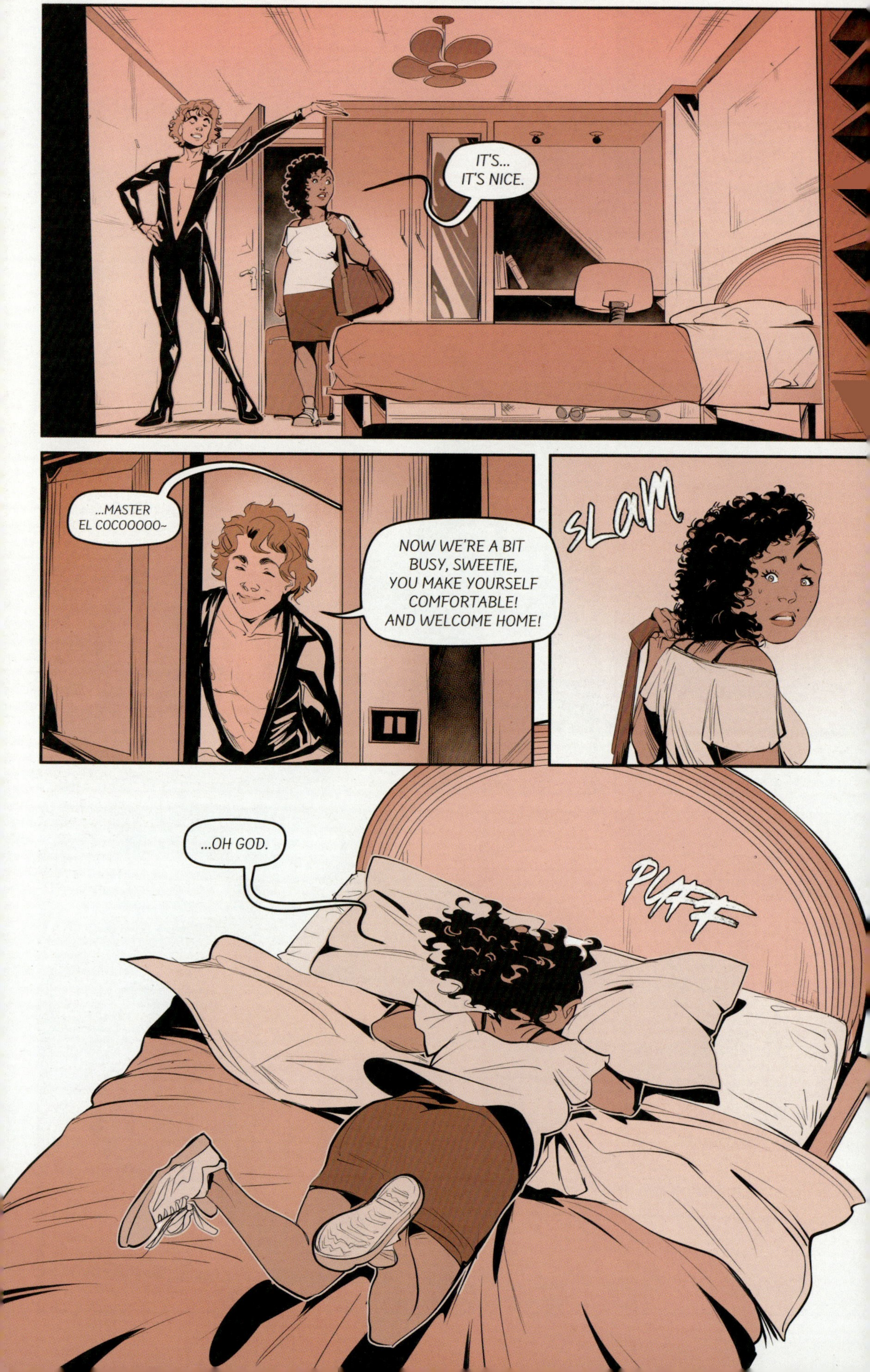
IT'S...
IT'S NICE.
...MASTER
EL COCOOOOO~
NOW WE'RE A BIT
BUSY, SWEETIE,
YOU MAKE YOURSELF
COMFORTABLE!
AND WELCOME HOME!
SLAM
...OH GOD.
PUFF

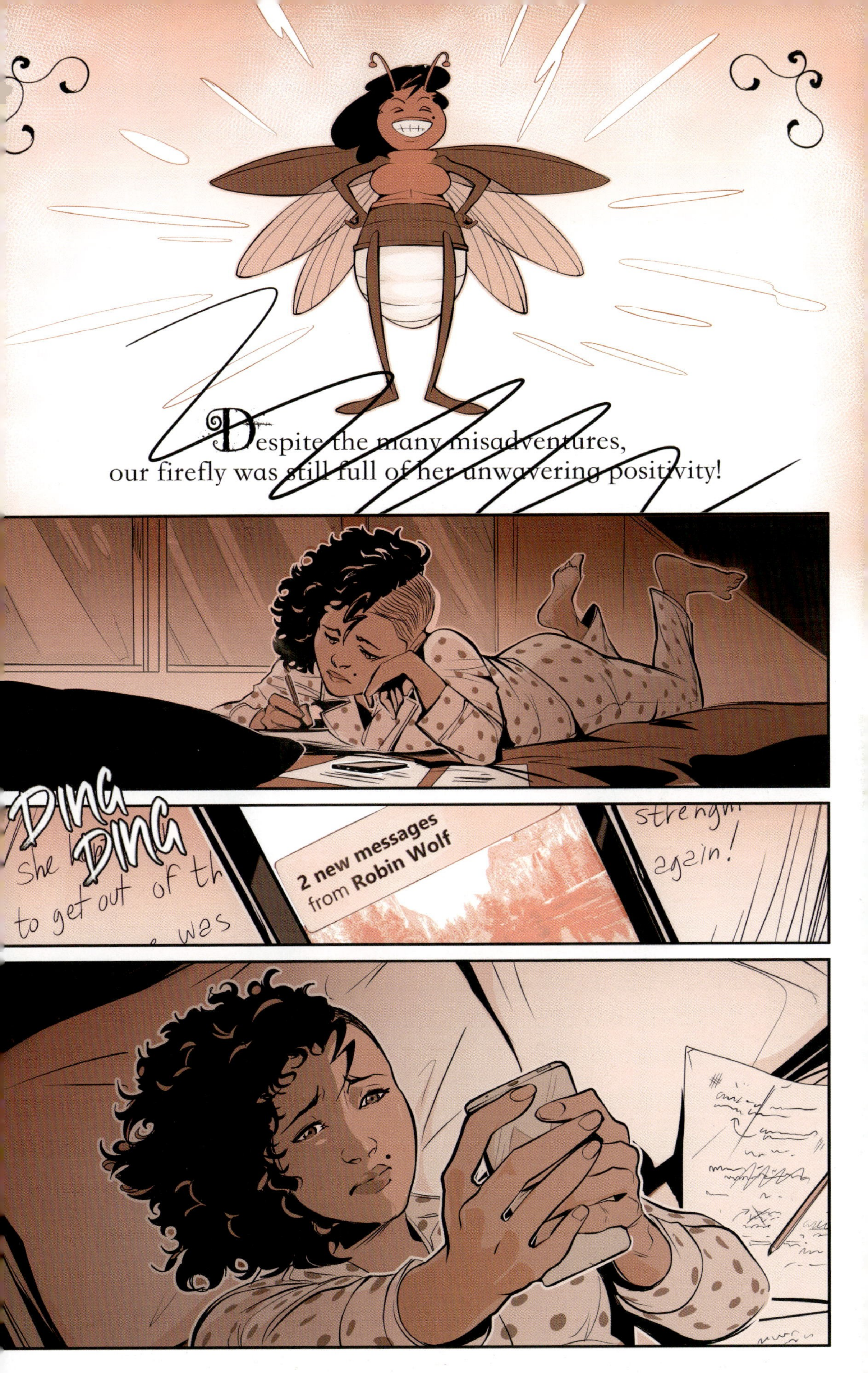
Despite the many misadventures,
our firefly was still full of her unwavering positivity!
DING DING
2 new messages
from Robin Wolf
again!

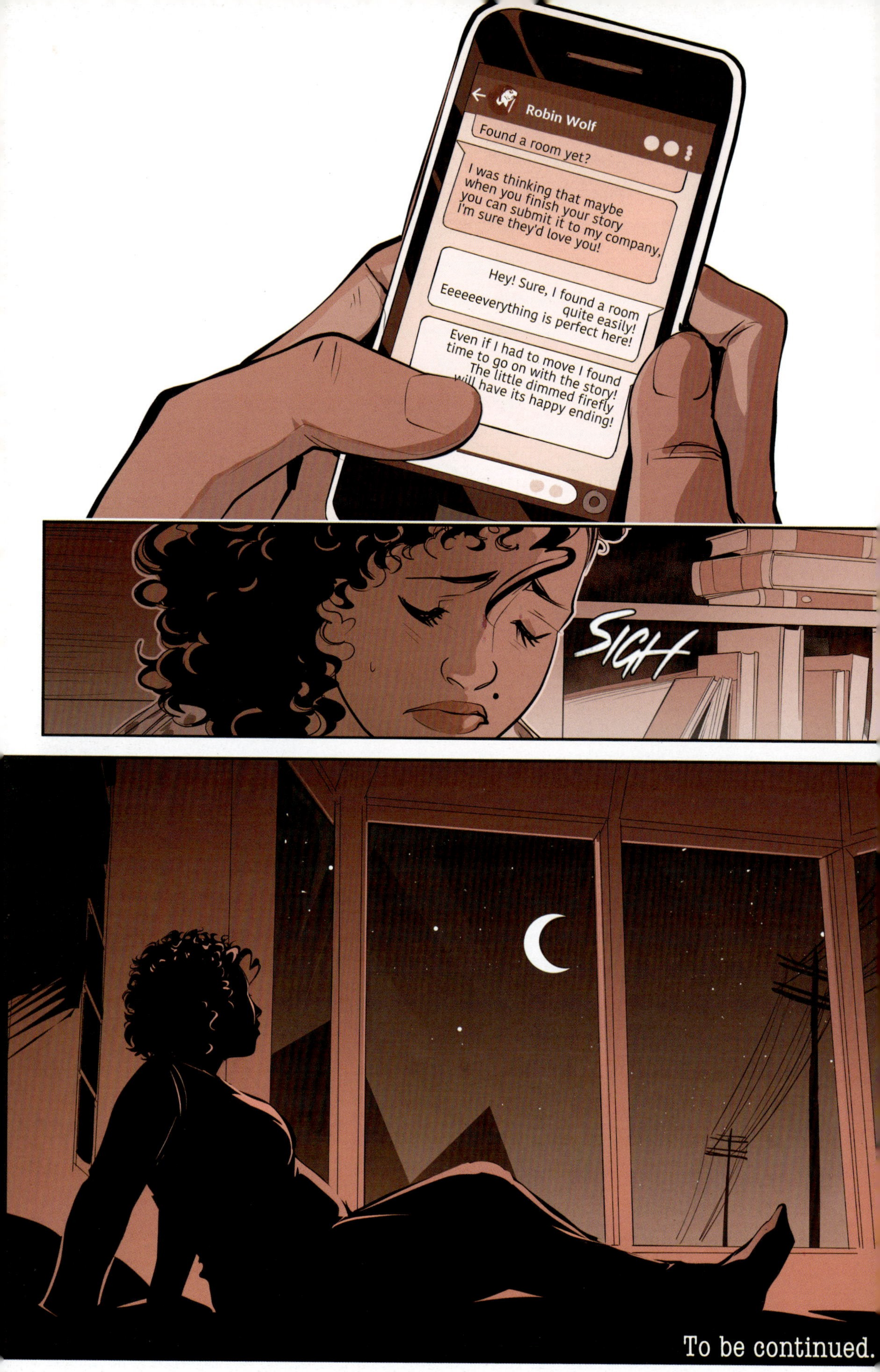
Robin Wolf
Found a room yet?
I was thinking that maybe when you finish your story you can submit it to my company, I'm sure they'd love you!
Hey! Sure, I found a room quite easily! Eeeeeeverything is perfect here!
Even if I had to move I found time to go on with the story! The little dimmed firefly will have its happy ending!
SIGH
To be continued.

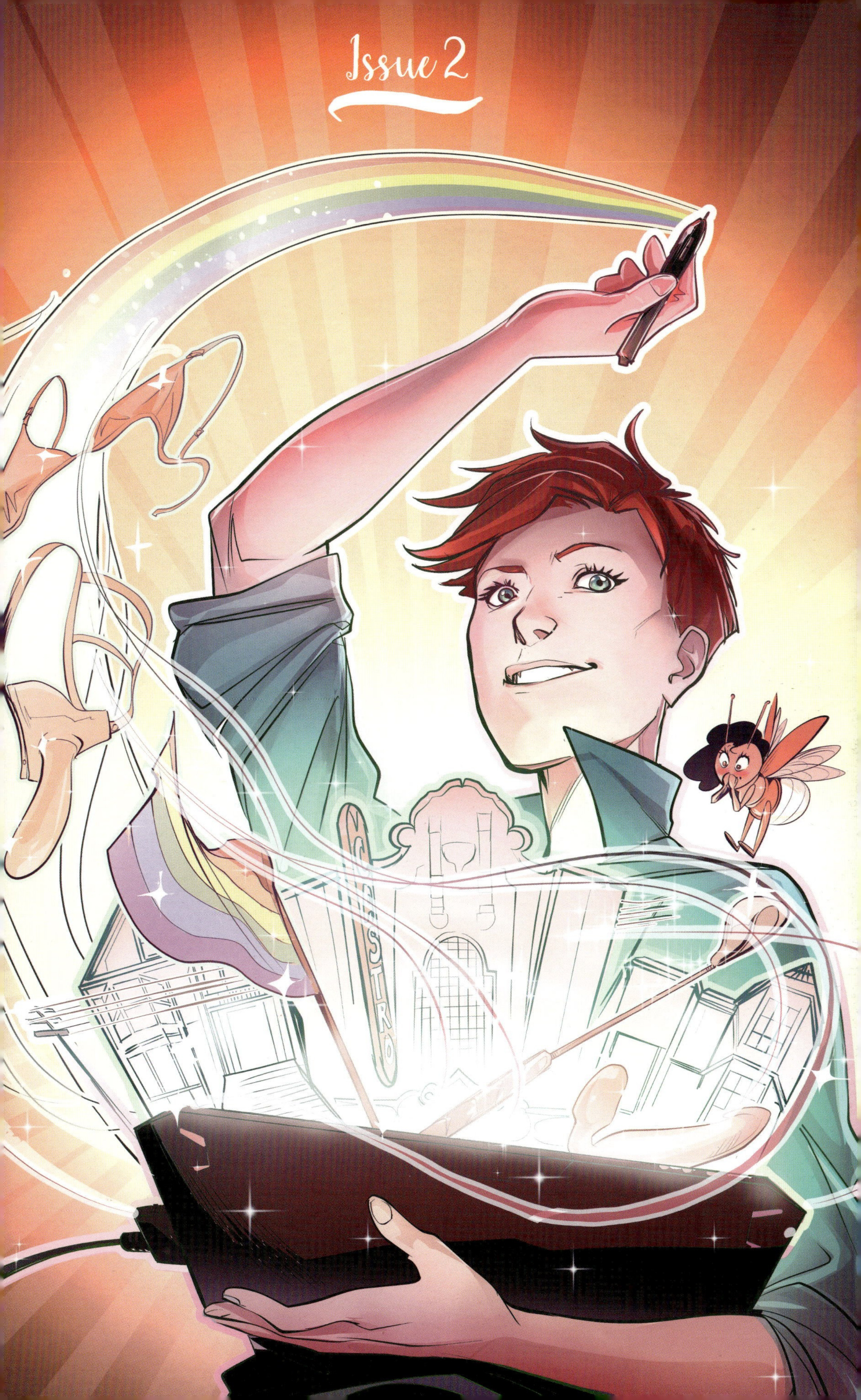
Issue 2

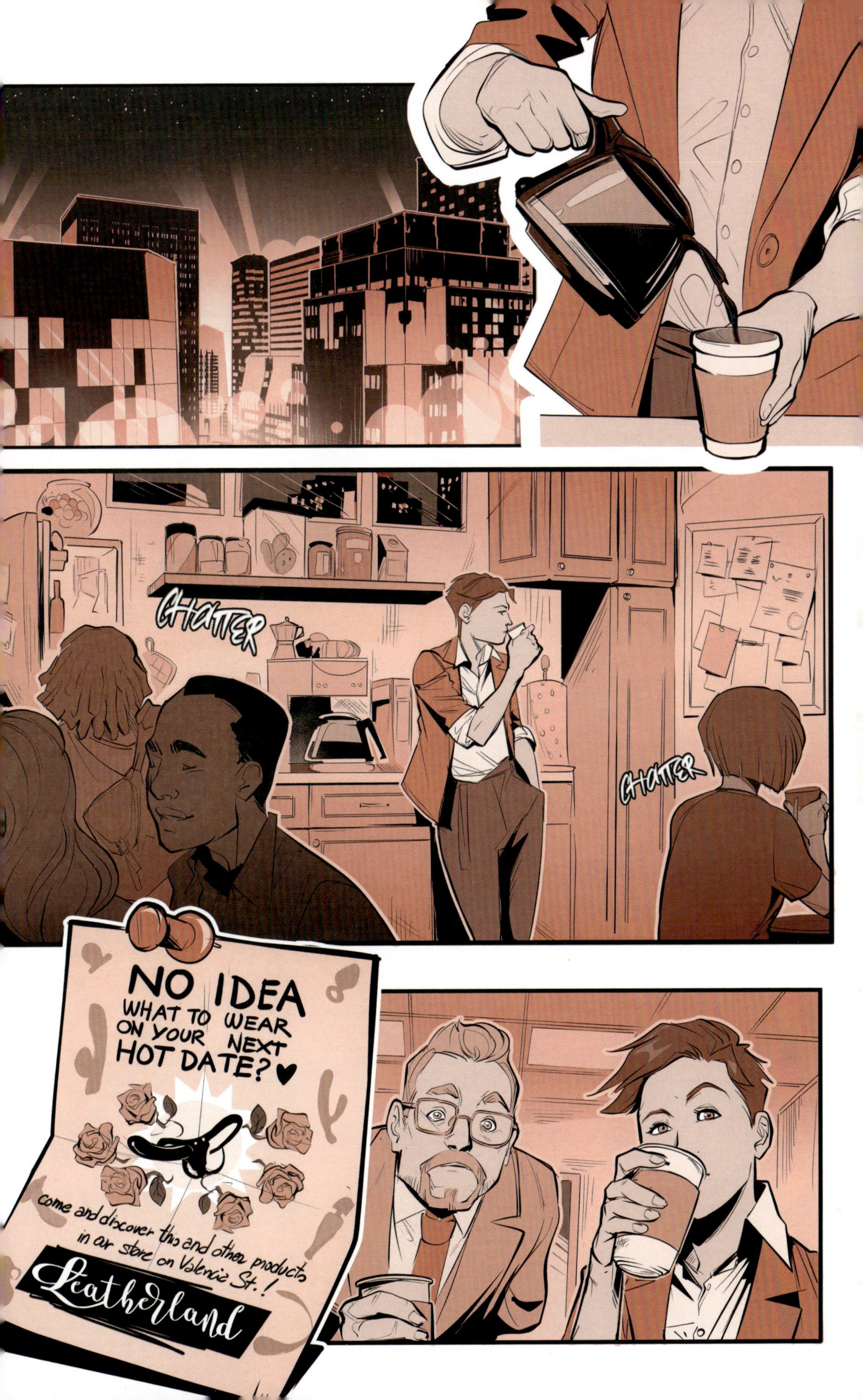
CHATTER
CHATTER
NO IDEA WHAT TO WEAR ON YOUR NEXT HOT DATE? ♥
come and discover this and other products in our store on Valencia St.!
Leatherland

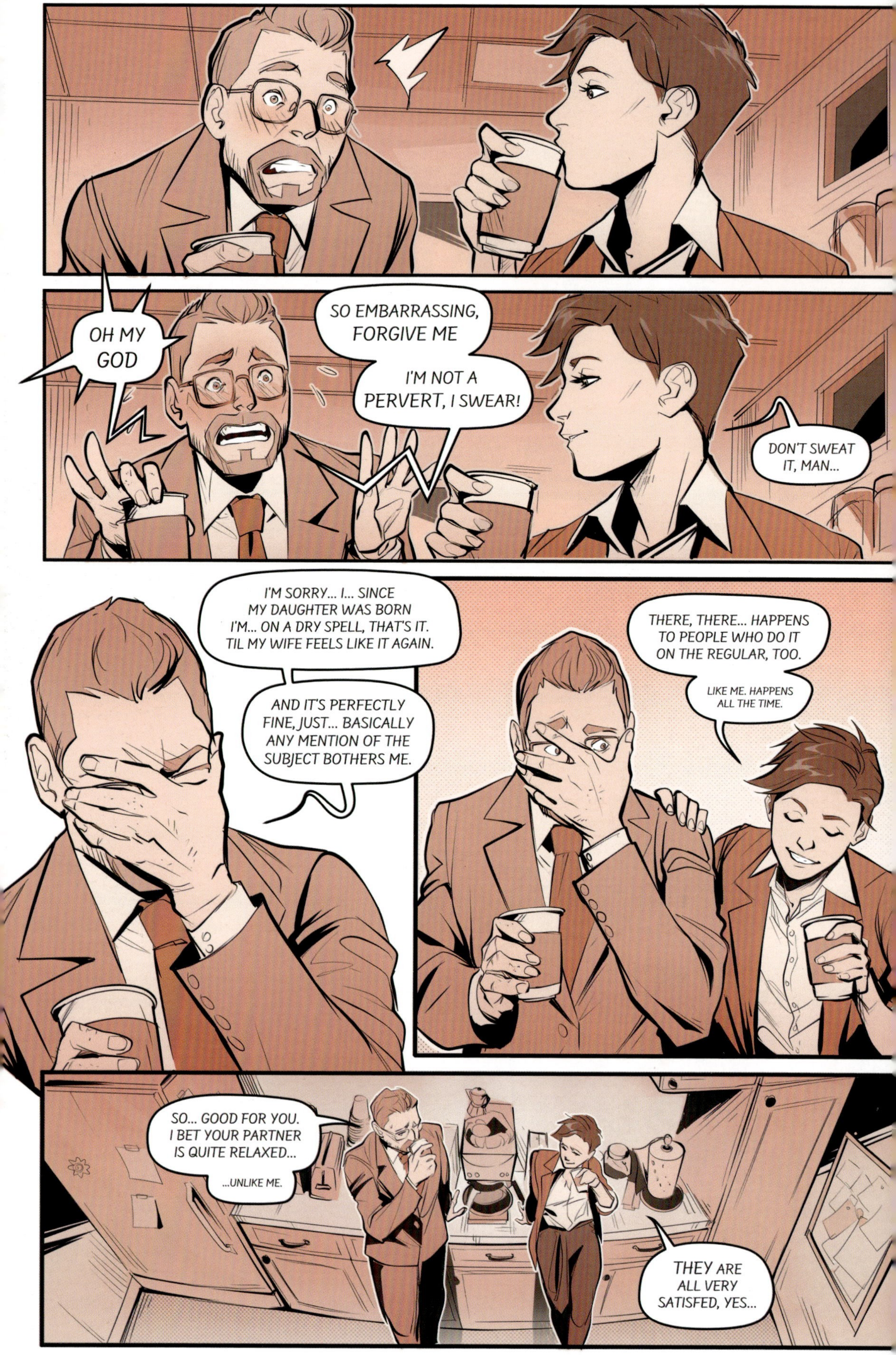
OH MY GOD
SO EMBARRASSING, FORGIVE ME
I'M NOT A PERVERT, I SWEAR!
DON'T SWEAT IT, MAN...
I'M SORRY... I... SINCE MY DAUGHTER WAS BORN I'M... ON A DRY SPELL, THAT'S IT. TIL MY WIFE FEELS LIKE IT AGAIN.
AND IT'S PERFECTLY FINE, JUST... BASICALLY ANY MENTION OF THE SUBJECT BOTHERS ME.
THERE, THERE... HAPPENS TO PEOPLE WHO DO IT ON THE REGULAR, TOO.
LIKE ME. HAPPENS ALL THE TIME.
SO... GOOD FOR YOU. I BET YOUR PARTNER IS QUITE RELAXED...
...UNLIKE ME.
THEY ARE ALL VERY SATISFED, YES...

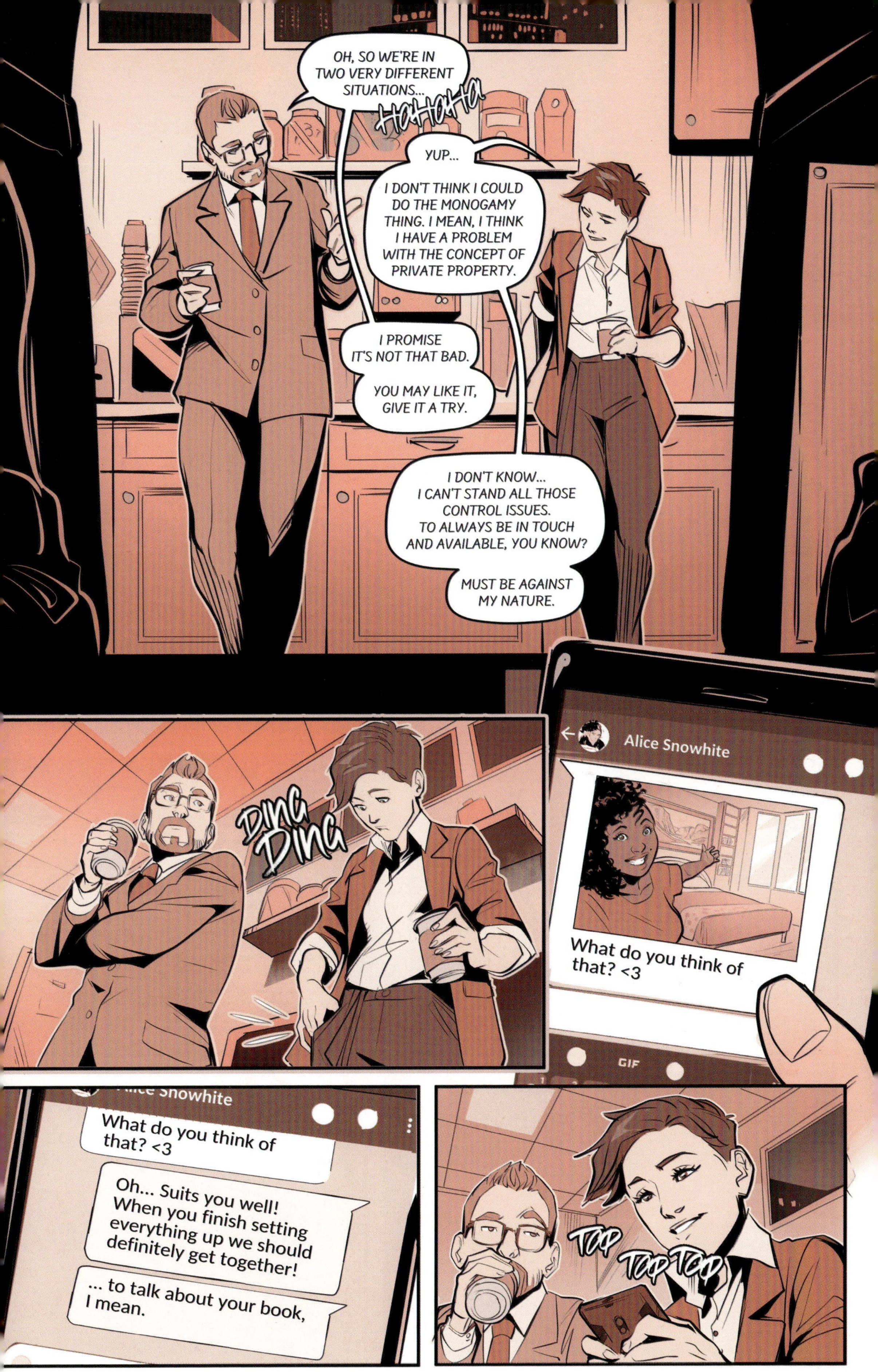
OH, SO WE'RE IN TWO VERY DIFFERENT SITUATIONS...
HAHAHA
YUP...
I DON'T THINK I COULD DO THE MONOGAMY THING. I MEAN, I THINK I HAVE A PROBLEM WITH THE CONCEPT OF PRIVATE PROPERTY.
I PROMISE IT'S NOT THAT BAD.
YOU MAY LIKE IT, GIVE IT A TRY.
I DON'T KNOW... I CAN'T STAND ALL THOSE CONTROL ISSUES. TO ALWAYS BE IN TOUCH AND AVAILABLE, YOU KNOW?
MUST BE AGAINST MY NATURE.
DING DING
Alice Snowhite
What do you think of that? <3
GIF
Alice Snowhite
What do you think of that? <3
Oh... Suits you well! When you finish setting everything up we should definitely get together!
... to talk about your book, I mean.
TAP
TAP TAP

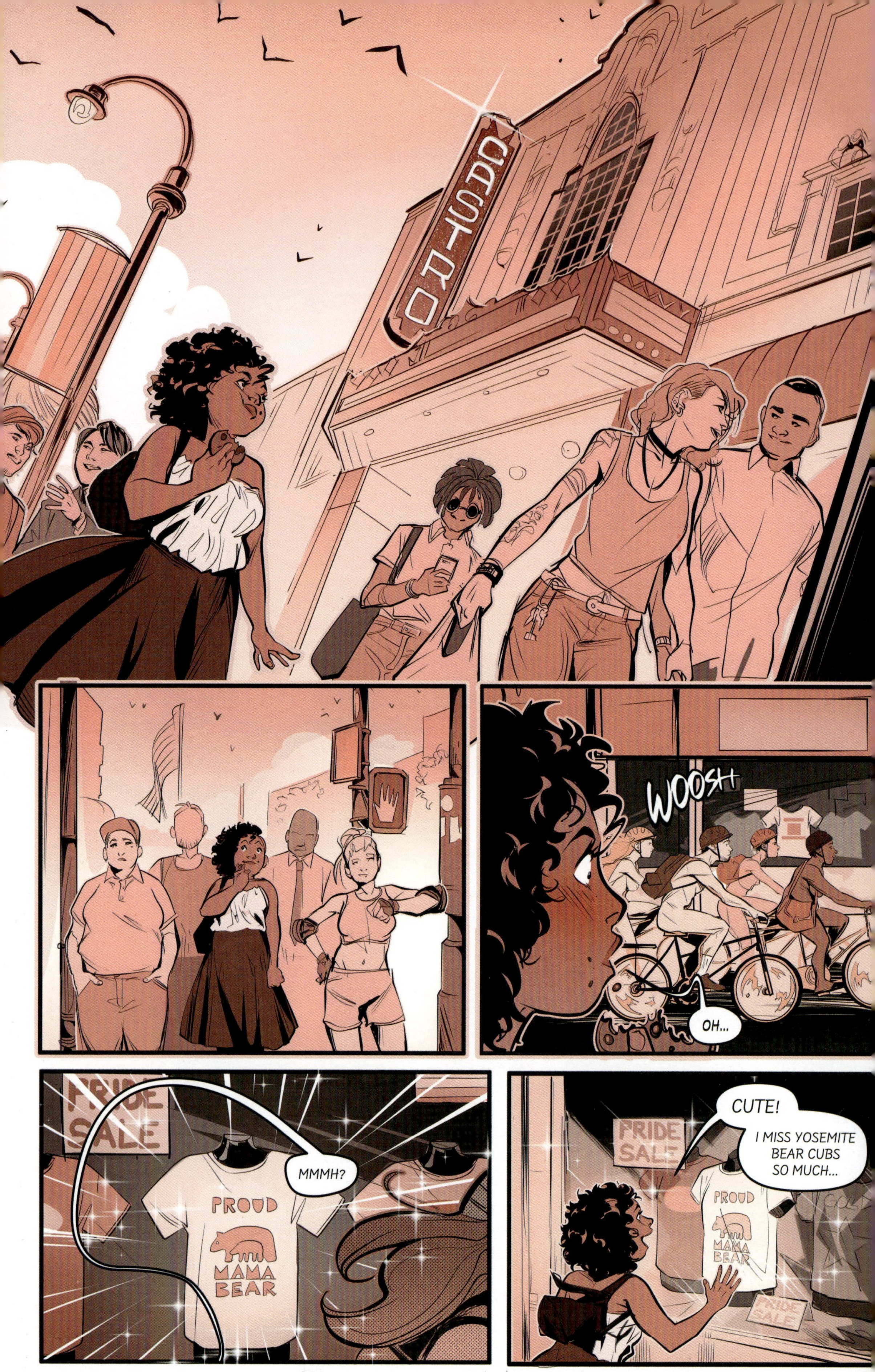
CASTRO
WOOSH
OH...
PRIDE SALE
PROUD MAMA BEAR
MMMH?
CUTE!
I MISS YOSEMITE BEAR CUBS SO MUCH...
PRIDE SALE
PROUD MAMA BEAR
PRIDE SALE

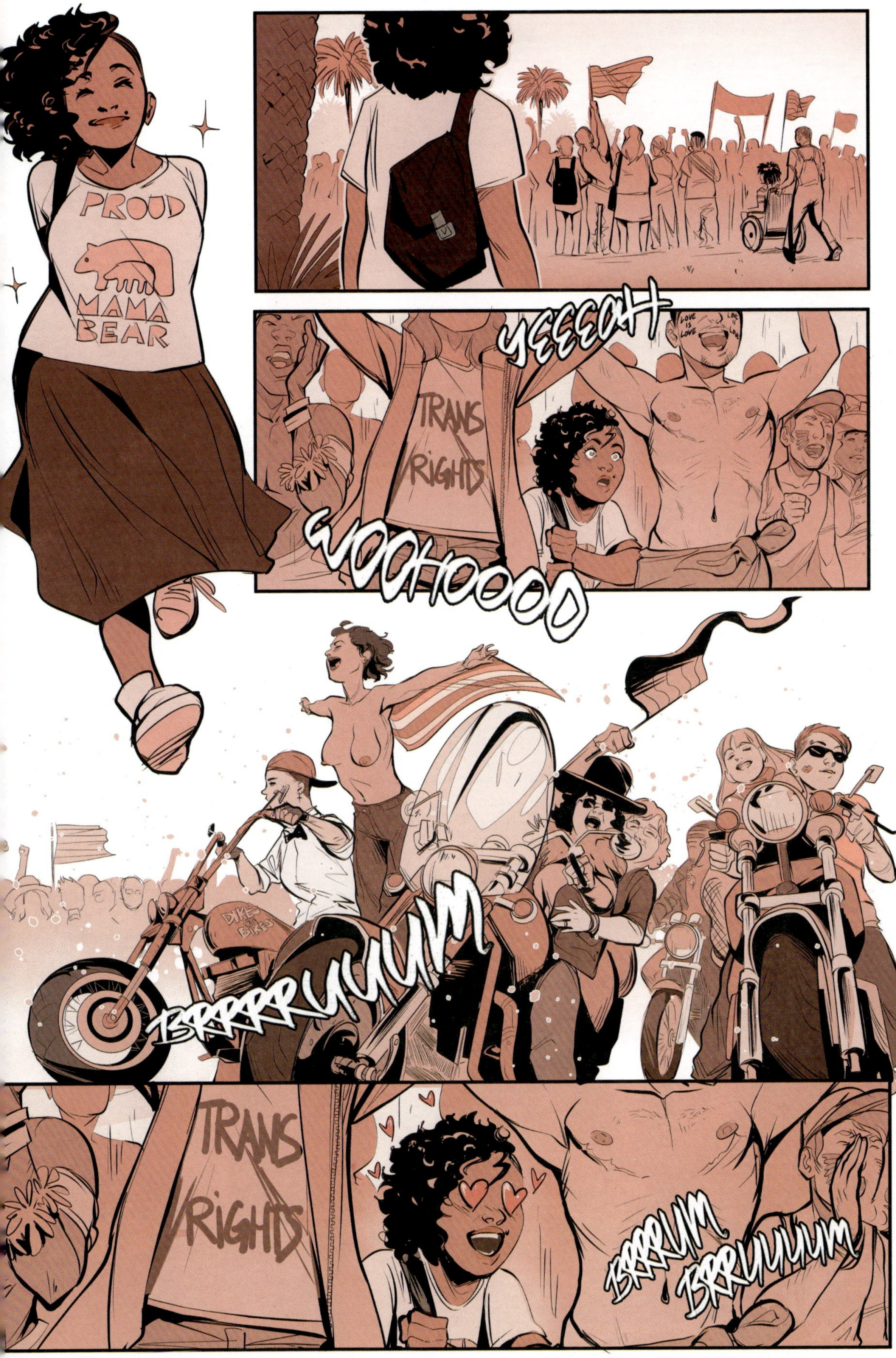
PROUD
MAMA
BEAR
YEEEAH
LOVE IS LOVE
TRANS RIGHTS
WOOHOOOO
DYKES ON BIKES
BRRRRRUUUUM
TRANS RIGHTS
BRRRUM BRRUUUUM

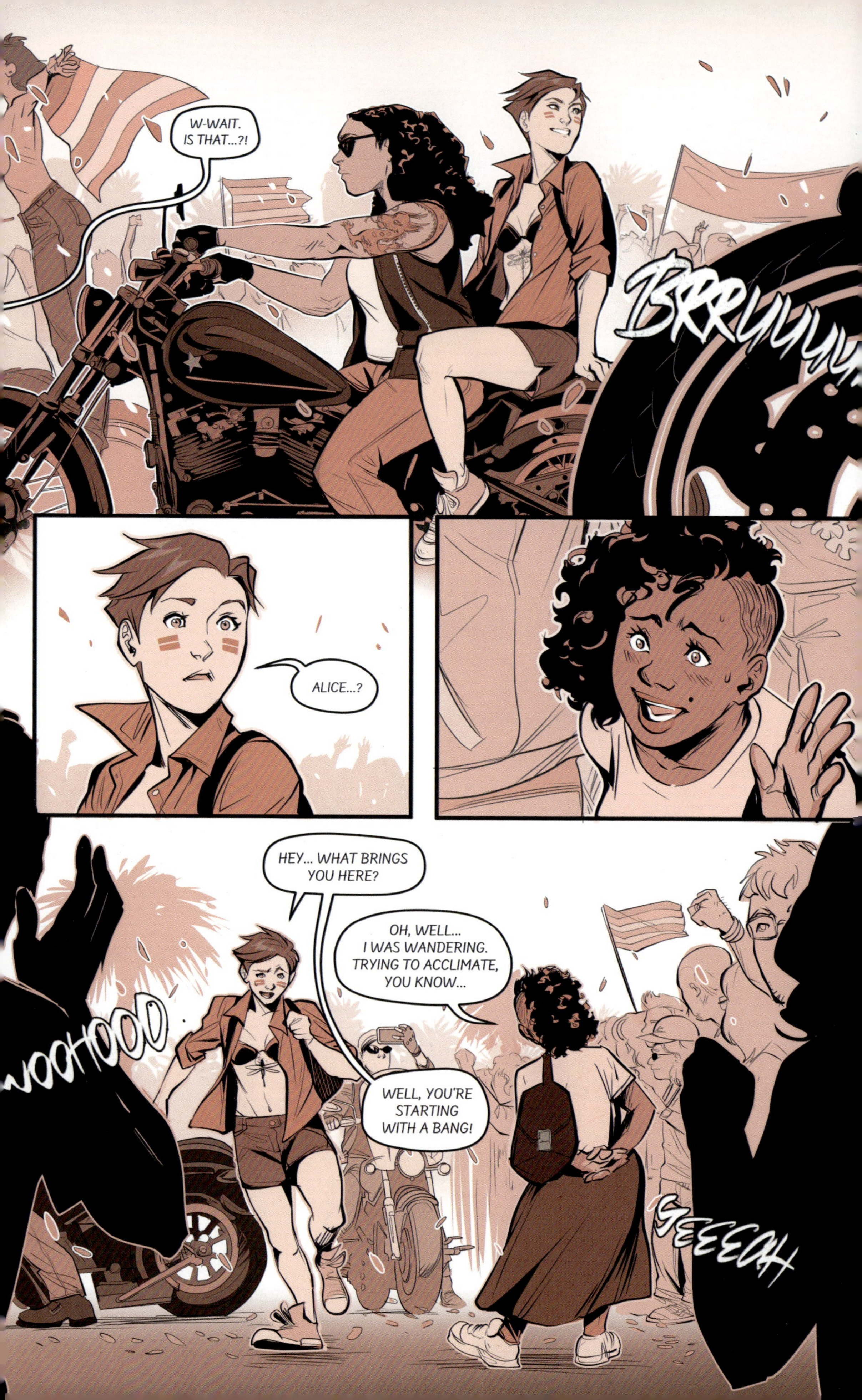
W-WAIT. IS THAT...?!
BRRYUUUM
ALICE...?
HEY... WHAT BRINGS YOU HERE?
OH, WELL... I WAS WANDERING. TRYING TO ACCLIMATE, YOU KNOW...
WELL, YOU'RE STARTING WITH A BANG!
WOOHOOO
YEEEOH

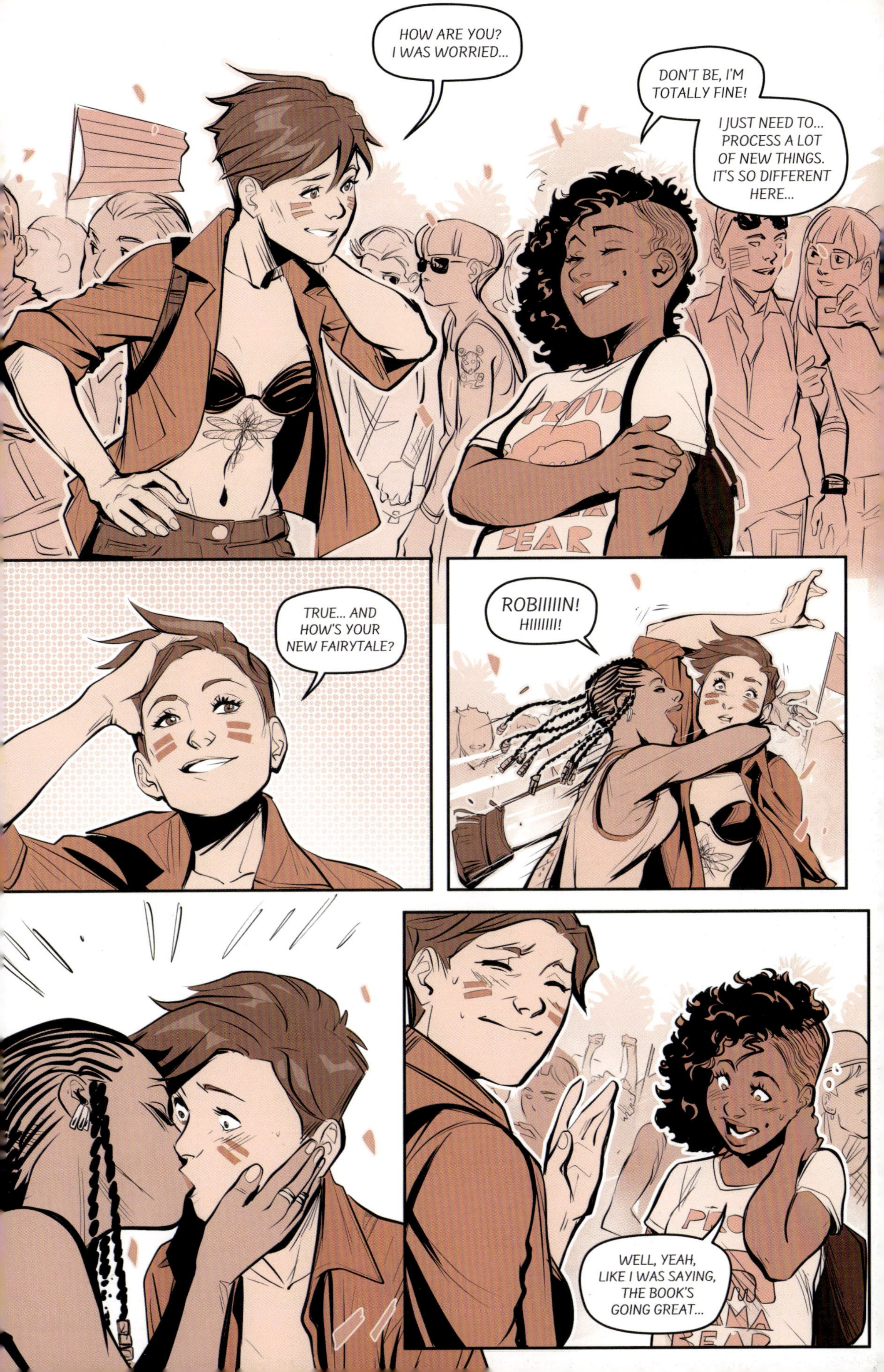
HOW ARE YOU? I WAS WORRIED...
DON'T BE, I'M TOTALLY FINE!
I JUST NEED TO... PROCESS A LOT OF NEW THINGS. IT'S SO DIFFERENT HERE...
PROUD
BEAR
TRUE... AND HOW'S YOUR NEW FAIRYTALE?
ROBIIIIIN! HIIIIIII!
WELL, YEAH, LIKE I WAS SAYING, THE BOOK'S GOING GREAT...

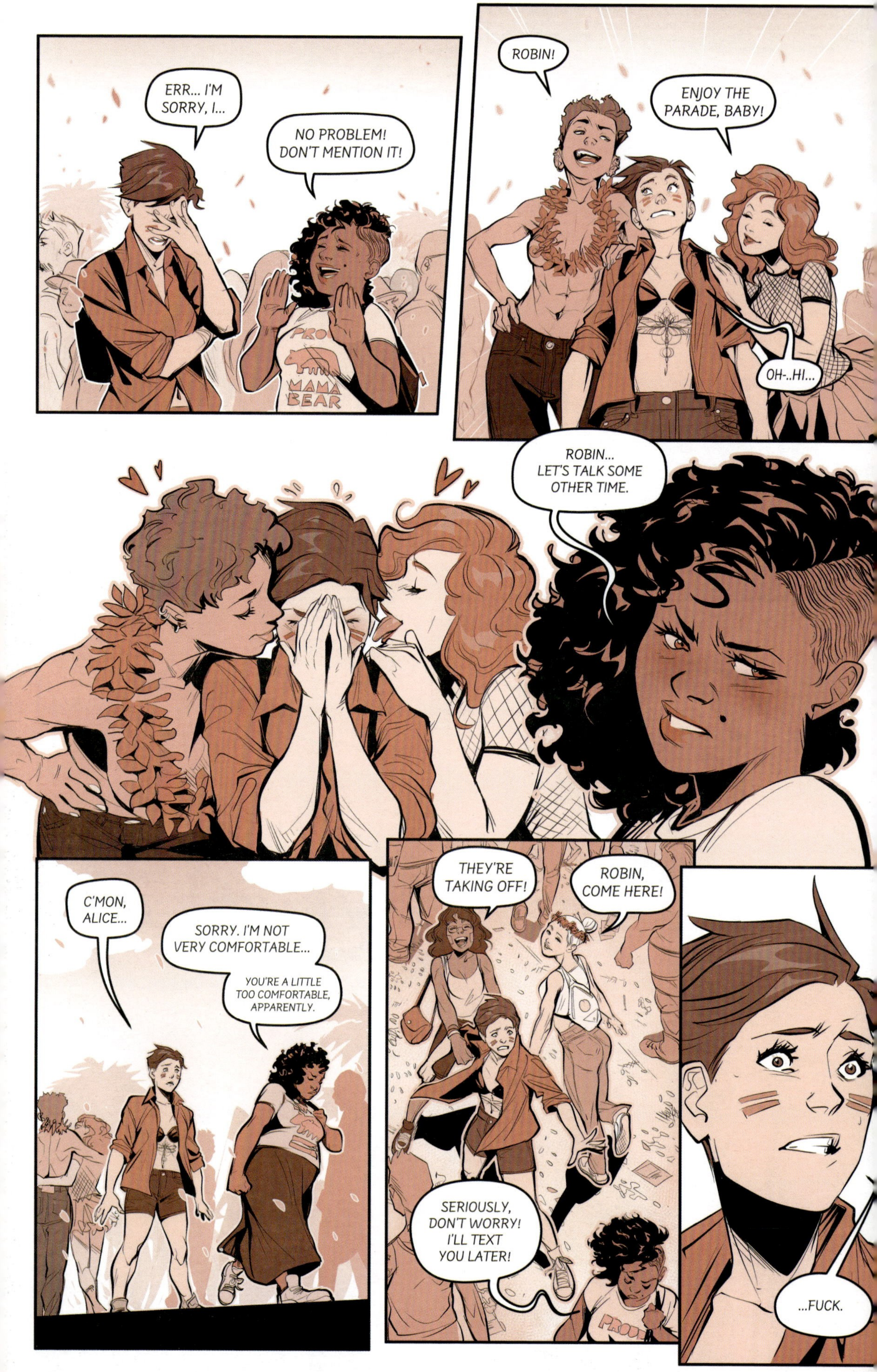
ERR... I'M SORRY, I...
NO PROBLEM! DON'T MENTION IT!
PROUD MAMA BEAR
ROBIN!
ENJOY THE PARADE, BABY!
OH-..HI...
ROBIN... LET'S TALK SOME OTHER TIME.
C'MON, ALICE...
SORRY. I'M NOT VERY COMFORTABLE...
YOU'RE A LITTLE TOO COMFORTABLE, APPARENTLY.
THEY'RE TAKING OFF!
ROBIN, COME HERE!
SERIOUSLY, DON'T WORRY! I'LL TEXT YOU LATER!
...FUCK.

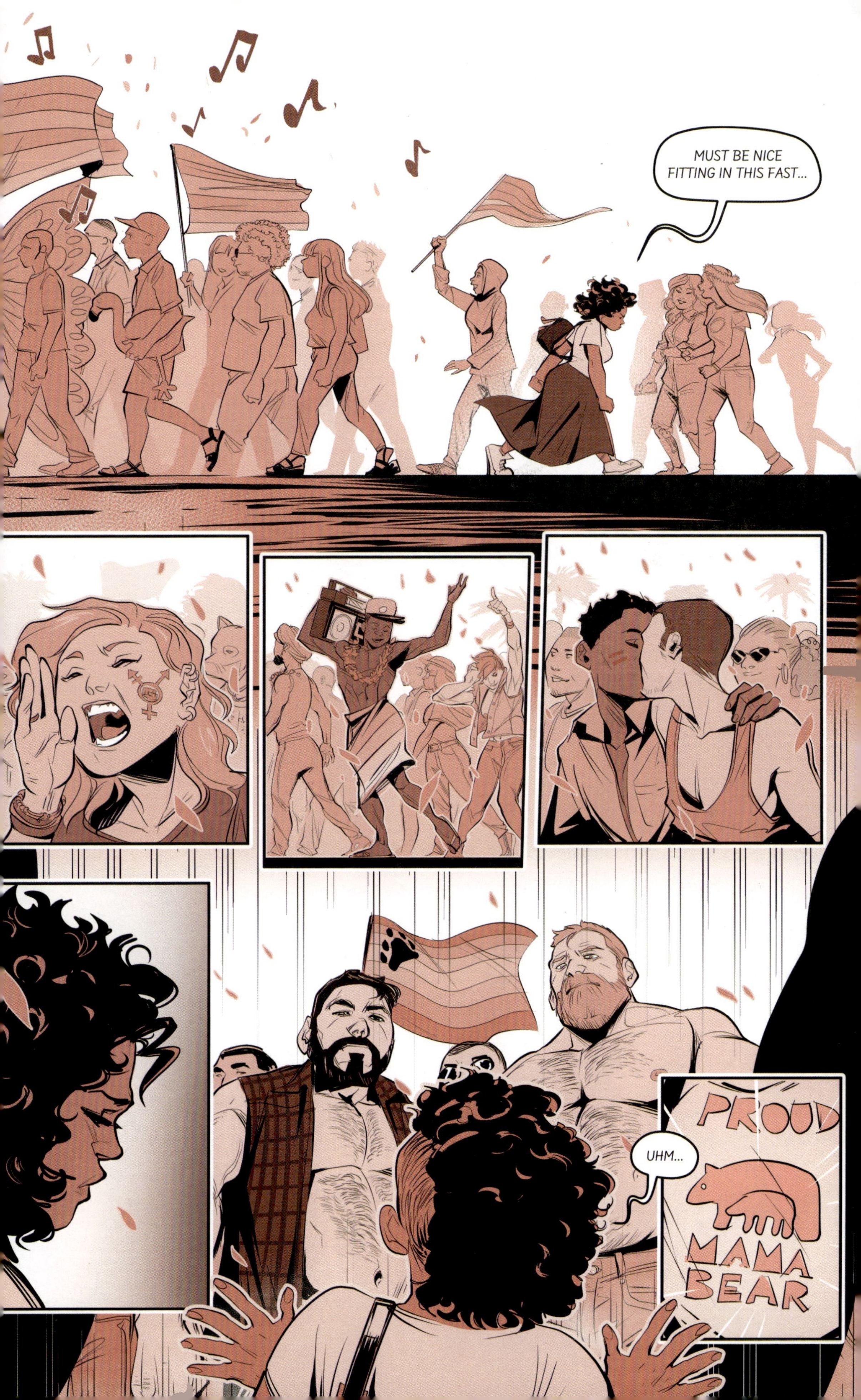
MUST BE NICE FITTING IN THIS FAST...
UHM...
PROUD MAMA BEAR

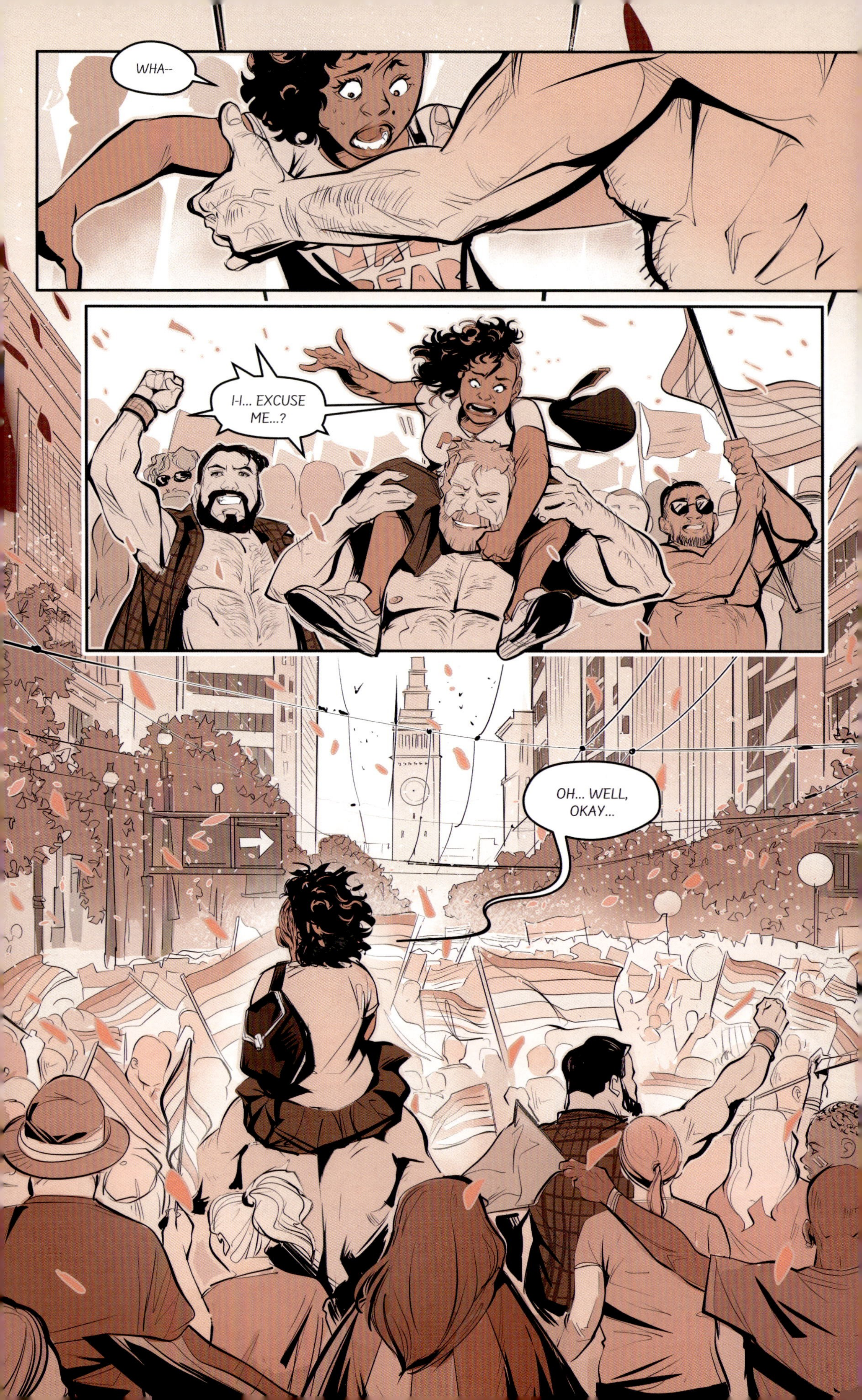
WHA--
I-I... EXCUSE ME...?
OH... WELL, OKAY...

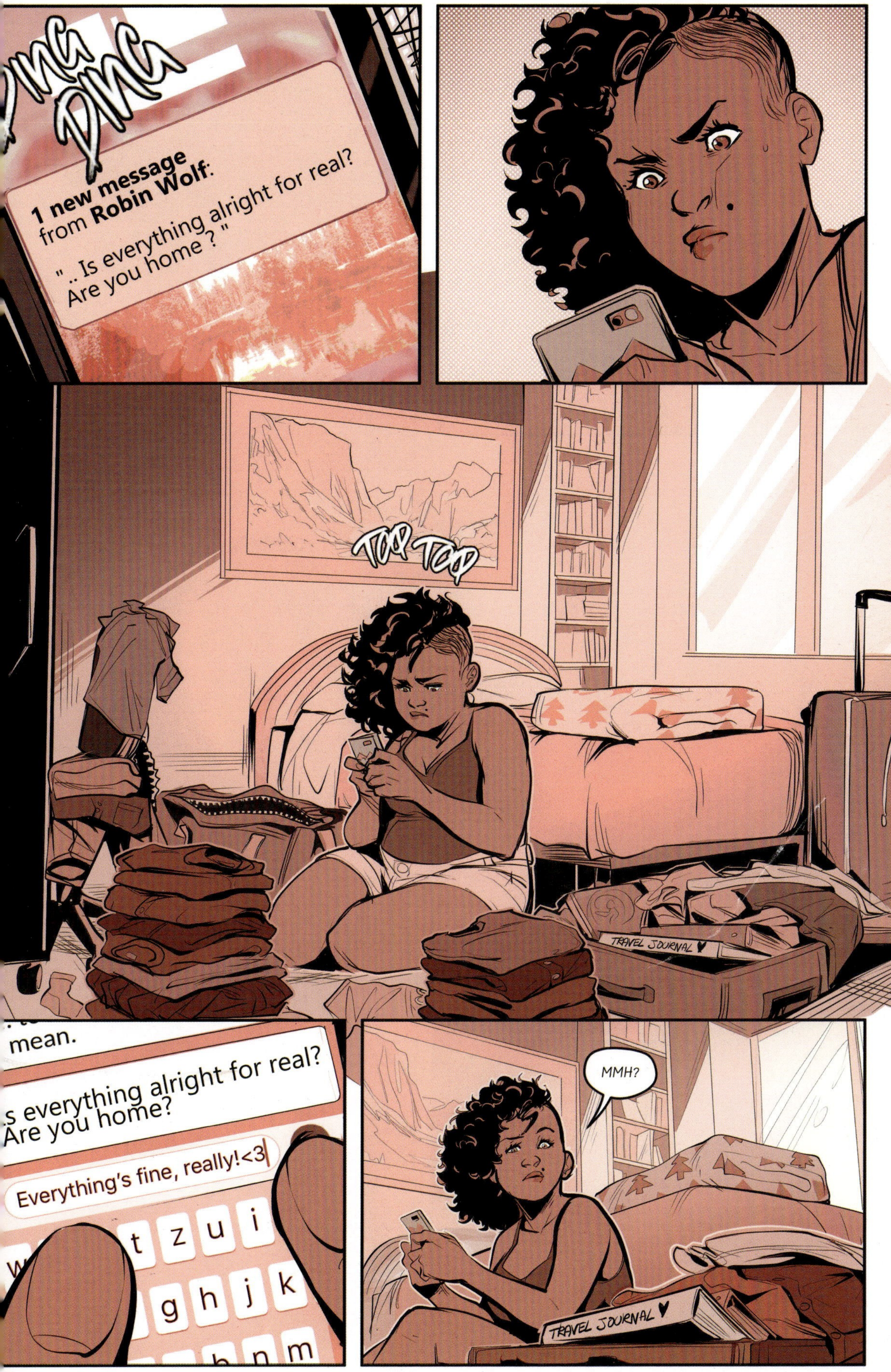
1 new message from Robin Wolf:
" .. Is everything alright for real? Are you home ? "
TOP TOP
TRAVEL JOURNAL ♥
mean.
s everything alright for real? Are you home?
Everything's fine, really!<3
MMH?
TRAVEL JOURNAL ♥

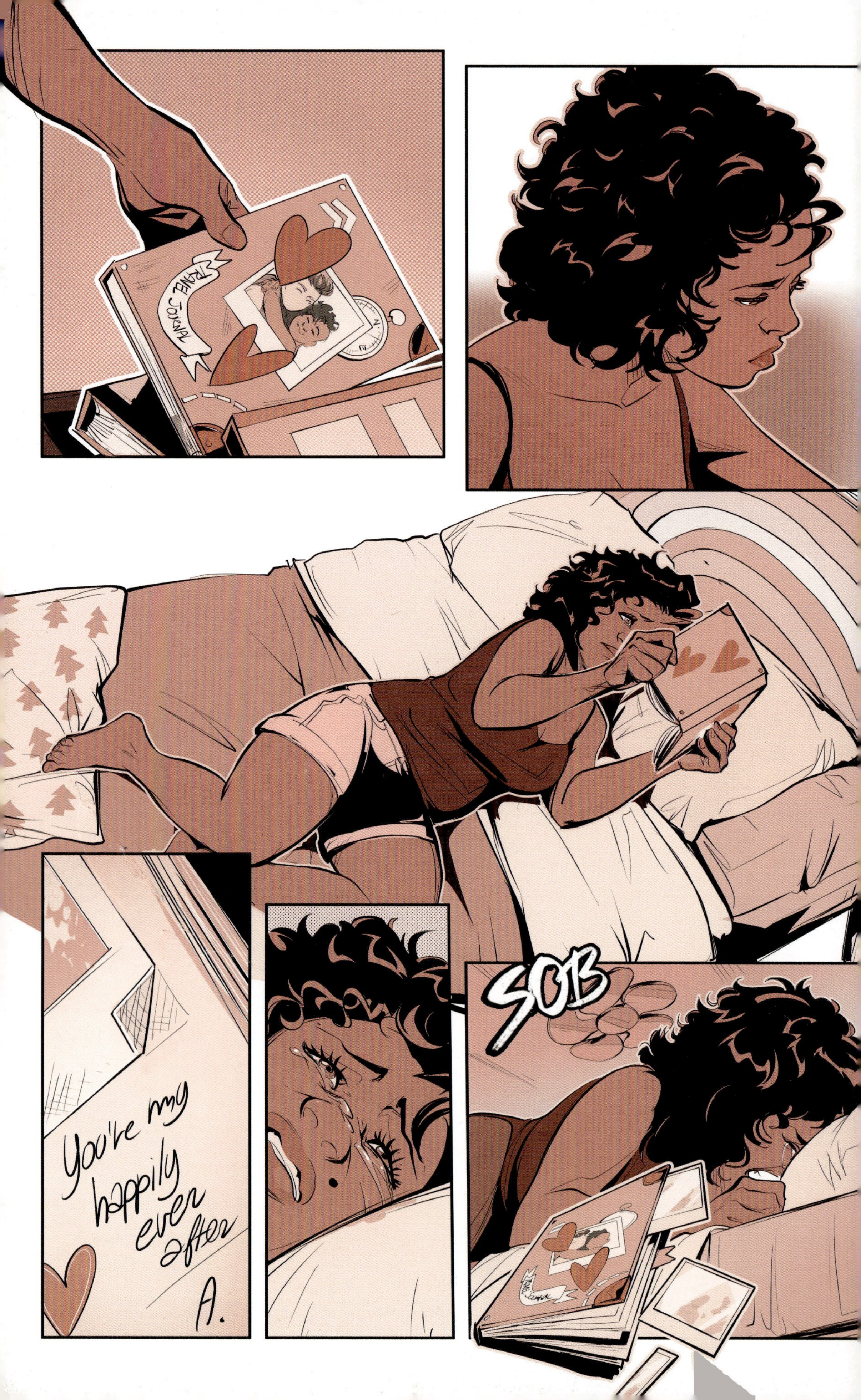
Travel Journal
You're my happily ever after
A.
SOB

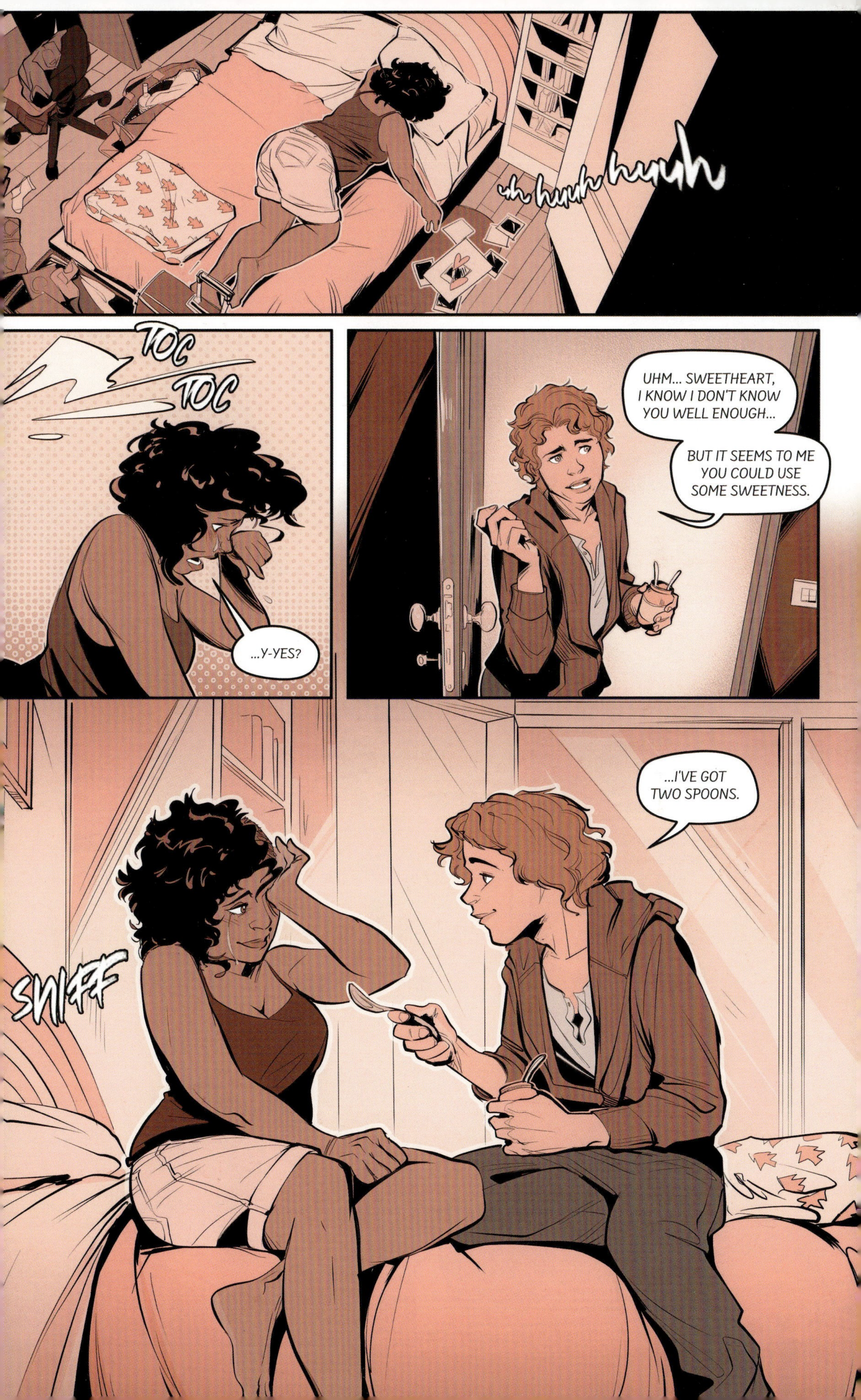
uh huuh huuh
TOC
TOC
...Y-YES?
UHM... SWEETHEART, I KNOW I DON'T KNOW YOU WELL ENOUGH...
BUT IT SEEMS TO ME YOU COULD USE SOME SWEETNESS.
SNIFF
...I'VE GOT TWO SPOONS.

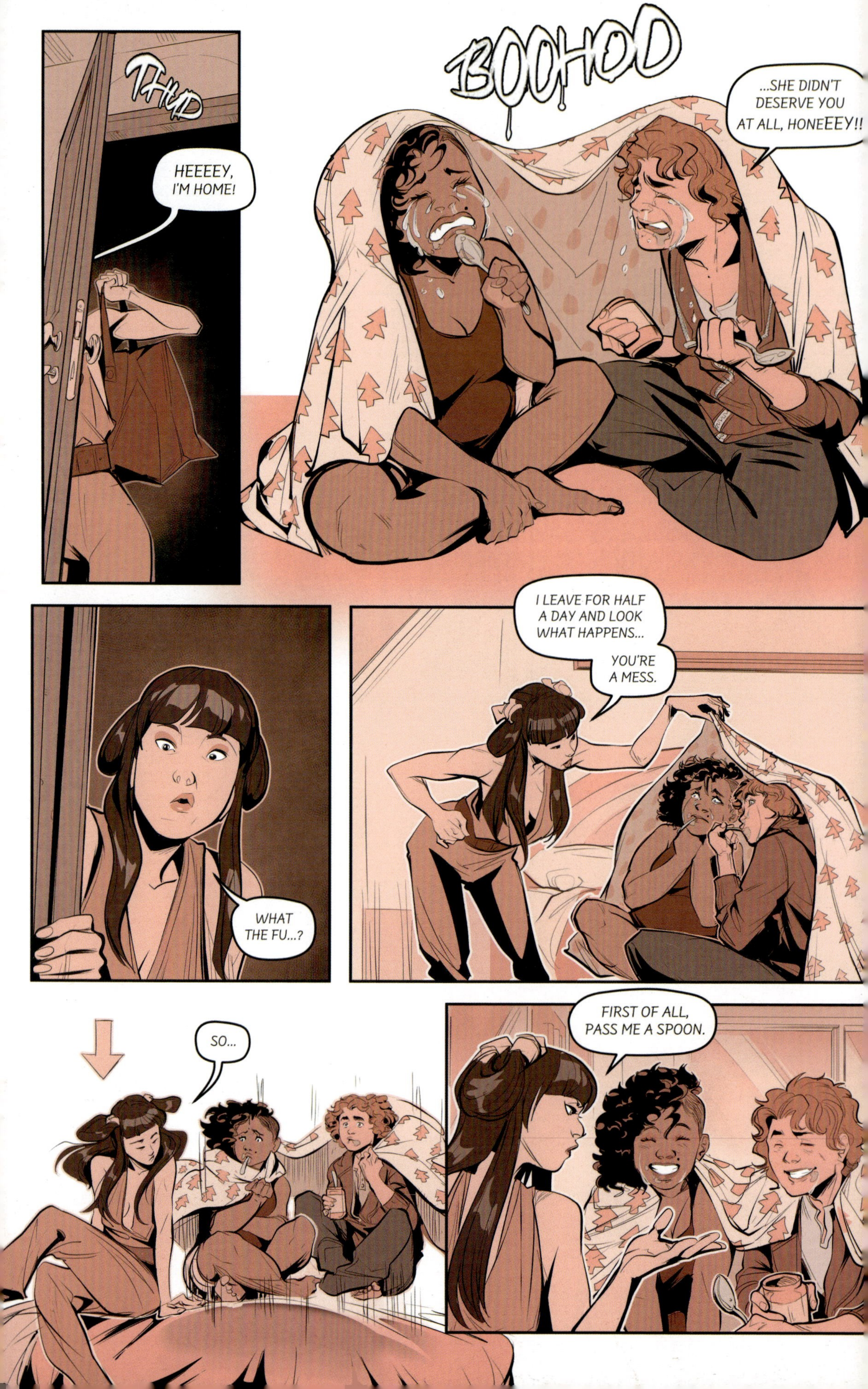
THUD
HEEEEY, I'M HOME!
BOOHOO
...SHE DIDN'T DESERVE YOU AT ALL, HONEEEY!!
WHAT THE FU...?
I LEAVE FOR HALF A DAY AND LOOK WHAT HAPPENS...
YOU'RE A MESS.
SO...
FIRST OF ALL, PASS ME A SPOON.

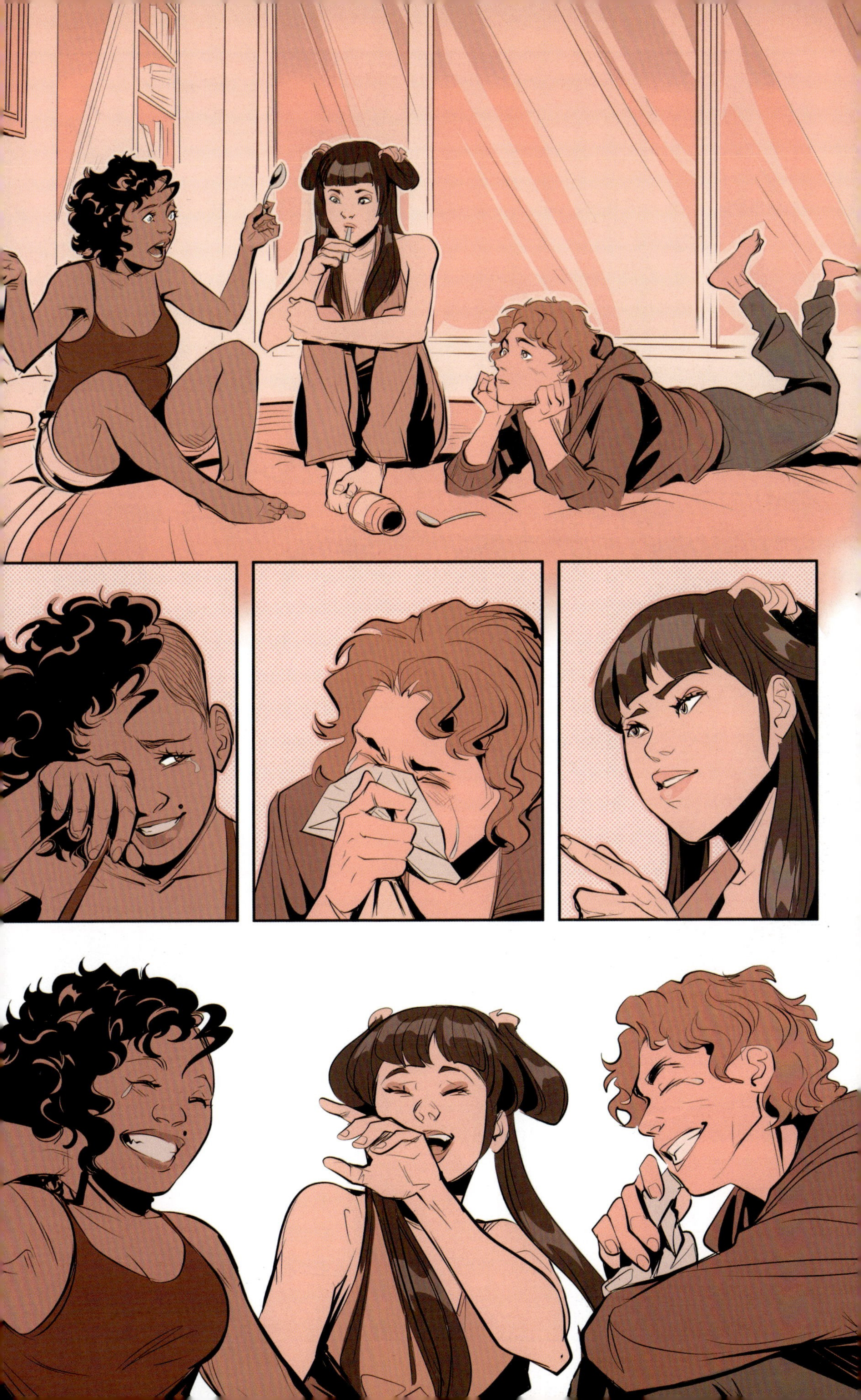

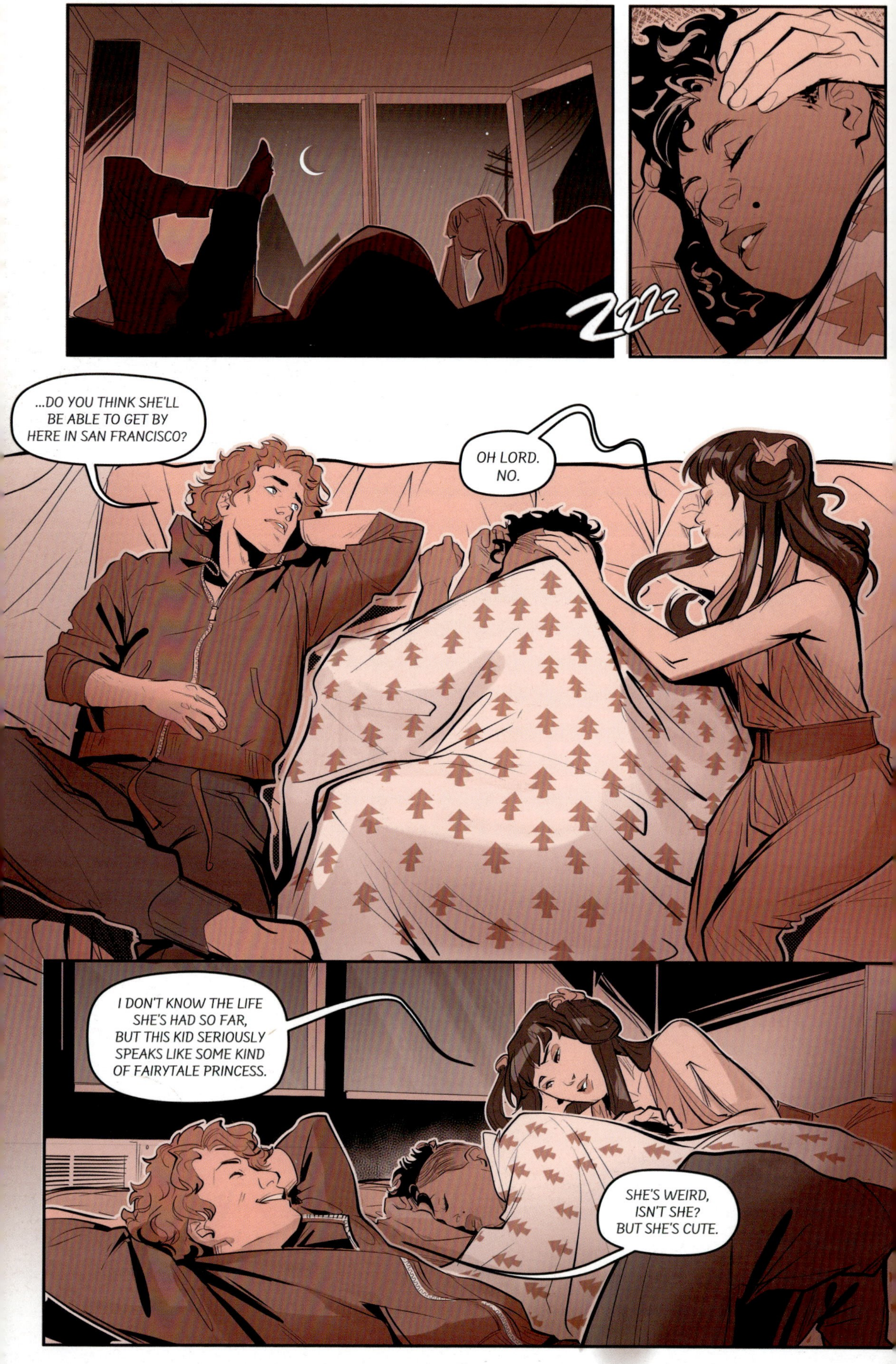
ZZZZ
...DO YOU THINK SHE'LL BE ABLE TO GET BY HERE IN SAN FRANCISCO?
OH LORD. NO.
I DON'T KNOW THE LIFE SHE'S HAD SO FAR, BUT THIS KID SERIOUSLY SPEAKS LIKE SOME KIND OF FAIRYTALE PRINCESS.
SHE'S WEIRD, ISN'T SHE? BUT SHE'S CUTE.

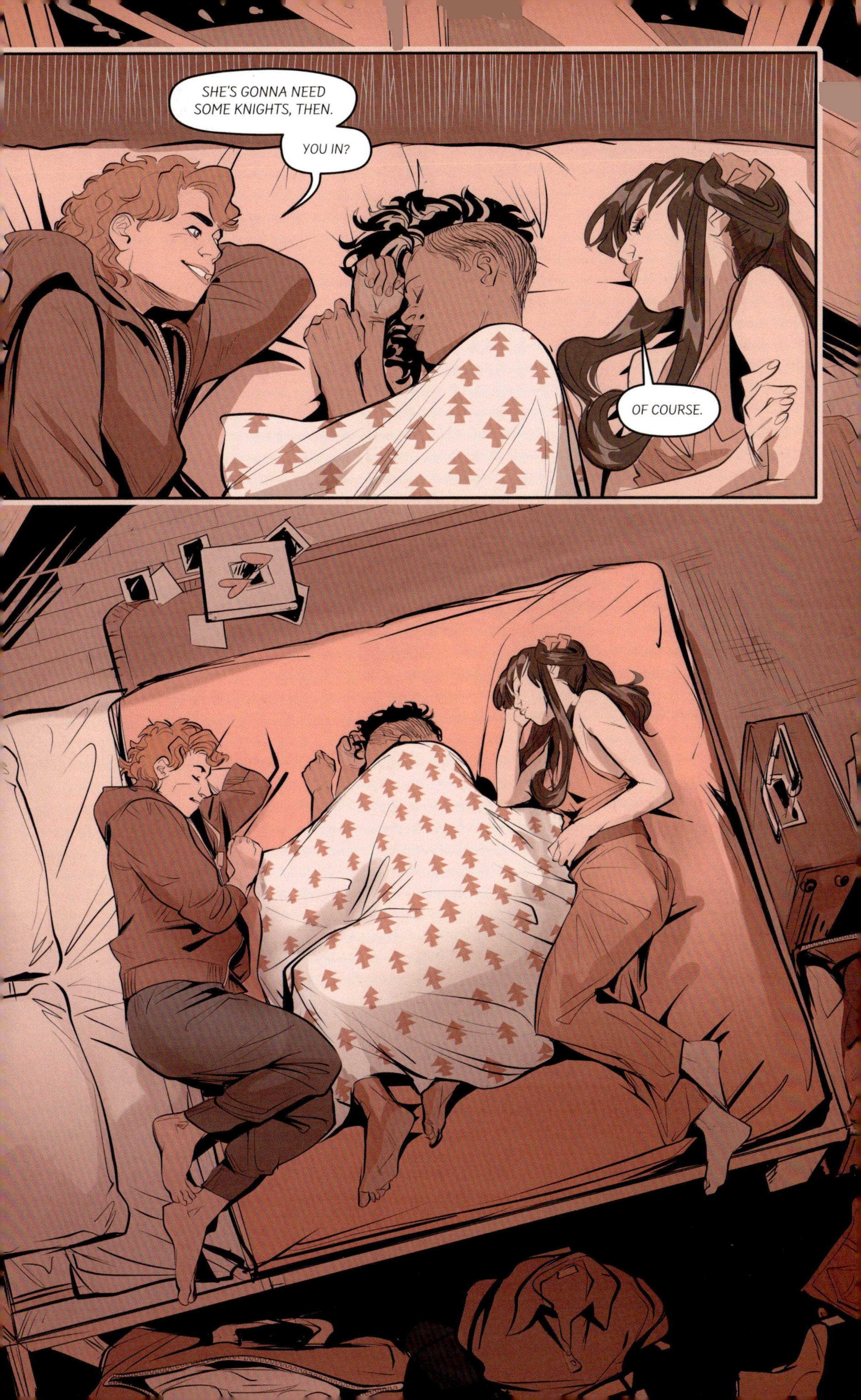
SHE'S GONNA NEED SOME KNIGHTS, THEN.
YOU IN?
OF COURSE.

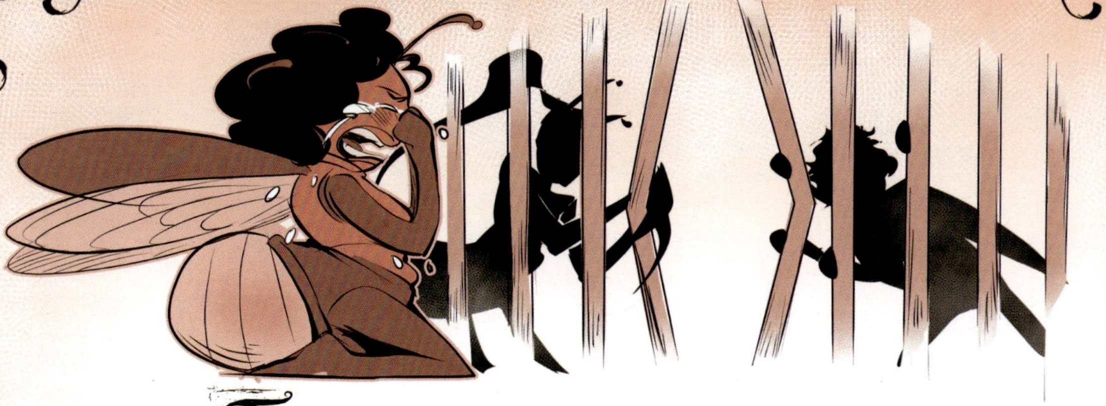

The firefly couldn't break free on her own...
She was feeling lost and desperate!
But her new friends, Mantis and Scarab, came to her rescue!

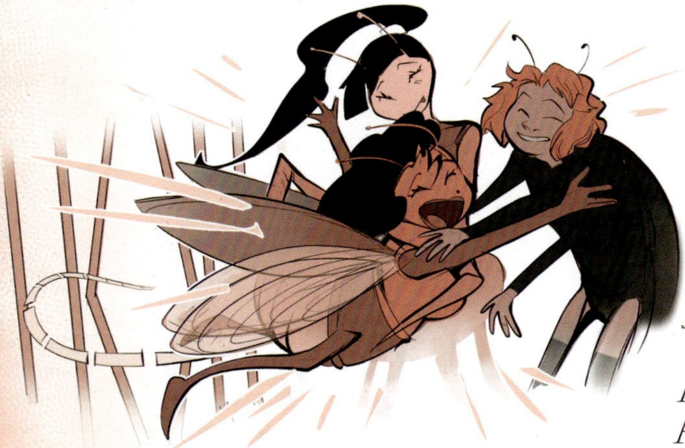

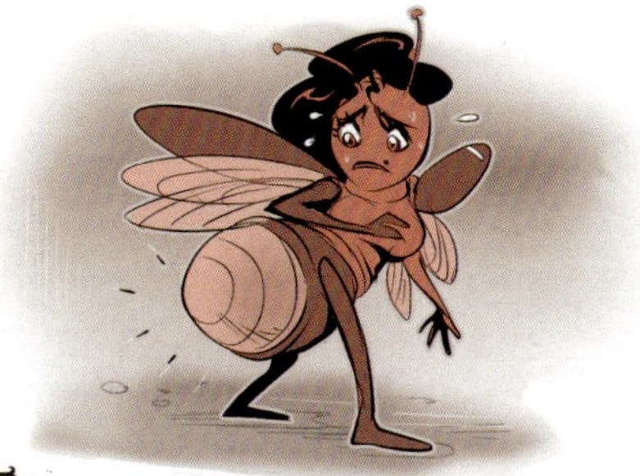

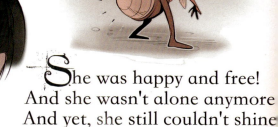

She was happy and free!
And she wasn't alone anymore
And yet, she still couldn't shine

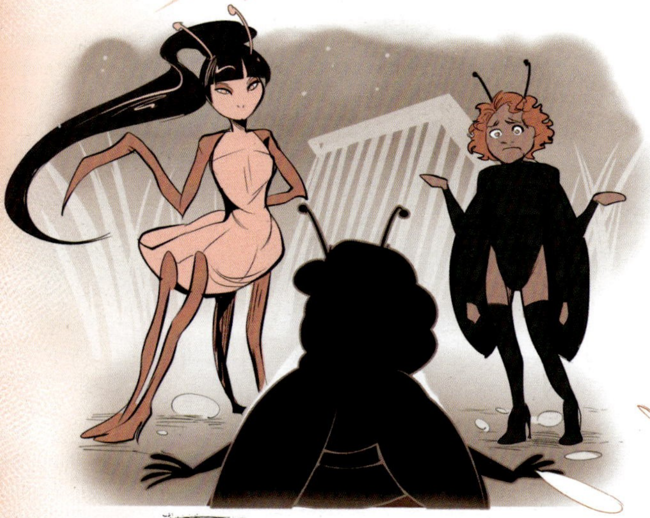

"We can't help you
with that, little firefly!"
Her wise friends said.
"You still have a long way
to go before you'll be able
to shine like you used to!"

The firefly was ready
to set of on her adventurous
journey to find her light again!
There still were many
things to discover, and she
couldn't wait to get started!

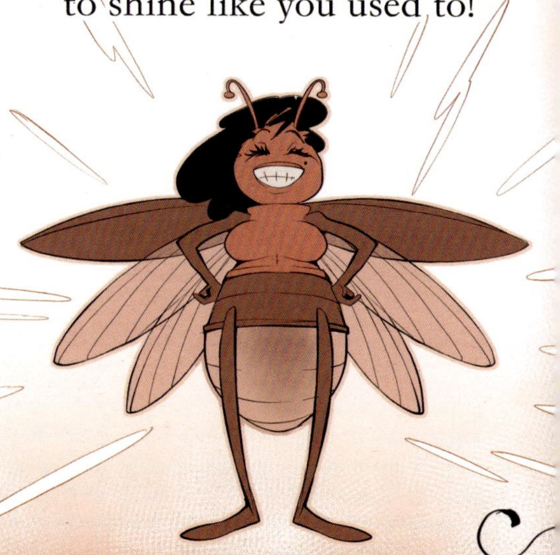

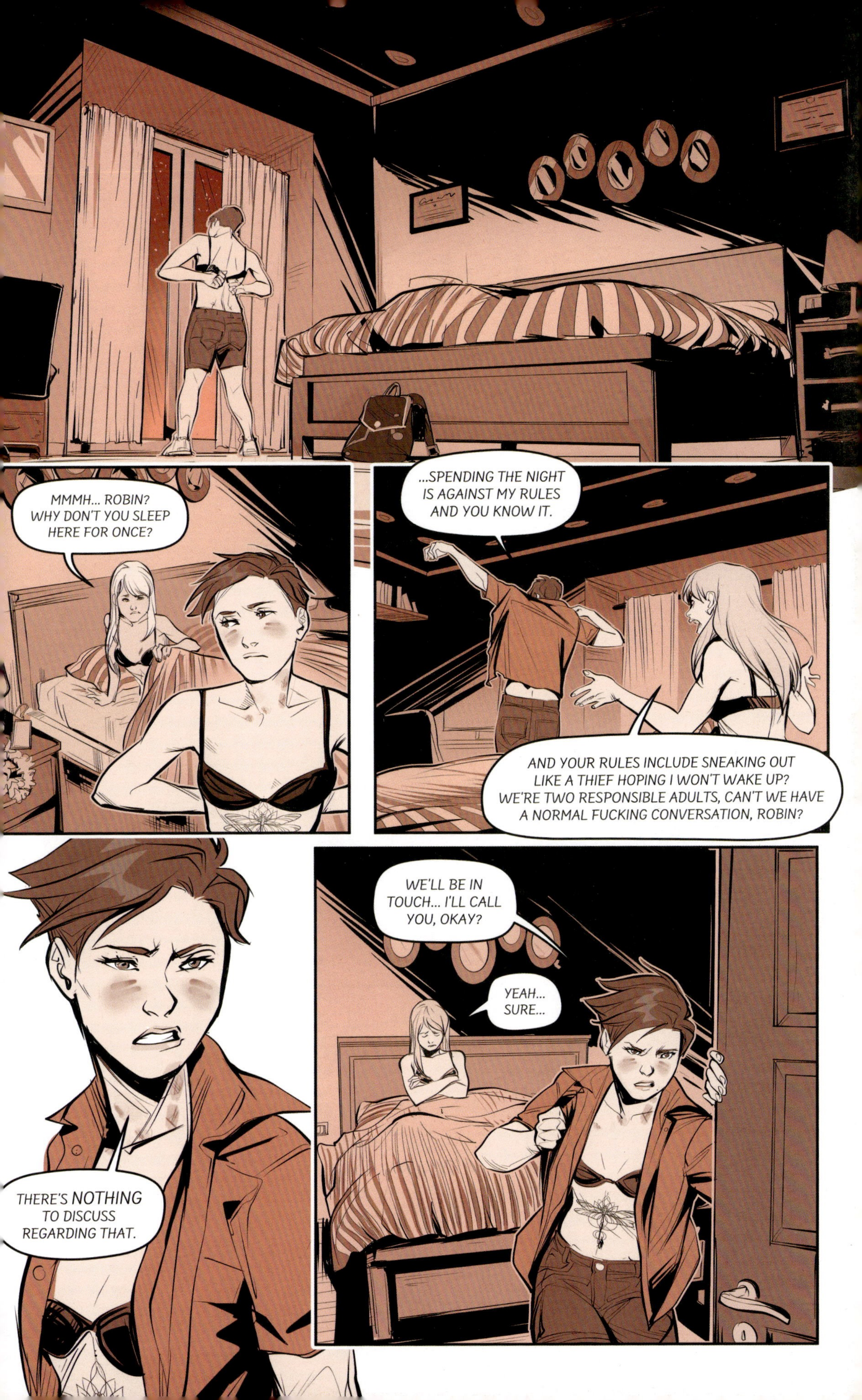
MMMH... ROBIN? WHY DON'T YOU SLEEP HERE FOR ONCE?
...SPENDING THE NIGHT IS AGAINST MY RULES AND YOU KNOW IT.
AND YOUR RULES INCLUDE SNEAKING OUT LIKE A THIEF HOPING I WON'T WAKE UP? WE'RE TWO RESPONSIBLE ADULTS, CAN'T WE HAVE A NORMAL FUCKING CONVERSATION, ROBIN?
THERE'S NOTHING TO DISCUSS REGARDING THAT.
WE'LL BE IN TOUCH... I'LL CALL YOU, OKAY?
YEAH... SURE...

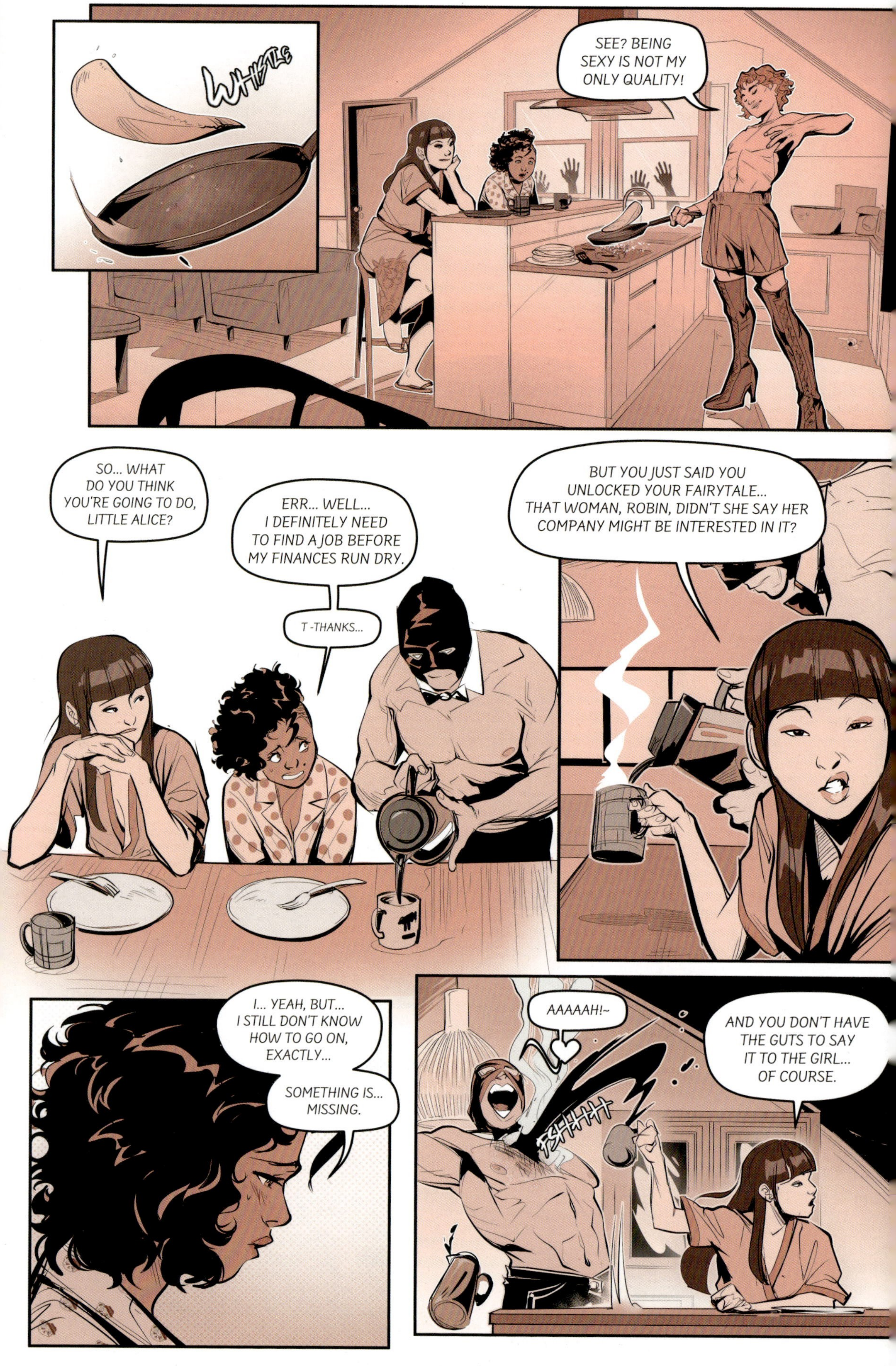
WHISTLE
SEE? BEING SEXY IS NOT MY ONLY QUALITY!
SO... WHAT DO YOU THINK YOU'RE GOING TO DO, LITTLE ALICE?
ERR... WELL... I DEFINITELY NEED TO FIND A JOB BEFORE MY FINANCES RUN DRY.
T-THANKS...
BUT YOU JUST SAID YOU UNLOCKED YOUR FAIRYTALE... THAT WOMAN, ROBIN, DIDN'T SHE SAY HER COMPANY MIGHT BE INTERESTED IN IT?
I... YEAH, BUT... I STILL DON'T KNOW HOW TO GO ON, EXACTLY...
SOMETHING IS... MISSING.
AAAAAH!~
FSHHHH
AND YOU DON'T HAVE THE GUTS TO SAY IT TO THE GIRL... OF COURSE.

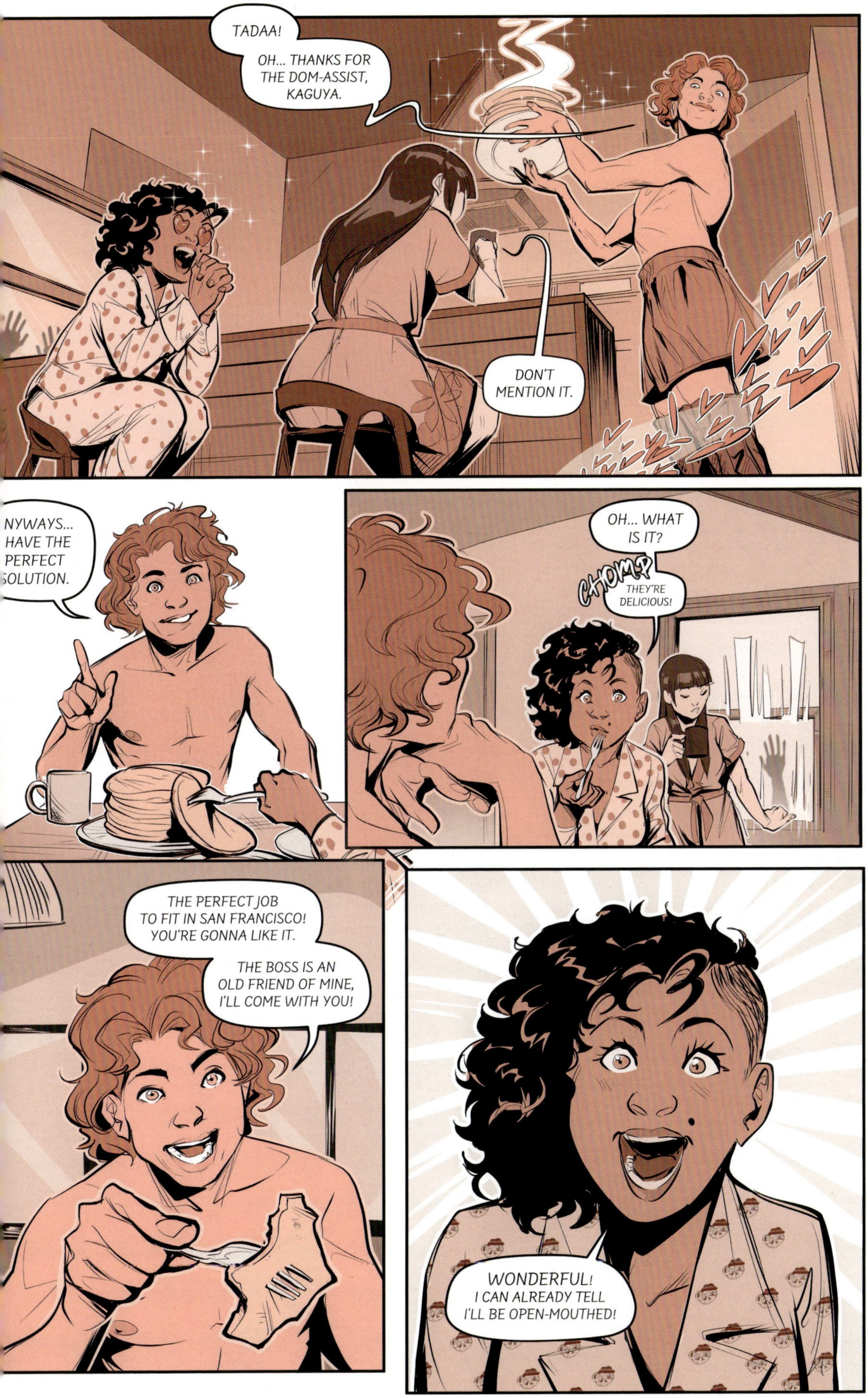
TADAA!
OH... THANKS FOR THE DOM-ASSIST, KAGUYA.
DON'T MENTION IT.
NYWAYS... HAVE THE PERFECT SOLUTION.
OH... WHAT IS IT?
CHOMP
THEY'RE DELICIOUS!
THE PERFECT JOB TO FIT IN SAN FRANCISCO! YOU'RE GONNA LIKE IT.
THE BOSS IS AN OLD FRIEND OF MINE, I'LL COME WITH YOU!
WONDERFUL! I CAN ALREADY TELL I'LL BE OPEN-MOUTHED!

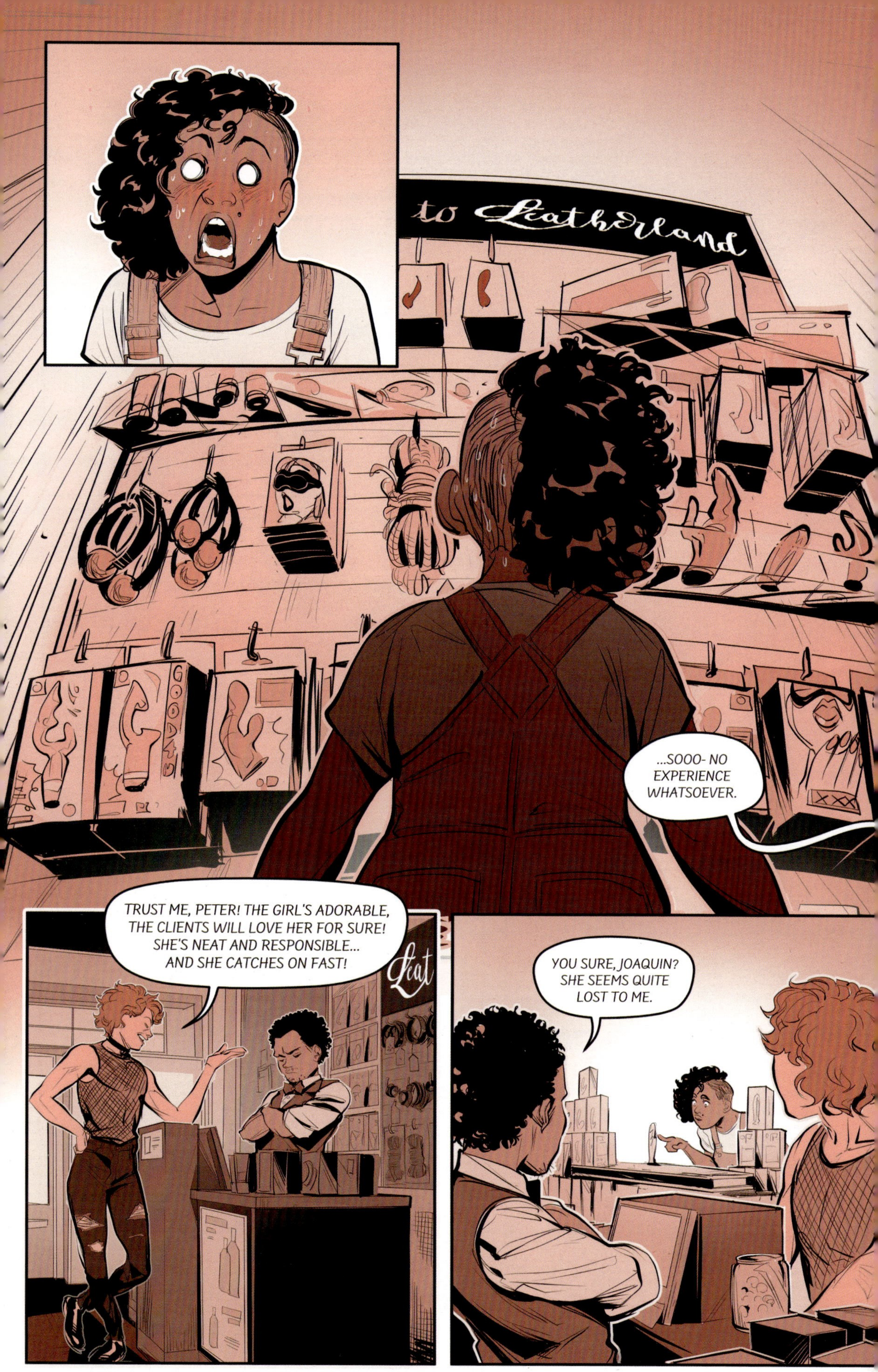
to Leatherland
...SOOO- NO EXPERIENCE WHATSOEVER.
TRUST ME, PETER! THE GIRL'S ADORABLE, THE CLIENTS WILL LOVE HER FOR SURE! SHE'S NEAT AND RESPONSIBLE... AND SHE CATCHES ON FAST!
YOU SURE, JOAQUIN? SHE SEEMS QUITE LOST TO ME.

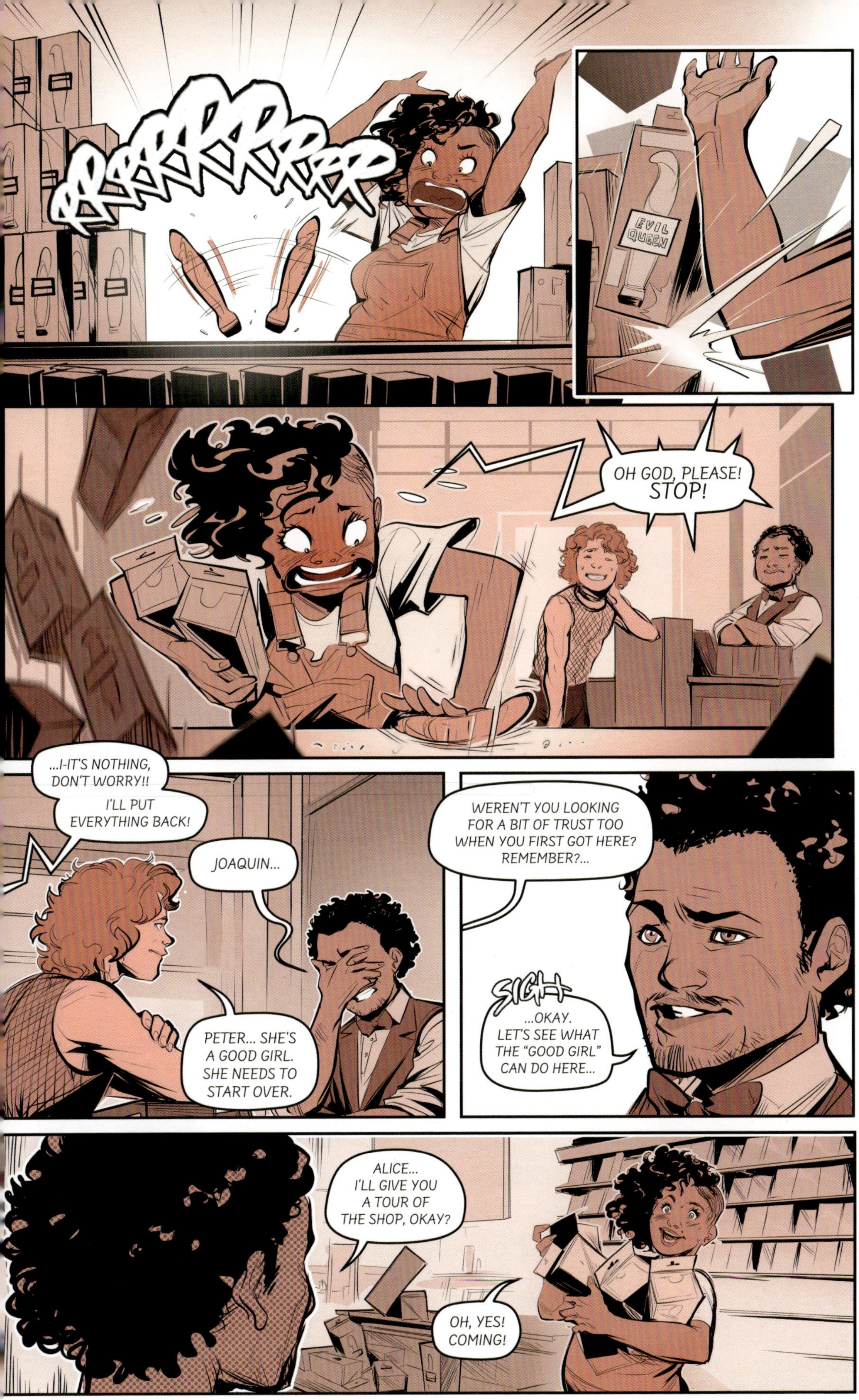
BRRRRRRRR
EVIL QUEEN
OH GOD, PLEASE! STOP!
...I-IT'S NOTHING, DON'T WORRY!!
I'LL PUT EVERYTHING BACK!
JOAQUIN...
PETER... SHE'S A GOOD GIRL. SHE NEEDS TO START OVER.
WEREN'T YOU LOOKING FOR A BIT OF TRUST TOO WHEN YOU FIRST GOT HERE? REMEMBER?...
SIGH
...OKAY. LET'S SEE WHAT THE "GOOD GIRL" CAN DO HERE...
ALICE... I'LL GIVE YOU A TOUR OF THE SHOP, OKAY?
OH, YES! COMING!

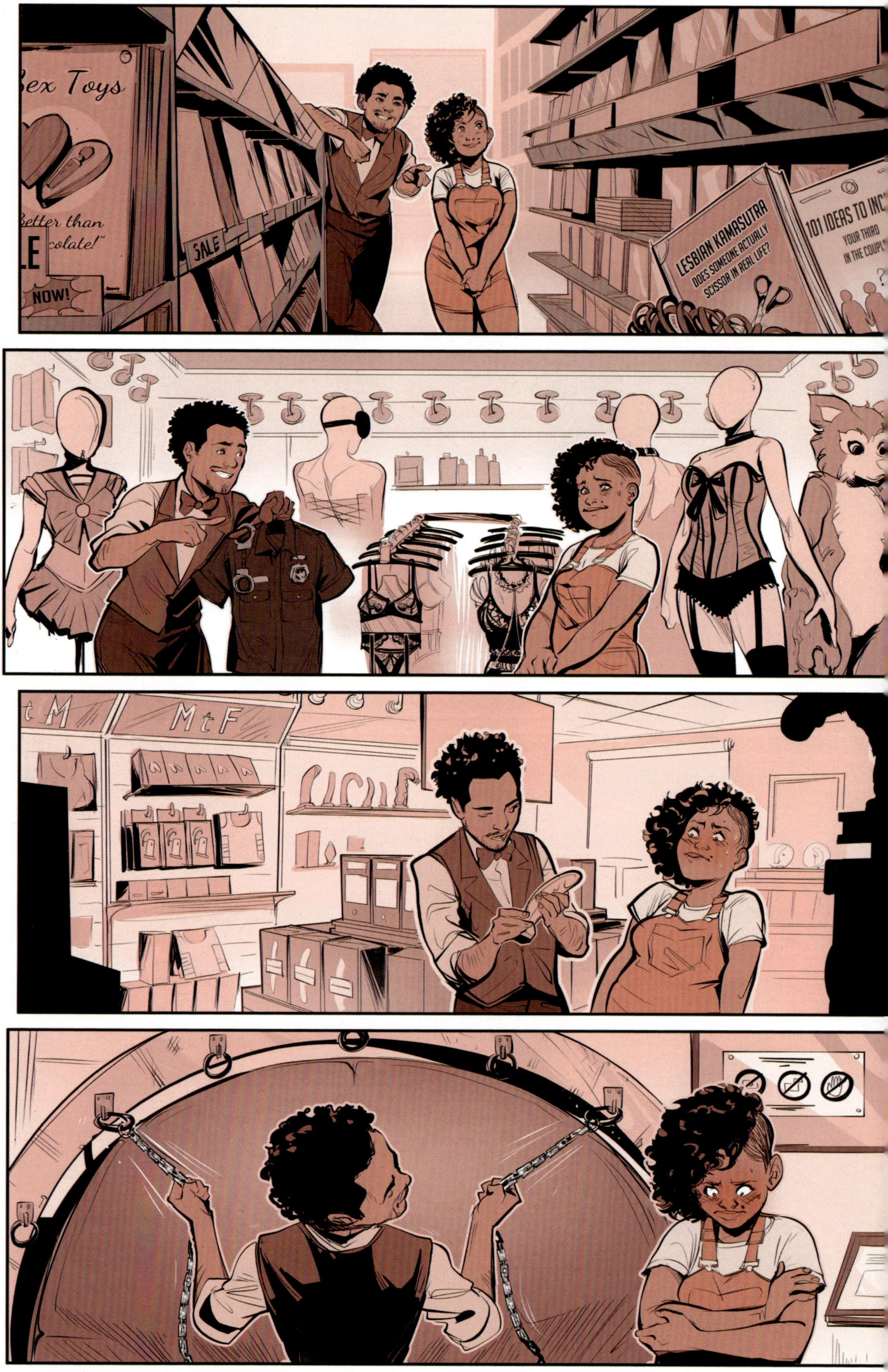

Sex Toys
NOW!
SALE
LESBIAN KAMASUTRA
DOES SOMEONE ACTUALLY SCISSOR IN REAL LIFE?
YOUR THIRD
MtF

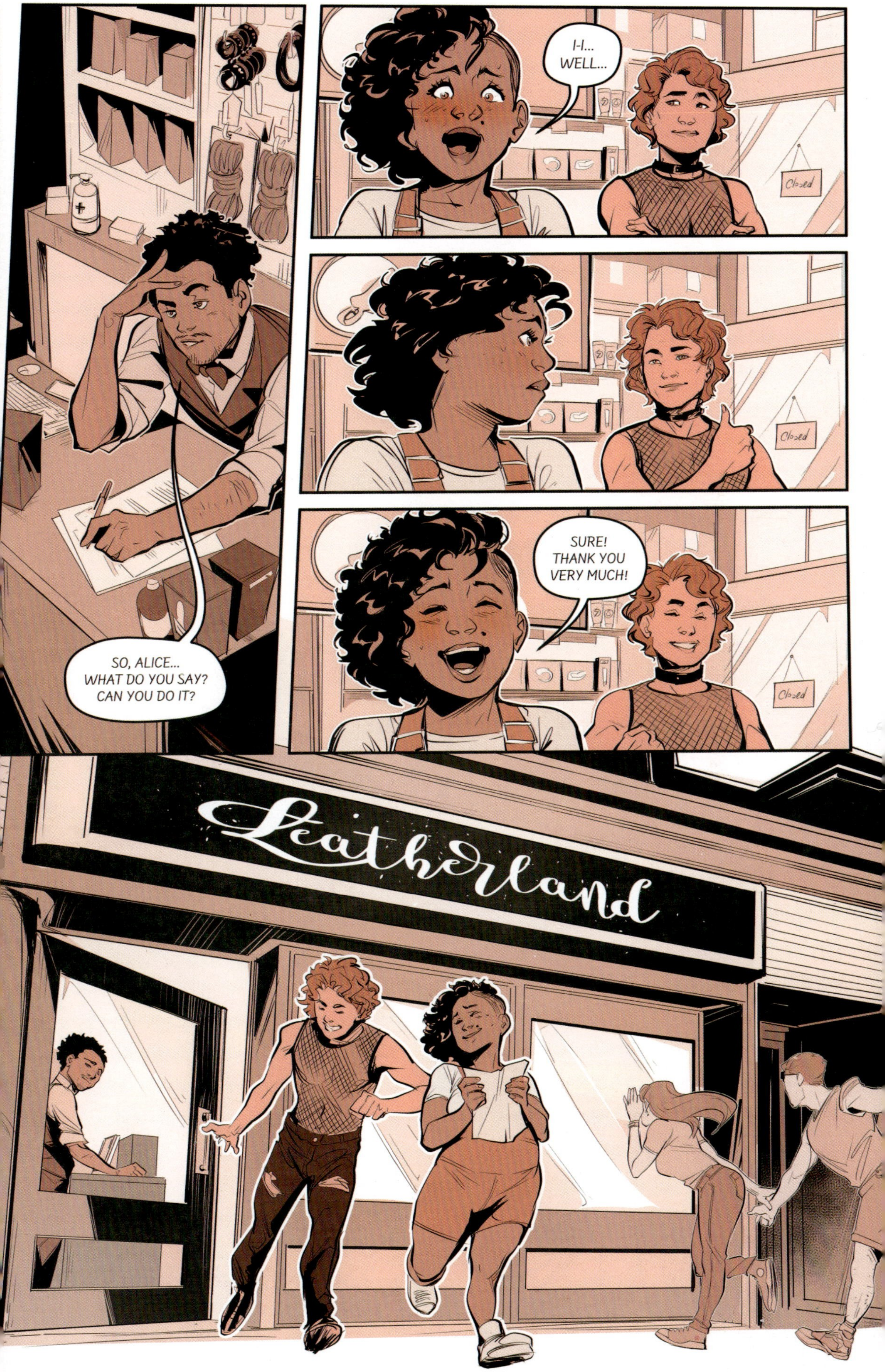
I-I... WELL...
Closed
Closed
SO, ALICE... WHAT DO YOU SAY? CAN YOU DO IT?
SURE! THANK YOU VERY MUCH!
Closed
Leatherland

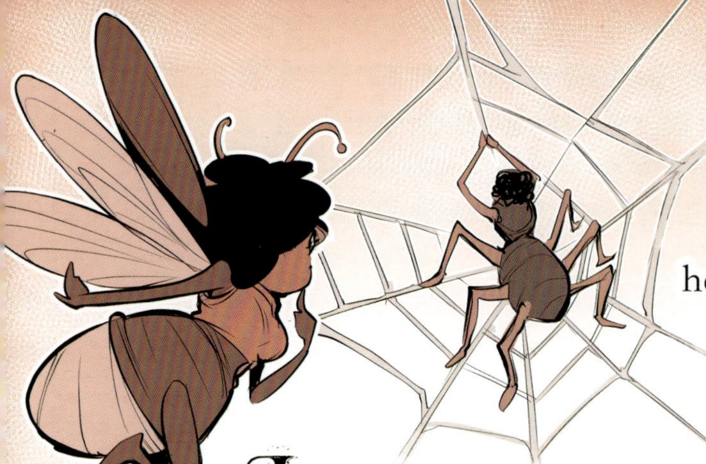

The firefly, on her path,
met an industrious spider.
Such an interesting web
he could manage around him!
But he looked like he
could use some help!

"Let me help you, eight-legged friend!
Can I do something for you?"
offered our little firefly cheerfully.

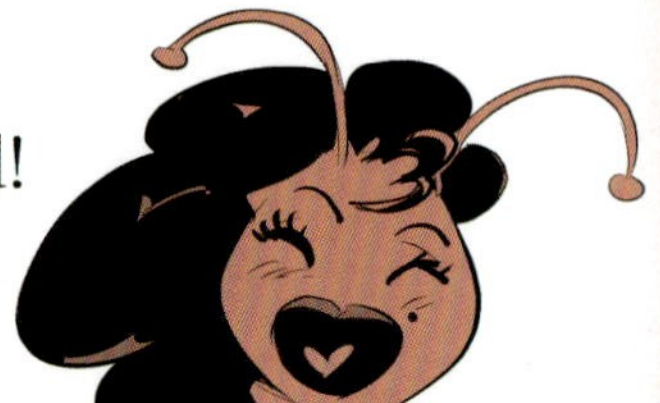

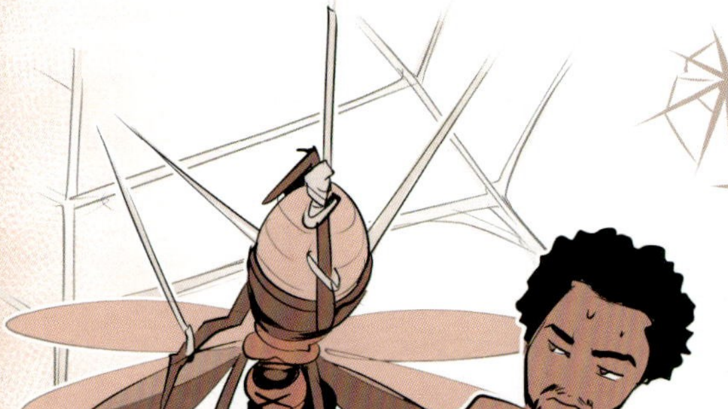

Alas, she really couldn't.
She kept causing trouble!

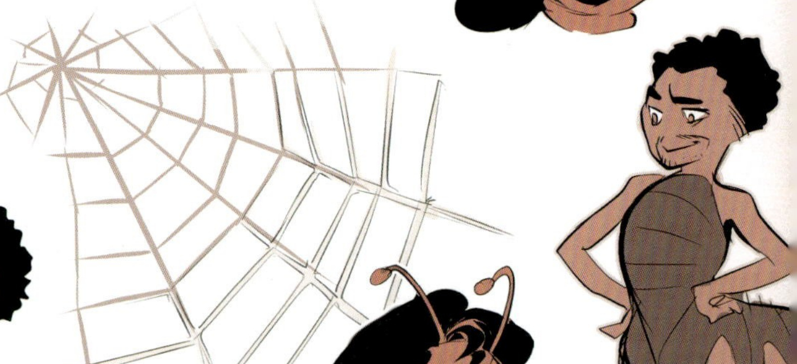

But she never gave up and
she found her way to be helpful!

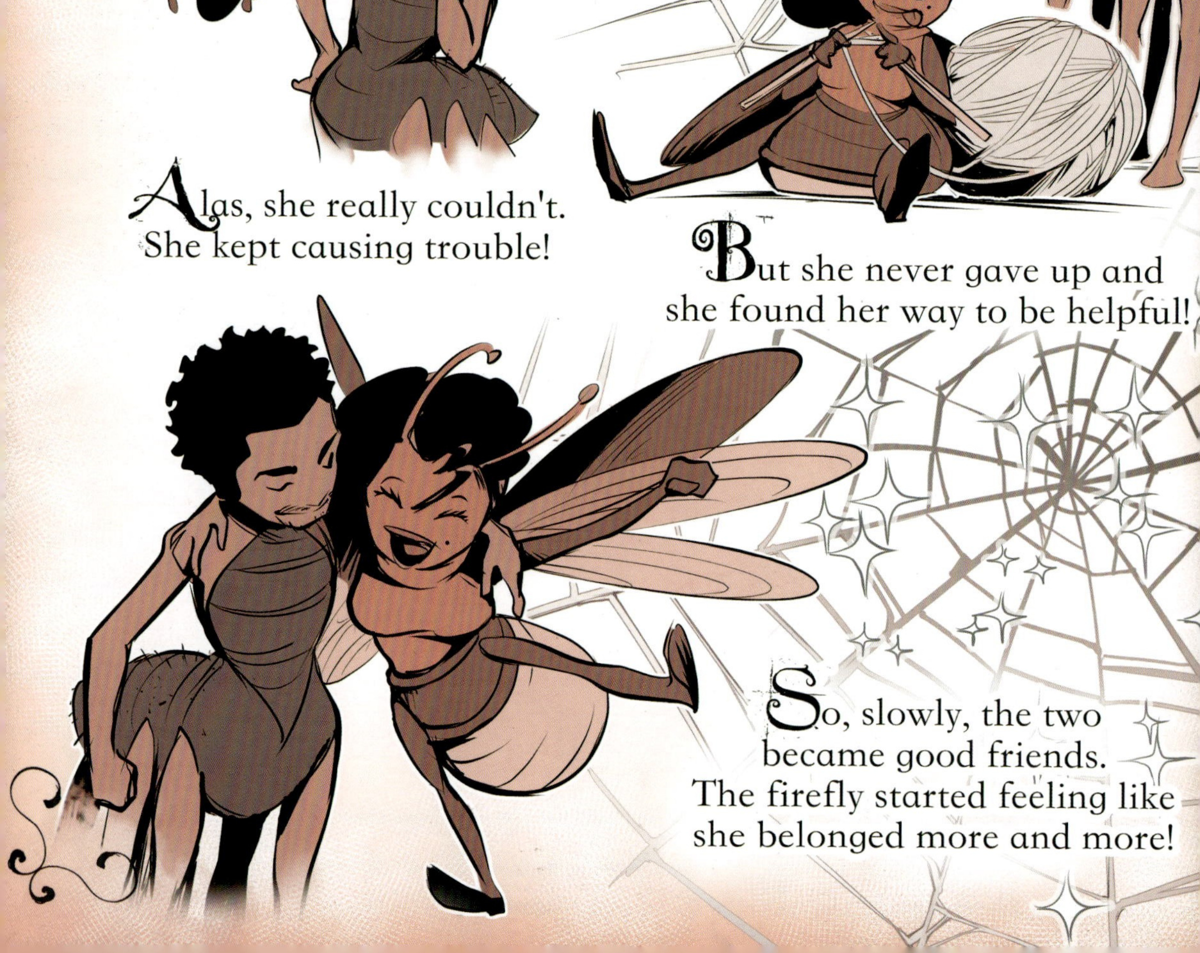

So, slowly, the two
became good friends.
The firefly started feeling like
she belonged more and more!

Issue 3

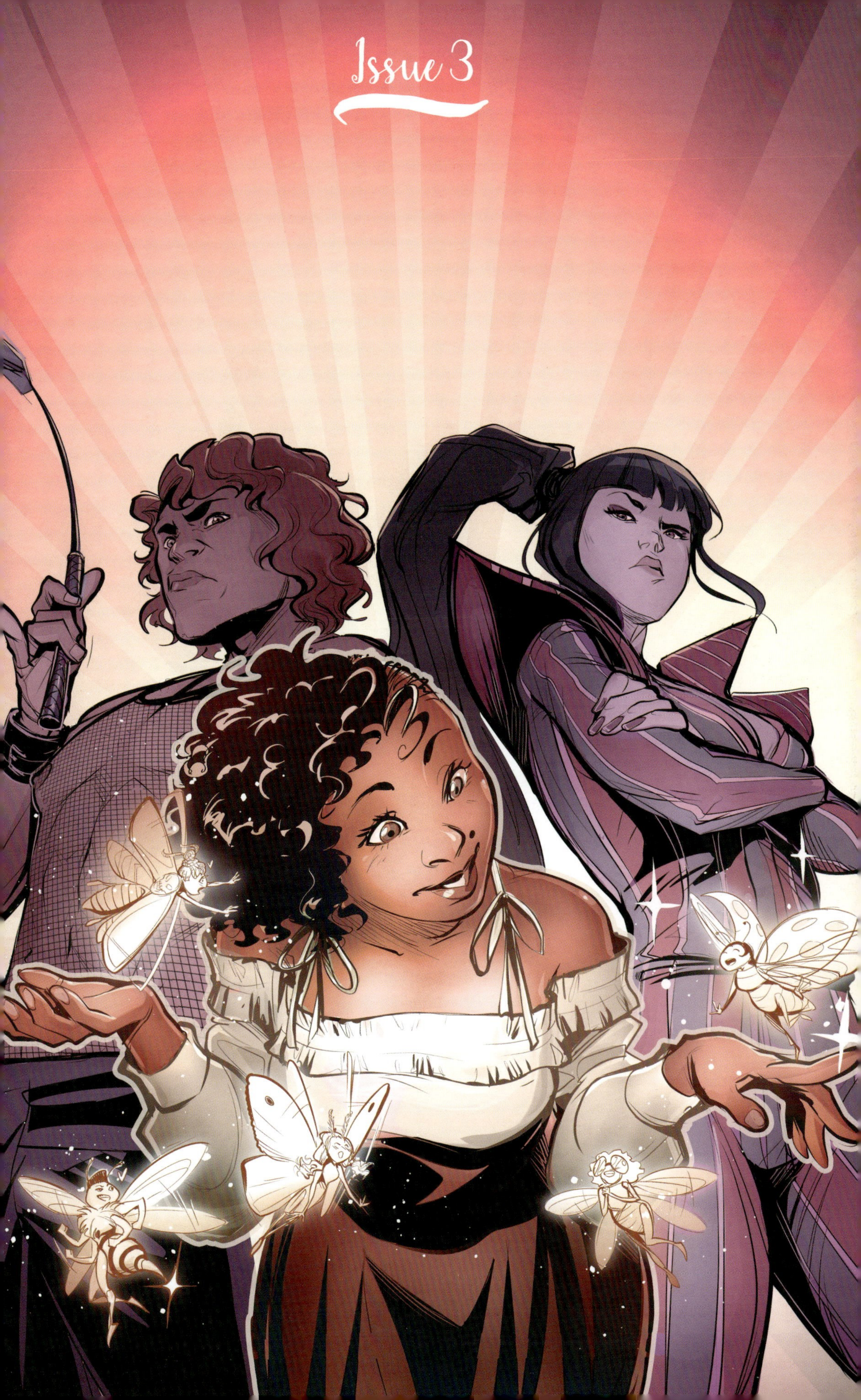

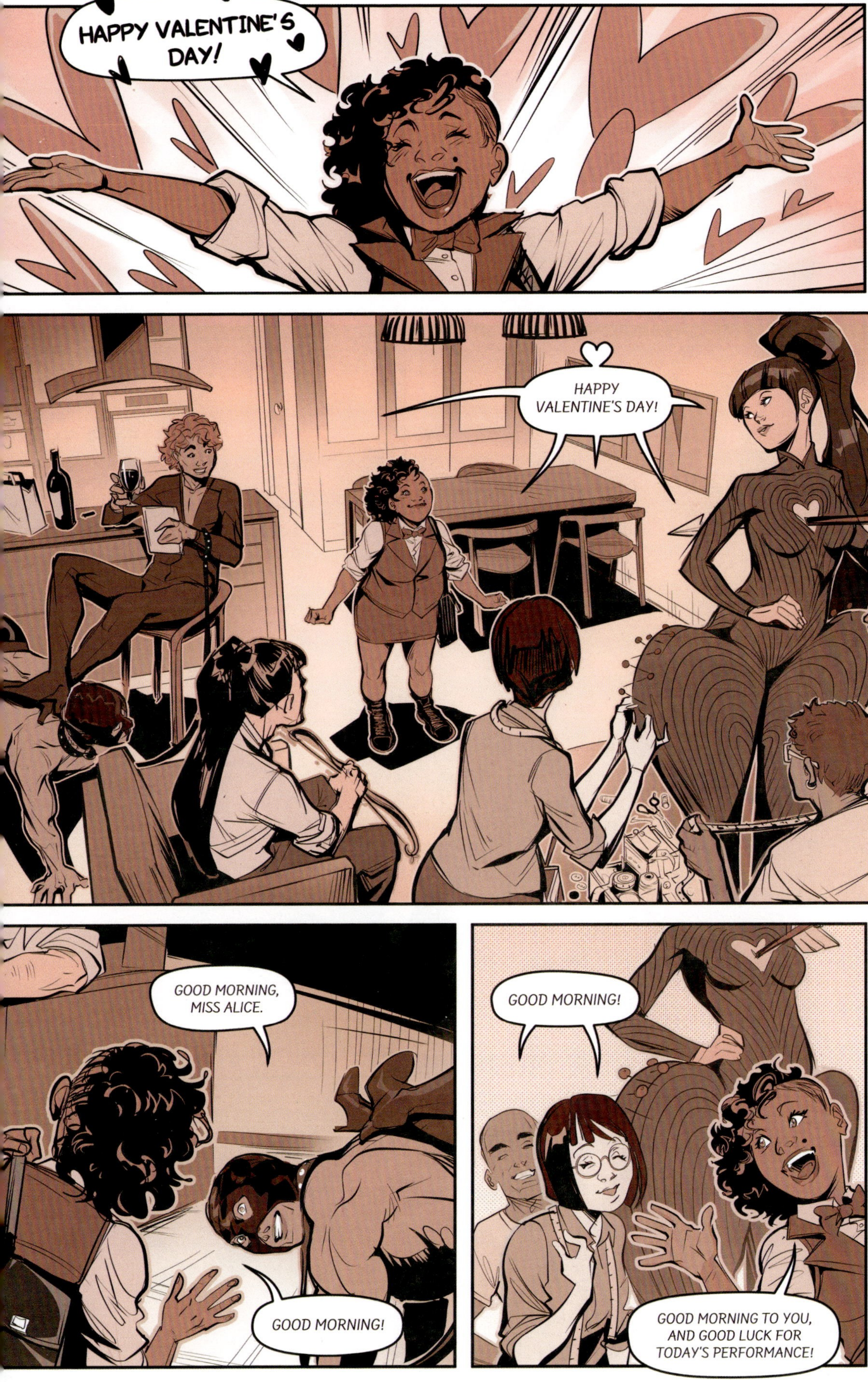
HAPPY VALENTINE'S DAY!
HAPPY VALENTINE'S DAY!
GOOD MORNING, MISS ALICE.
GOOD MORNING!
GOOD MORNING!
GOOD MORNING TO YOU, AND GOOD LUCK FOR TODAY'S PERFORMANCE!

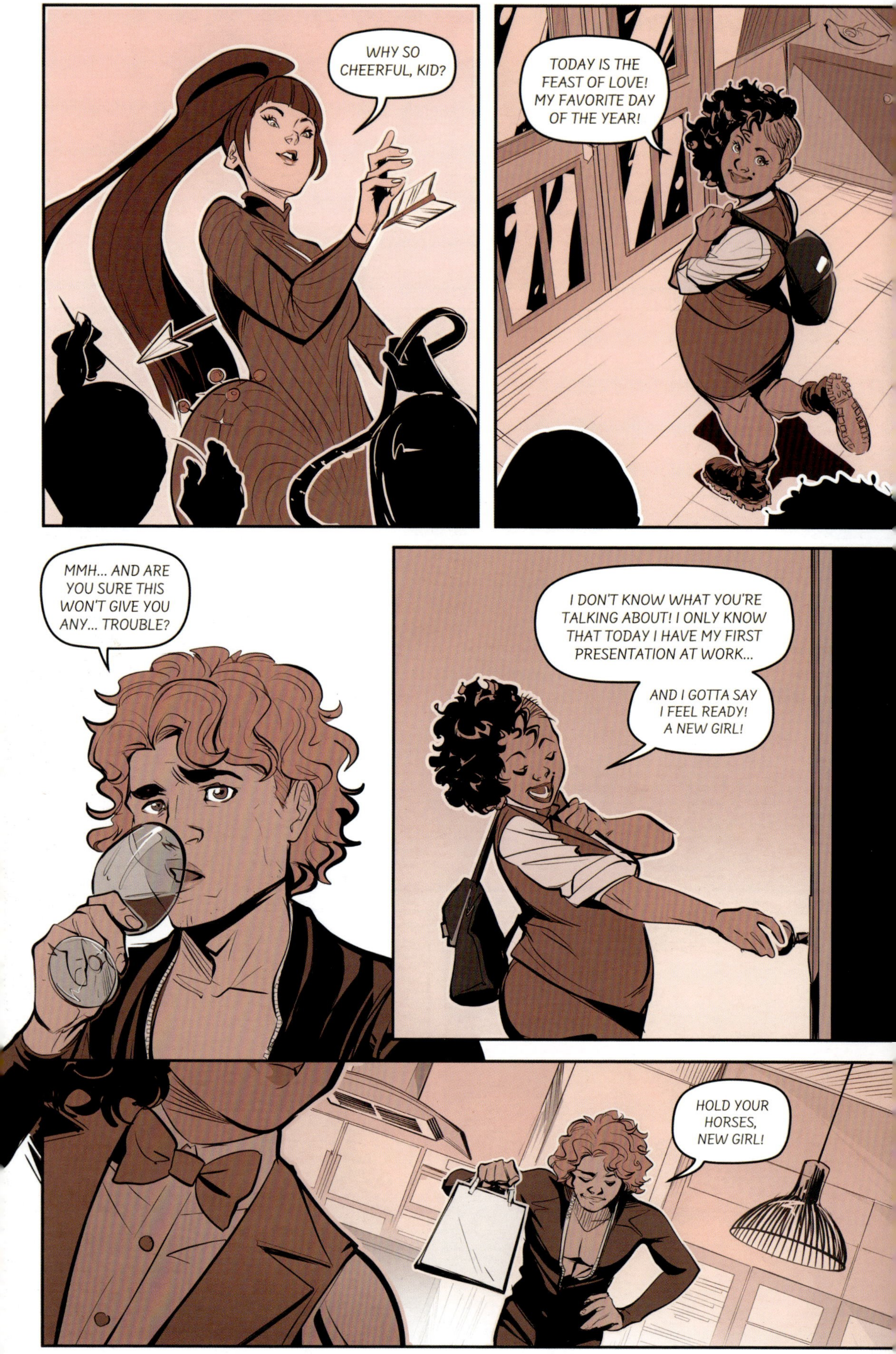
WHY SO CHEERFUL, KID?
TODAY IS THE FEAST OF LOVE! MY FAVORITE DAY OF THE YEAR!
MMH... AND ARE YOU SURE THIS WON'T GIVE YOU ANY... TROUBLE?
I DON'T KNOW WHAT YOU'RE TALKING ABOUT! I ONLY KNOW THAT TODAY I HAVE MY FIRST PRESENTATION AT WORK...
AND I GOTTA SAY I FEEL READY! A NEW GIRL!
HOLD YOUR HORSES, NEW GIRL!

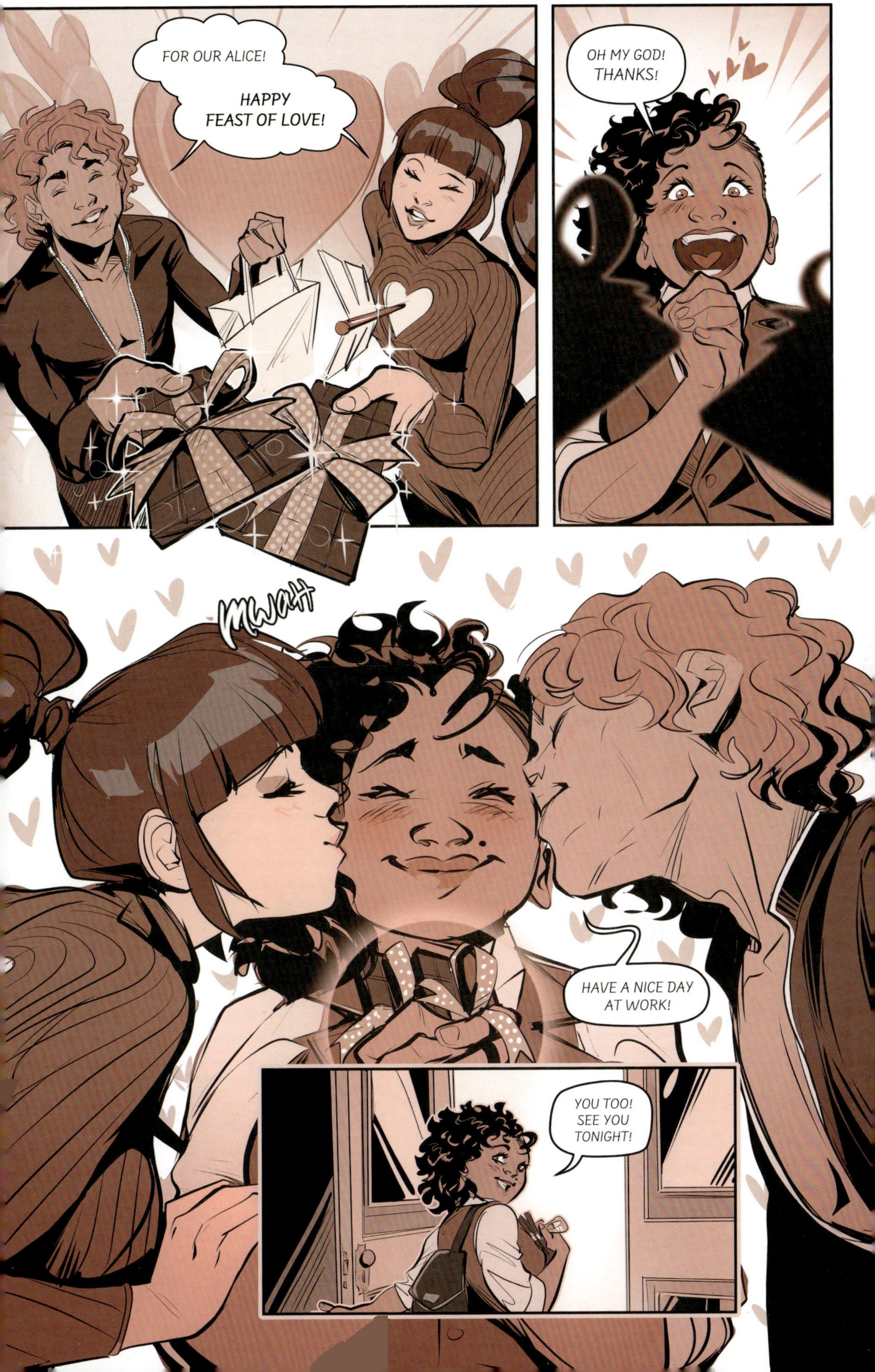
FOR OUR ALICE!
HAPPY FEAST OF LOVE!
OH MY GOD! THANKS!
MWAH
HAVE A NICE DAY AT WORK!
YOU TOO! SEE YOU TONIGHT!

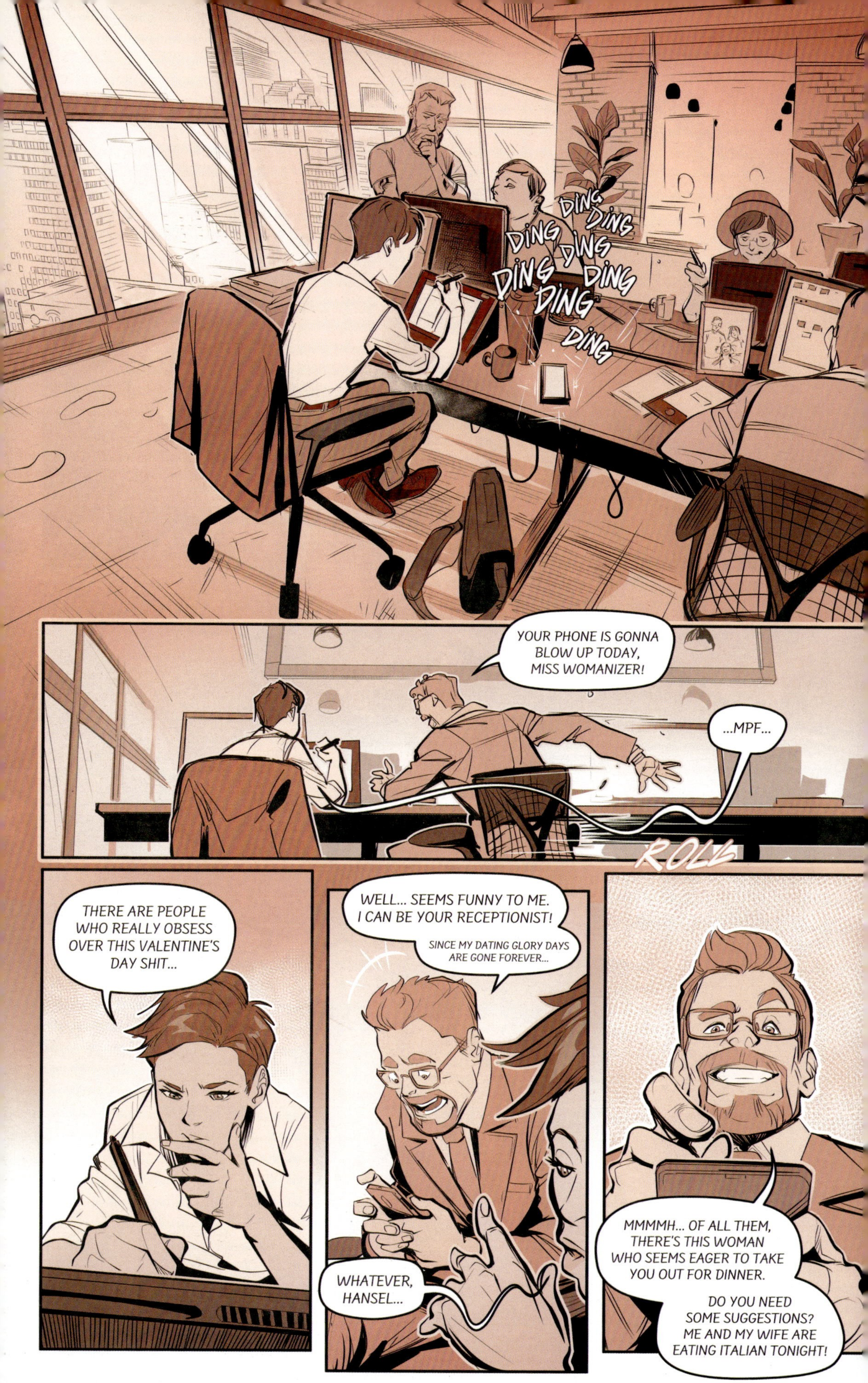
DING DING
DING DING
DING DING
DING
DING
YOUR PHONE IS GONNA BLOW UP TODAY, MISS WOMANIZER!
...MPF...
ROLL
THERE ARE PEOPLE WHO REALLY OBSESS OVER THIS VALENTINE'S DAY SHIT...
WELL... SEEMS FUNNY TO ME. I CAN BE YOUR RECEPTIONIST!
SINCE MY DATING GLORY DAYS ARE GONE FOREVER...
WHATEVER, HANSEL...
MMMMH... OF ALL THEM, THERE'S THIS WOMAN WHO SEEMS EAGER TO TAKE YOU OUT FOR DINNER.
DO YOU NEED SOME SUGGESTIONS? ME AND MY WIFE ARE EATING ITALIAN TONIGHT!

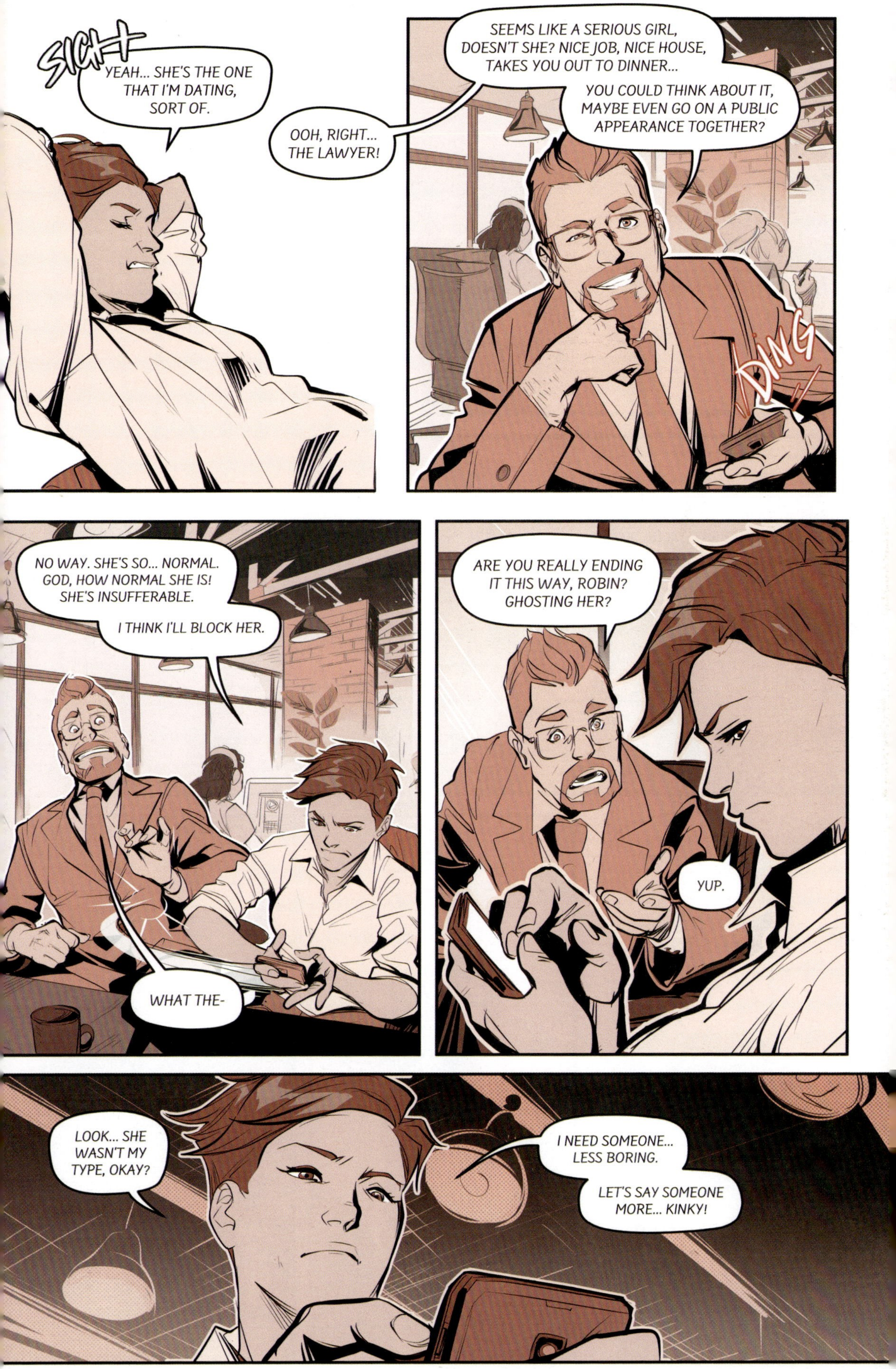
SIGH
YEAH... SHE'S THE ONE THAT I'M DATING, SORT OF.
OOH, RIGHT... THE LAWYER!
SEEMS LIKE A SERIOUS GIRL, DOESN'T SHE? NICE JOB, NICE HOUSE, TAKES YOU OUT TO DINNER...
YOU COULD THINK ABOUT IT, MAYBE EVEN GO ON A PUBLIC APPEARANCE TOGETHER?
DING
NO WAY. SHE'S SO... NORMAL. GOD, HOW NORMAL SHE IS! SHE'S INSUFFERABLE.
I THINK I'LL BLOCK HER.
WHAT THE-
ARE YOU REALLY ENDING IT THIS WAY, ROBIN? GHOSTING HER?
YUP.
LOOK... SHE WASN'T MY TYPE, OKAY?
I NEED SOMEONE... LESS BORING.
LET'S SAY SOMEONE MORE... KINKY!

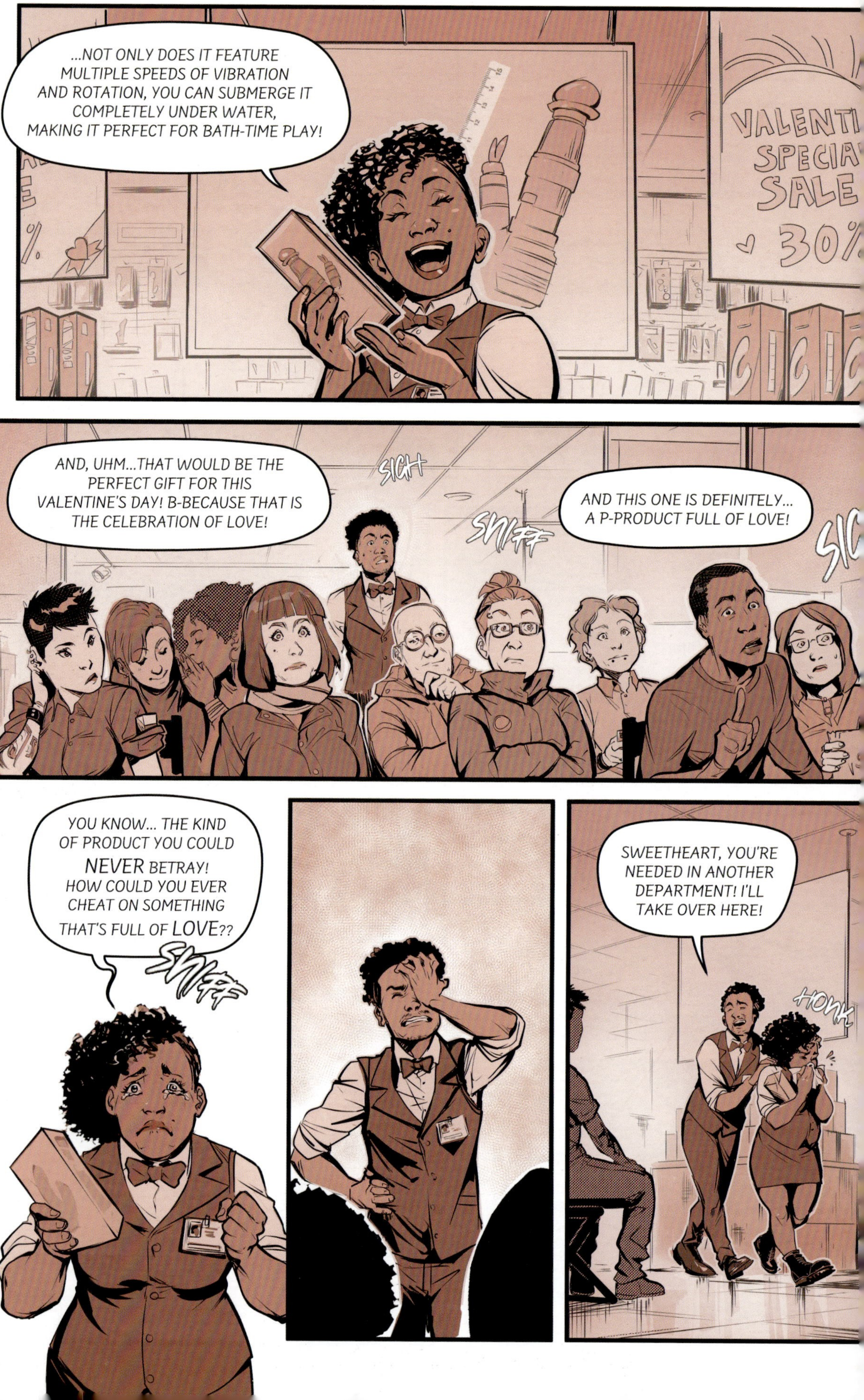
...NOT ONLY DOES IT FEATURE MULTIPLE SPEEDS OF VIBRATION AND ROTATION, YOU CAN SUBMERGE IT COMPLETELY UNDER WATER, MAKING IT PERFECT FOR BATH-TIME PLAY!
VALENTI SPECIA SALE
30%
AND, UHM...THAT WOULD BE THE PERFECT GIFT FOR THIS VALENTINE'S DAY! B-BECAUSE THAT IS THE CELEBRATION OF LOVE!
SIGH
SNIFF
AND THIS ONE IS DEFINITELY... A P-PRODUCT FULL OF LOVE!
YOU KNOW... THE KIND OF PRODUCT YOU COULD NEVER BETRAY! HOW COULD YOU EVER CHEAT ON SOMETHING THAT'S FULL OF LOVE??
SNIFF
SWEETHEART, YOU'RE NEEDED IN ANOTHER DEPARTMENT! I'LL TAKE OVER HERE!
HONK

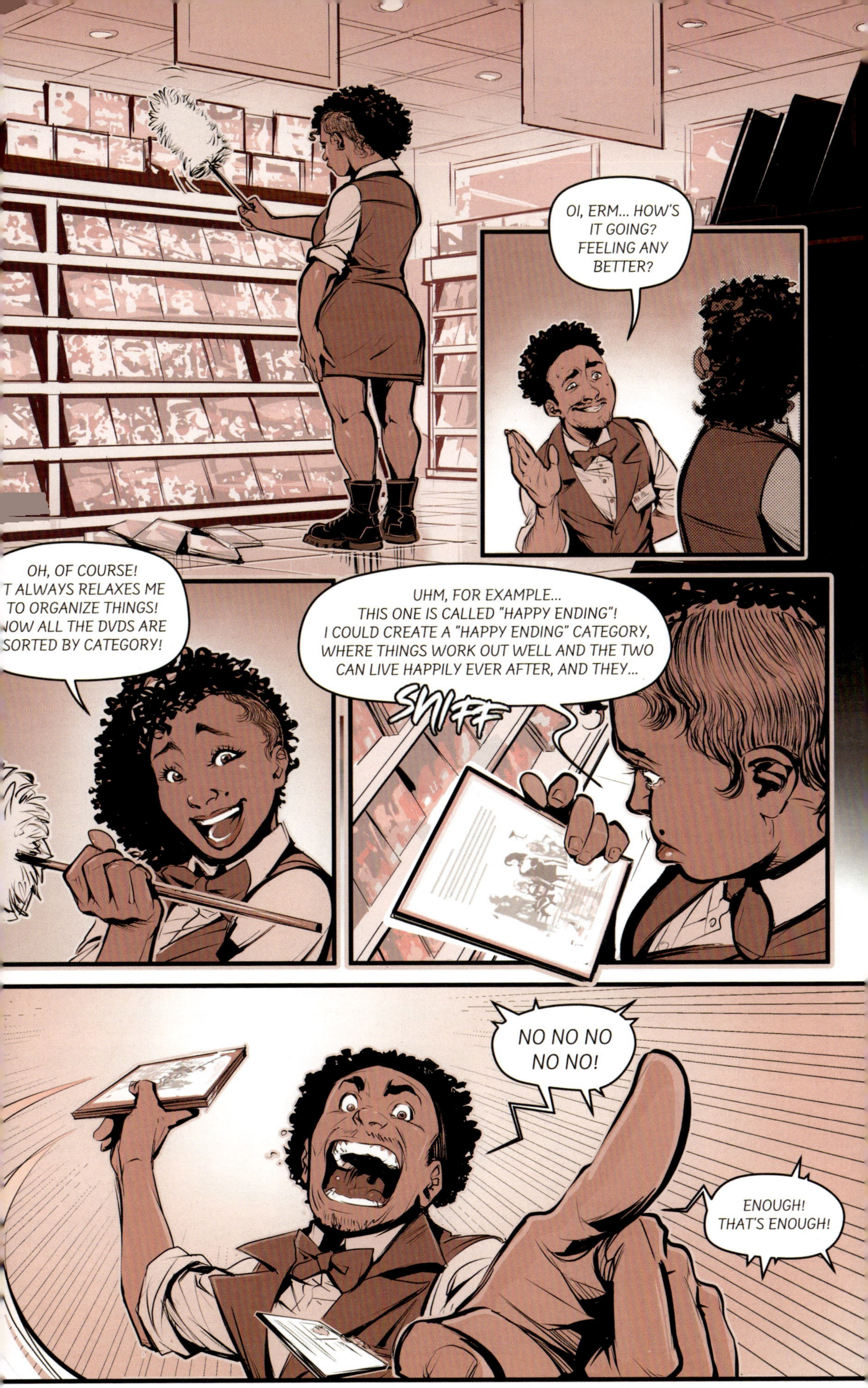
OI, ERM... HOW'S IT GOING? FEELING ANY BETTER?
OH, OF COURSE! T ALWAYS RELAXES ME TO ORGANIZE THINGS! NOW ALL THE DVDS ARE SORTED BY CATEGORY!
UHM, FOR EXAMPLE... THIS ONE IS CALLED "HAPPY ENDING"! I COULD CREATE A "HAPPY ENDING" CATEGORY, WHERE THINGS WORK OUT WELL AND THE TWO CAN LIVE HAPPILY EVER AFTER, AND THEY...
SNIFF
NO NO NO NO NO!
ENOUGH! THAT'S ENOUGH!

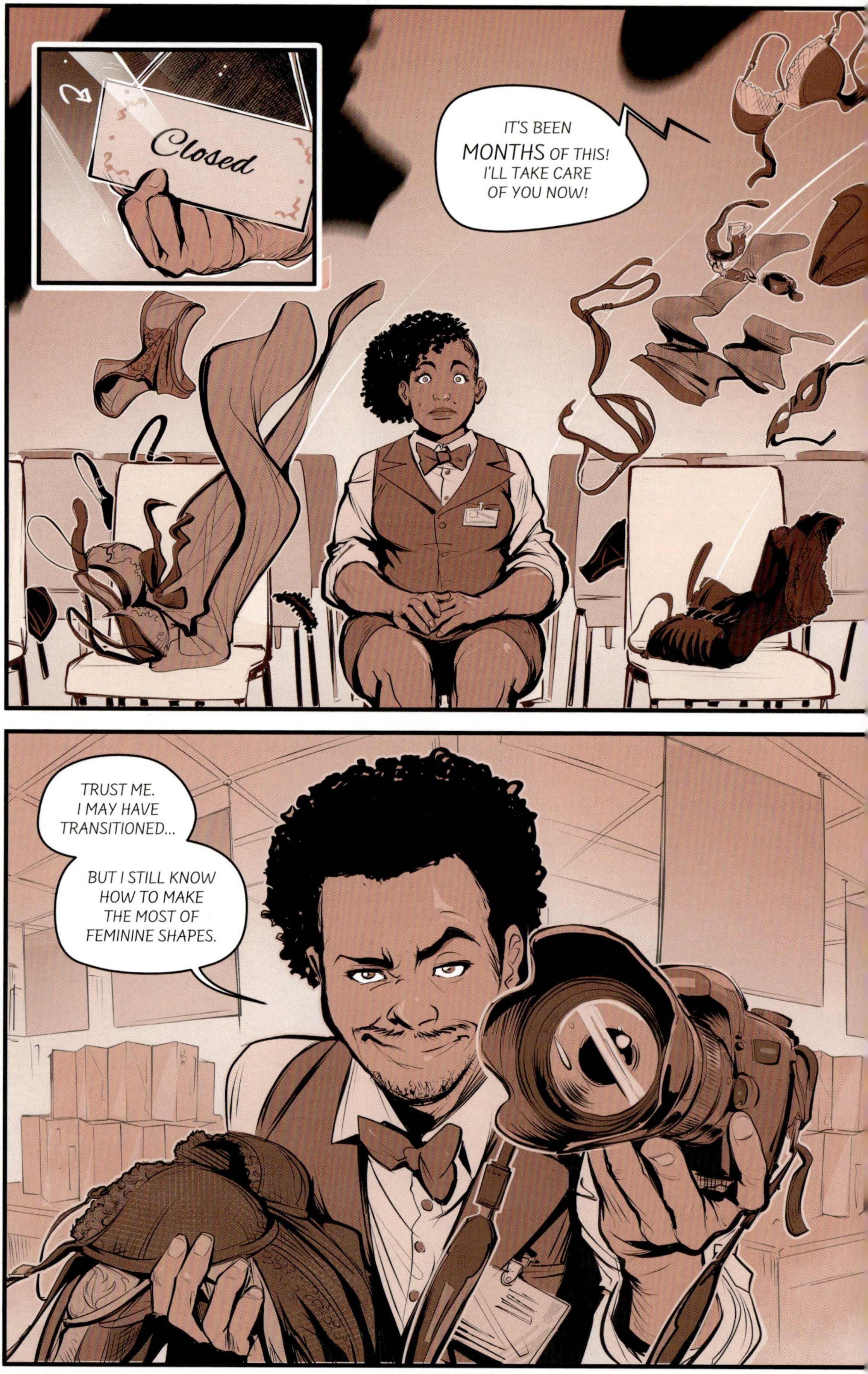
Closed
IT'S BEEN MONTHS OF THIS! I'LL TAKE CARE OF YOU NOW!
TRUST ME. I MAY HAVE TRANSITIONED...
BUT I STILL KNOW HOW TO MAKE THE MOST OF FEMININE SHAPES.

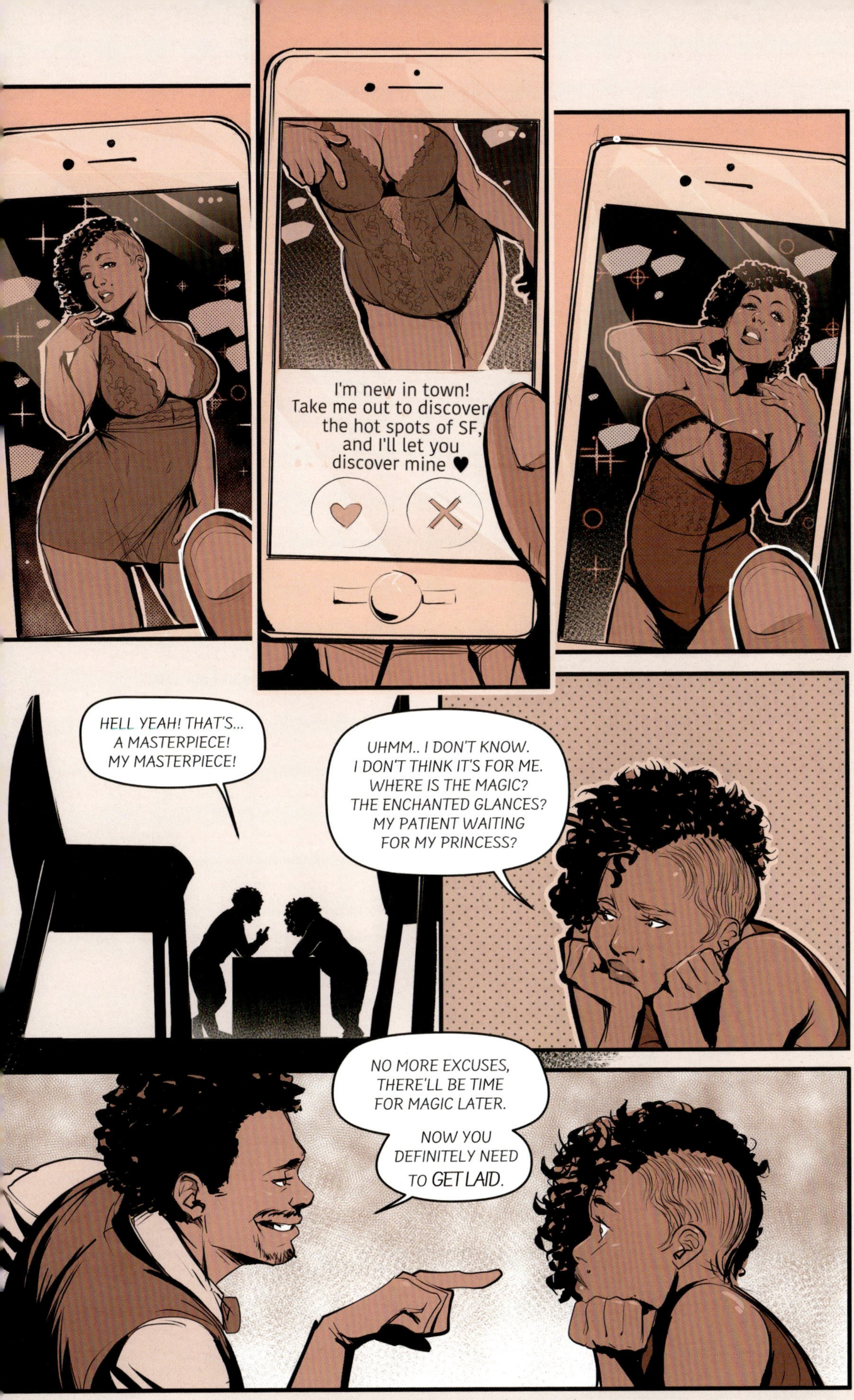
I'm new in town! Take me out to discover the hot spots of SF, and I'll let you discover mine ♥
HELL YEAH! THAT'S... A MASTERPIECE! MY MASTERPIECE!
UHMM.. I DON'T KNOW. I DON'T THINK IT'S FOR ME. WHERE IS THE MAGIC? THE ENCHANTED GLANCES? MY PATIENT WAITING FOR MY PRINCESS?
NO MORE EXCUSES, THERE'LL BE TIME FOR MAGIC LATER.
NOW YOU DEFINITELY NEED TO GET LAID.

HA HA HA

WHAT A GREAT PROFILE!

YEAH... WE JUST NEED TO UPLOAD NORMAL PHOTOS AND WRITE SOMETHING DECENT.

WELL! NOW IS THE TIM[E] FOR MY TUTORIAL O[N] HOW TO AVOID CREEP[Y] DATES ON THE APPS

TADAA!

It's easy! You just need to avoid the profiles with descriptions such as:
- Self-declaration of fun like "I am a very funny and self-ironic girl"
- Weight, height and other exact datas as if they were selling themselves on craigslist
- Too many Emojis
- Dad jokes
- Googled bio like this was a school test
- Indiana Jones staments such as "seeking new adventures"
- Mysterious types like "I don't open up easily, you have to discover me slowly"
- The constantly hurt: "I don't know if I will ever be able to feel emotions after my last relationsh[ip]"

OH and then, about chats...
- The ones texting you more than once after an unanswered message
- The ones asking you out after 3 texts
- The ones telling you the story of their lives after 3 texts
- The ones tracing your real social network profil[e] using just your nickname
- The hikikomoris
- The TERFs

ALL CLEAR?

ERR... YES?

AND, SHOULD YOU HA[VE] ANY PROBLEM... YOU CA[LL] AND WE DEAL WITH I[T]

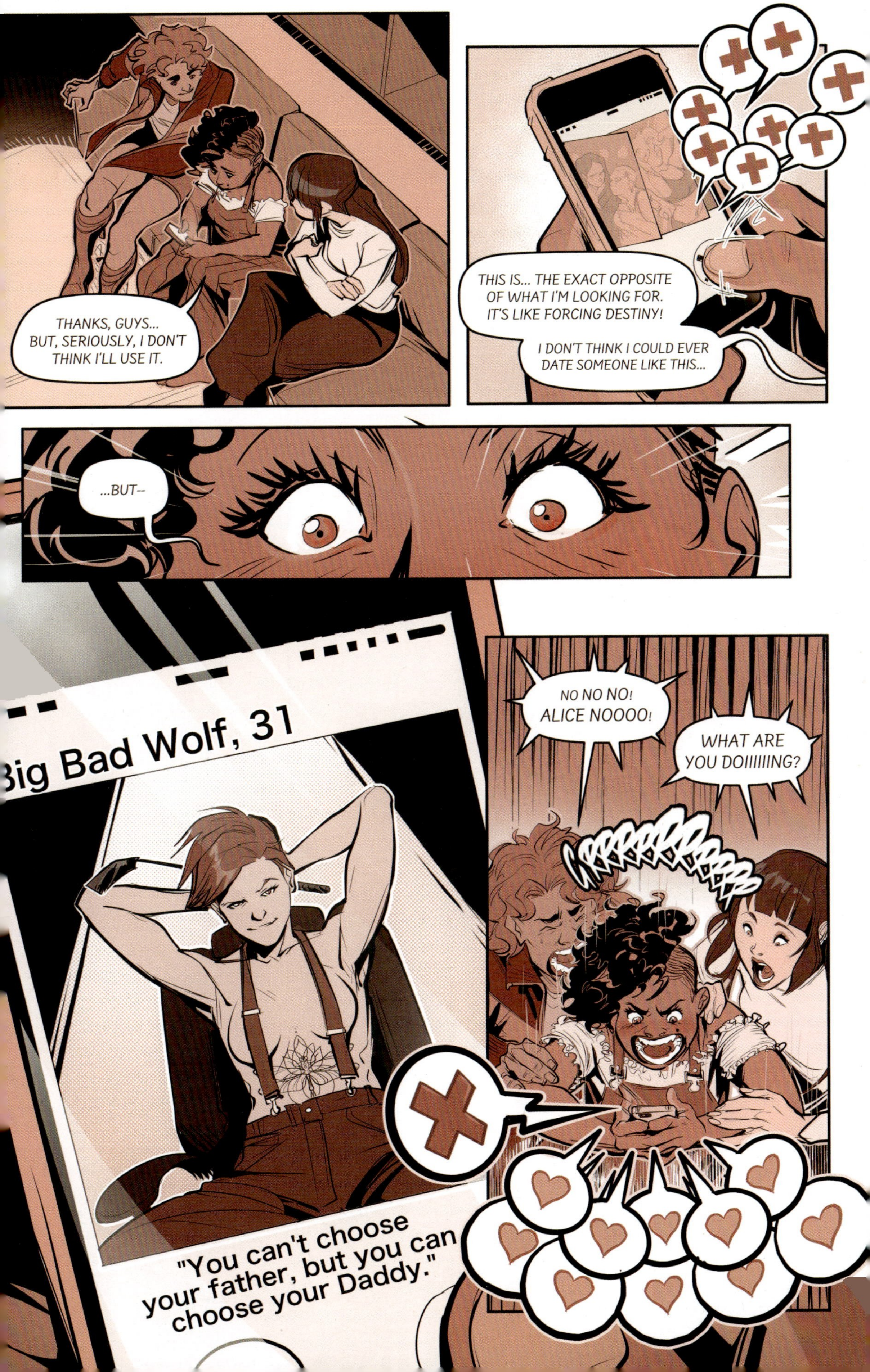
THANKS, GUYS... BUT, SERIOUSLY, I DON'T THINK I'LL USE IT.
THIS IS... THE EXACT OPPOSITE OF WHAT I'M LOOKING FOR. IT'S LIKE FORCING DESTINY!
I DON'T THINK I COULD EVER DATE SOMEONE LIKE THIS...
...BUT--
Big Bad Wolf, 31
"You can't choose your father, but you can choose your Daddy."
NO NO NO! ALICE NOOOO!
WHAT ARE YOU DOIIIIIING?

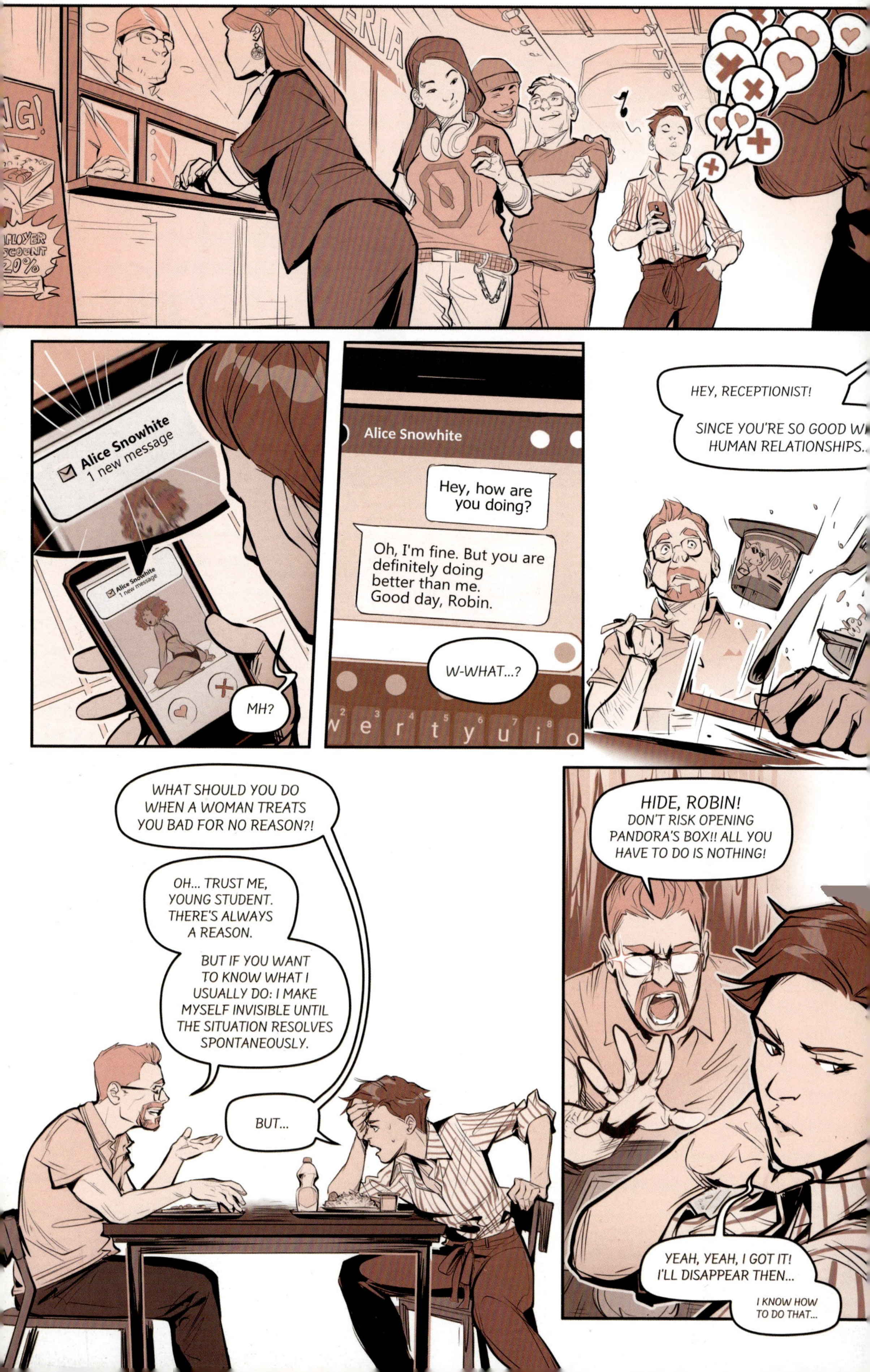

ERIA
IG!
EMPLOYER DISCOUNT 20%
Alice Snowhite
1 new message
MH?
Alice Snowhite
Hey, how are you doing?
Oh, I'm fine. But you are definitely doing better than me. Good day, Robin.
W-WHAT...?
HEY, RECEPTIONIST!
SINCE YOU'RE SO GOOD W
HUMAN RELATIONSHIPS...
WHAT SHOULD YOU DO WHEN A WOMAN TREATS YOU BAD FOR NO REASON?!
OH... TRUST ME, YOUNG STUDENT. THERE'S ALWAYS A REASON.
BUT IF YOU WANT TO KNOW WHAT I USUALLY DO: I MAKE MYSELF INVISIBLE UNTIL THE SITUATION RESOLVES SPONTANEOUSLY.
BUT...
HIDE, ROBIN!
DON'T RISK OPENING PANDORA'S BOX!! ALL YOU HAVE TO DO IS NOTHING!
YEAH, YEAH, I GOT IT! I'LL DISAPPEAR THEN...
I KNOW HOW TO DO THAT...

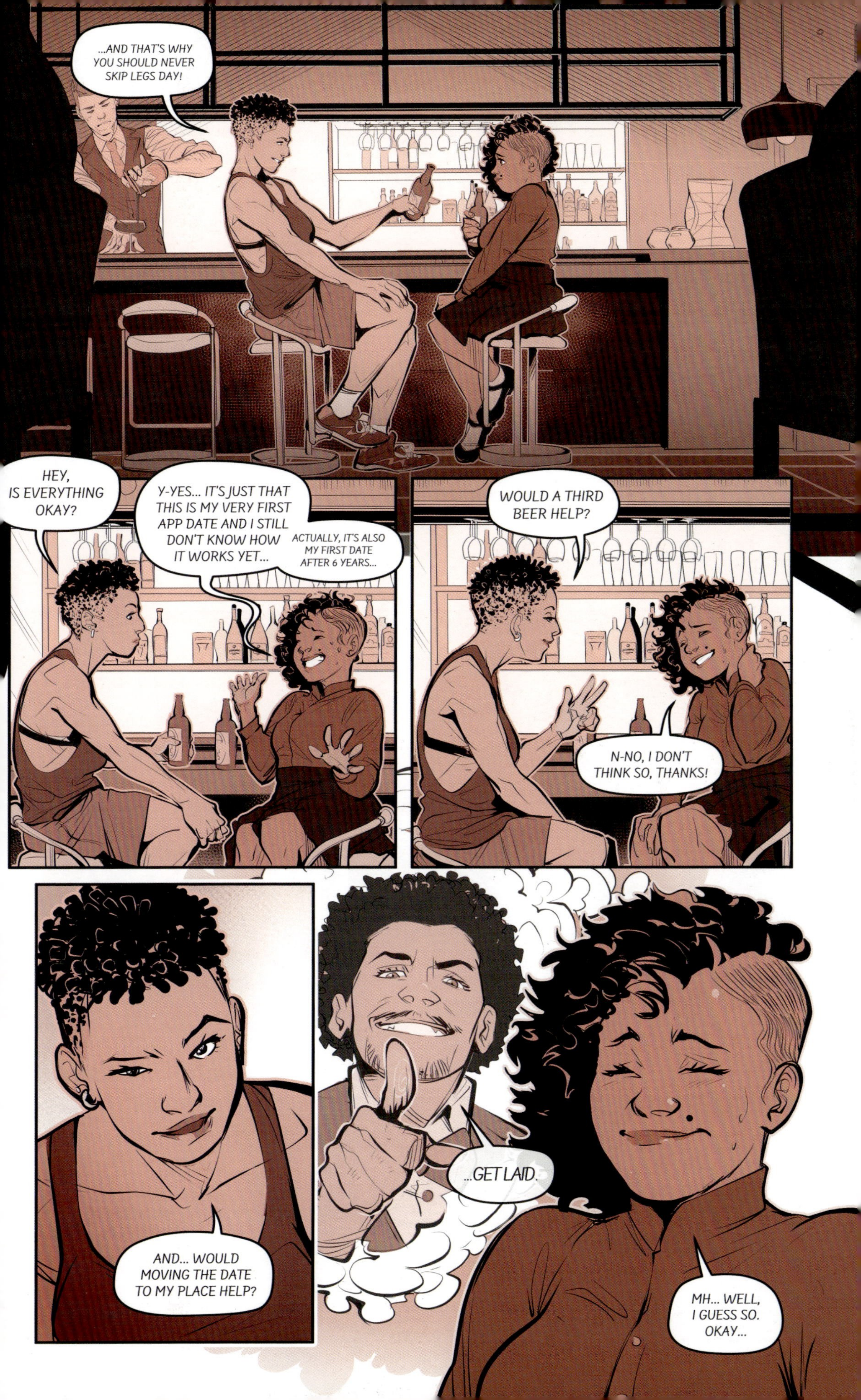
...AND THAT'S WHY YOU SHOULD NEVER SKIP LEGS DAY!
HEY, IS EVERYTHING OKAY?
Y-YES... IT'S JUST THAT THIS IS MY VERY FIRST APP DATE AND I STILL DON'T KNOW HOW IT WORKS YET...
ACTUALLY, IT'S ALSO MY FIRST DATE AFTER 6 YEARS...
WOULD A THIRD BEER HELP?
N-NO, I DON'T THINK SO, THANKS!
AND... WOULD MOVING THE DATE TO MY PLACE HELP?
...GET LAID.
MH... WELL, I GUESS SO. OKAY...

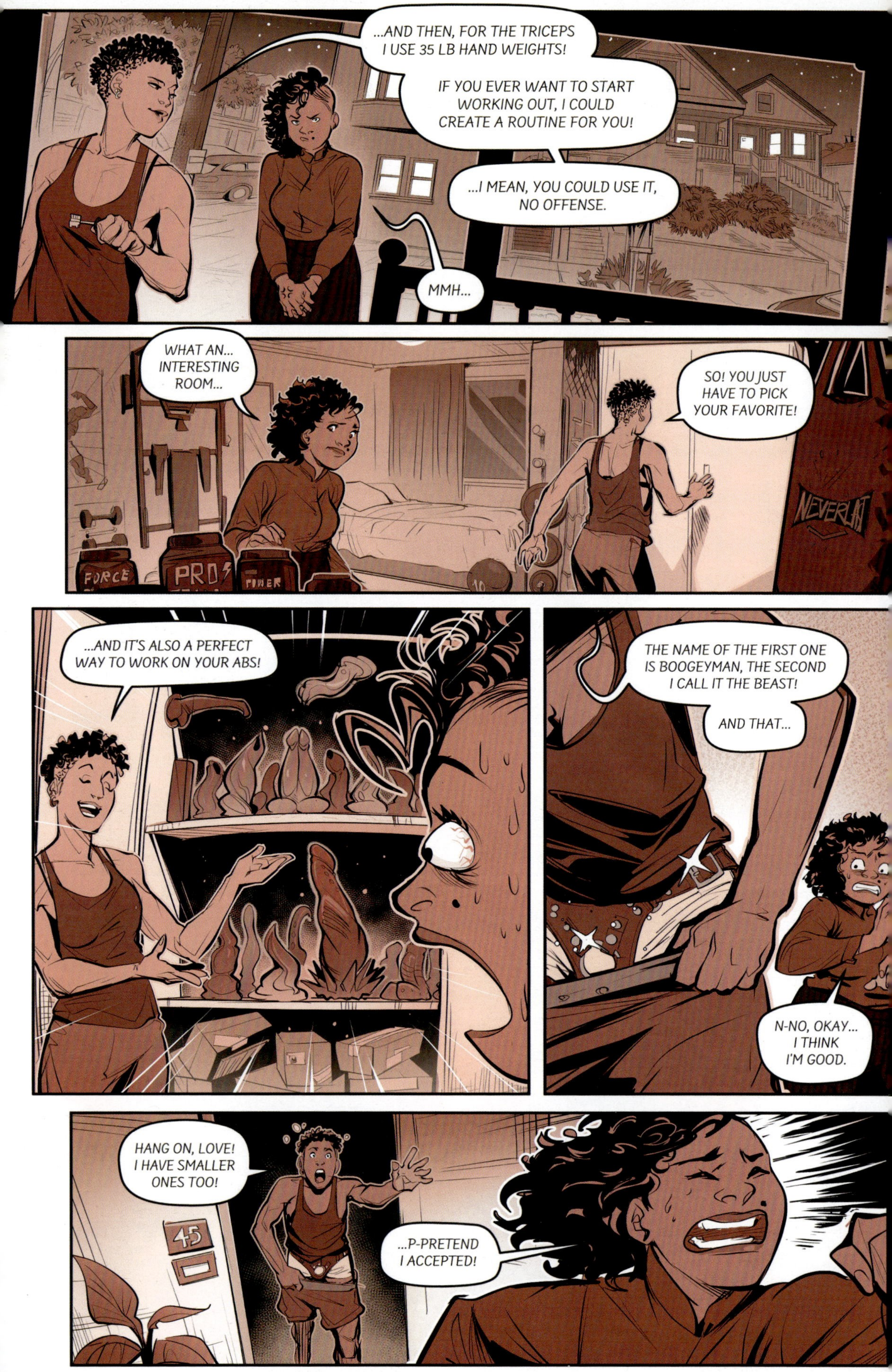
...AND THEN, FOR THE TRICEPS I USE 35 LB HAND WEIGHTS!
IF YOU EVER WANT TO START WORKING OUT, I COULD CREATE A ROUTINE FOR YOU!
...I MEAN, YOU COULD USE IT, NO OFFENSE.
MMH...
WHAT AN... INTERESTING ROOM...
SO! YOU JUST HAVE TO PICK YOUR FAVORITE!
NEVERLAST
FORCE
PRO
POWER
...AND IT'S ALSO A PERFECT WAY TO WORK ON YOUR ABS!
THE NAME OF THE FIRST ONE IS BOOGEYMAN, THE SECOND I CALL IT THE BEAST!
AND THAT...
N-NO, OKAY... I THINK I'M GOOD.
HANG ON, LOVE! I HAVE SMALLER ONES TOO!
45
...P-PRETEND I ACCEPTED!

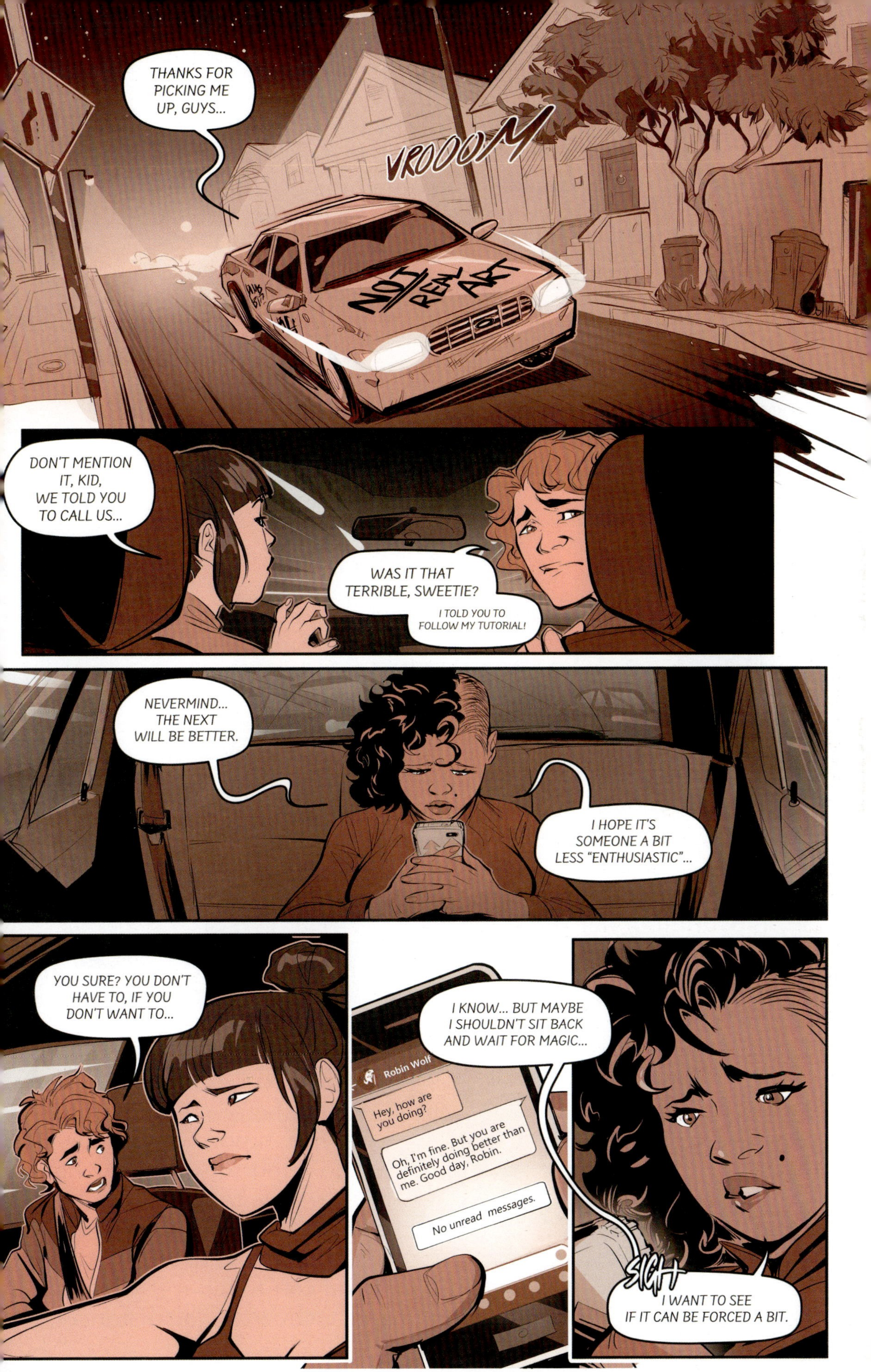
THANKS FOR PICKING ME UP, GUYS...
VROOOM
NOT REAL ART
DON'T MENTION IT, KID, WE TOLD YOU TO CALL US...
WAS IT THAT TERRIBLE, SWEETIE?
I TOLD YOU TO FOLLOW MY TUTORIAL!
NEVERMIND... THE NEXT WILL BE BETTER.
I HOPE IT'S SOMEONE A BIT LESS "ENTHUSIASTIC"...
YOU SURE? YOU DON'T HAVE TO, IF YOU DON'T WANT TO...
I KNOW... BUT MAYBE I SHOULDN'T SIT BACK AND WAIT FOR MAGIC...
Robin Wolf
Hey, how are you doing?
Oh, I'm fine. But you are definitely doing better than me. Good day, Robin.
No unread messages.
SIGH
I WANT TO SEE IF IT CAN BE FORCED A BIT.

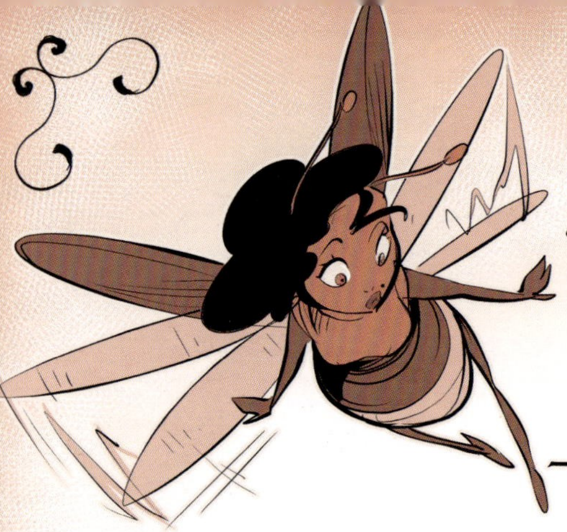

On her journey,
the firefly heard a call.
"Hey! Hey, little firefly!",
shouted the bee,
trying to be noticed.

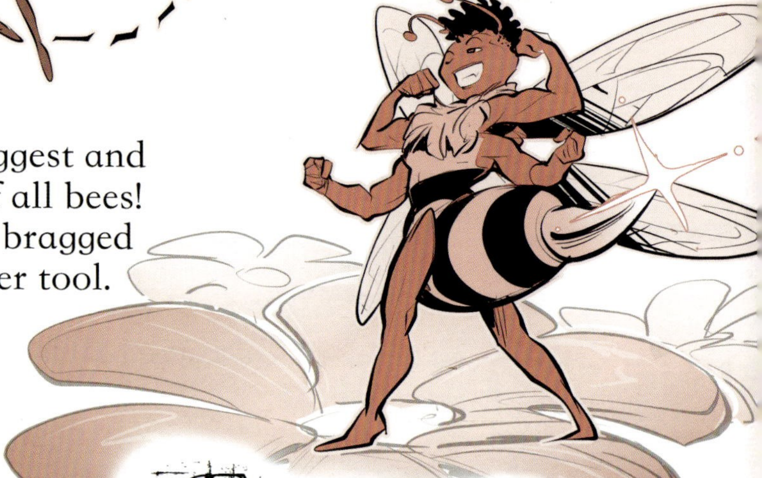

"My sting is the biggest and
most awe-inspiring of all bees!
What do you think?" bragged
the bee, flaunting her tool.

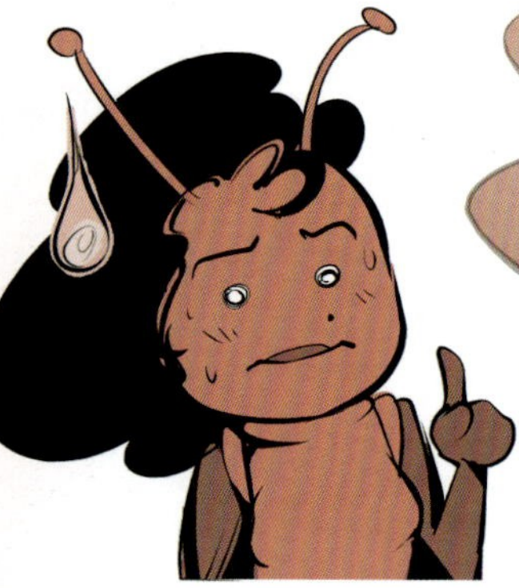

"Err... Sure, Ms. Bee,
but I don't think your supremacy could
help me." Our firefly replied politely.

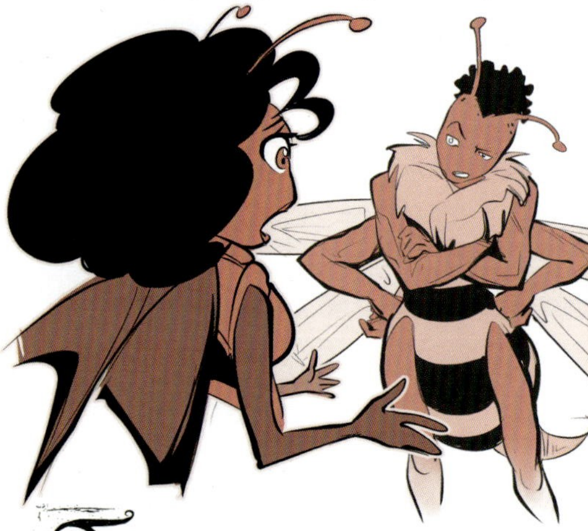

"Speaking of which...I'm looking
for a way to shine again.
Could you help me?" she asked
with interest, but, unfortunately,
in spite of all of her titles, the bee
seemed quite useless to the purpose.
"Um... I have no idea what you're
talking about," she replied.

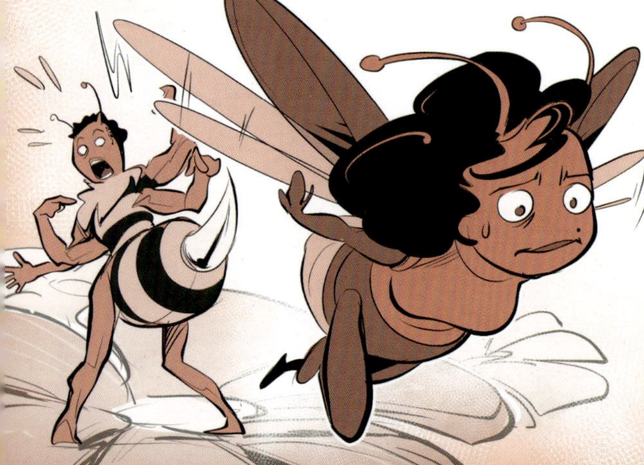

"Thanks anyway!" the firefly
said, before taking off for
her important journey.
So important that she had
no time to listen to other
proposals. "Wait! Don't you want
to take a look at my sting?
You can touch it if you want!"
echoed in the distance.

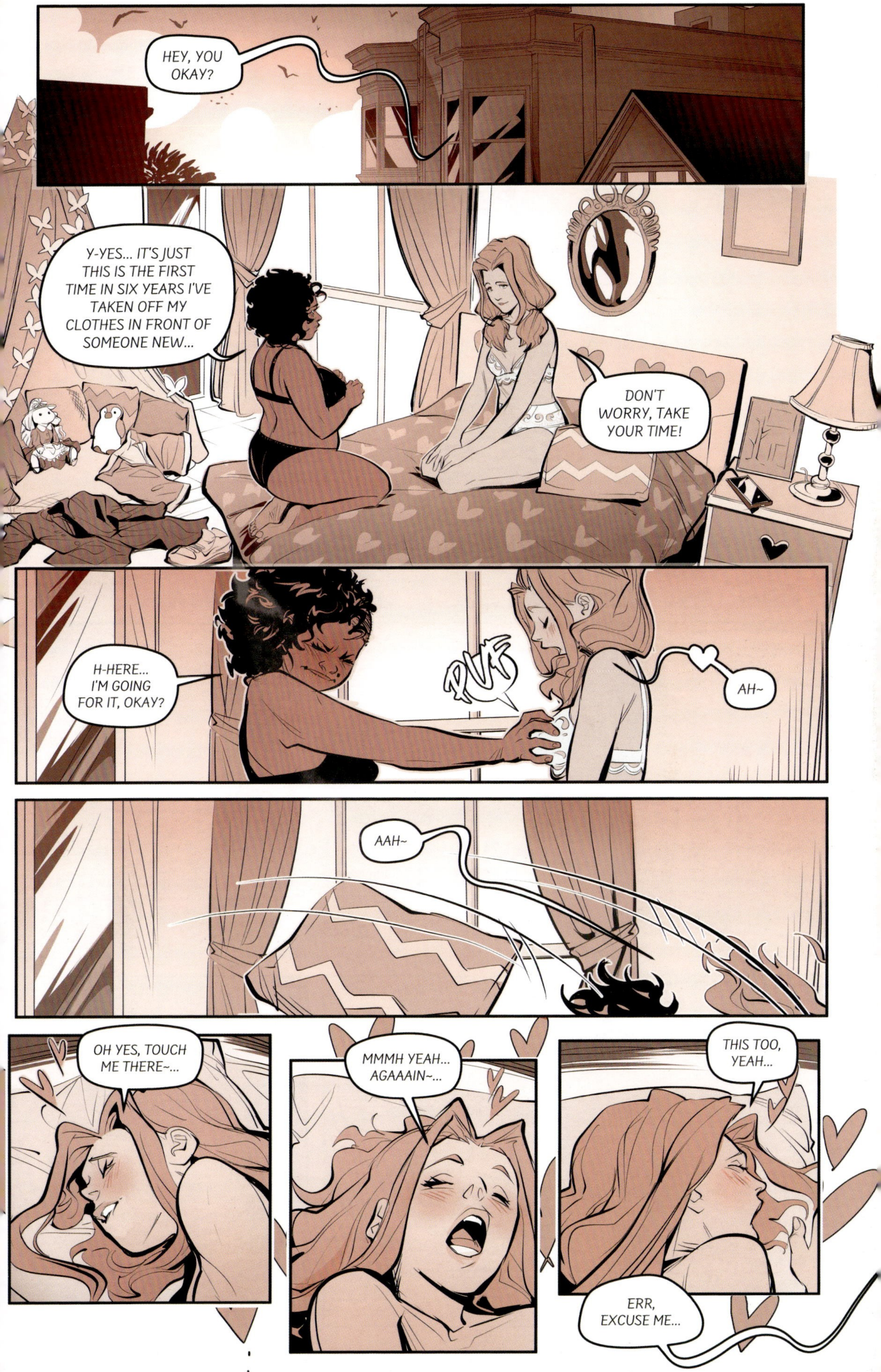
HEY, YOU OKAY?
Y-YES... IT'S JUST THIS IS THE FIRST TIME IN SIX YEARS I'VE TAKEN OFF MY CLOTHES IN FRONT OF SOMEONE NEW...
DON'T WORRY, TAKE YOUR TIME!
H-HERE... I'M GOING FOR IT, OKAY?
PUF
AH~
AAH~
OH YES, TOUCH ME THERE~...
MMMH YEAH... AGAAAIN~...
THIS TOO, YEAH...
ERR, EXCUSE ME...

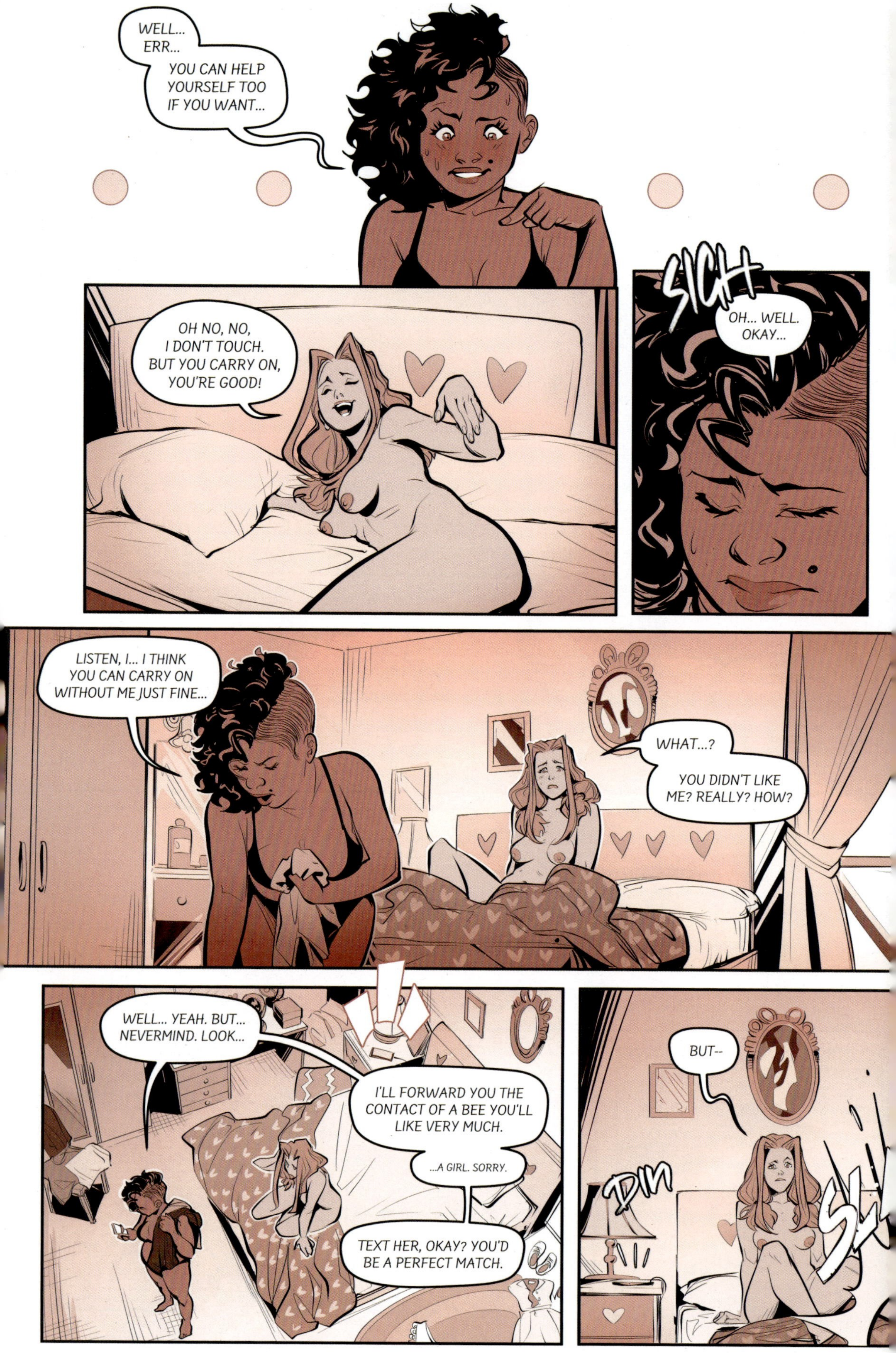
WELL... ERR...
YOU CAN HELP YOURSELF TOO IF YOU WANT...
OH NO, NO, I DON'T TOUCH. BUT YOU CARRY ON, YOU'RE GOOD!
SIGH
OH... WELL. OKAY...
LISTEN, I... I THINK YOU CAN CARRY ON WITHOUT ME JUST FINE...
WHAT...?
YOU DIDN'T LIKE ME? REALLY? HOW?
WELL... YEAH. BUT... NEVERMIND. LOOK...
I'LL FORWARD YOU THE CONTACT OF A BEE YOU'LL LIKE VERY MUCH.
...A GIRL. SORRY.
TEXT HER, OKAY? YOU'D BE A PERFECT MATCH.
BUT--
DIN

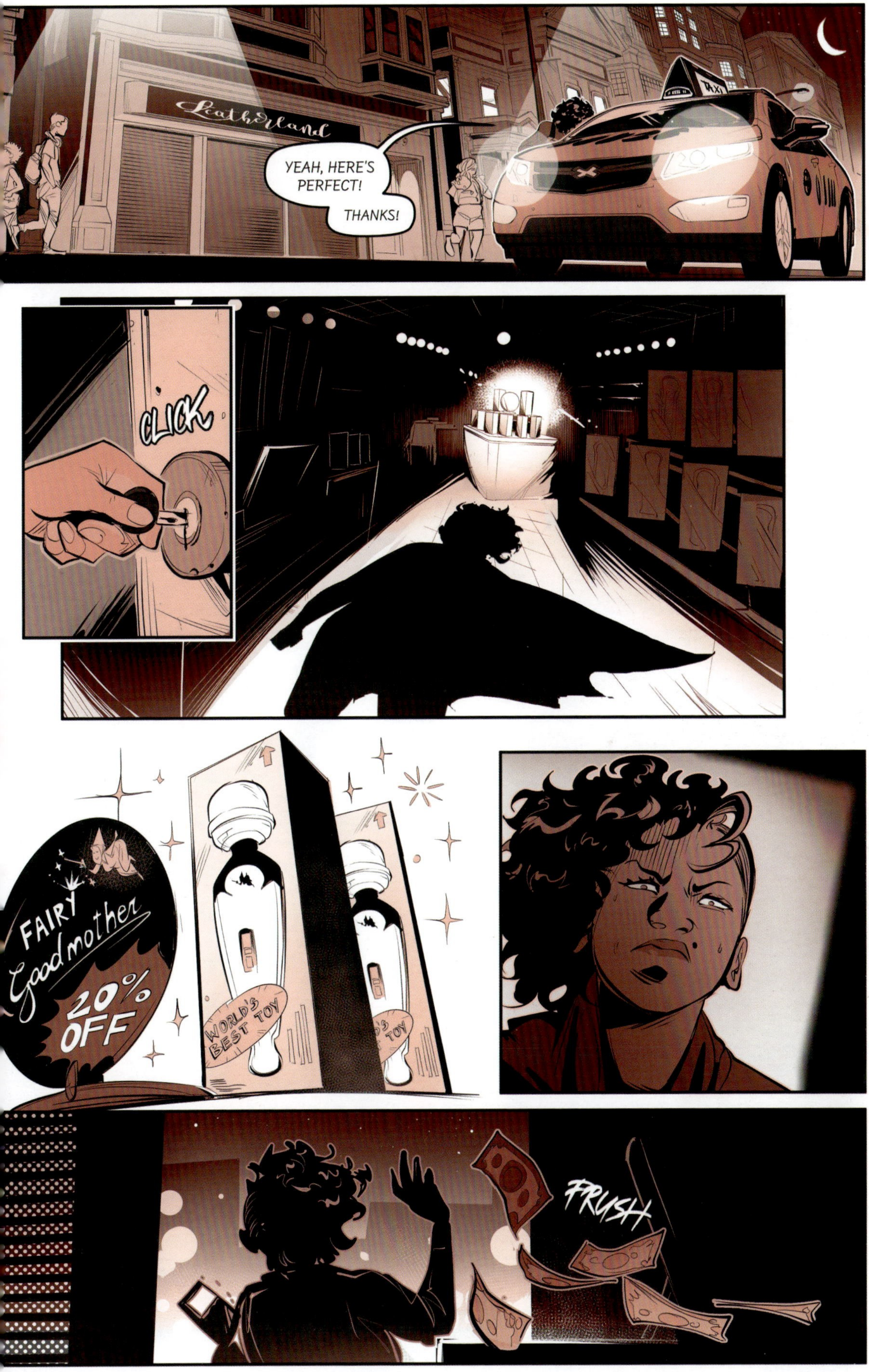
Leatherland
YEAH, HERE'S PERFECT!
THANKS!
TAXI
CLICK
FAIRY Goodmother
20% OFF
WORLD'S BEST TOY
FRUSH

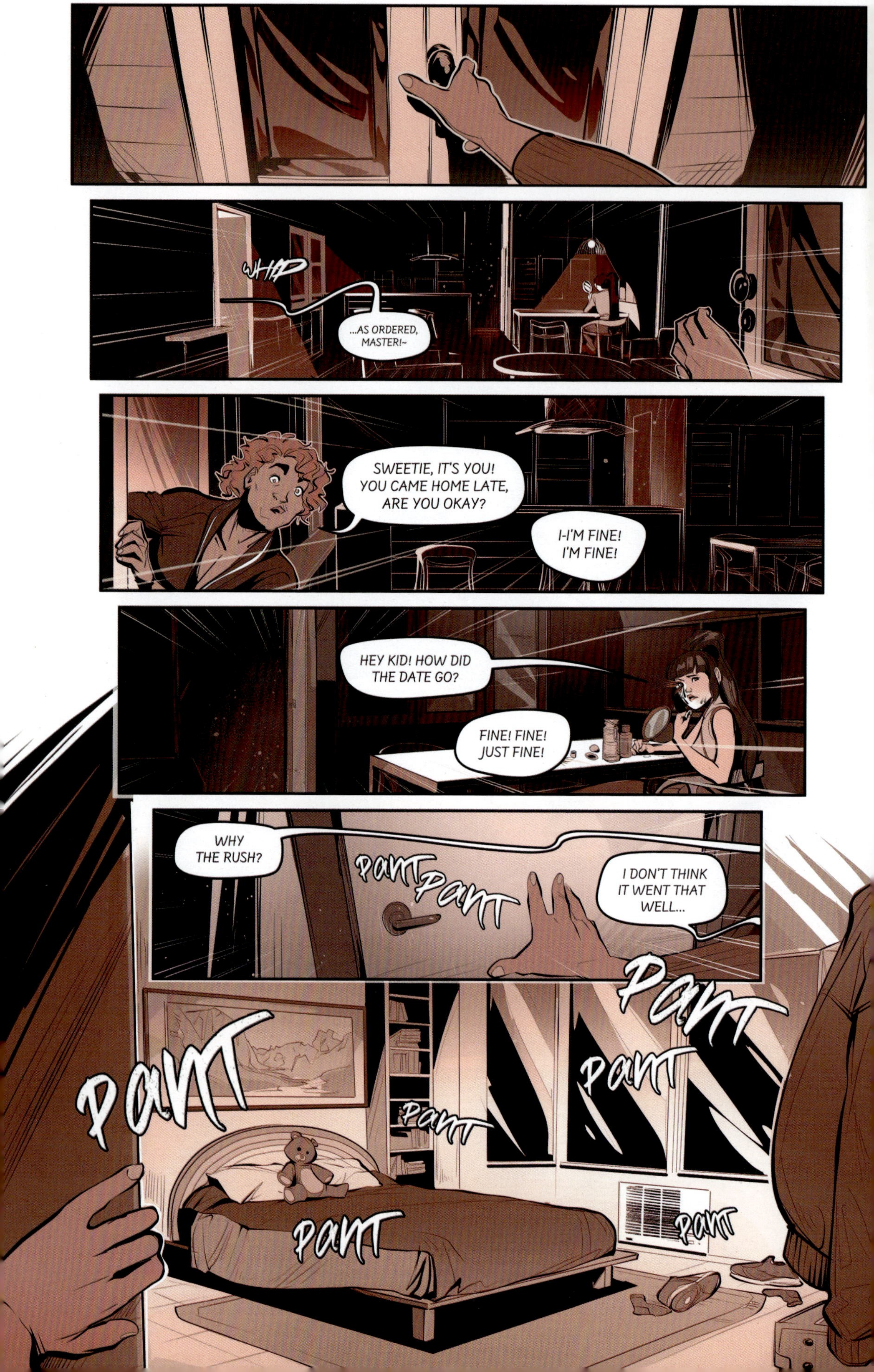
WHIP
...AS ORDERED, MASTER!~
SWEETIE, IT'S YOU! YOU CAME HOME LATE, ARE YOU OKAY?
I-I'M FINE! I'M FINE!
HEY KID! HOW DID THE DATE GO?
FINE! FINE! JUST FINE!
WHY THE RUSH?
PANT PANT
I DON'T THINK IT WENT THAT WELL...
PANT
PANT
PANT
PANT
PANT
PANT

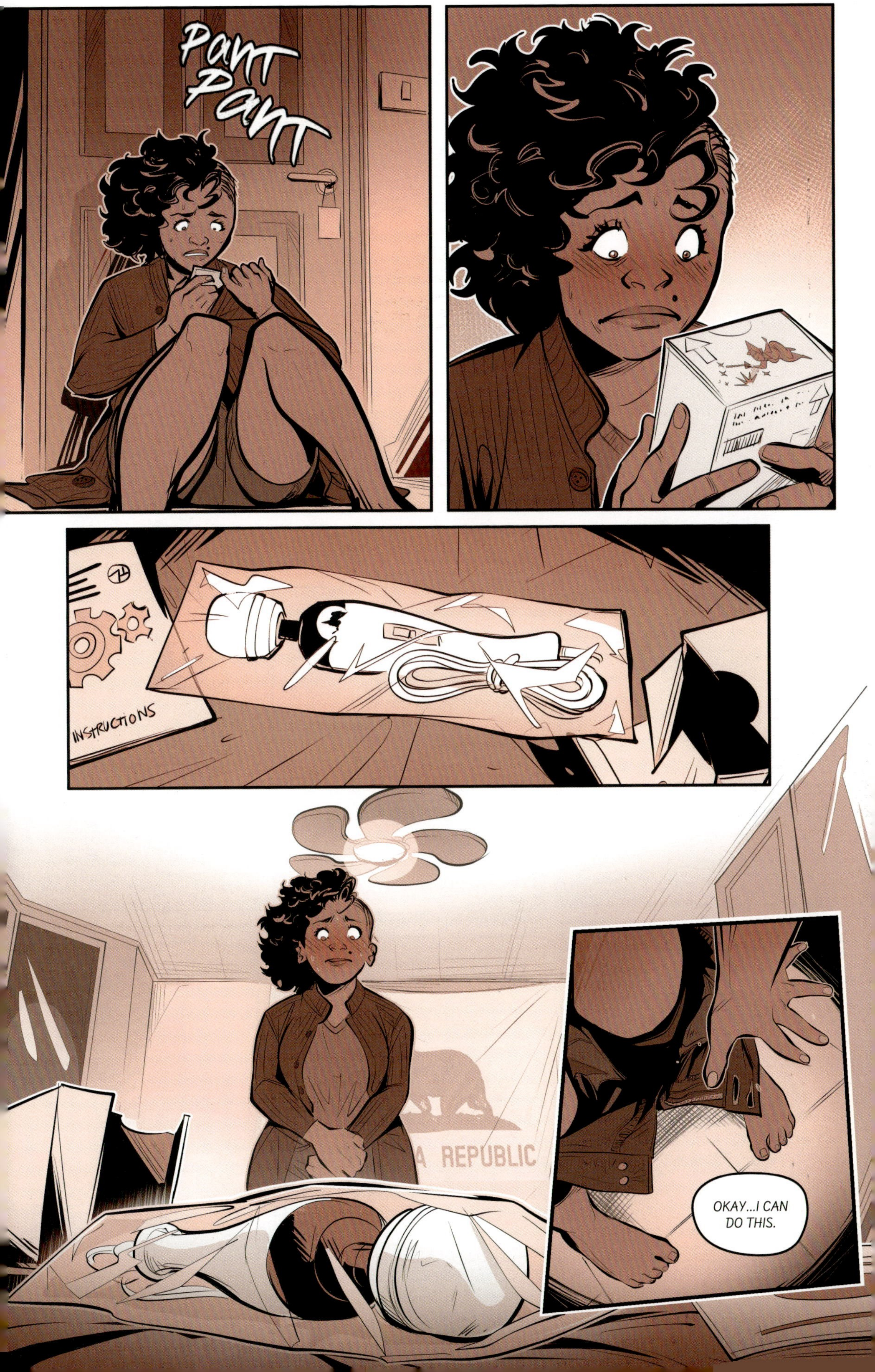
PANT PANT
INSTRUCTIONS
A REPUBLIC
OKAY...I CAN DO THIS.

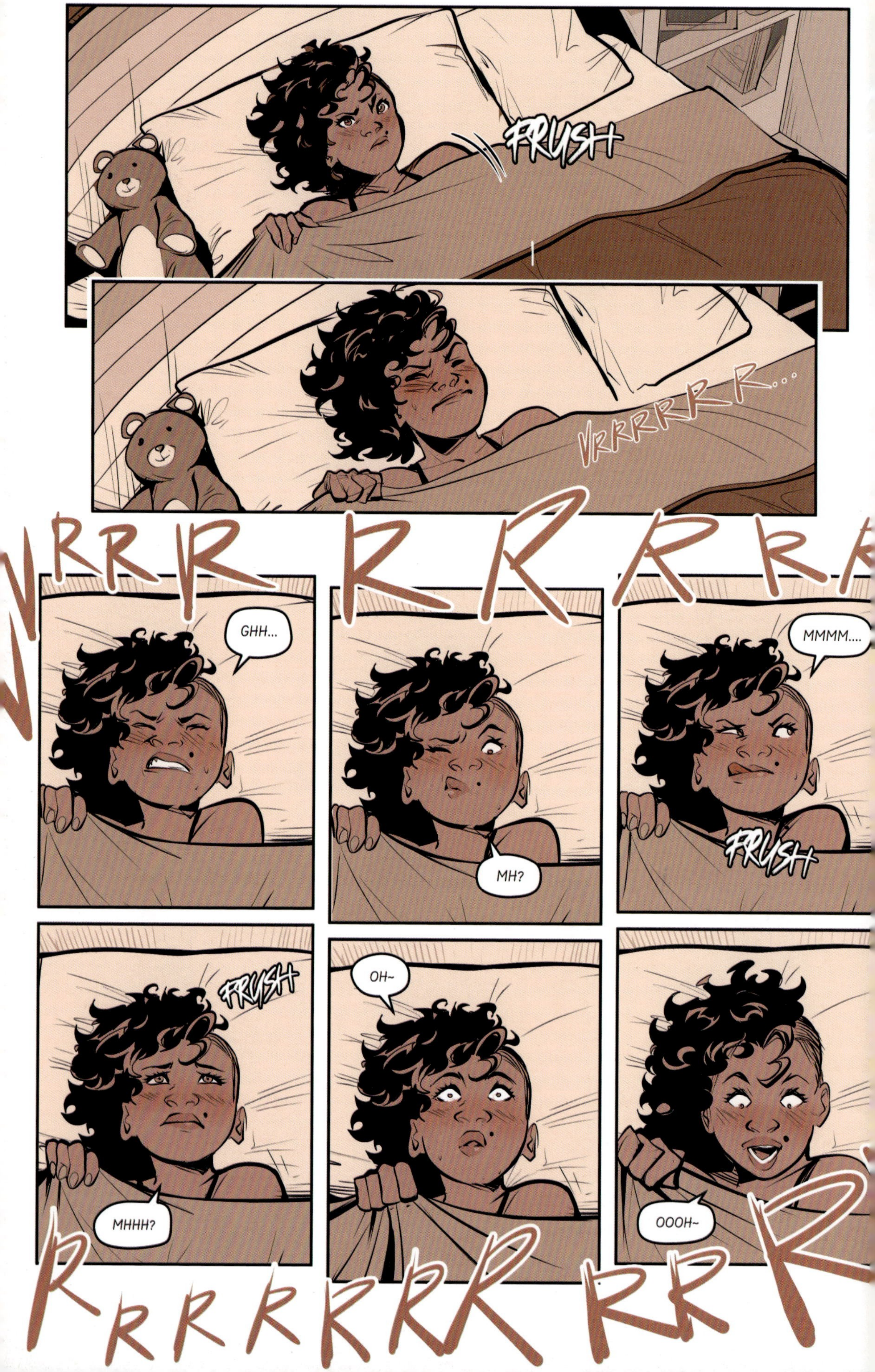
FRUSH
VRRRRRR...
VRRR RRRRR
GHH...
MH?
MMMM....
FRUSH
FRUSH
MHHH?
OH~
OOOH~
RRRRRRRRRR

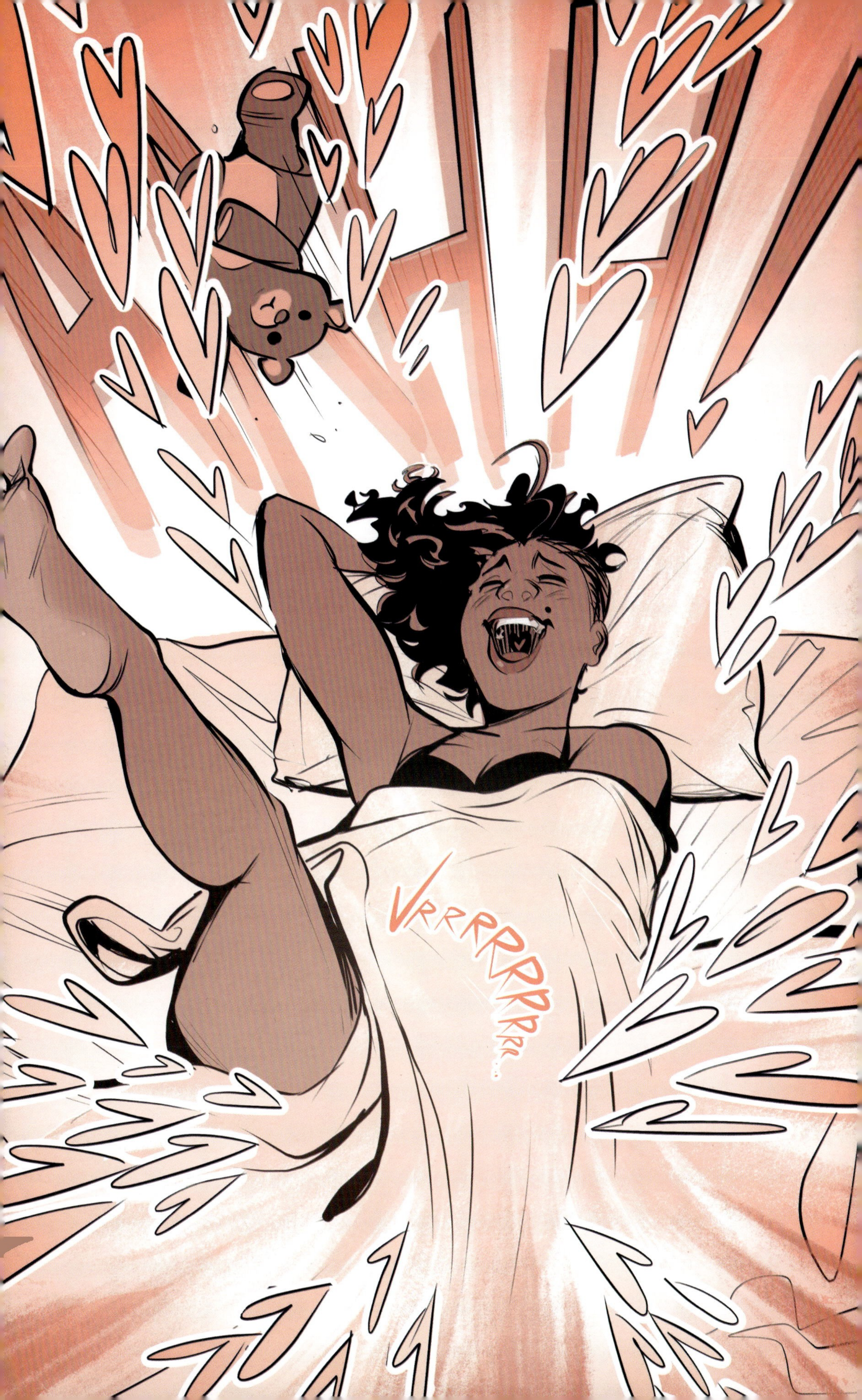
VRRRRRRRRRR...

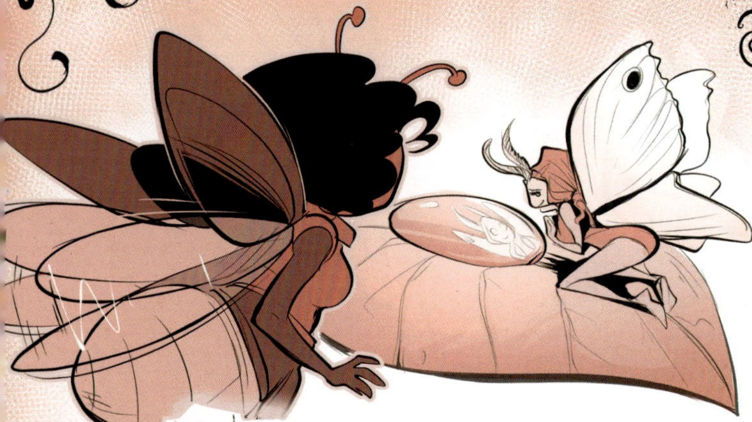

The firefly was focused on her mission but she allowed herself to peer quickly at a beautiful butterfly on a leaf.

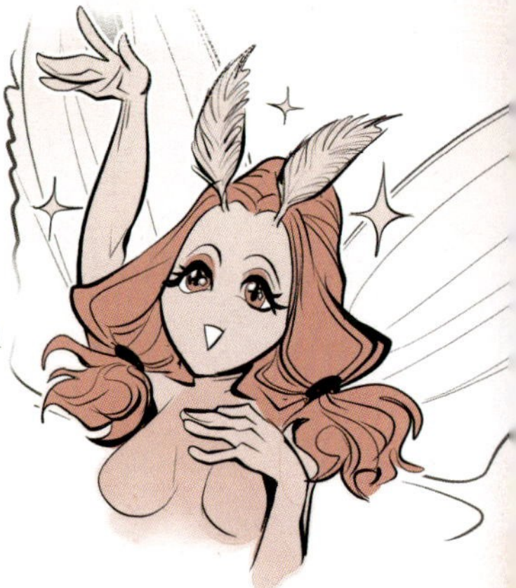

"Hey, you, little firefly!" the beautiful butterfly called out, catching her attention before she could go back to her journey.

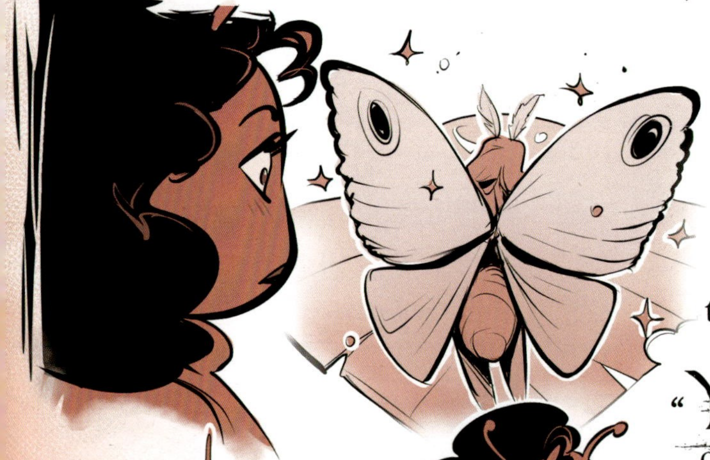

"I saw you looking at me... Do you think I'm beautiful? Am I the prettiest butterfly you've ever met?" asked the butterfly in a mellow voice

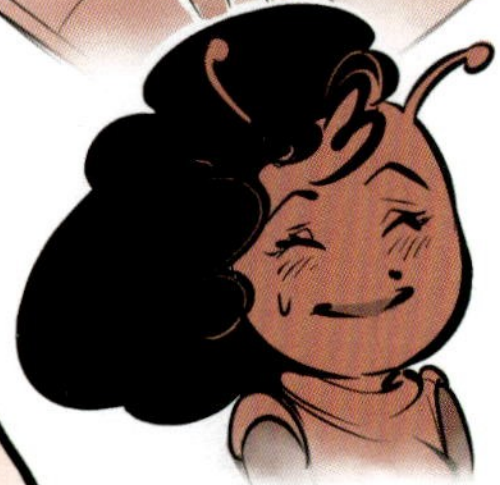

"Yes, you are beautiful, Miss," confirmed our firefly politely. But her mission had priority over everything so she asked: "Do you have any ideas on how to make a firefly shine again?"

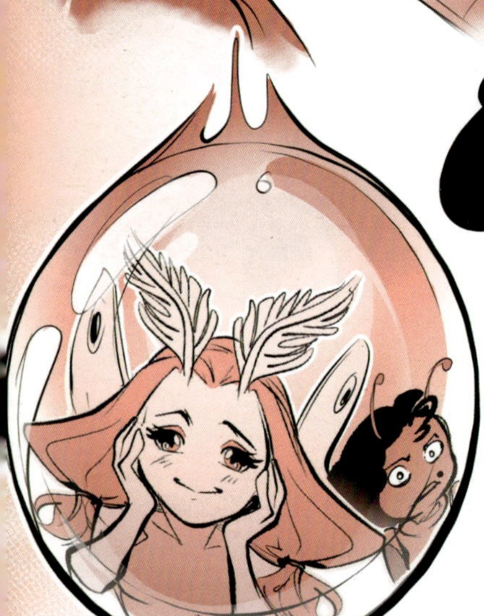

"Mmh? Why would you want to shine wher you already have the chance to admire me?" "What do you say? Do you think I am beautifu Am I the prettiest butterfy you've ever met?"

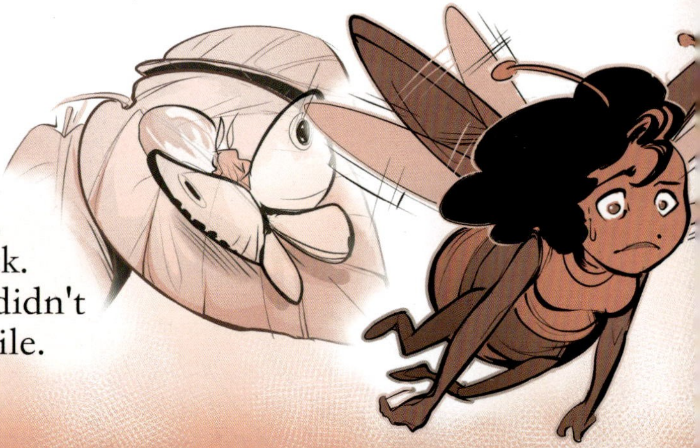

Without a word, the firefly walked back. The butterfly, probably, didn't even notice it for a while.

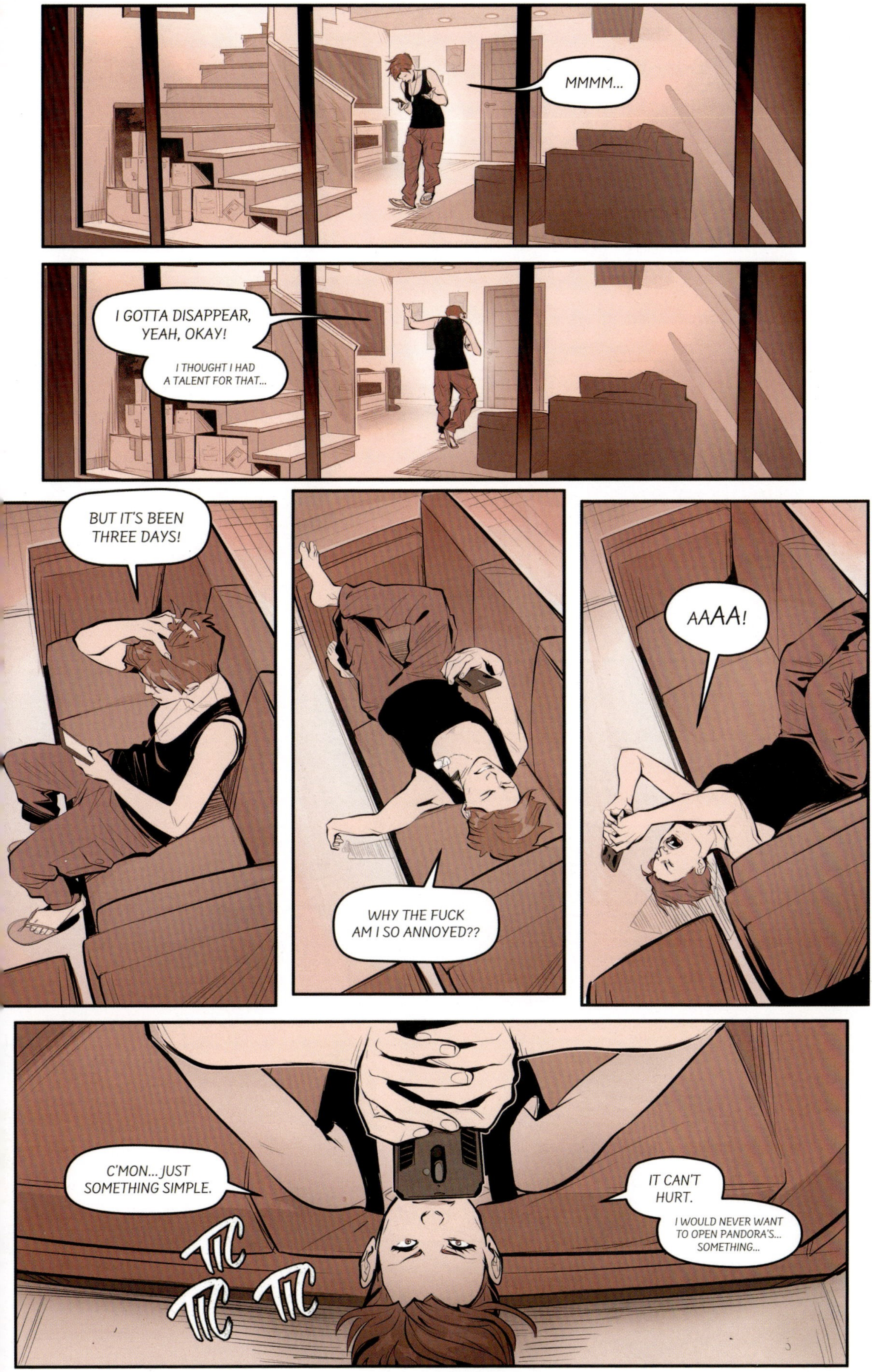
MMMM...
I GOTTA DISAPPEAR, YEAH, OKAY!
I THOUGHT I HAD A TALENT FOR THAT...
BUT IT'S BEEN THREE DAYS!
WHY THE FUCK AM I SO ANNOYED??
AAAA!
C'MON... JUST SOMETHING SIMPLE.
TIC
TIC TIC
IT CAN'T HURT.
I WOULD NEVER WANT TO OPEN PANDORA'S... SOMETHING...

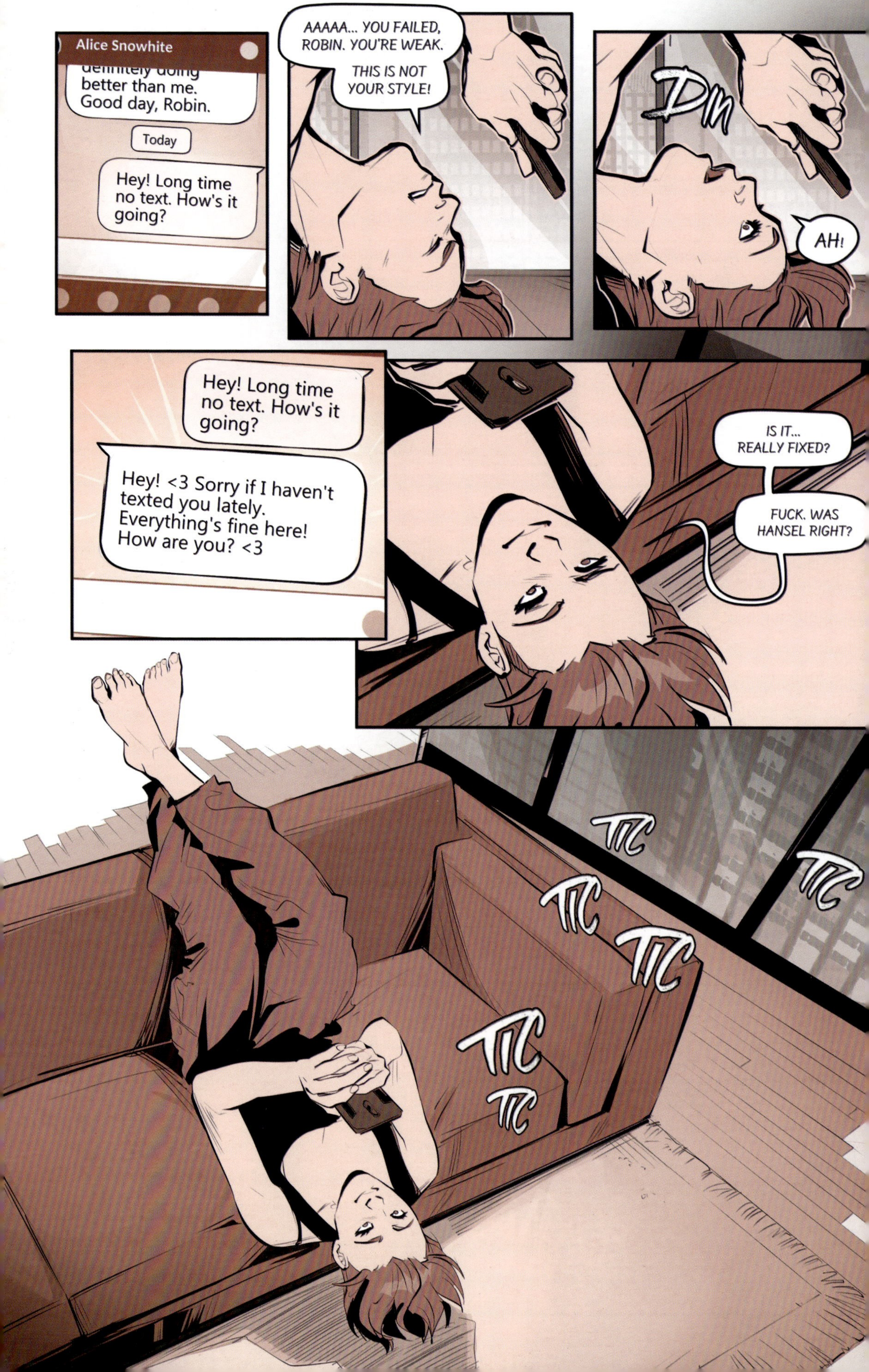
Alice Snowhite
definitely doing better than me. Good day, Robin.
Today
Hey! Long time no text. How's it going?
AAAAA... YOU FAILED, ROBIN. YOU'RE WEAK.
THIS IS NOT YOUR STYLE!
DIN
AH!
Hey! Long time no text. How's it going?
Hey! <3 Sorry if I haven't texted you lately. Everything's fine here! How are you? <3
IS IT... REALLY FIXED?
FUCK. WAS HANSEL RIGHT?
TIC
TIC
TIC
TIC
TIC
TIC

Issue 4

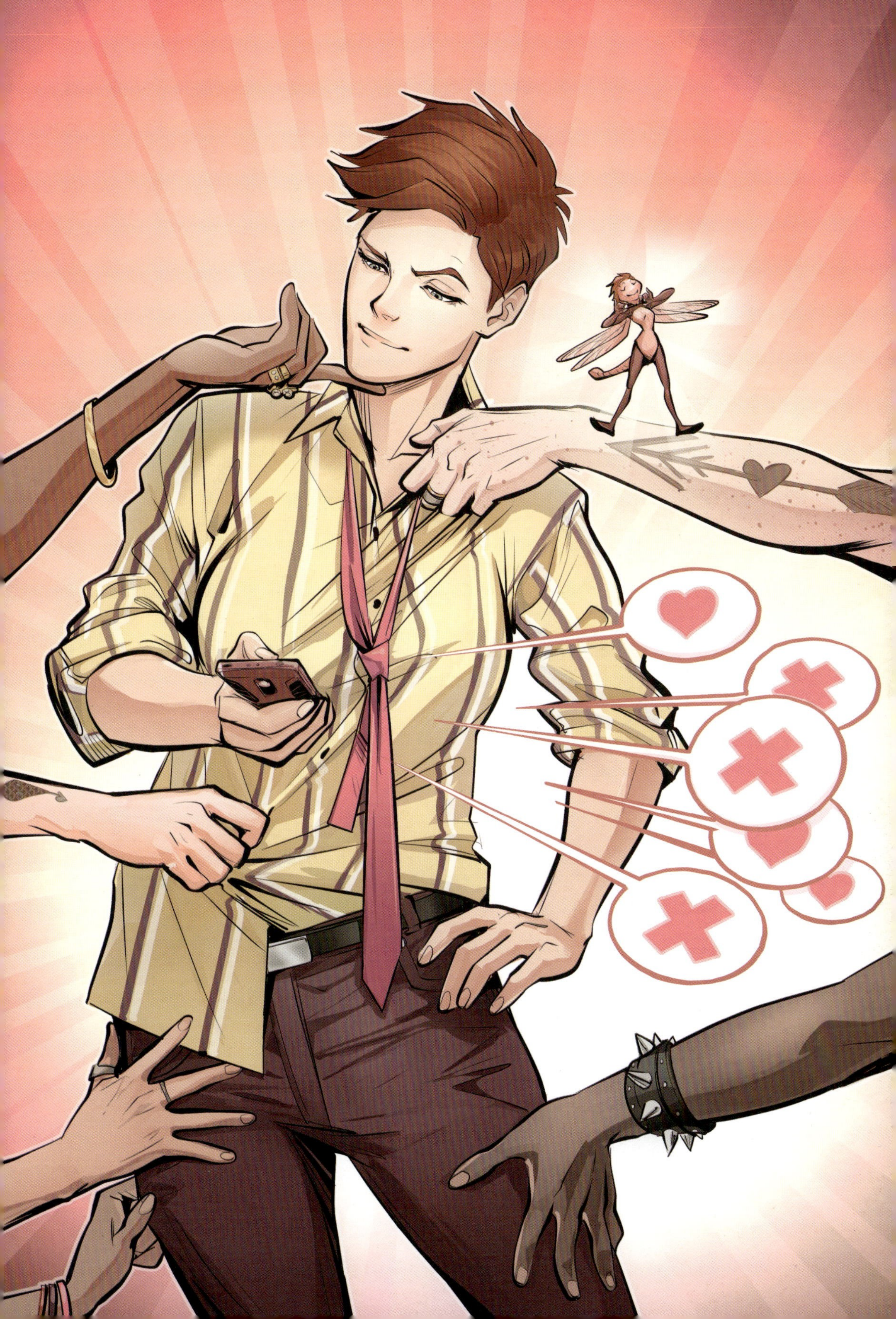

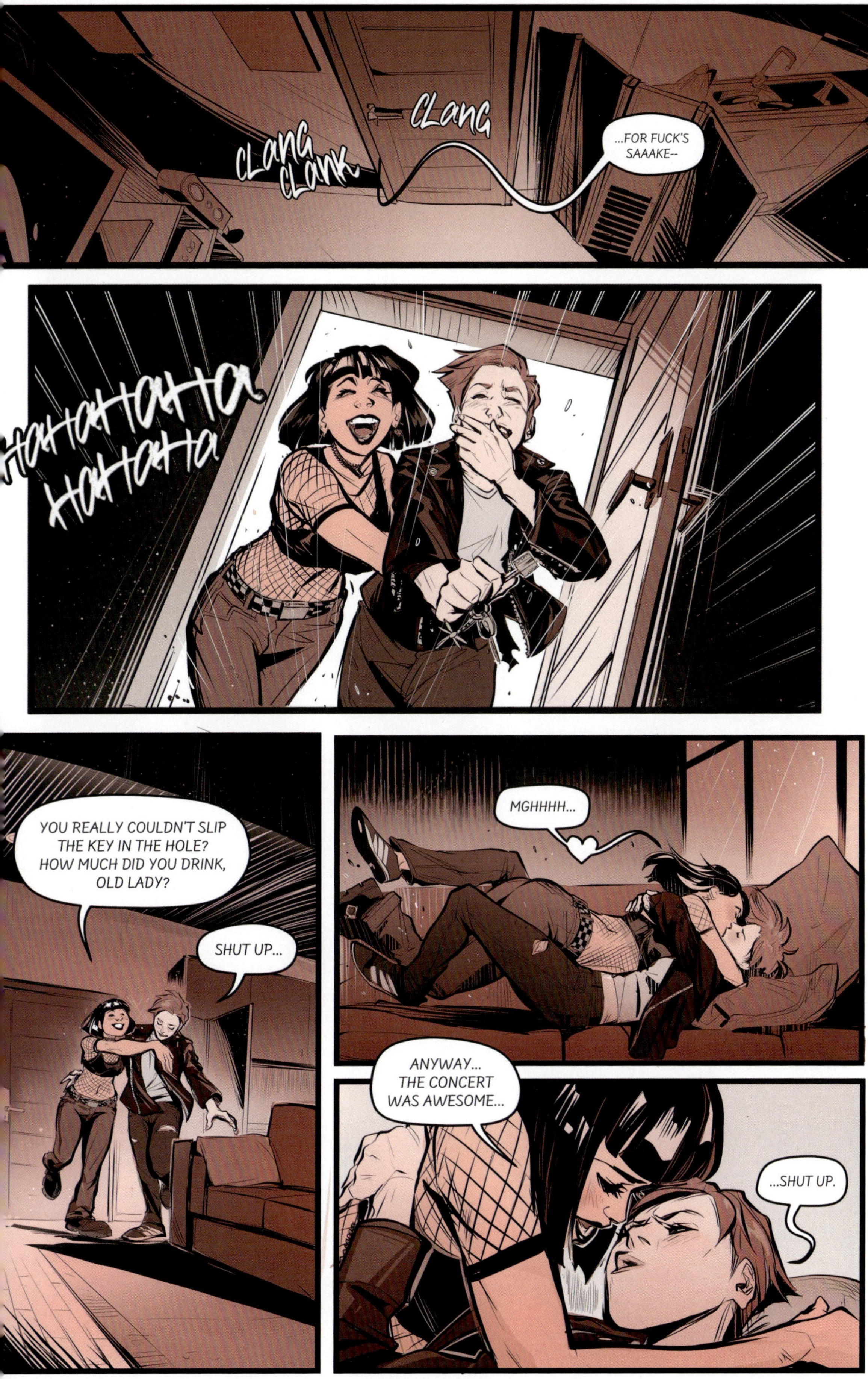
CLANG
CLANK
CLANG
...FOR FUCK'S SAAAKE--
HAHAHAHAHA
HAHAHAHA
YOU REALLY COULDN'T SLIP THE KEY IN THE HOLE? HOW MUCH DID YOU DRINK, OLD LADY?
SHUT UP...
MGHHHH...
ANYWAY... THE CONCERT WAS AWESOME...
...SHUT UP.

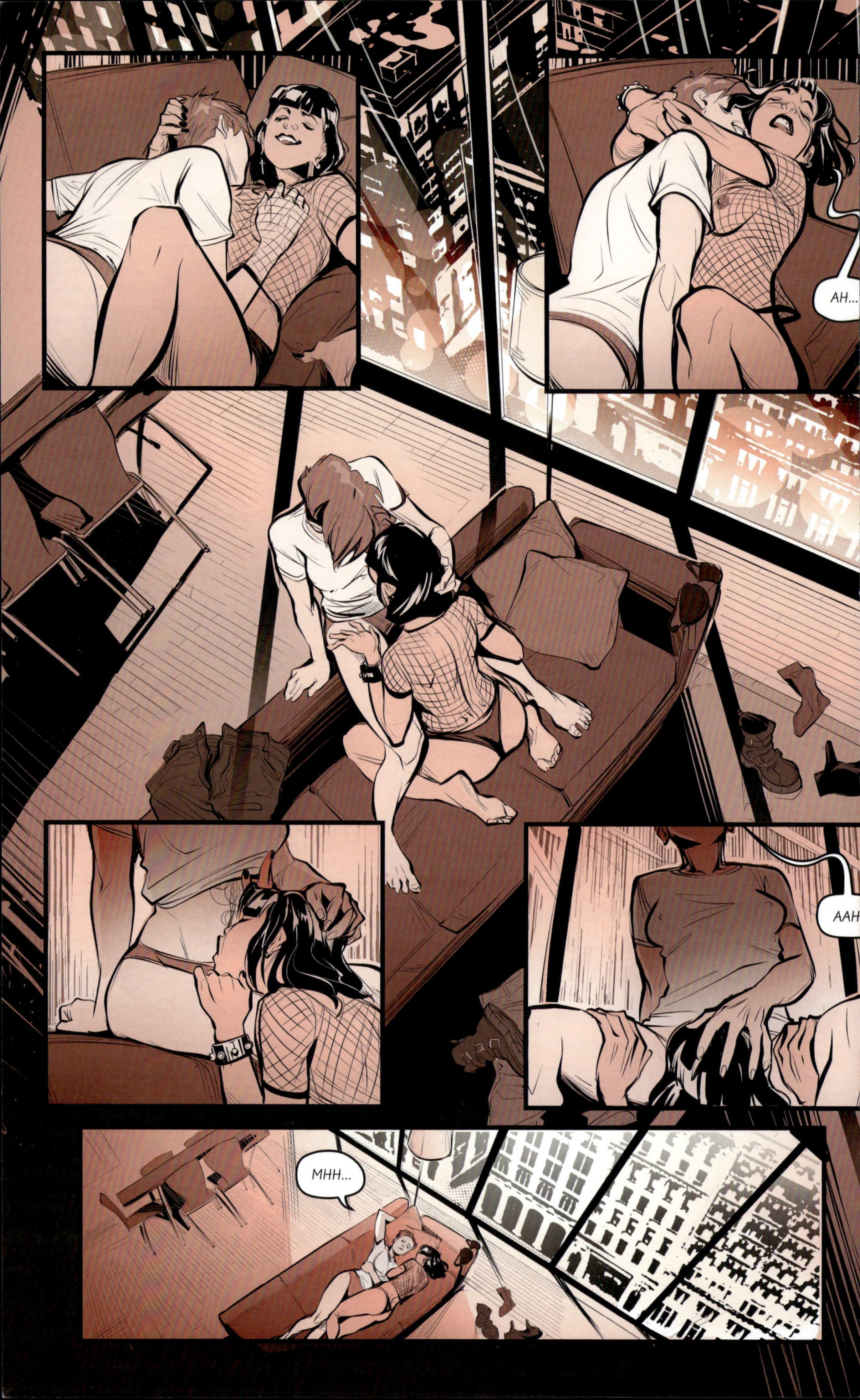
AH...
AAH
MHH...

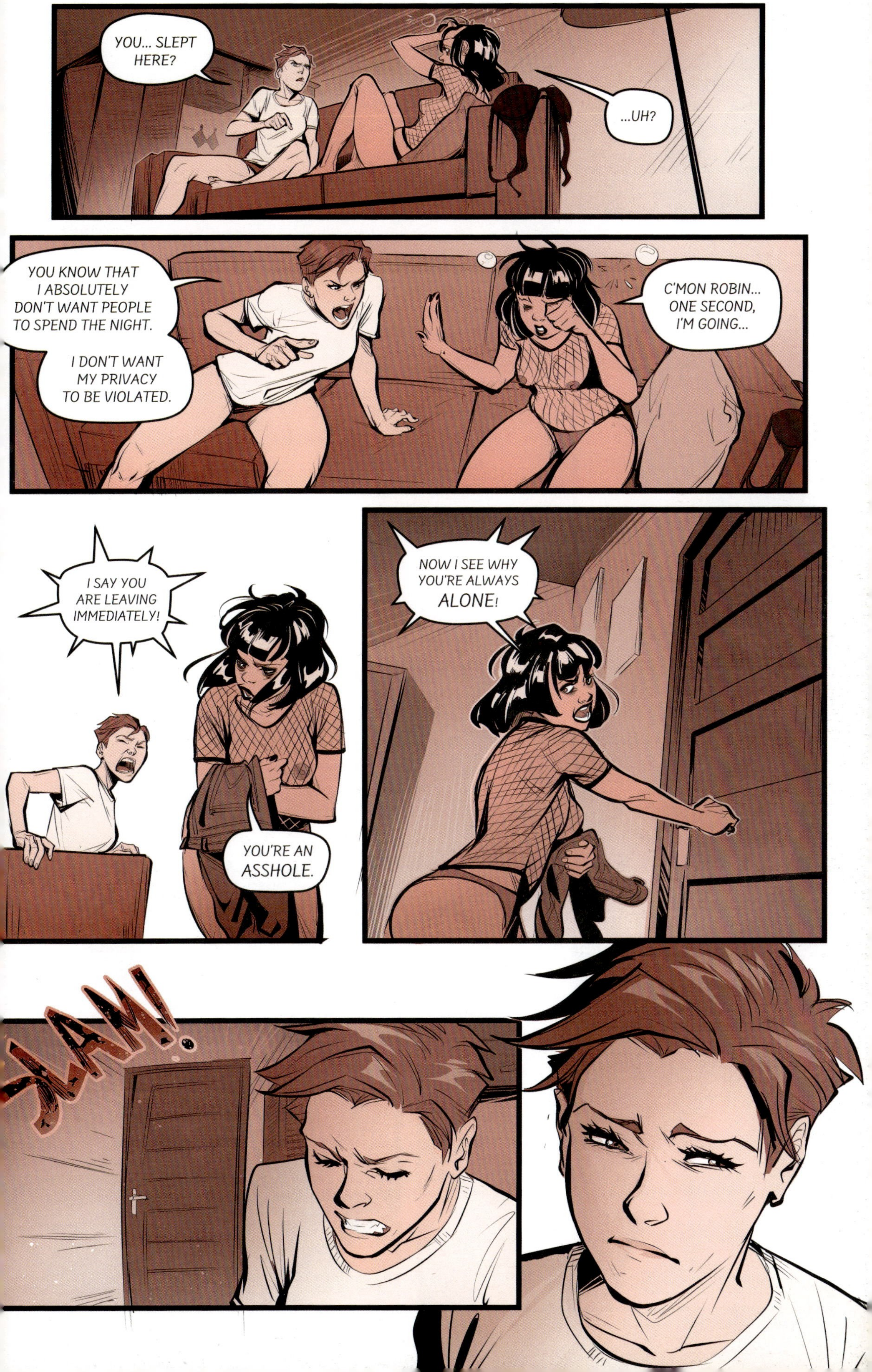
YOU... SLEPT HERE?
...UH?
YOU KNOW THAT I ABSOLUTELY DON'T WANT PEOPLE TO SPEND THE NIGHT.
I DON'T WANT MY PRIVACY TO BE VIOLATED.
C'MON ROBIN... ONE SECOND, I'M GOING...
I SAY YOU ARE LEAVING IMMEDIATELY!
YOU'RE AN ASSHOLE.
NOW I SEE WHY YOU'RE ALWAYS ALONE!
SLAM!

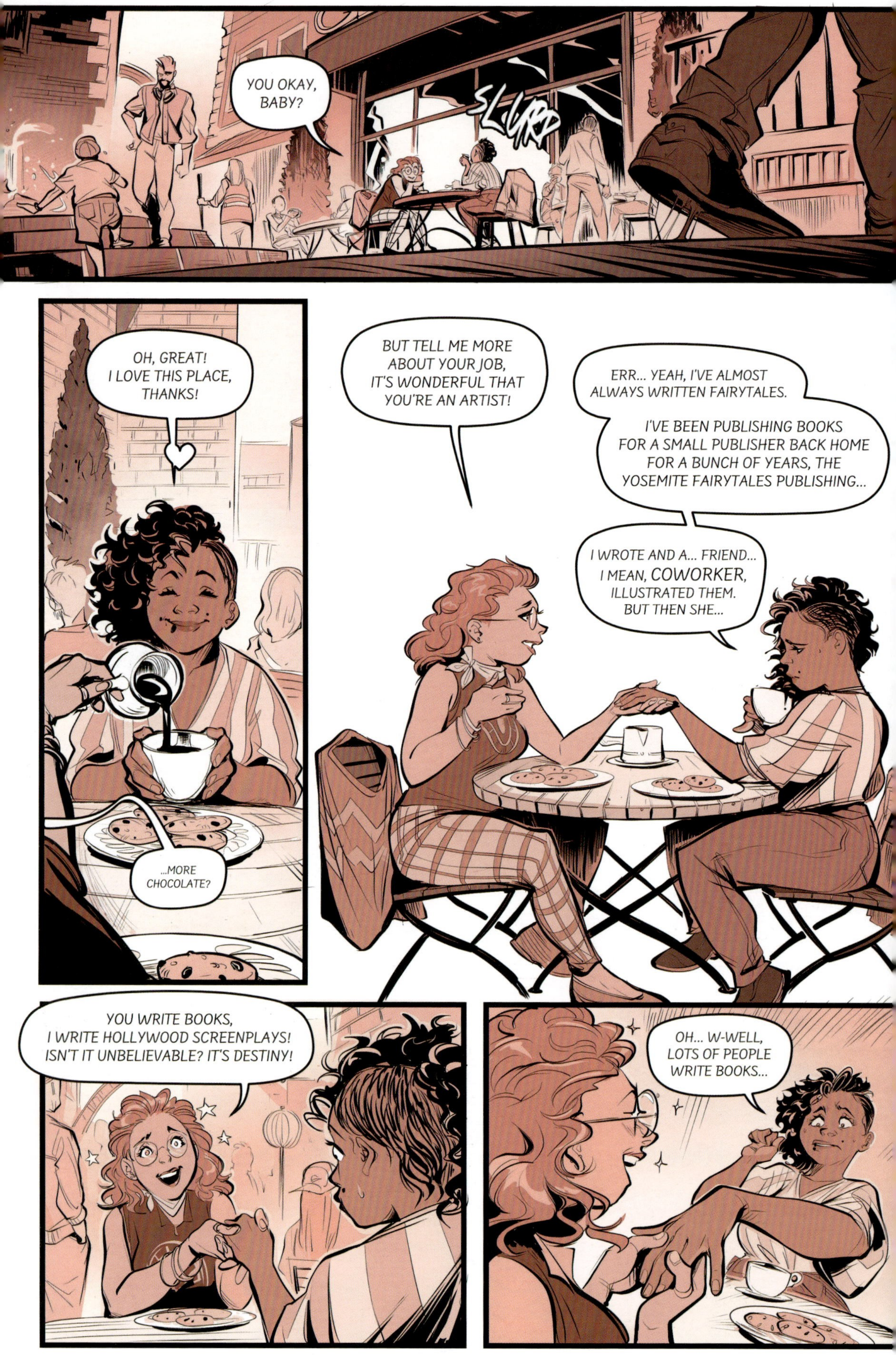
YOU OKAY, BABY?
SLURP
OH, GREAT! I LOVE THIS PLACE, THANKS!
...MORE CHOCOLATE?
BUT TELL ME MORE ABOUT YOUR JOB, IT'S WONDERFUL THAT YOU'RE AN ARTIST!
ERR... YEAH, I'VE ALMOST ALWAYS WRITTEN FAIRYTALES.
I'VE BEEN PUBLISHING BOOKS FOR A SMALL PUBLISHER BACK HOME FOR A BUNCH OF YEARS, THE YOSEMITE FAIRYTALES PUBLISHING...
I WROTE AND A... FRIEND... I MEAN, COWORKER, ILLUSTRATED THEM. BUT THEN SHE...
YOU WRITE BOOKS, I WRITE HOLLYWOOD SCREENPLAYS! ISN'T IT UNBELIEVABLE? IT'S DESTINY!
OH... W-WELL, LOTS OF PEOPLE WRITE BOOKS...

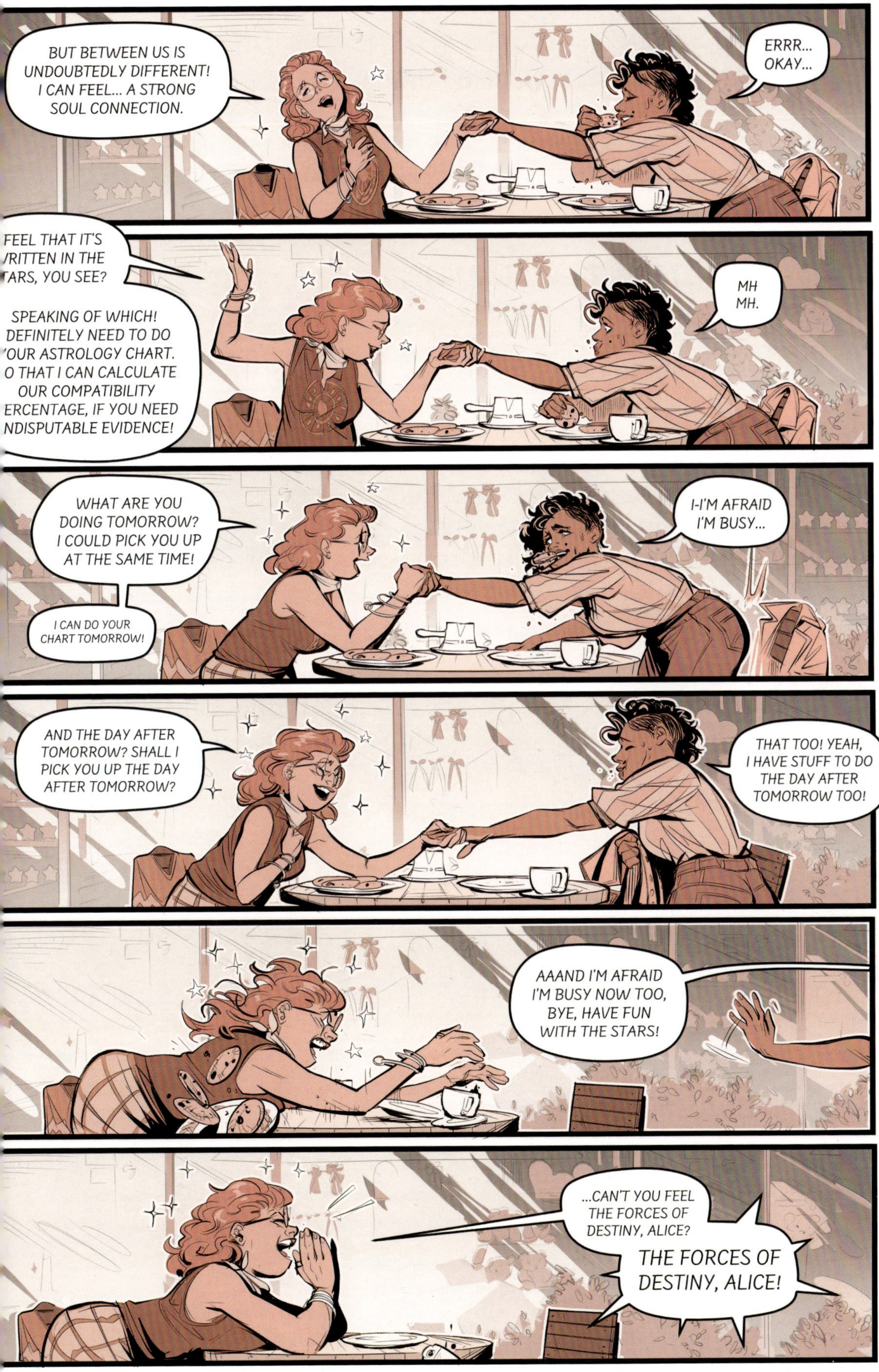

BUT BETWEEN US IS UNDOUBTEDLY DIFFERENT! I CAN FEEL... A STRONG SOUL CONNECTION.
ERRR... OKAY...
FEEL THAT IT'S /RITTEN IN THE ARS, YOU SEE?
SPEAKING OF WHICH! DEFINITELY NEED TO DO 'OUR ASTROLOGY CHART. O THAT I CAN CALCULATE OUR COMPATIBILITY ERCENTAGE, IF YOU NEED NDISPUTABLE EVIDENCE!
MH MH.
WHAT ARE YOU DOING TOMORROW? I COULD PICK YOU UP AT THE SAME TIME!
I CAN DO YOUR CHART TOMORROW!
I-I'M AFRAID I'M BUSY...
AND THE DAY AFTER TOMORROW? SHALL I PICK YOU UP THE DAY AFTER TOMORROW?
THAT TOO! YEAH, I HAVE STUFF TO DO THE DAY AFTER TOMORROW TOO!
AAAND I'M AFRAID I'M BUSY NOW TOO, BYE, HAVE FUN WITH THE STARS!
...CAN'T YOU FEEL THE FORCES OF DESTINY, ALICE?
THE FORCES OF DESTINY, ALICE!

While proceeding on her journey, our firefly got distracted by an insistent buzzing that awoke her curiosity.

BZZZZ ZZZ ZZZZ

Hi firefly! I heard you need help!" she enthusiastically exclaimed, coming from above. "Oh... Yes! Can you help me shine again?" our firefly asked hopefully. She felt so lucky to have found someone offering their help! "I wouldn't know how, but I would do anything to help you! Let me come with you on your journey!" the fly proposed.

BZZZ MNZZ

And she did! But, alas, the fly was so noisy and always so close that our little firefly couldn't even hear her own thoughts!

BZZ BZZ BZZ BZZZZ BZZ

"**D**estiny has pulled us together! We're two flying bugs, of all things! Such an unbelievable and mysterious coincidence!" buzzed the fly, more often than needed, flying around her.

BZZZ BZZZZZ

And like that, our firefly decided to continue her journey looking for her light in peaceful loneliness. Oh my, such odd bugs existed in the world!

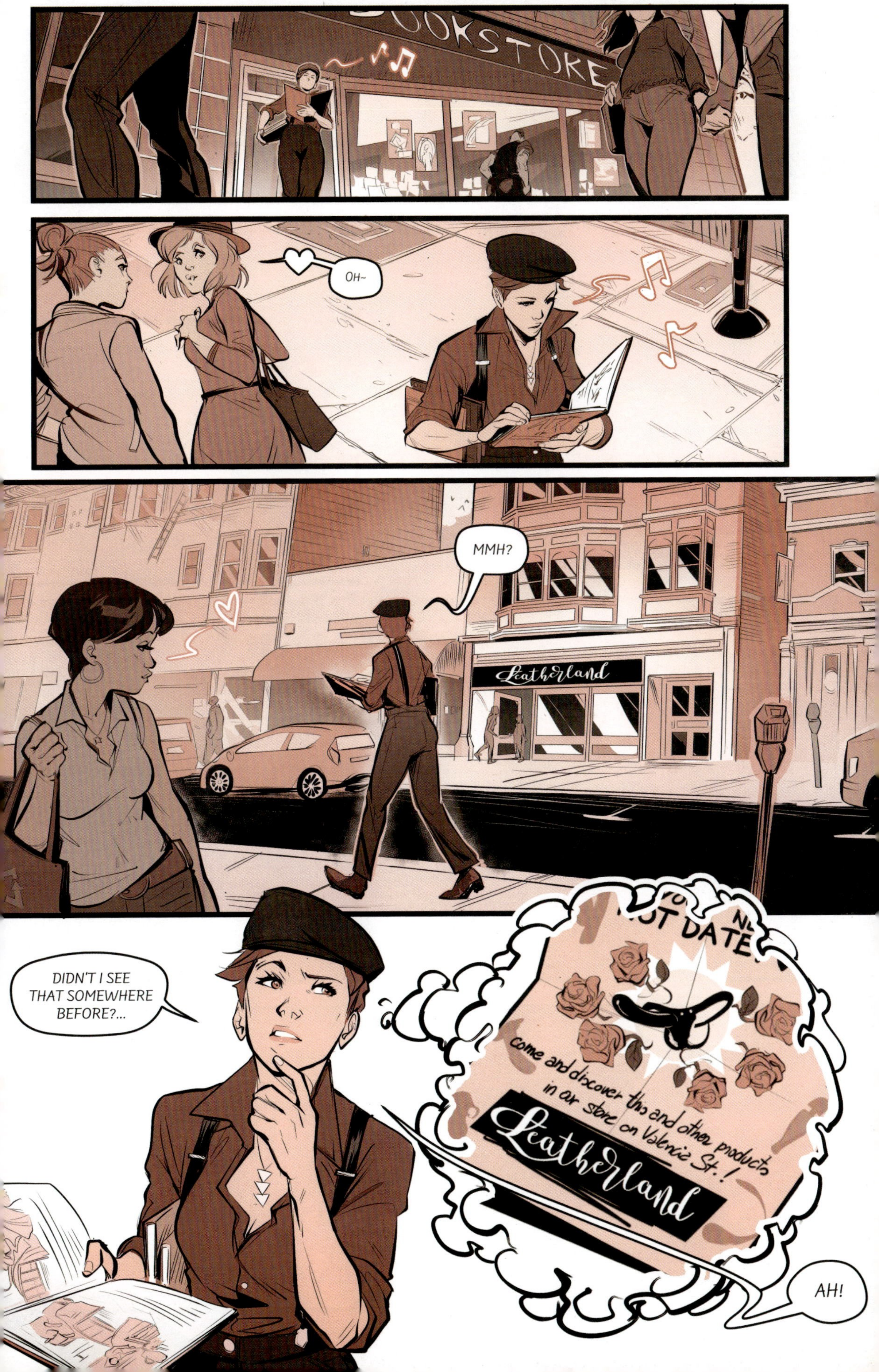
OOKSTORE
OH~
MMH?
Leatherland
DIDN'T I SEE THAT SOMEWHERE BEFORE?...
come and discover this and other products in our store on Valencia St.!
Leatherland
AH!

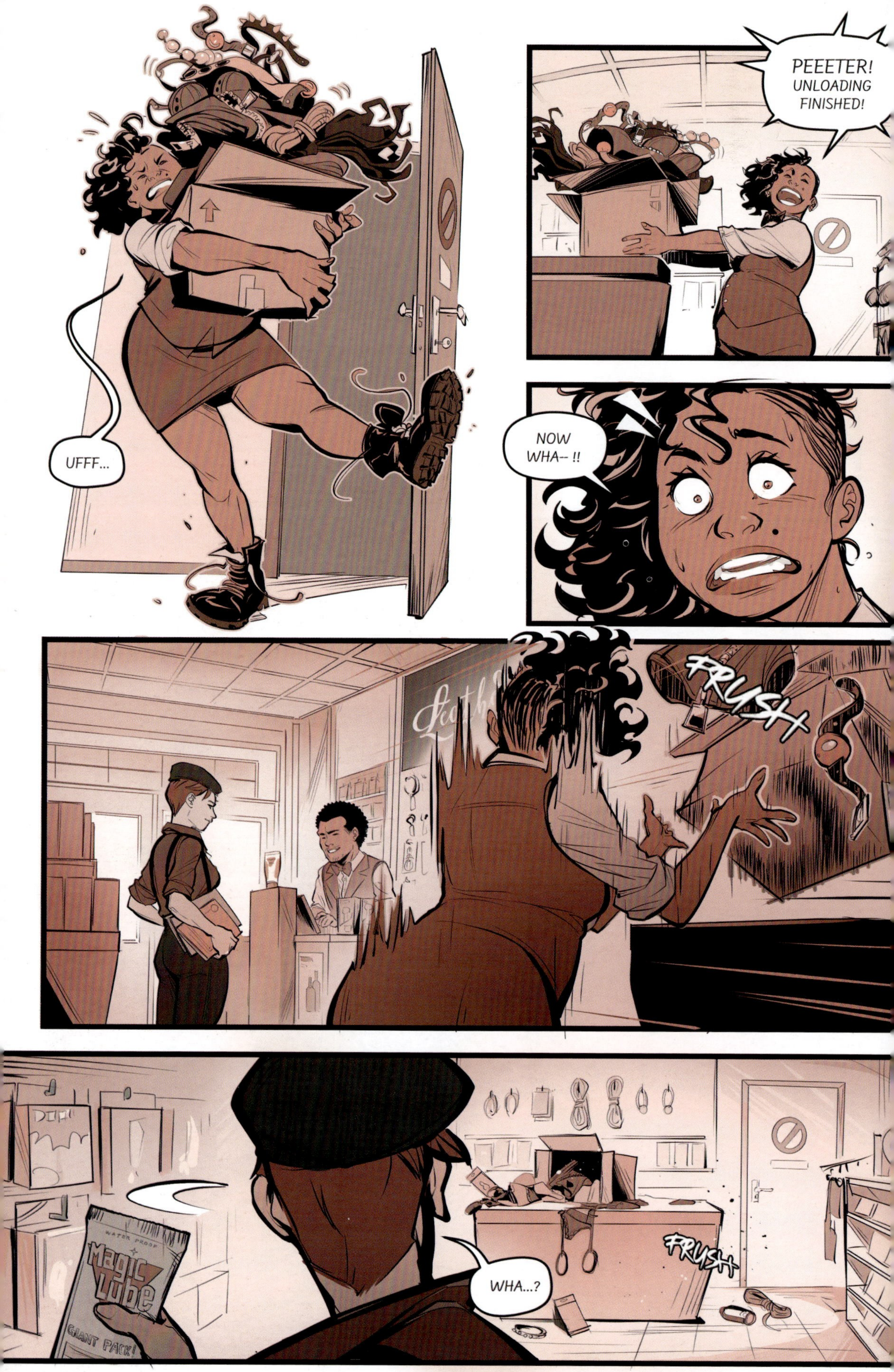
UFFF...
PEEETER! UNLOADING FINISHED!
NOW WHA-- !!
FRUSH
WHA...?
FRUSH
WATER PROOF
Magic Lube
GIANT PACK!

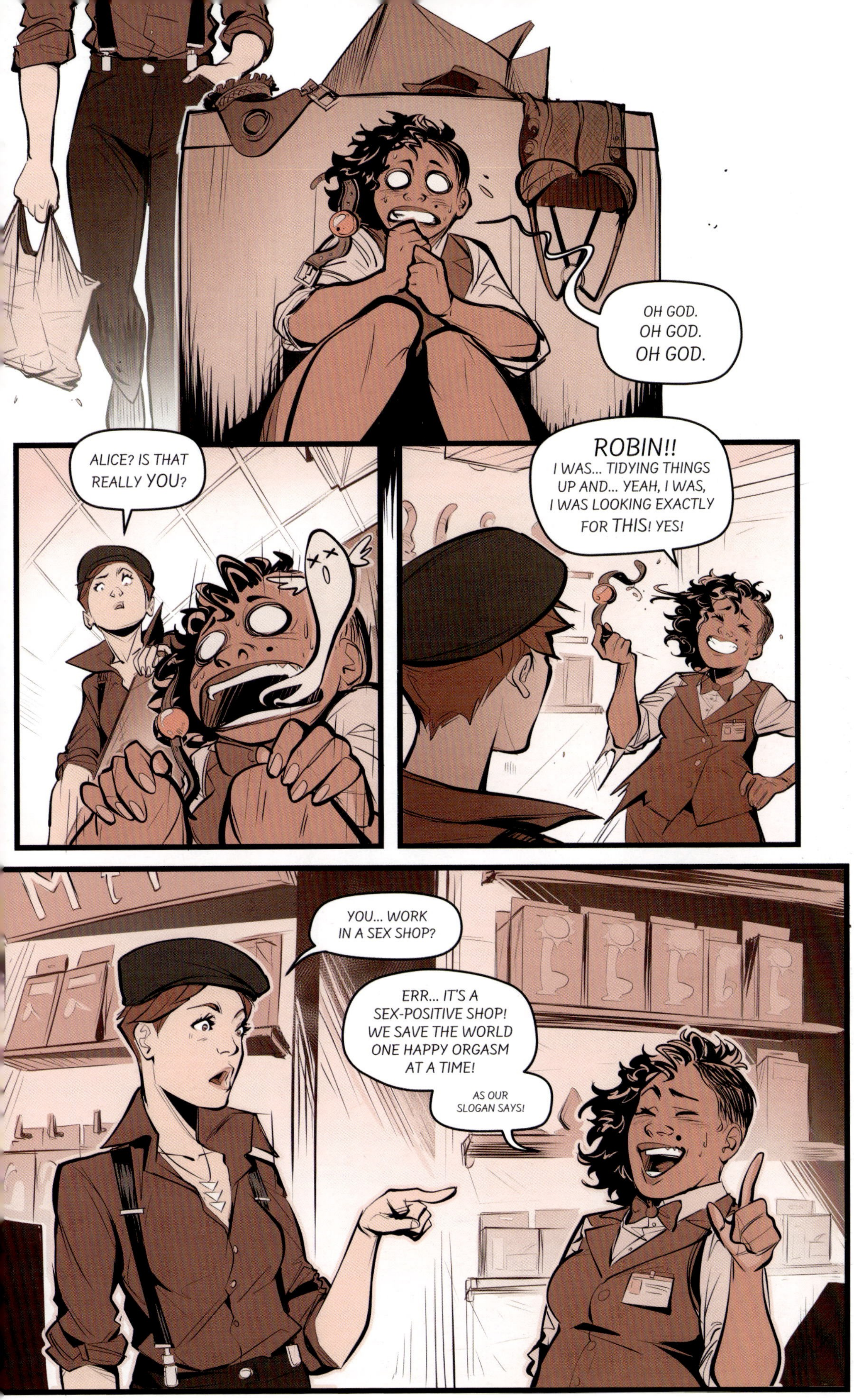
OH GOD.
OH GOD.
OH GOD.
ALICE? IS THAT REALLY YOU?
ROBIN!! I WAS... TIDYING THINGS UP AND... YEAH, I WAS, I WAS LOOKING EXACTLY FOR THIS! YES!
YOU... WORK IN A SEX SHOP?
ERR... IT'S A SEX-POSITIVE SHOP! WE SAVE THE WORLD ONE HAPPY ORGASM AT A TIME!
AS OUR SLOGAN SAYS!

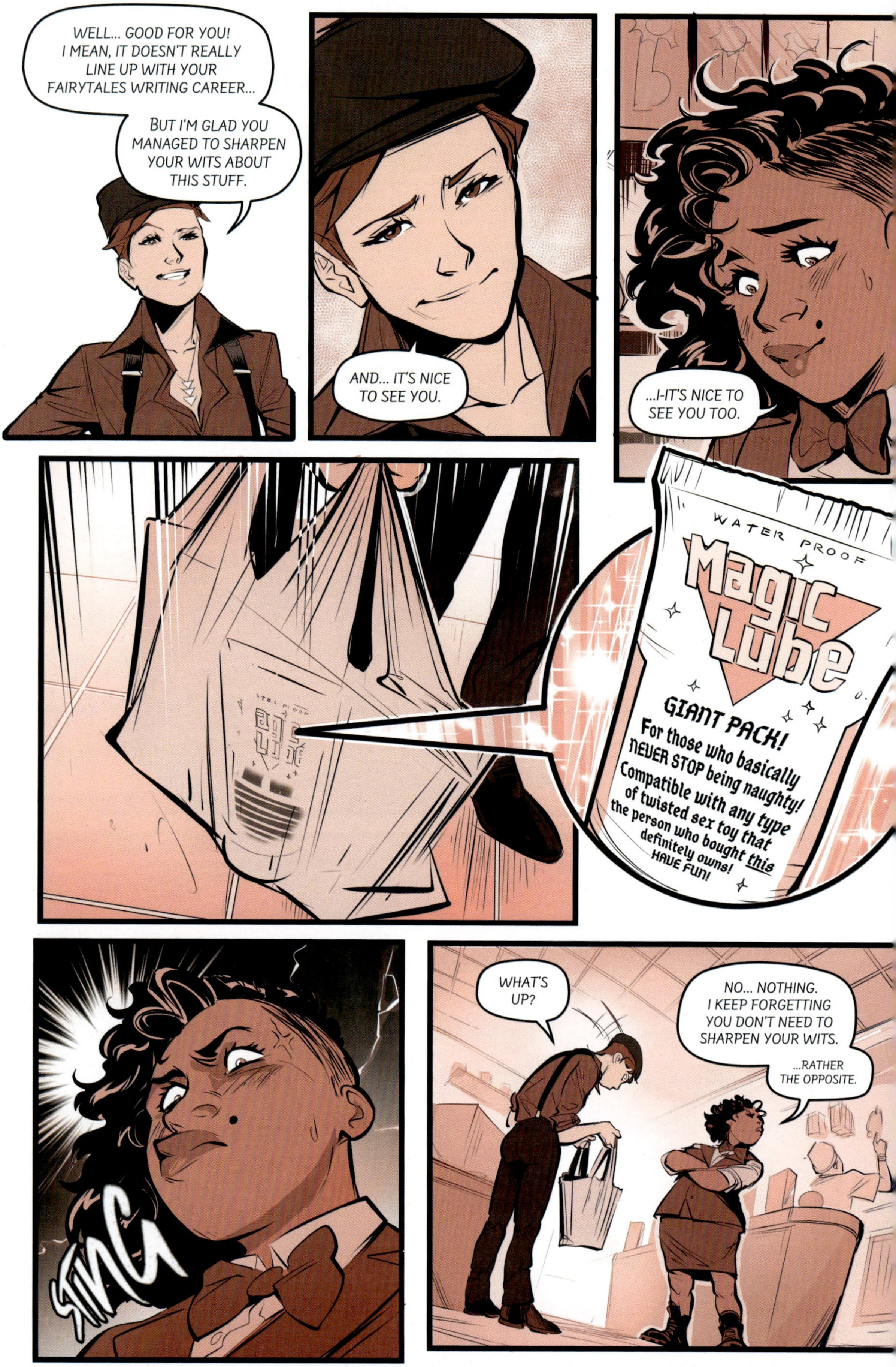
WELL... GOOD FOR YOU! I MEAN, IT DOESN'T REALLY LINE UP WITH YOUR FAIRYTALES WRITING CAREER...
BUT I'M GLAD YOU MANAGED TO SHARPEN YOUR WITS ABOUT THIS STUFF.
AND... IT'S NICE TO SEE YOU.
...I-IT'S NICE TO SEE YOU TOO.
WATER PROOF
Magic Lube
GIANT PACK!
For those who basically NEVER STOP being naughty! Compatible with any type of twisted sex toy that the person who bought this definitely owns! HAVE FUN!
STING
WHAT'S UP?
NO... NOTHING. I KEEP FORGETTING YOU DON'T NEED TO SHARPEN YOUR WITS.
...RATHER THE OPPOSITE.

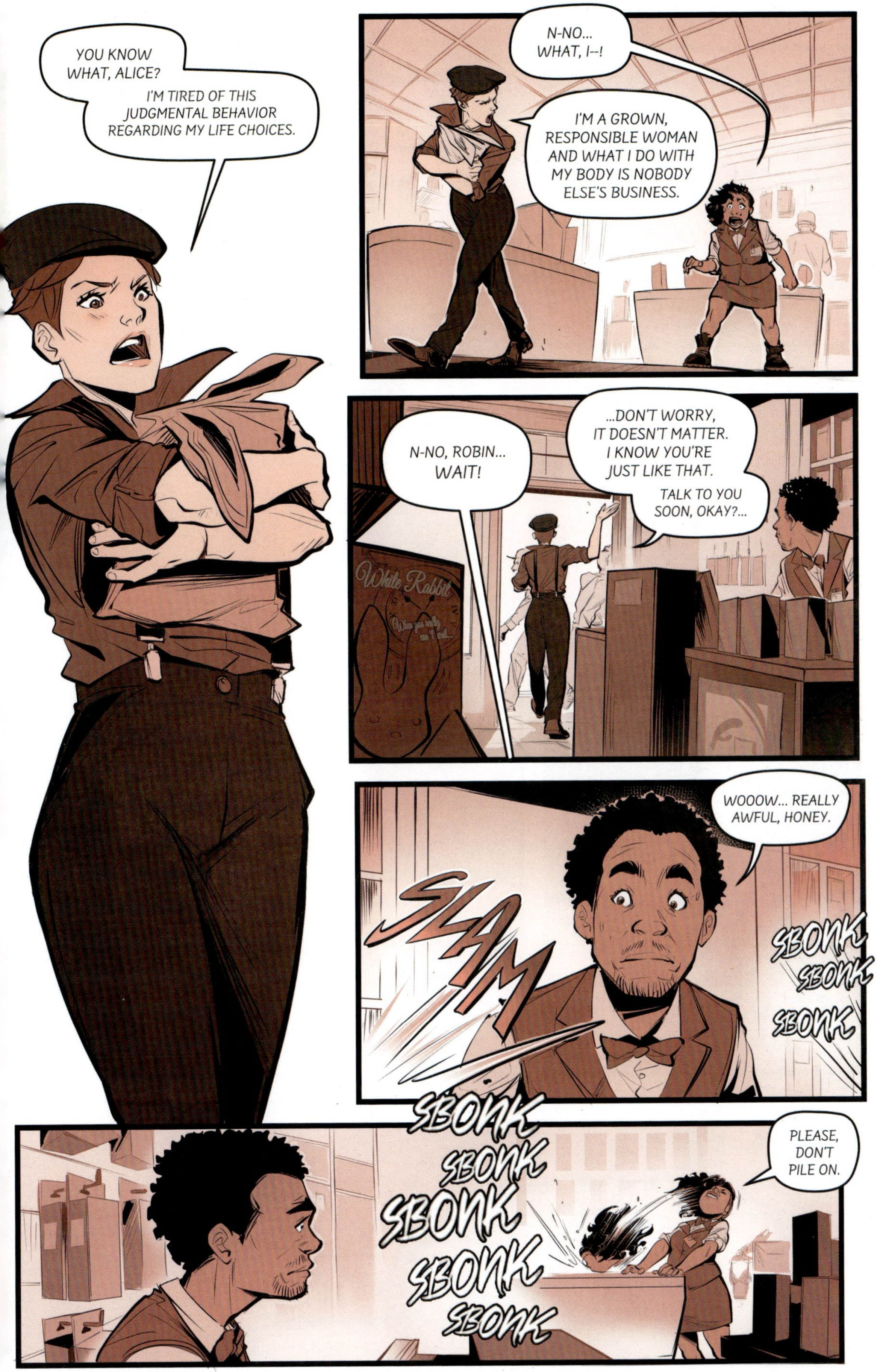
YOU KNOW WHAT, ALICE?
I'M TIRED OF THIS JUDGMENTAL BEHAVIOR REGARDING MY LIFE CHOICES.
N-NO... WHAT, I--!
I'M A GROWN, RESPONSIBLE WOMAN AND WHAT I DO WITH MY BODY IS NOBODY ELSE'S BUSINESS.
N-NO, ROBIN... WAIT!
...DON'T WORRY, IT DOESN'T MATTER. I KNOW YOU'RE JUST LIKE THAT.
TALK TO YOU SOON, OKAY?...
White Rabbit
WOOOW... REALLY AWFUL, HONEY.
SLAM
SBONK
SBONK
SBONK
SBONK
SBONK
SBONK
SBONK
SBONK
PLEASE, DON'T PILE ON.

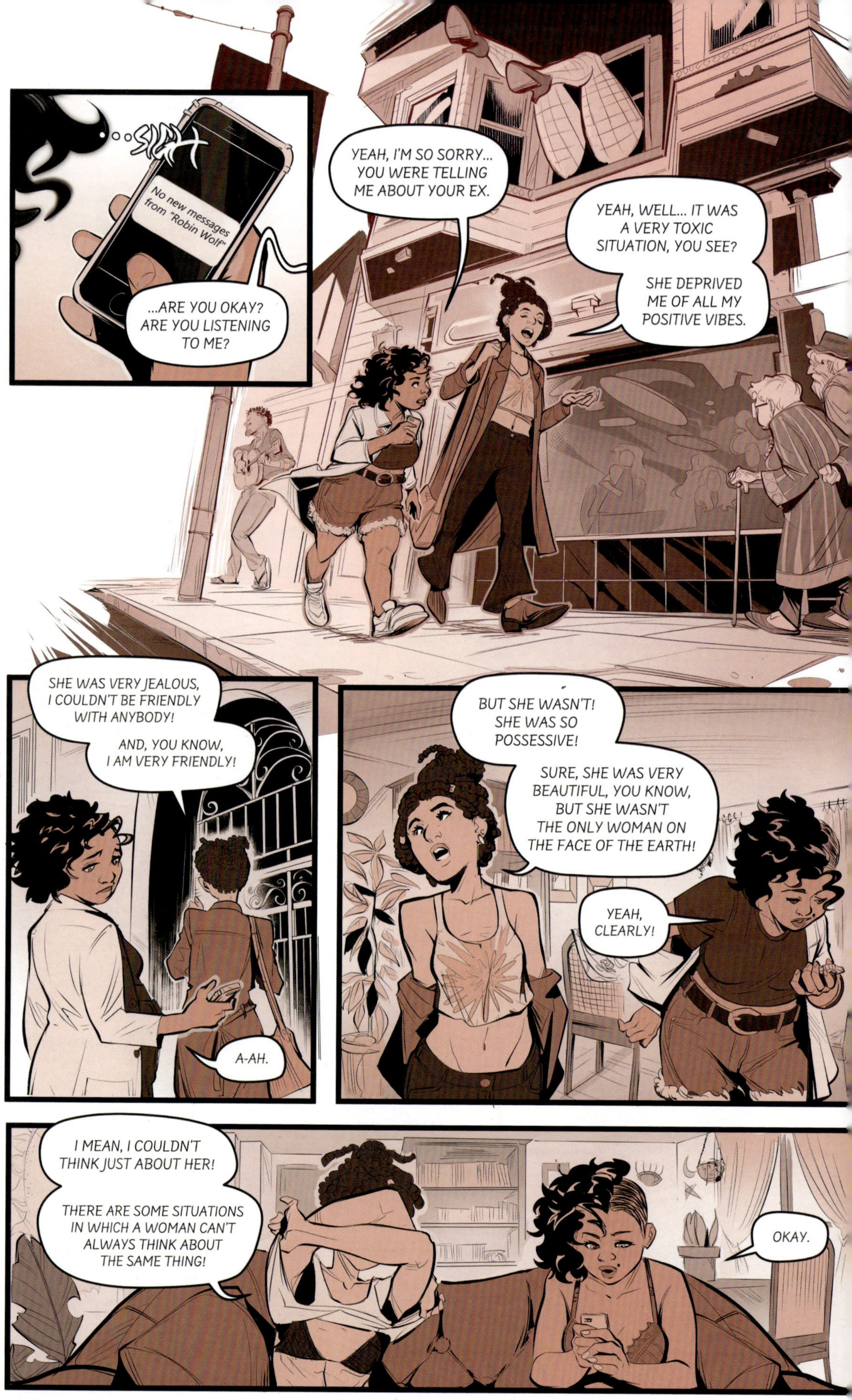
SIGH
No new messages from "Robin Wolf"
...ARE YOU OKAY? ARE YOU LISTENING TO ME?
YEAH, I'M SO SORRY... YOU WERE TELLING ME ABOUT YOUR EX.
YEAH, WELL... IT WAS A VERY TOXIC SITUATION, YOU SEE?
SHE DEPRIVED ME OF ALL MY POSITIVE VIBES.
SHE WAS VERY JEALOUS, I COULDN'T BE FRIENDLY WITH ANYBODY!
AND, YOU KNOW, I AM VERY FRIENDLY!
A-AH.
BUT SHE WASN'T! SHE WAS SO POSSESSIVE!
SURE, SHE WAS VERY BEAUTIFUL, YOU KNOW, BUT SHE WASN'T THE ONLY WOMAN ON THE FACE OF THE EARTH!
YEAH, CLEARLY!
I MEAN, I COULDN'T THINK JUST ABOUT HER!
THERE ARE SOME SITUATIONS IN WHICH A WOMAN CAN'T ALWAYS THINK ABOUT THE SAME THING!
OKAY.

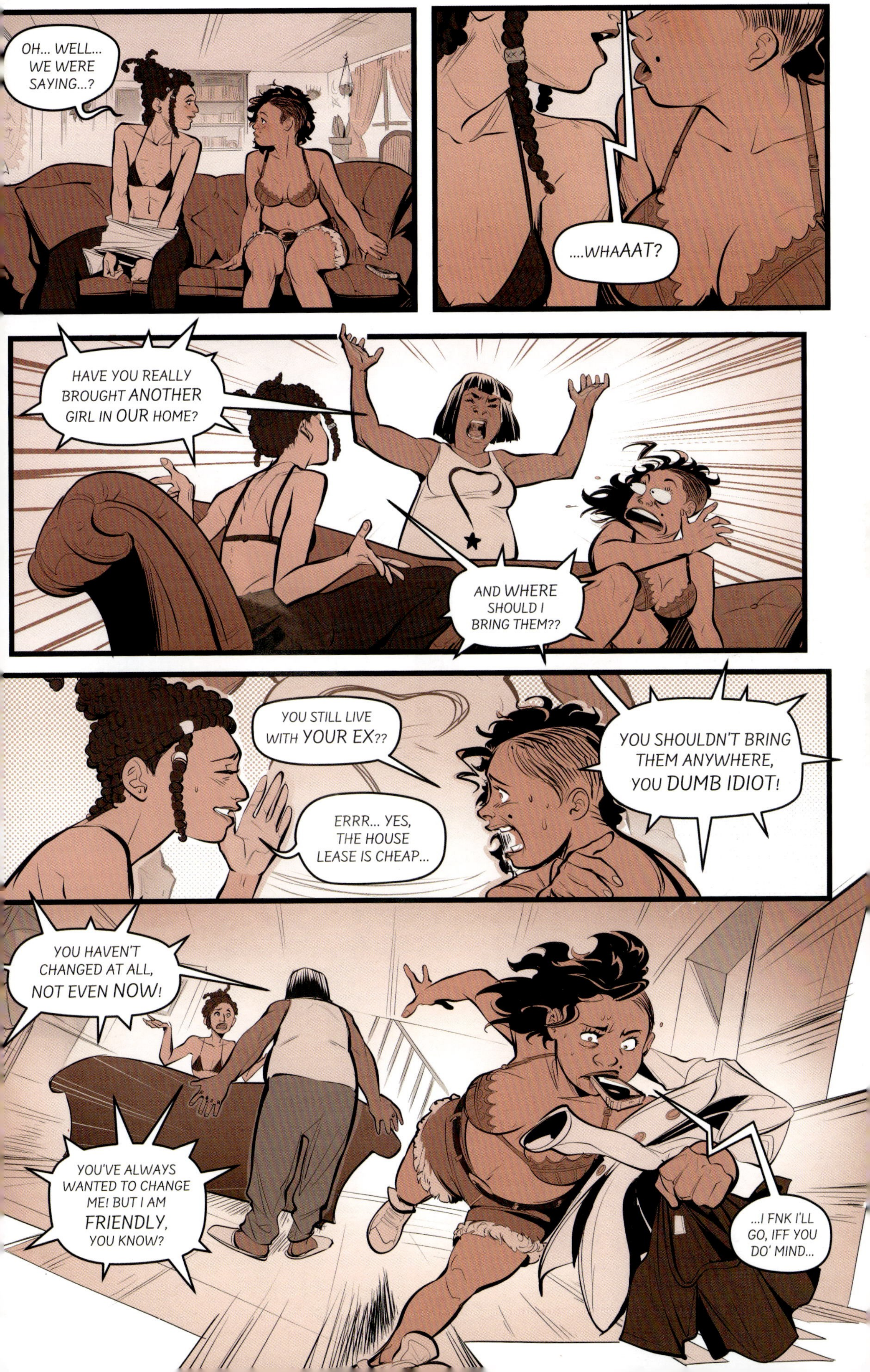
OH... WELL... WE WERE SAYING...?
....WHAAAT?
HAVE YOU REALLY BROUGHT ANOTHER GIRL IN OUR HOME?
AND WHERE SHOULD I BRING THEM??
YOU STILL LIVE WITH YOUR EX??
ERRR... YES, THE HOUSE LEASE IS CHEAP...
YOU SHOULDN'T BRING THEM ANYWHERE, YOU DUMB IDIOT!
YOU HAVEN'T CHANGED AT ALL, NOT EVEN NOW!
YOU'VE ALWAYS WANTED TO CHANGE ME! BUT I AM FRIENDLY, YOU KNOW?
...I FNK I'LL GO, IFF YOU DO' MIND...

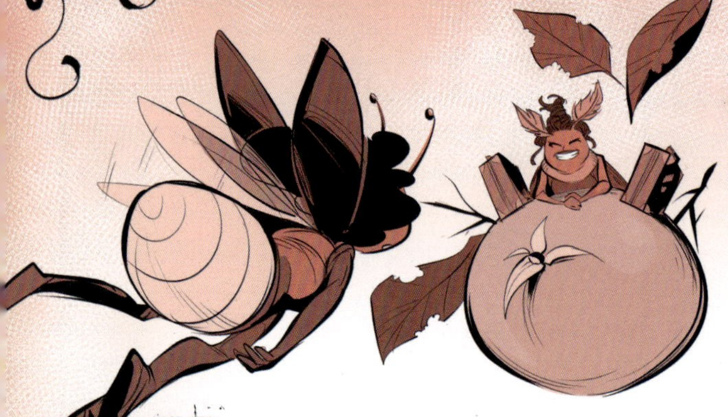

On her journey, the firefly met yet another little bug trying to catch her attention.

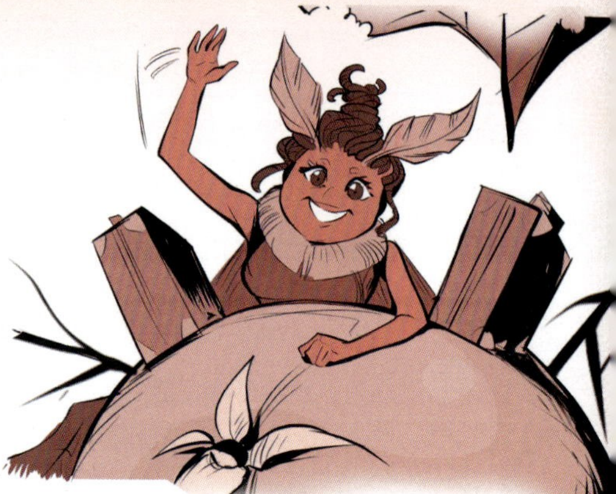

"Hi beautiful firefly! Are you going in this direction too?" asked the strange, exuberant gray butterfy. "Would you like to keep traveling together?" she immediately proposed.

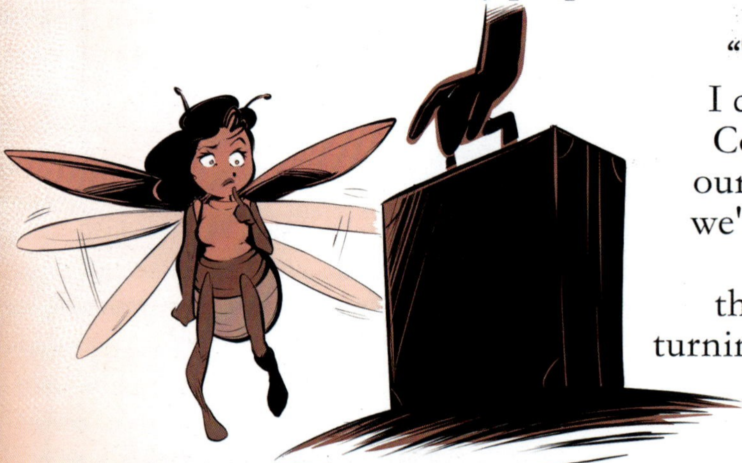

"Okay, miss... butterfly? I am trying to shine again... Could you help me?" asked our firefly politely. "We'll see, we'll see! Now let me grab my stuff so we can leave!" the moth said dismissively, turning to load her great baggage

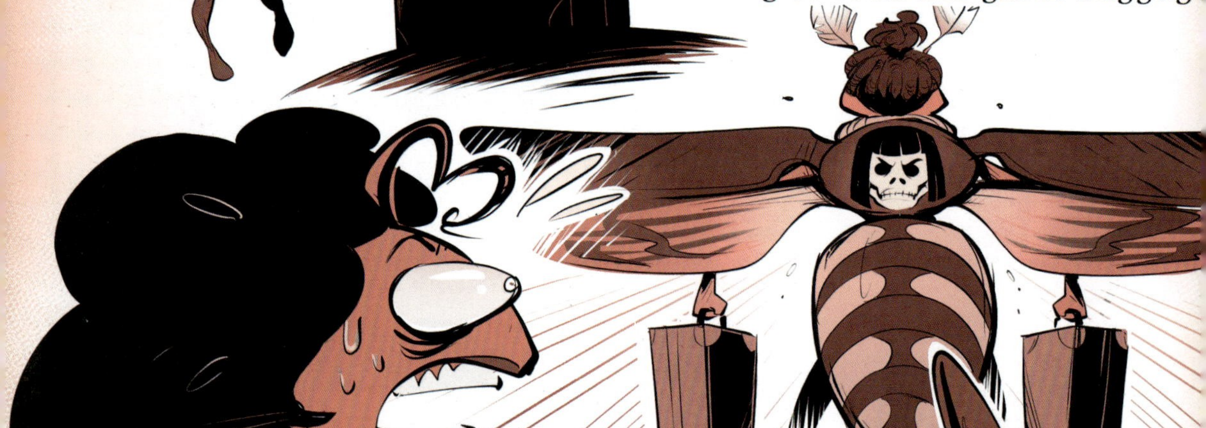

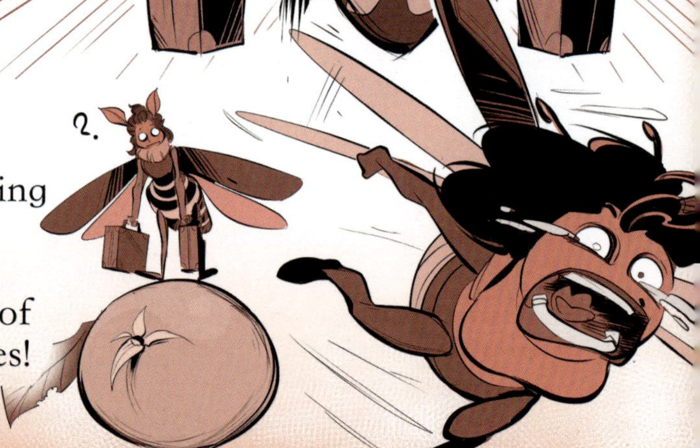

Oh God! The firefly didn't see that coming! She flew away without saying goodbye, despite her impeccable politeness. The world really was full of bugs with strange surprises!

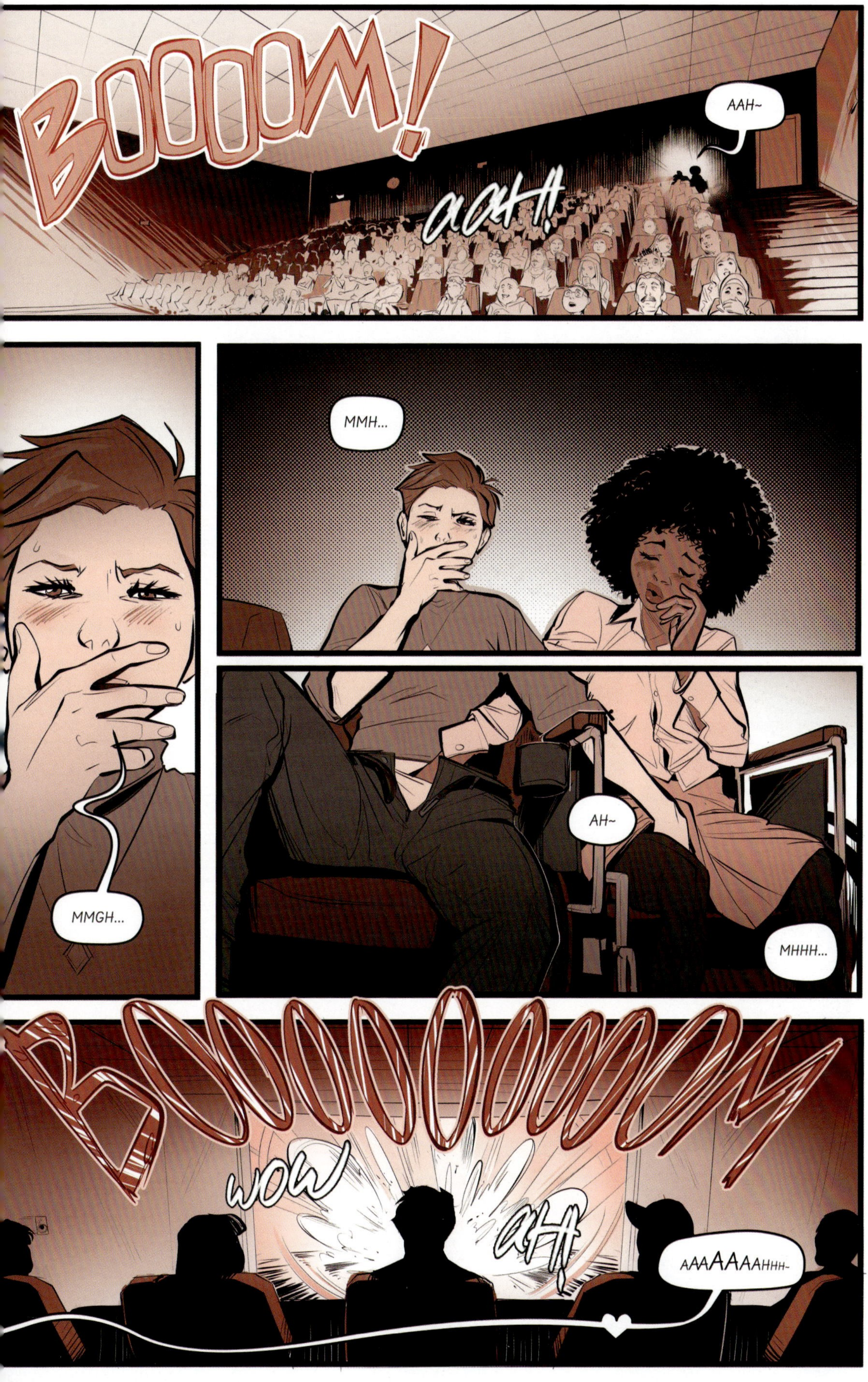
BOOOOM!
AAH~
AAH!!
MMH...
MMGH...
AH~
MHHH...
BOOOOOOOOM
WOW
AH!
AAAAAAAHHH-

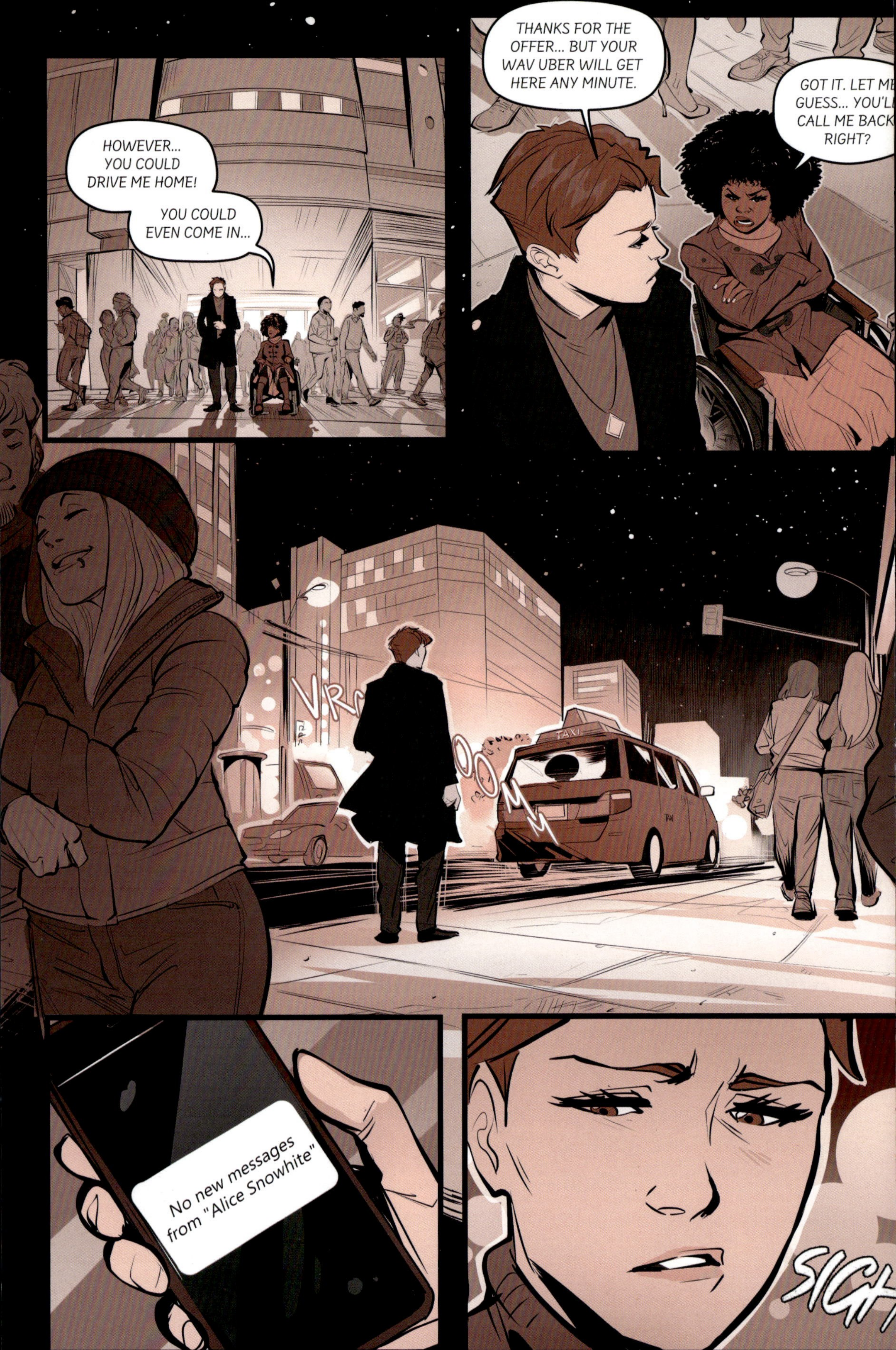
HOWEVER... YOU COULD DRIVE ME HOME!
YOU COULD EVEN COME IN...
THANKS FOR THE OFFER... BUT YOUR WAV UBER WILL GET HERE ANY MINUTE.
GOT IT. LET ME GUESS... YOU'LL CALL ME BACK RIGHT?
VROOOOMM
No new messages from "Alice Snowhite"
SIGH

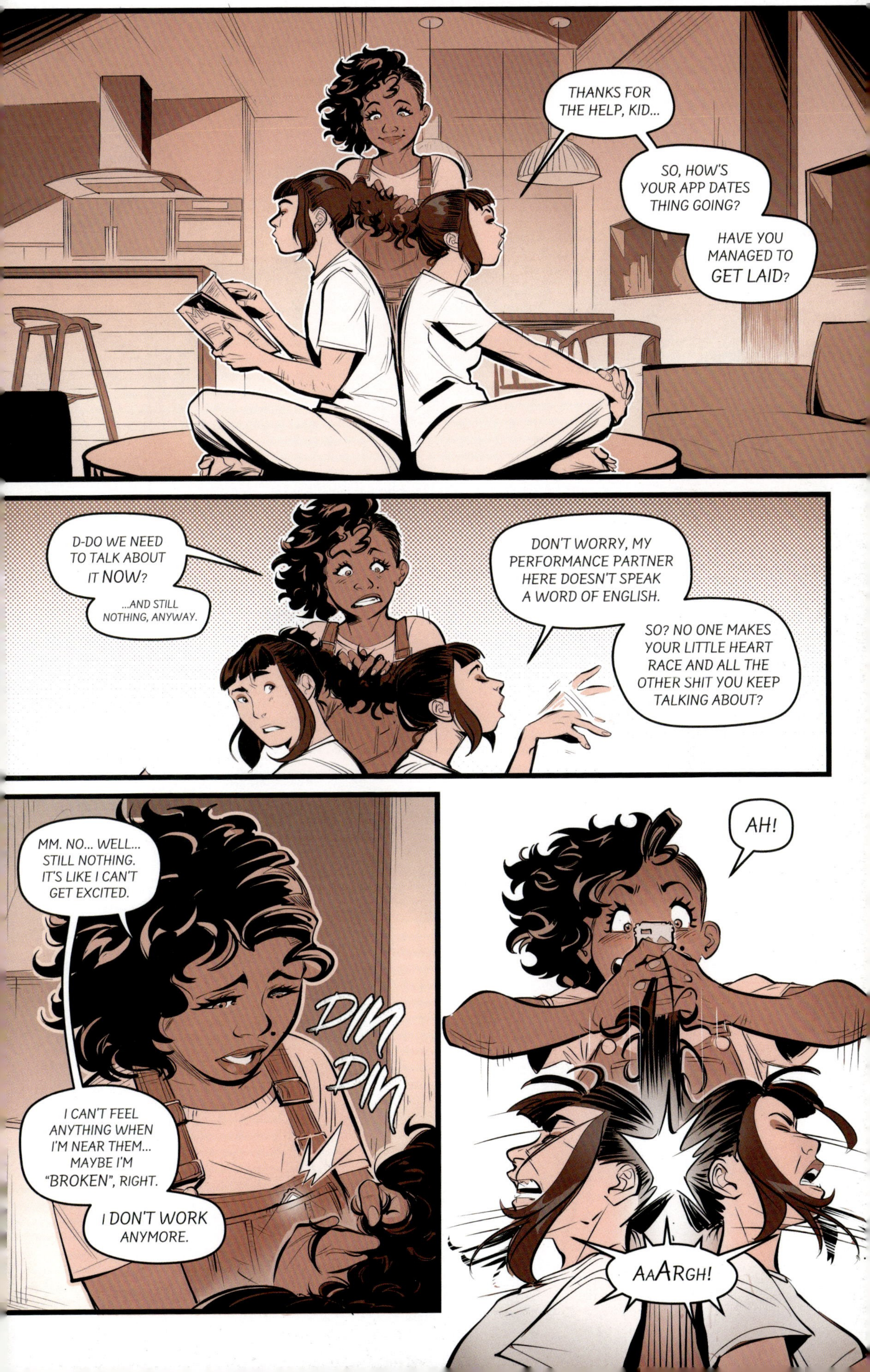
THANKS FOR THE HELP, KID...
SO, HOW'S YOUR APP DATES THING GOING?
HAVE YOU MANAGED TO GET LAID?
D-DO WE NEED TO TALK ABOUT IT NOW?
...AND STILL NOTHING, ANYWAY.
DON'T WORRY, MY PERFORMANCE PARTNER HERE DOESN'T SPEAK A WORD OF ENGLISH.
SO? NO ONE MAKES YOUR LITTLE HEART RACE AND ALL THE OTHER SHIT YOU KEEP TALKING ABOUT?
MM. NO... WELL... STILL NOTHING. IT'S LIKE I CAN'T GET EXCITED.
DIN DIN
I CAN'T FEEL ANYTHING WHEN I'M NEAR THEM... MAYBE I'M "BROKEN", RIGHT.
I DON'T WORK ANYMORE.
AH!
AAARGH!

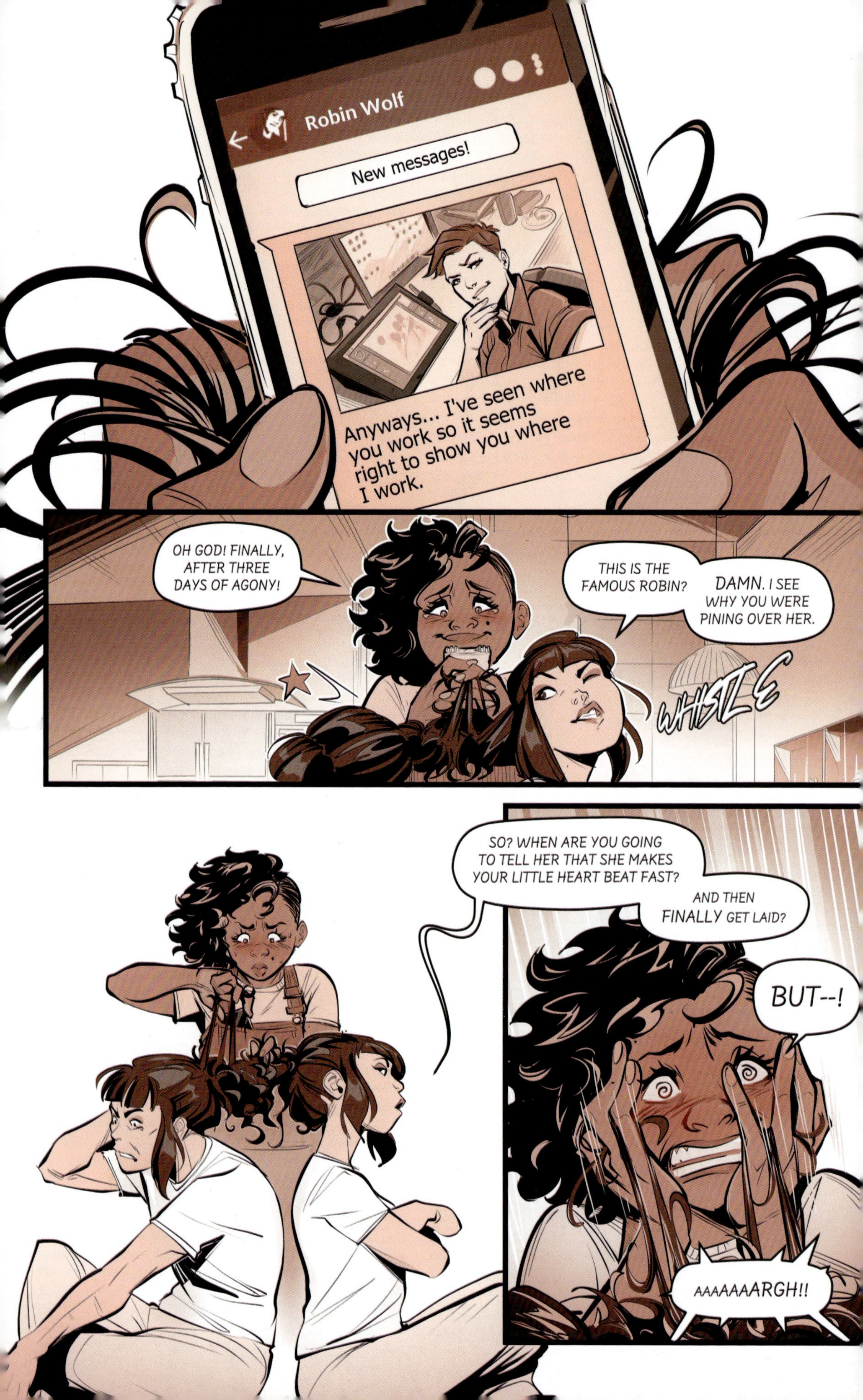
Robin Wolf
New messages!
Anyways... I've seen where you work so it seems right to show you where I work.
OH GOD! FINALLY, AFTER THREE DAYS OF AGONY!
THIS IS THE FAMOUS ROBIN?
DAMN. I SEE WHY YOU WERE PINING OVER HER.
WHISTLE
SO? WHEN ARE YOU GOING TO TELL HER THAT SHE MAKES YOUR LITTLE HEART BEAT FAST?
AND THEN FINALLY GET LAID?
BUT--!
AAAAAAARGH!!

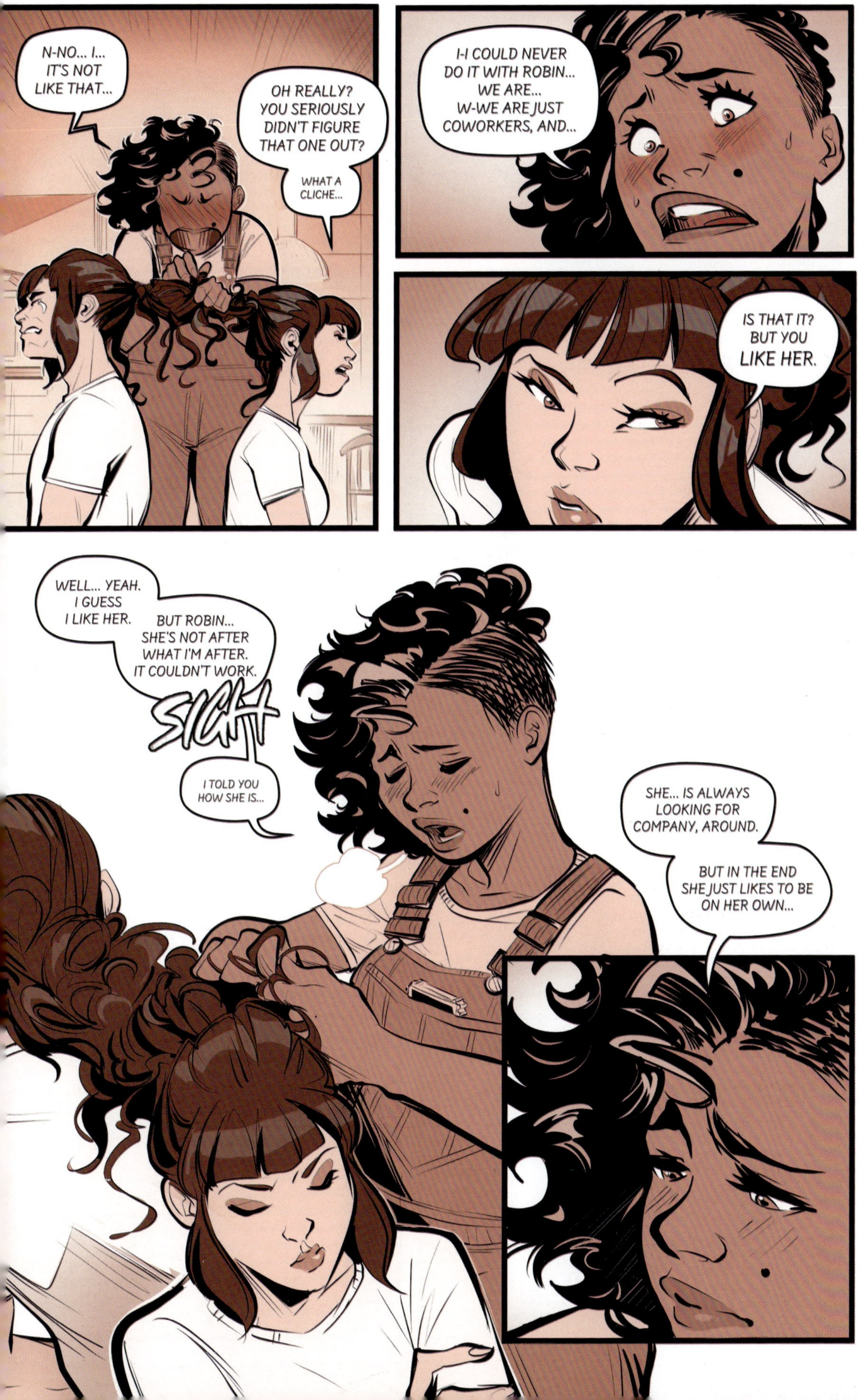
N-NO... I... IT'S NOT LIKE THAT...
OH REALLY? YOU SERIOUSLY DIDN'T FIGURE THAT ONE OUT?
WHAT A CLICHE...
I-I COULD NEVER DO IT WITH ROBIN... WE ARE... W-WE ARE JUST COWORKERS, AND...
IS THAT IT? BUT YOU LIKE HER.
WELL... YEAH. I GUESS I LIKE HER.
BUT ROBIN... SHE'S NOT AFTER WHAT I'M AFTER. IT COULDN'T WORK.
SIGH
I TOLD YOU HOW SHE IS...
SHE... IS ALWAYS LOOKING FOR COMPANY, AROUND.
BUT IN THE END SHE JUST LIKES TO BE ON HER OWN...

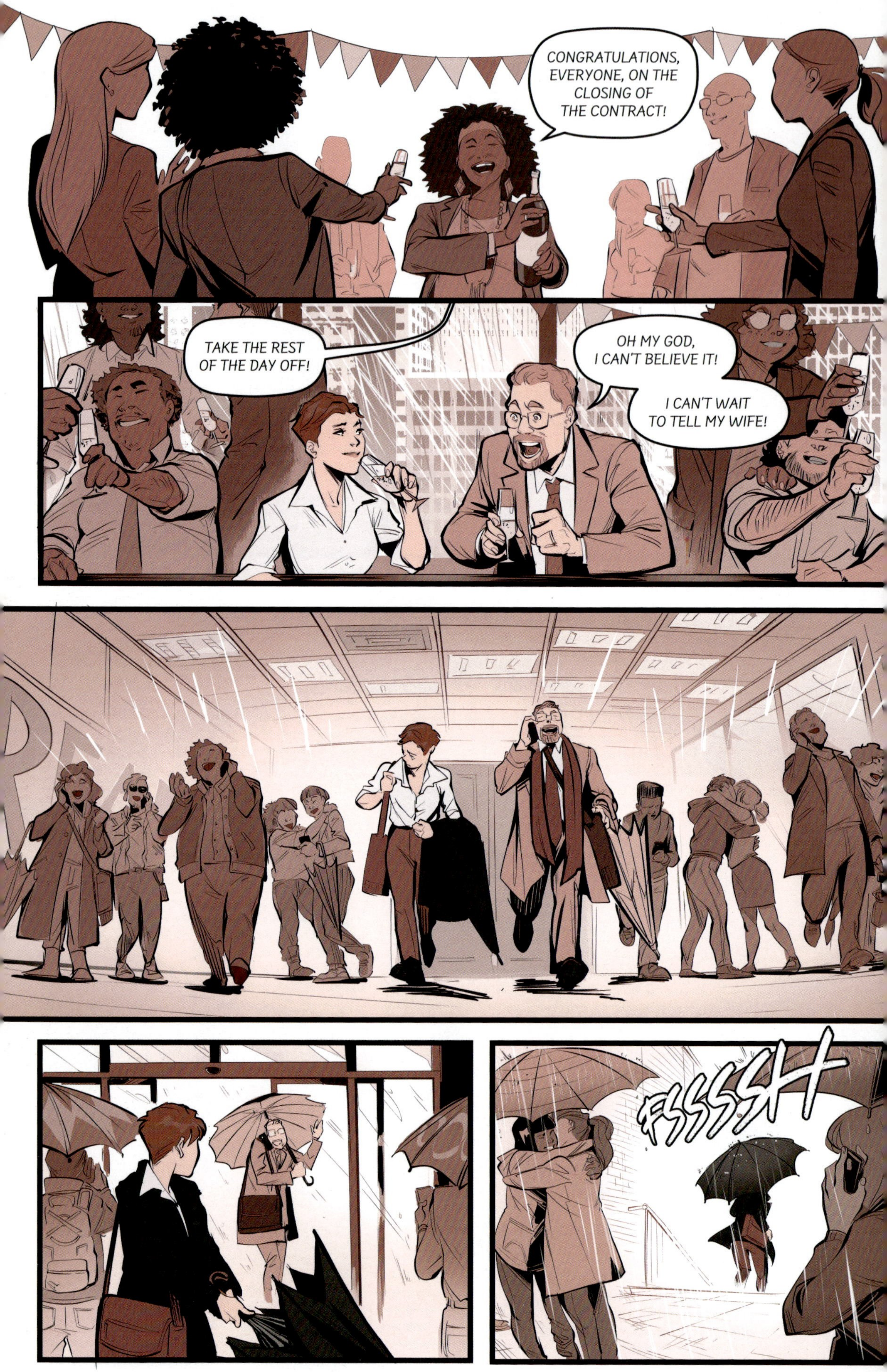
CONGRATULATIONS, EVERYONE, ON THE CLOSING OF THE CONTRACT!
TAKE THE REST OF THE DAY OFF!
OH MY GOD, I CAN'T BELIEVE IT!
I CAN'T WAIT TO TELL MY WIFE!
FSSSSSH

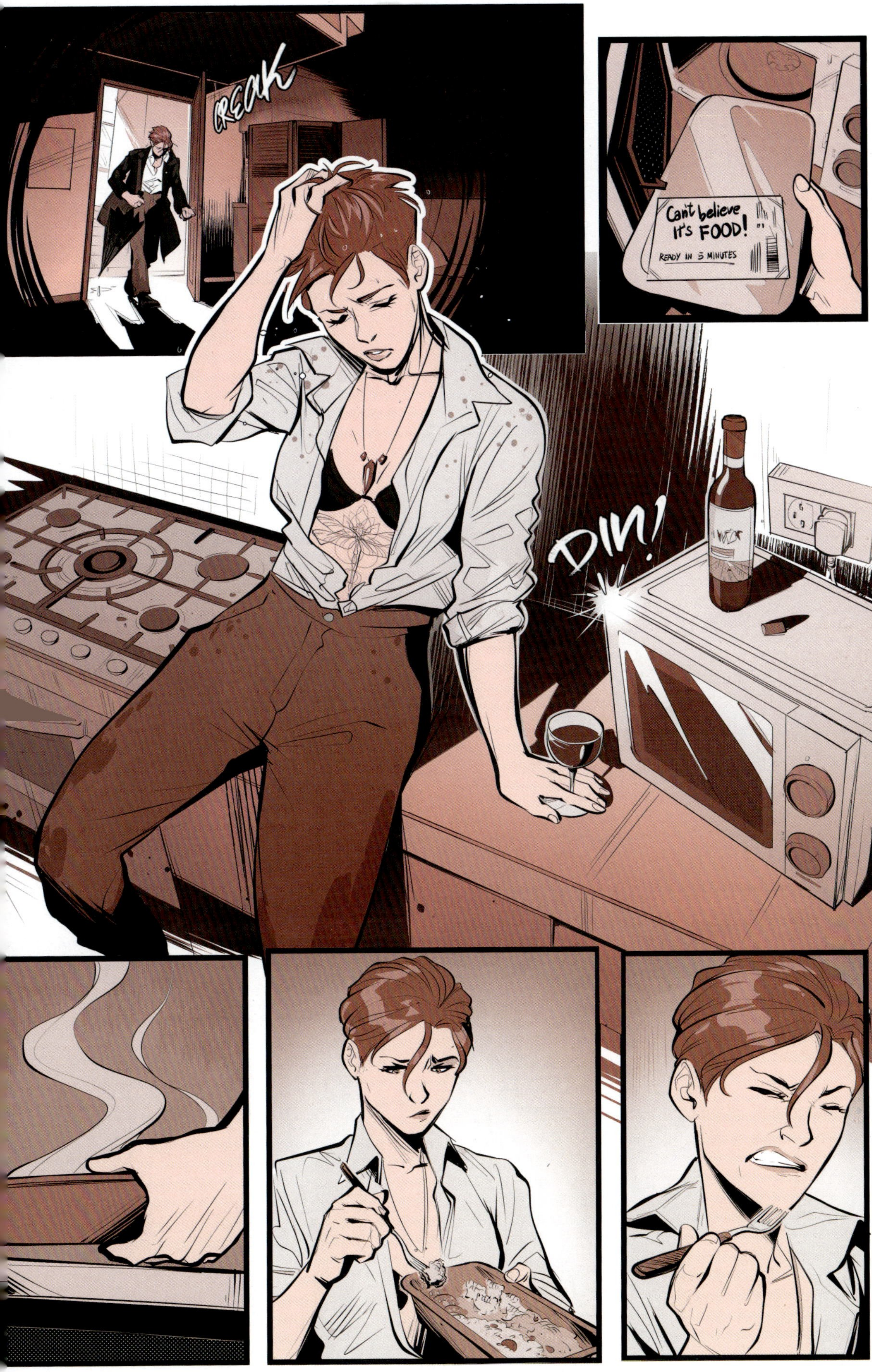

CREAK
Can't believe It's FOOD!
READY IN 5 MINUTES
DIN!

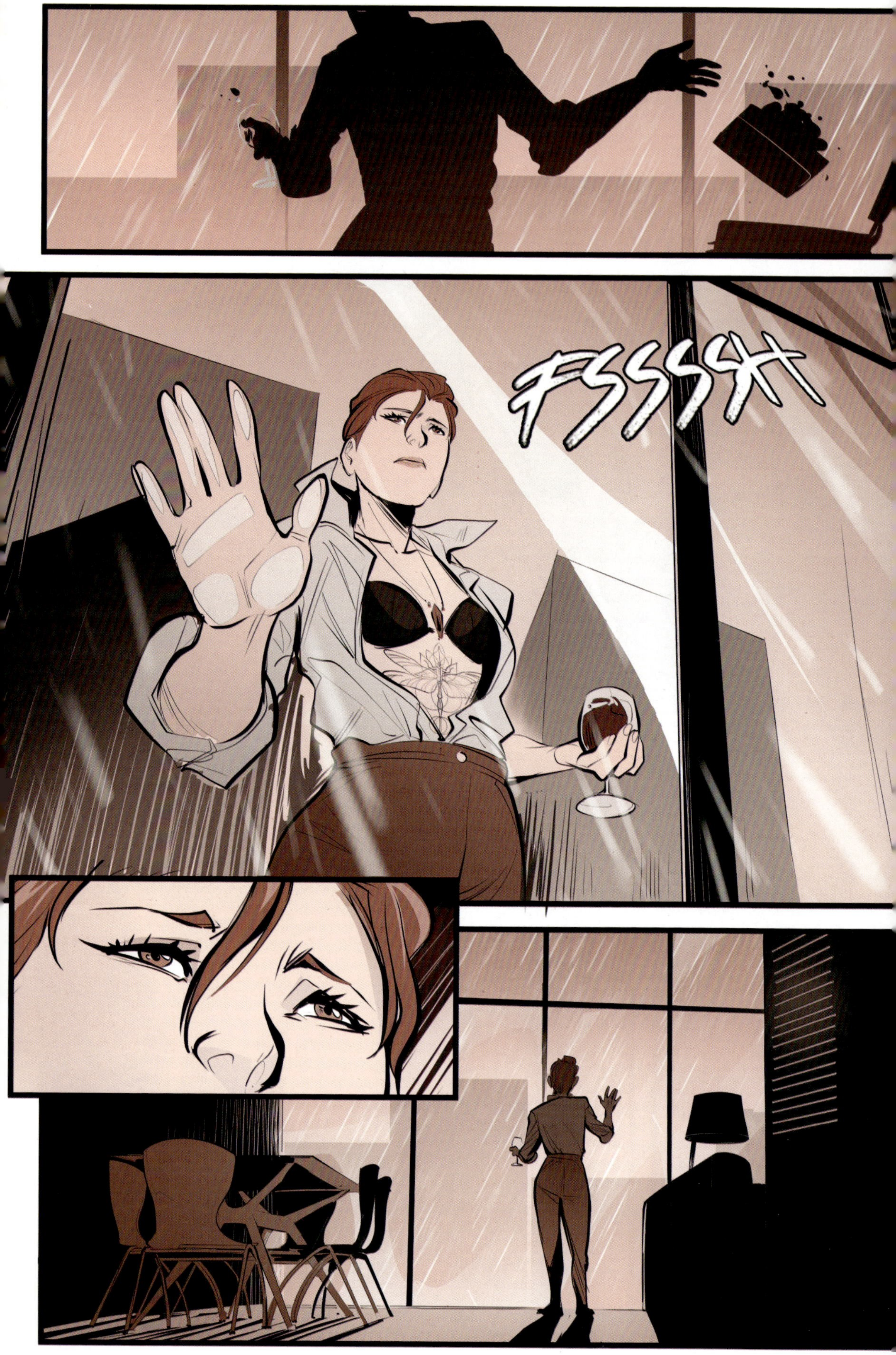
FSSSSH

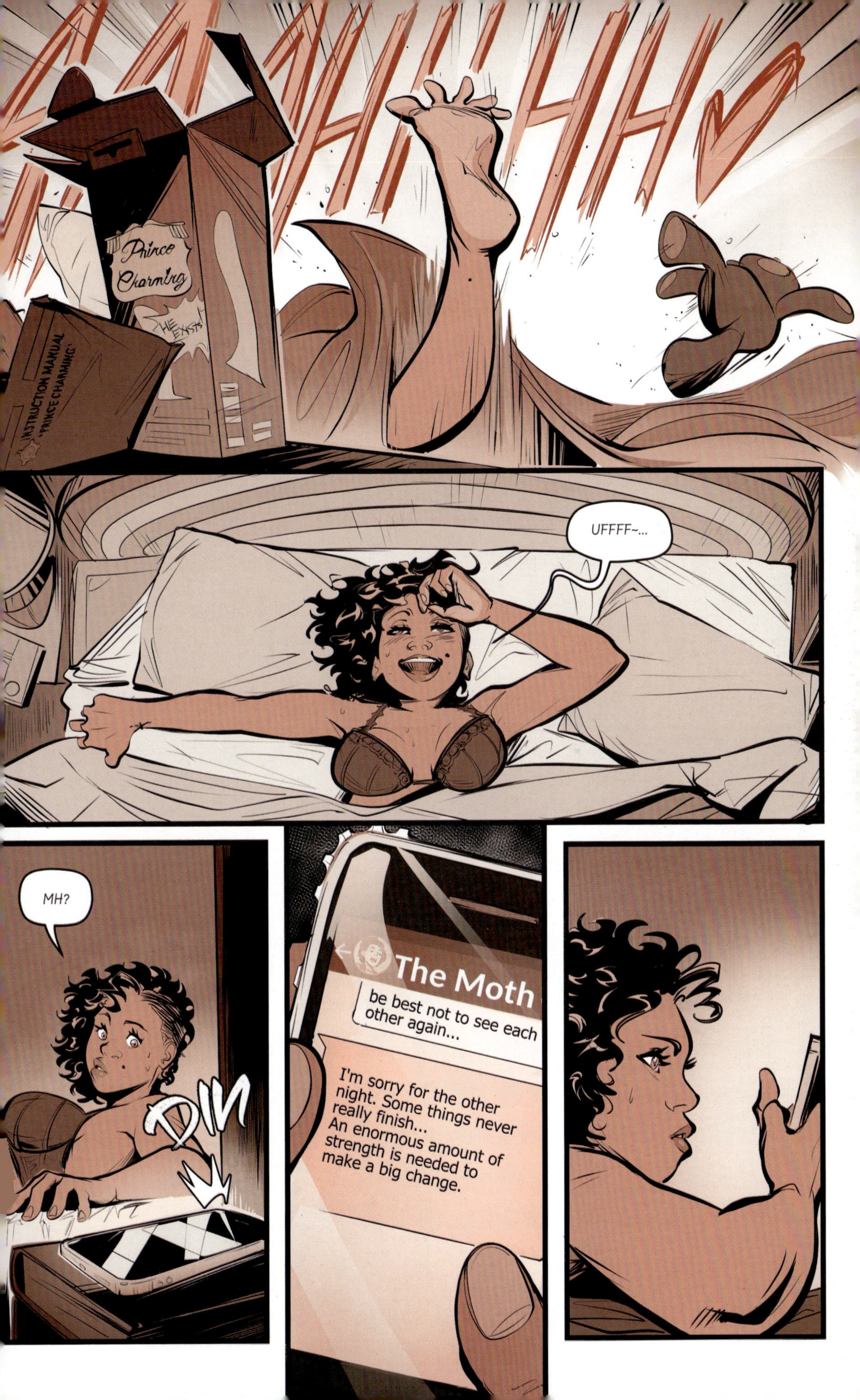
Prince Charming
HE EXISTS!
INSTRUCTION MANUAL "PRINCE CHARMING"
UFFFF~...
MH?
DIN
The Moth
be best not to see each other again...
I'm sorry for the other night. Some things never really finish...
An enormous amount of strength is needed to make a big change.

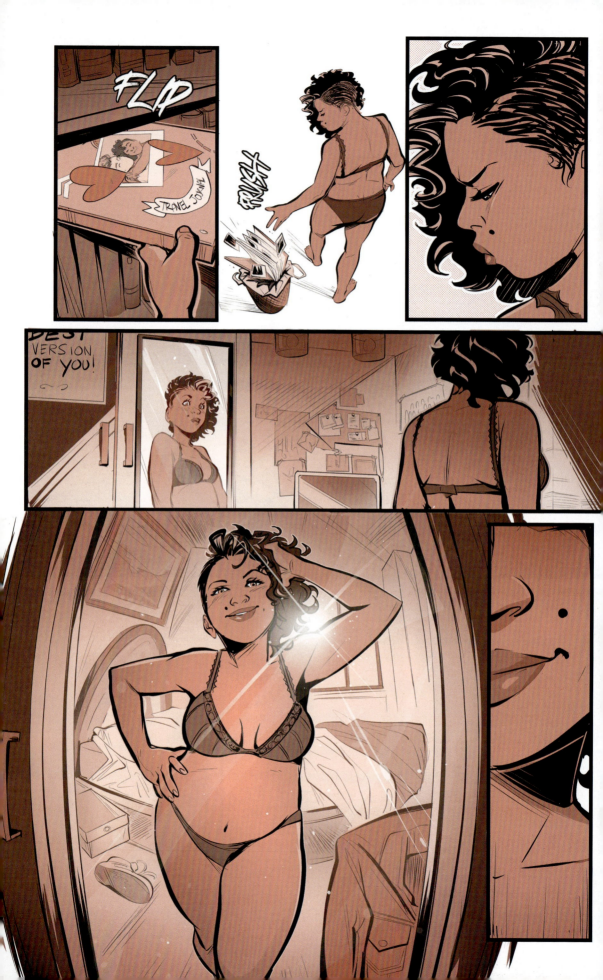

FLIP

TRAVEL JOURNAL

BEST VERSION OF YOU!

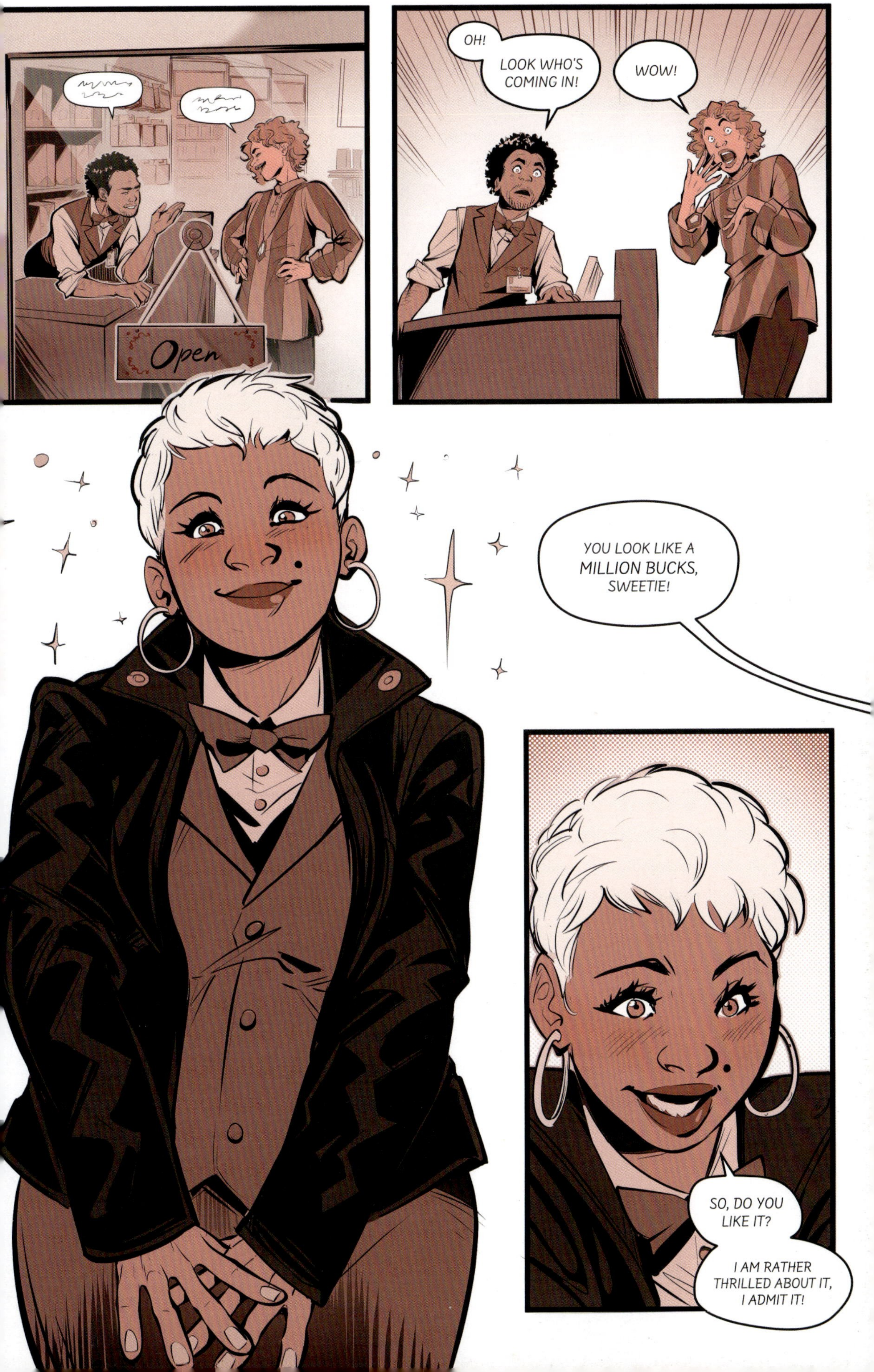

Open
OH!
LOOK WHO'S COMING IN!
WOW!
YOU LOOK LIKE A MILLION BUCKS, SWEETIE!
SO, DO YOU LIKE IT?
I AM RATHER THRILLED ABOUT IT, I ADMIT IT!

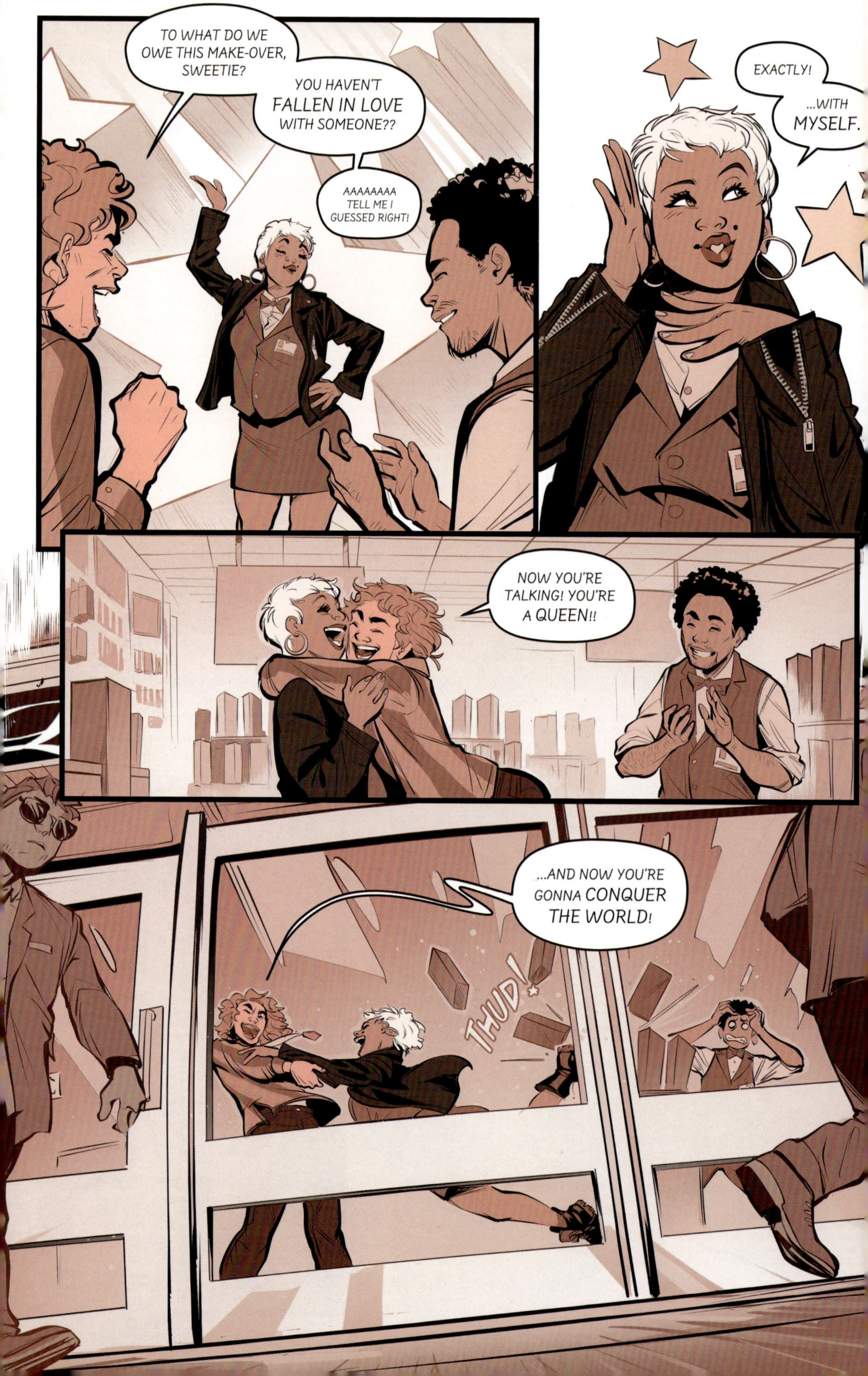
TO WHAT DO WE OWE THIS MAKE-OVER, SWEETIE?
YOU HAVEN'T FALLEN IN LOVE WITH SOMEONE??
AAAAAAAA TELL ME I GUESSED RIGHT!
EXACTLY!
...WITH MYSELF.
NOW YOU'RE TALKING! YOU'RE A QUEEN!!
...AND NOW YOU'RE GONNA CONQUER THE WORLD!
THUD!

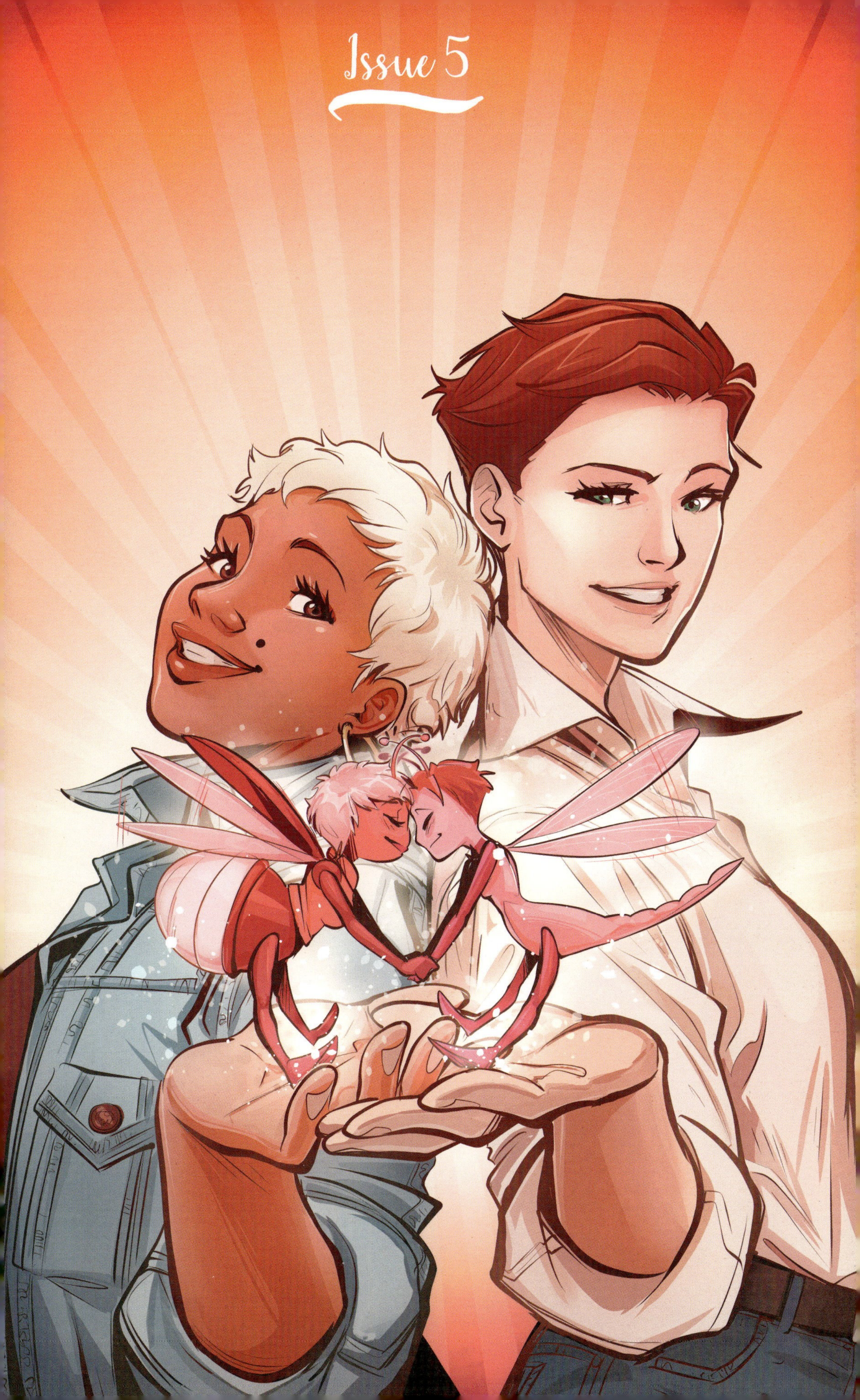
Issue 5

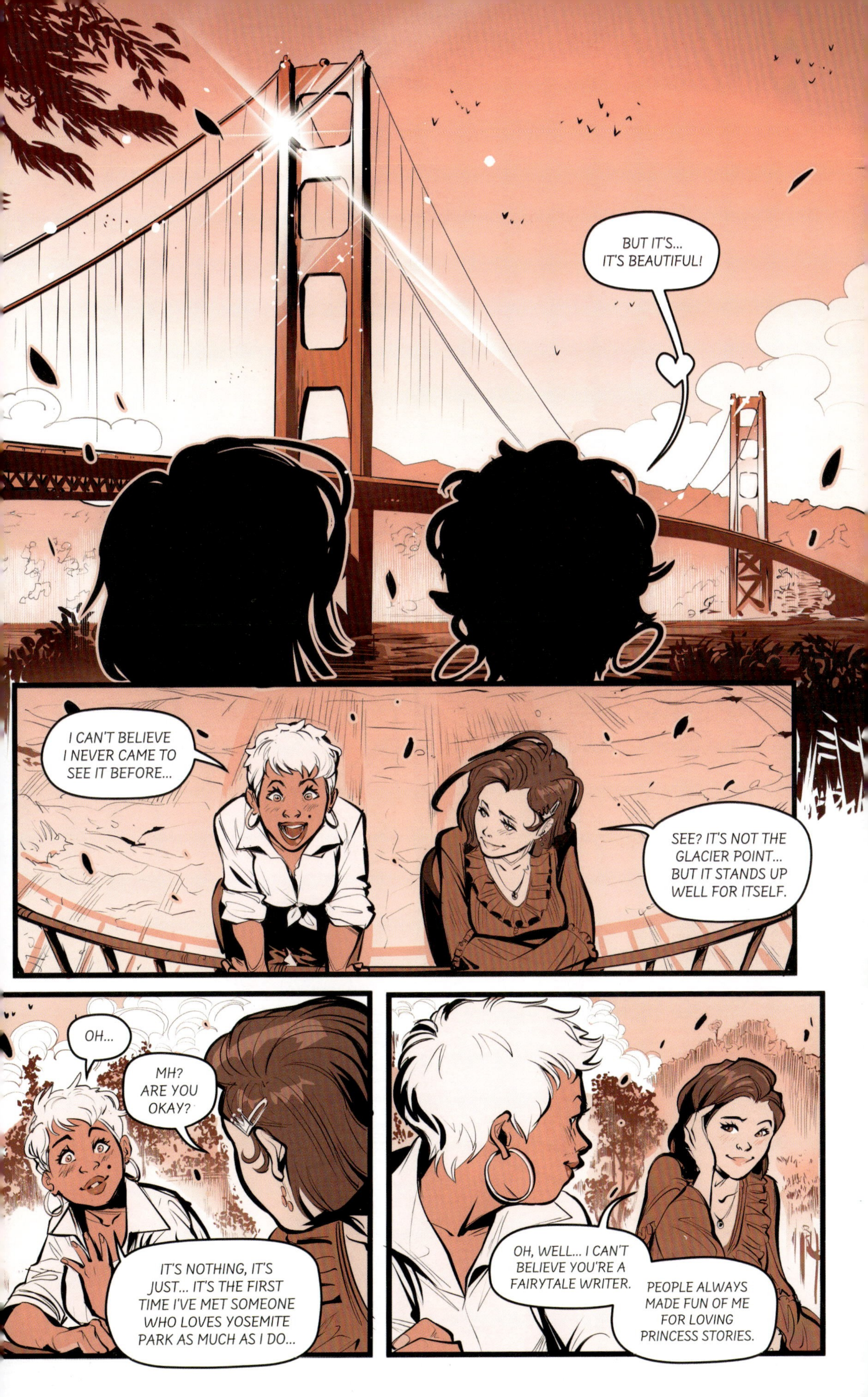
BUT IT'S... IT'S BEAUTIFUL!
I CAN'T BELIEVE I NEVER CAME TO SEE IT BEFORE...
SEE? IT'S NOT THE GLACIER POINT... BUT IT STANDS UP WELL FOR ITSELF.
OH...
MH? ARE YOU OKAY?
IT'S NOTHING, IT'S JUST... IT'S THE FIRST TIME I'VE MET SOMEONE WHO LOVES YOSEMITE PARK AS MUCH AS I DO...
OH, WELL... I CAN'T BELIEVE YOU'RE A FAIRYTALE WRITER.
PEOPLE ALWAYS MADE FUN OF ME FOR LOVING PRINCESS STORIES.

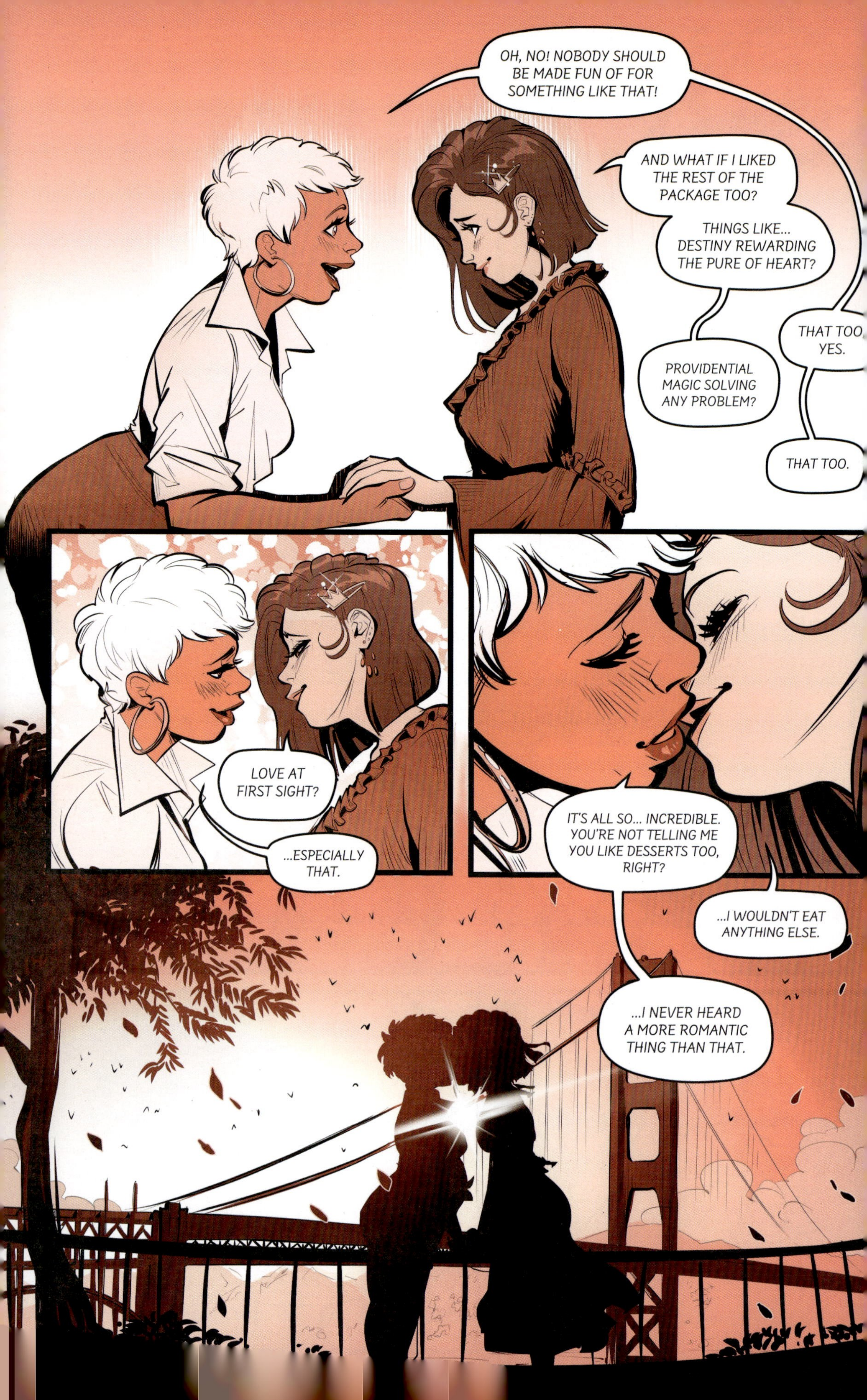
OH, NO! NOBODY SHOULD BE MADE FUN OF FOR SOMETHING LIKE THAT!
AND WHAT IF I LIKED THE REST OF THE PACKAGE TOO?
THINGS LIKE... DESTINY REWARDING THE PURE OF HEART?
THAT TOO, YES.
PROVIDENTIAL MAGIC SOLVING ANY PROBLEM?
THAT TOO.
LOVE AT FIRST SIGHT?
...ESPECIALLY THAT.
IT'S ALL SO... INCREDIBLE. YOU'RE NOT TELLING ME YOU LIKE DESSERTS TOO, RIGHT?
...I WOULDN'T EAT ANYTHING ELSE.
...I NEVER HEARD A MORE ROMANTIC THING THAN THAT.

Finally our firefly seemed to have found someone who really wanted to help her! “I am good luck, you know? If we're together everything will be fine!” said the ladybug smiling.

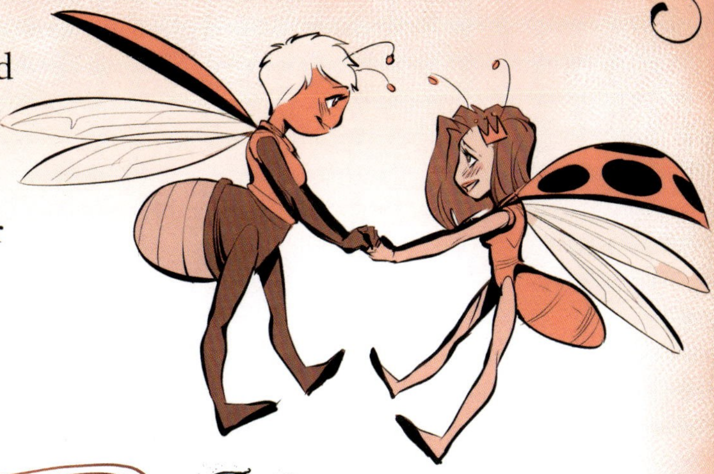

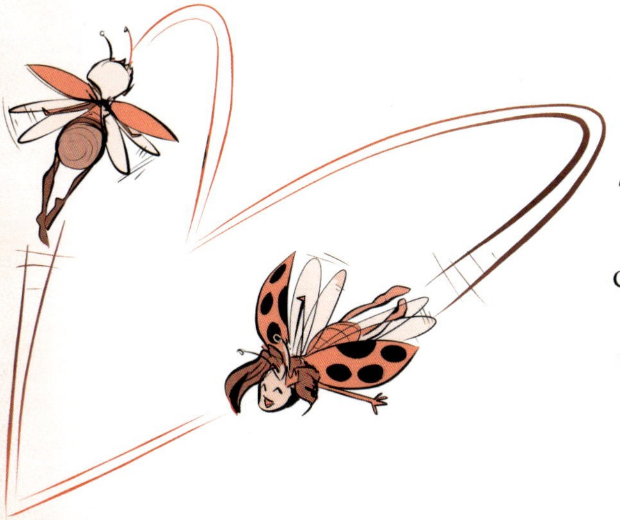

It was incredible... They were so much alike! It seemed like nothing could go wrong! And yet... When it came to trying to make our firefly shine, they didn't seem to be able to do any good!

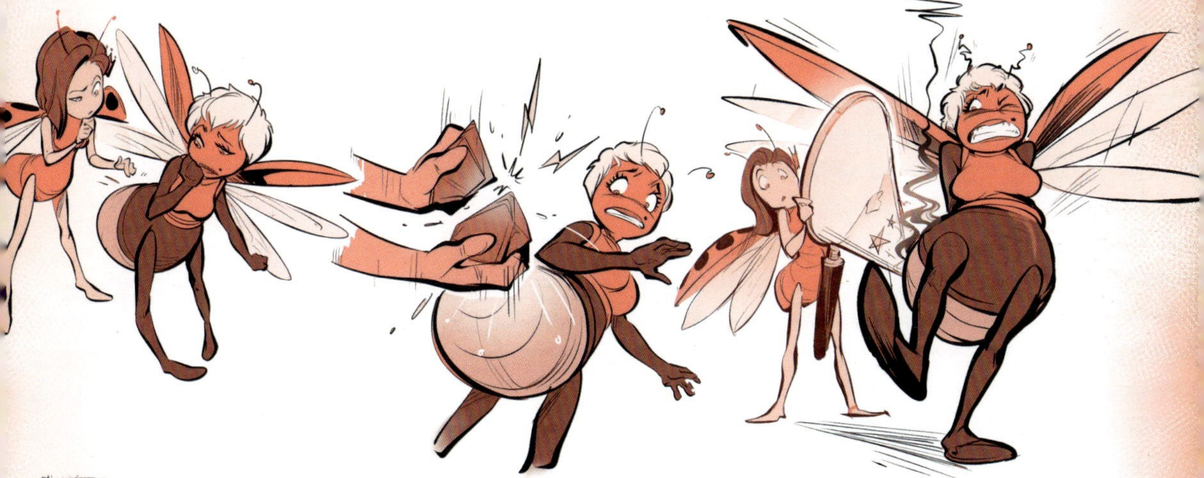

The two little bugs couldn't figure out what the problem was... And yet, on paper everything was perfect! What was missing?

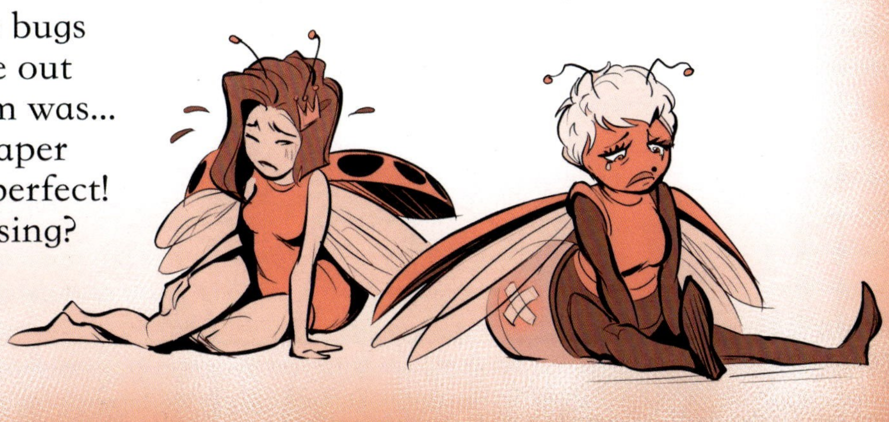

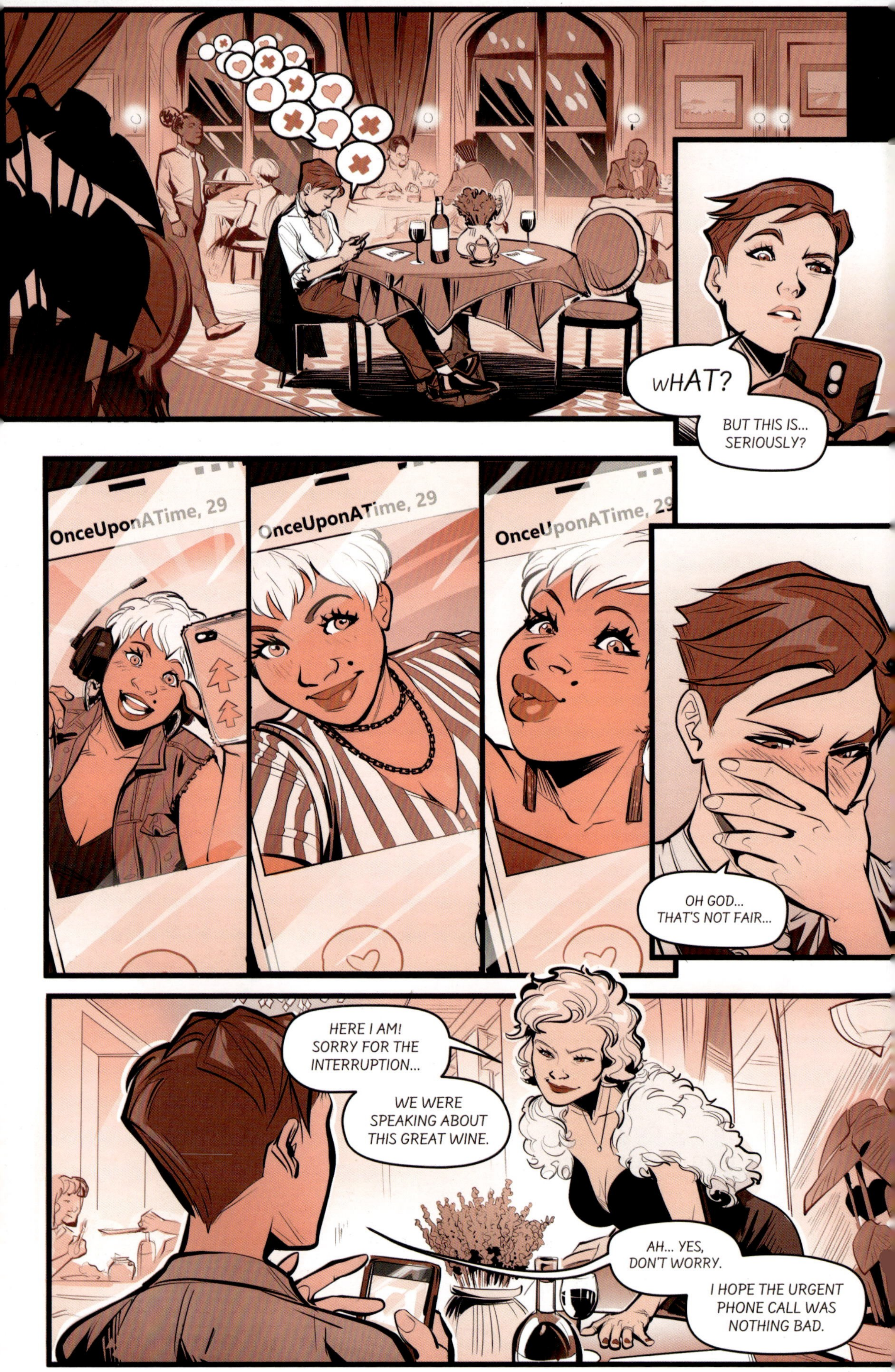
WHAT?
BUT THIS IS... SERIOUSLY?
OnceUponATime, 29
OnceUponATime, 29
OnceUponATime, 29
OH GOD... THAT'S NOT FAIR...
HERE I AM! SORRY FOR THE INTERRUPTION...
WE WERE SPEAKING ABOUT THIS GREAT WINE.
AH... YES, DON'T WORRY.
I HOPE THE URGENT PHONE CALL WAS NOTHING BAD.

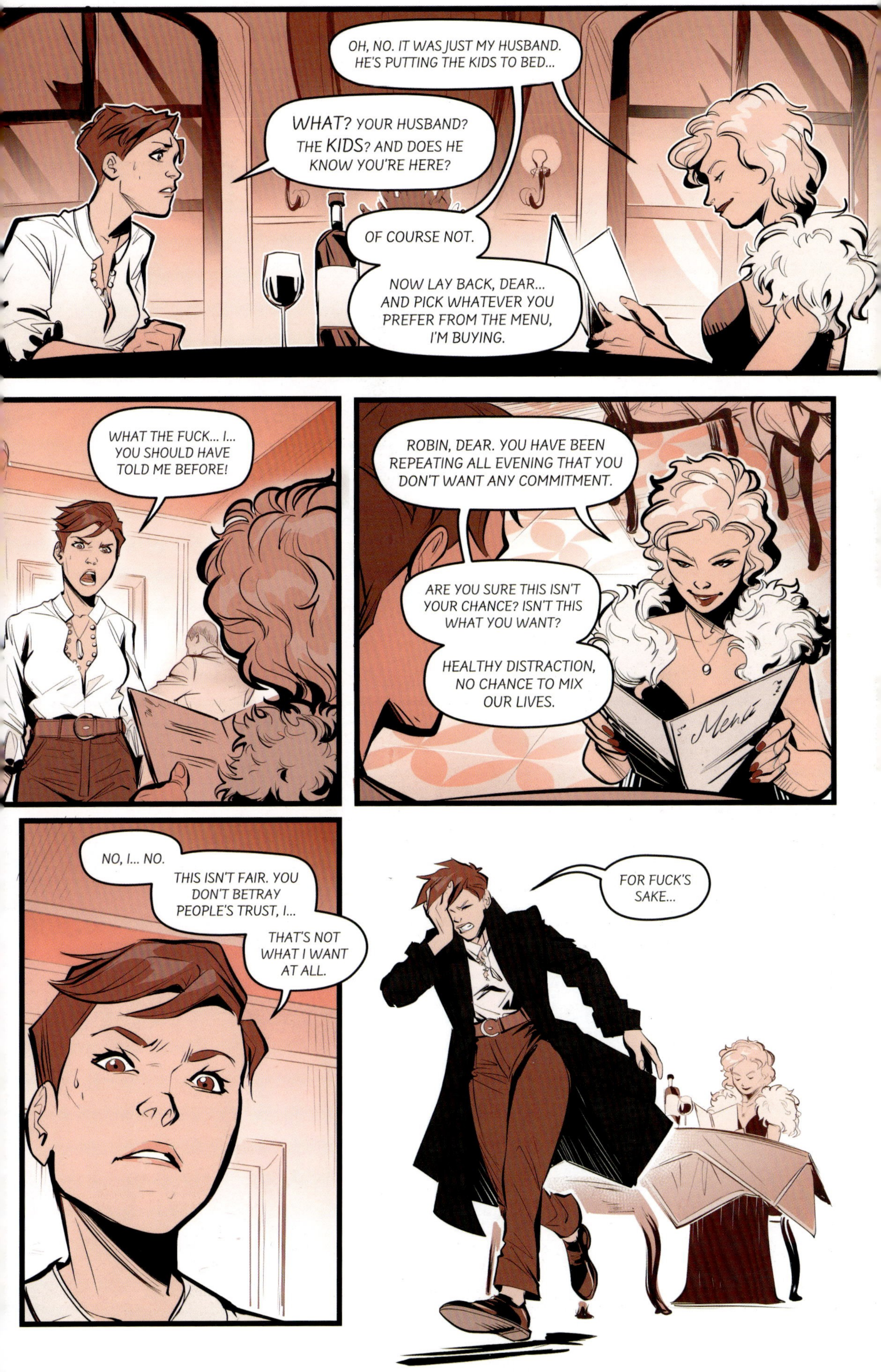

OH, NO. IT WAS JUST MY HUSBAND. HE'S PUTTING THE KIDS TO BED...
WHAT? YOUR HUSBAND? THE KIDS? AND DOES HE KNOW YOU'RE HERE?
OF COURSE NOT.
NOW LAY BACK, DEAR... AND PICK WHATEVER YOU PREFER FROM THE MENU, I'M BUYING.
WHAT THE FUCK... I... YOU SHOULD HAVE TOLD ME BEFORE!
ROBIN, DEAR. YOU HAVE BEEN REPEATING ALL EVENING THAT YOU DON'T WANT ANY COMMITMENT.
ARE YOU SURE THIS ISN'T YOUR CHANCE? ISN'T THIS WHAT YOU WANT?
HEALTHY DISTRACTION, NO CHANCE TO MIX OUR LIVES.
Menu
NO, I... NO.
THIS ISN'T FAIR. YOU DON'T BETRAY PEOPLE'S TRUST, I...
THAT'S NOT WHAT I WANT AT ALL.
FOR FUCK'S SAKE...

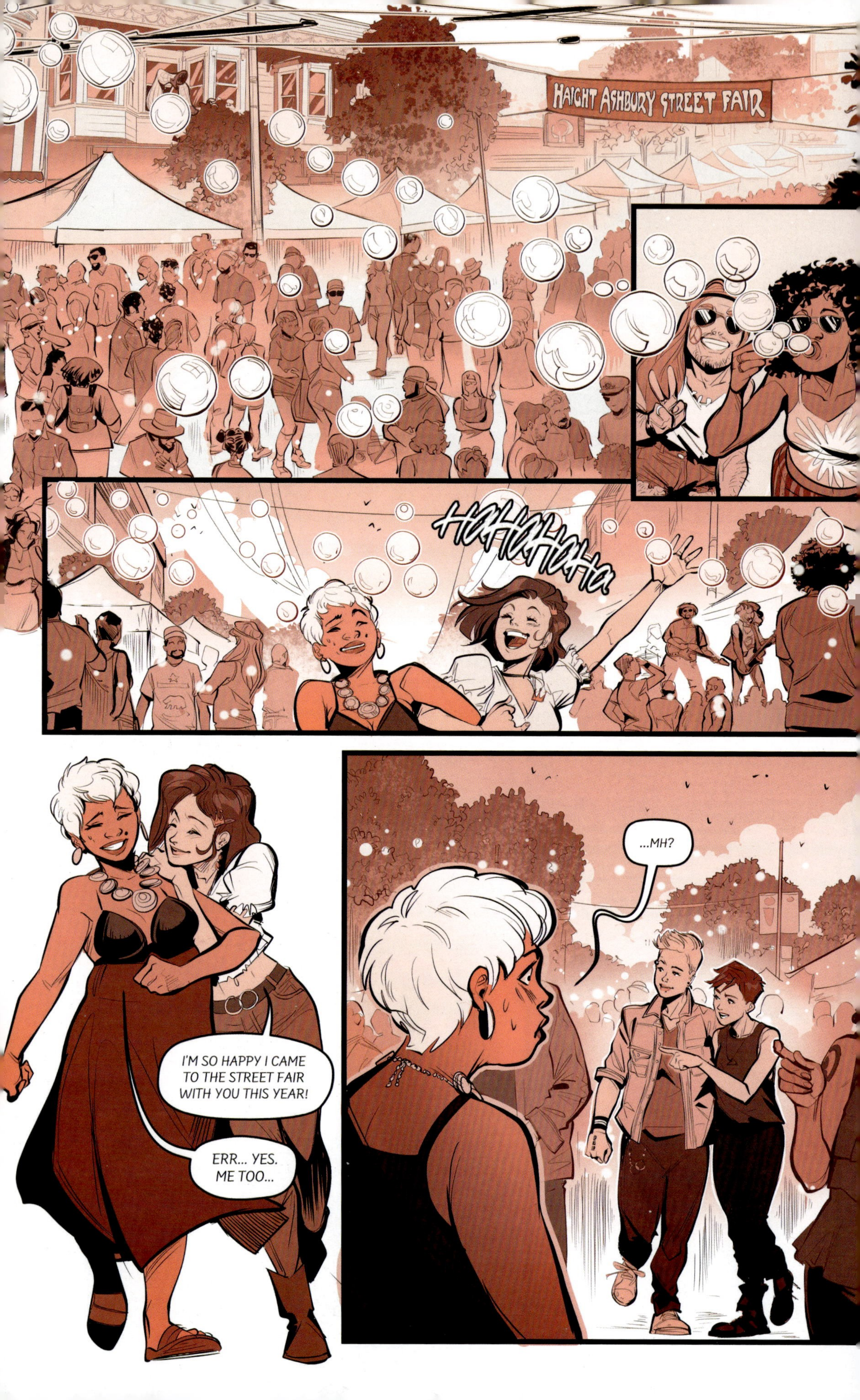
HAIGHT ASHBURY STREET FAIR
HAHAHAHA
I'M SO HAPPY I CAME TO THE STREET FAIR WITH YOU THIS YEAR!
ERR... YES. ME TOO...
...MH?

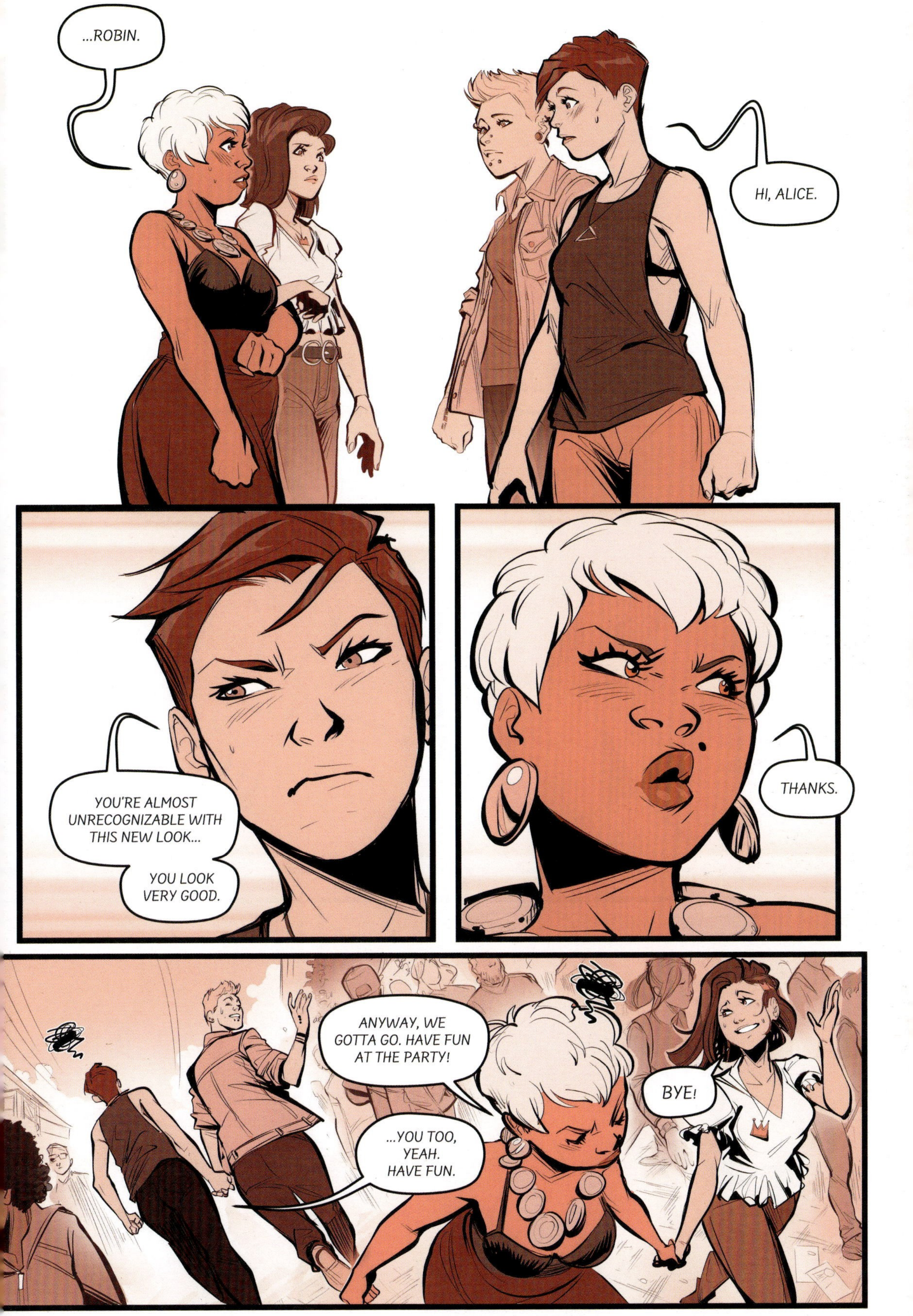
...ROBIN.
HI, ALICE.
YOU'RE ALMOST UNRECOGNIZABLE WITH THIS NEW LOOK...
YOU LOOK VERY GOOD.
THANKS.
ANYWAY, WE GOTTA GO. HAVE FUN AT THE PARTY!
...YOU TOO, YEAH. HAVE FUN.
BYE!

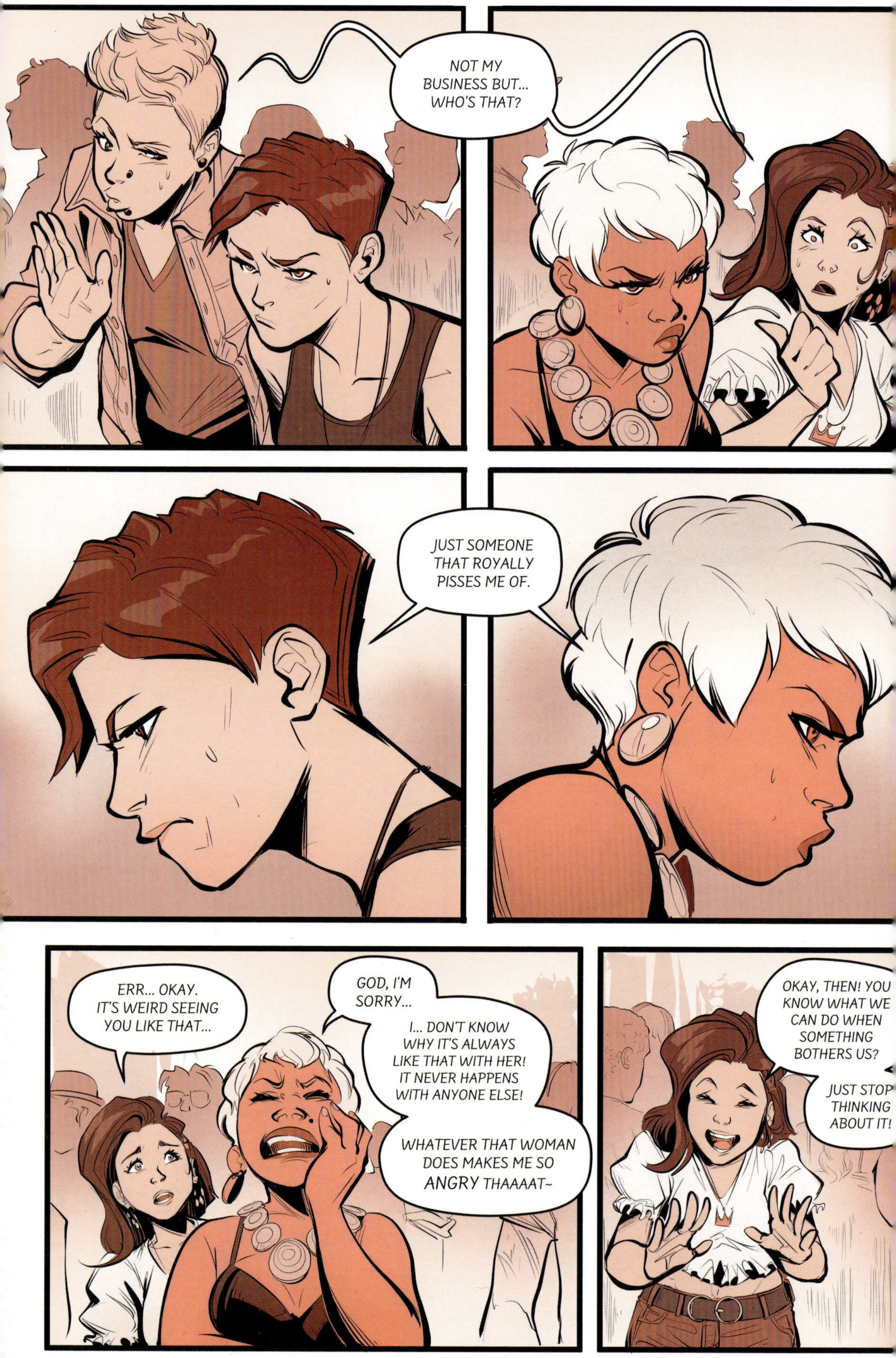
NOT MY BUSINESS BUT... WHO'S THAT?
JUST SOMEONE THAT ROYALLY PISSES ME OF.
ERR... OKAY. IT'S WEIRD SEEING YOU LIKE THAT...
GOD, I'M SORRY...
I... DON'T KNOW WHY IT'S ALWAYS LIKE THAT WITH HER! IT NEVER HAPPENS WITH ANYONE ELSE!
WHATEVER THAT WOMAN DOES MAKES ME SO ANGRY THAAAAT~
OKAY, THEN! YOU KNOW WHAT WE CAN DO WHEN SOMETHING BOTHERS US?
JUST STOP THINKING ABOUT IT!

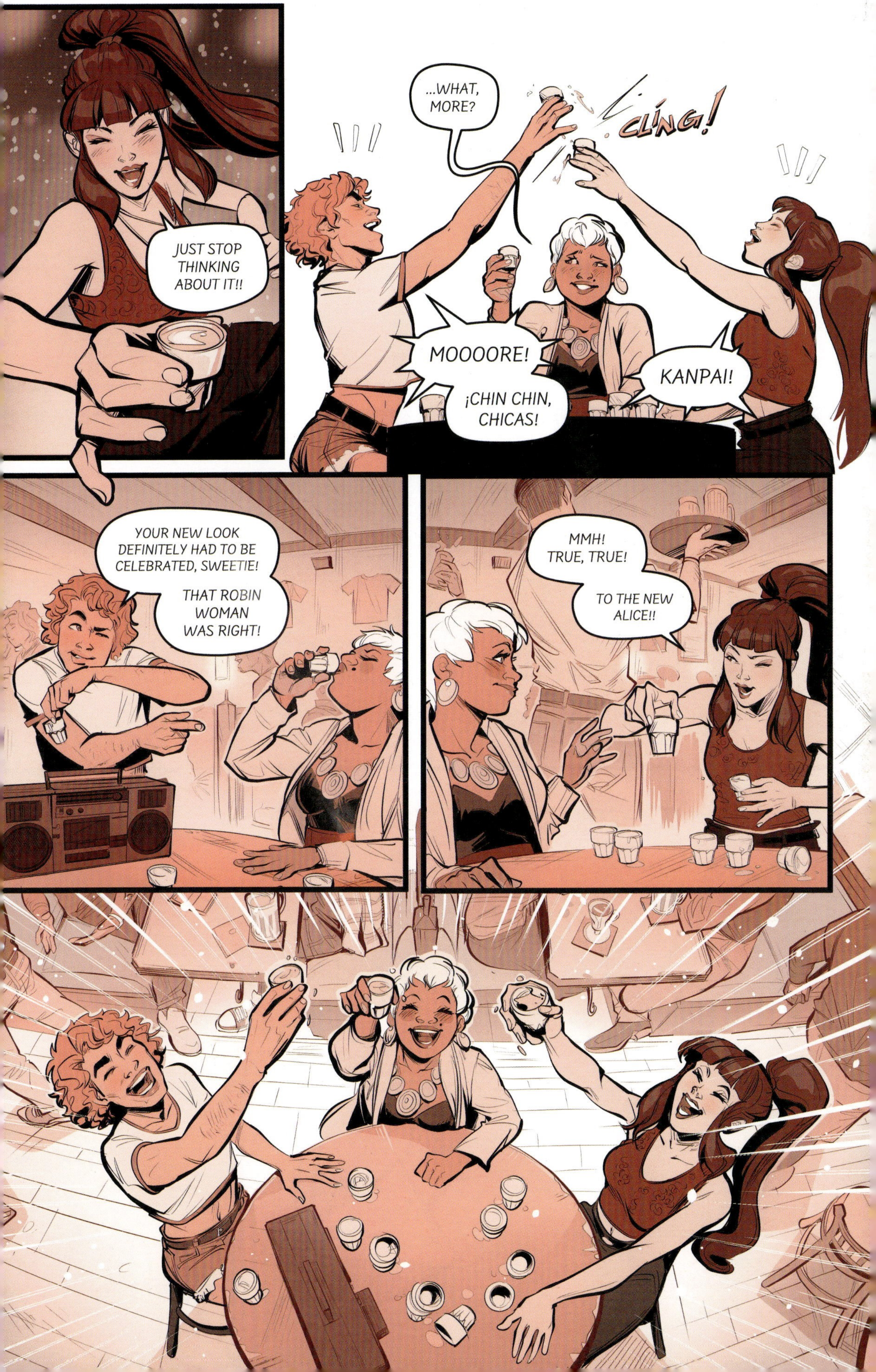
JUST STOP THINKING ABOUT IT!!
...WHAT, MORE?
CLING!
MOOOORE!
¡CHIN CHIN, CHICAS!
KANPAI!
YOUR NEW LOOK DEFINITELY HAD TO BE CELEBRATED, SWEETIE!
THAT ROBIN WOMAN WAS RIGHT!
MMH! TRUE, TRUE!
TO THE NEW ALICE!!

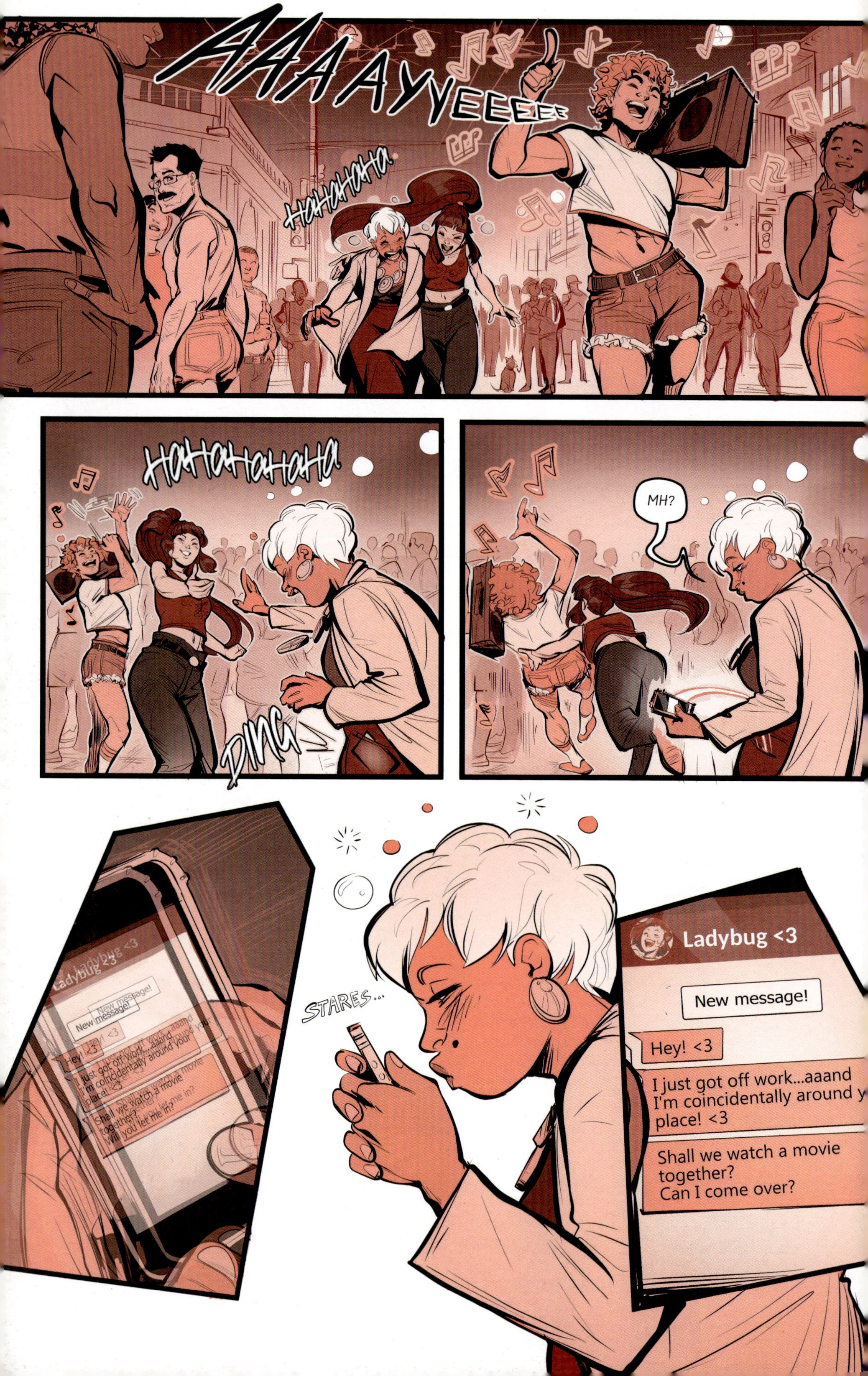
AAAAYYEEEEEE
HAHAHAHA
HAHAHAHAHAHA
DING
MH?
STARES...
Ladybug <3
New message!
Hey! <3
I just got off work...aaand I'm coincidentally around y place! <3
Shall we watch a movie together?
Can I come over?

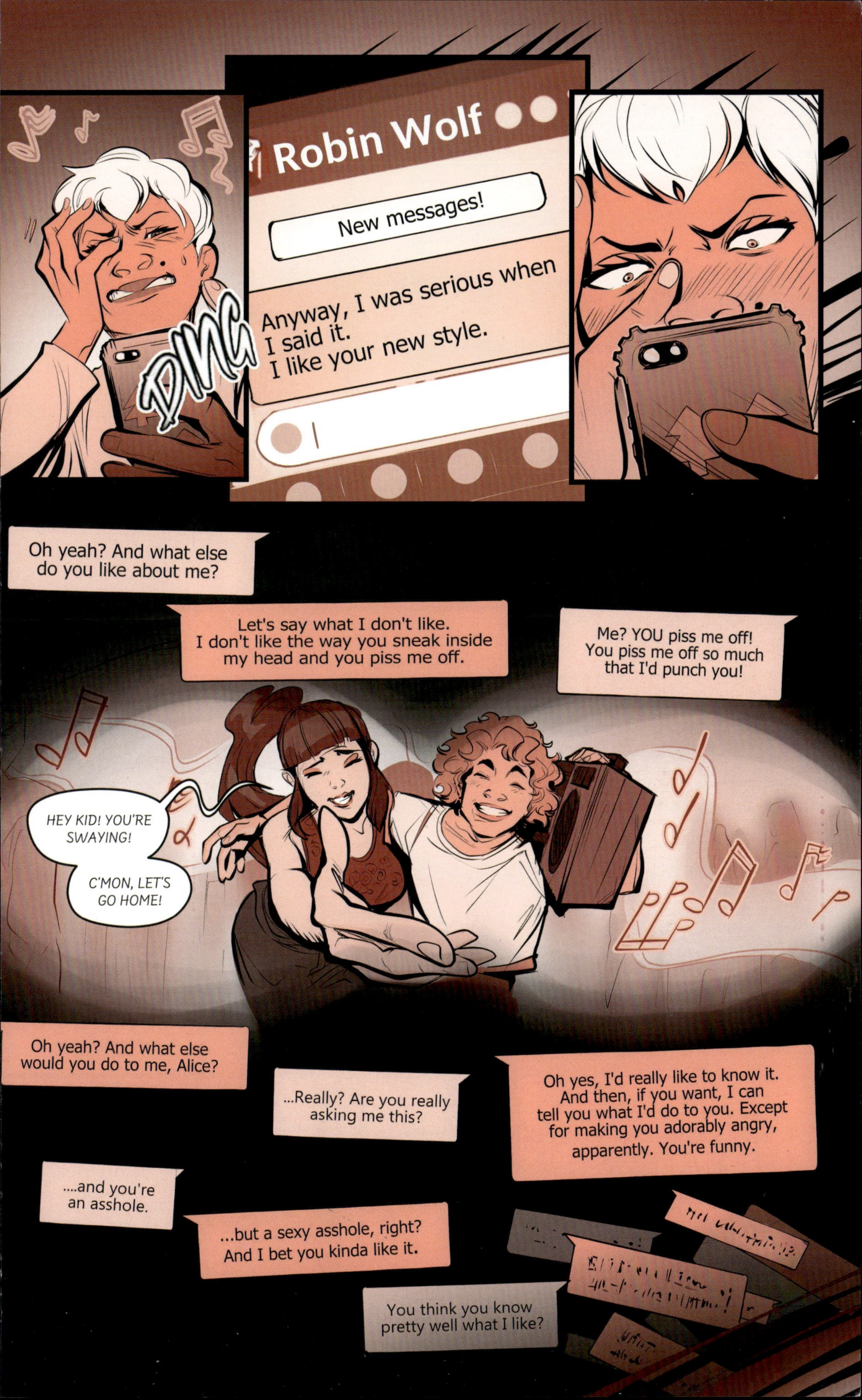
Robin Wolf
New messages!
Anyway, I was serious when I said it. I like your new style.
DING
Oh yeah? And what else do you like about me?
Let's say what I don't like. I don't like the way you sneak inside my head and you piss me off.
Me? YOU piss me off! You piss me off so much that I'd punch you!
HEY KID! YOU'RE SWAYING!
C'MON, LET'S GO HOME!
Oh yeah? And what else would you do to me, Alice?
...Really? Are you really asking me this?
Oh yes, I'd really like to know it. And then, if you want, I can tell you what I'd do to you. Except for making you adorably angry, apparently. You're funny.
....and you're an asshole.
...but a sexy asshole, right? And I bet you kinda like it.
You think you know pretty well what I like?

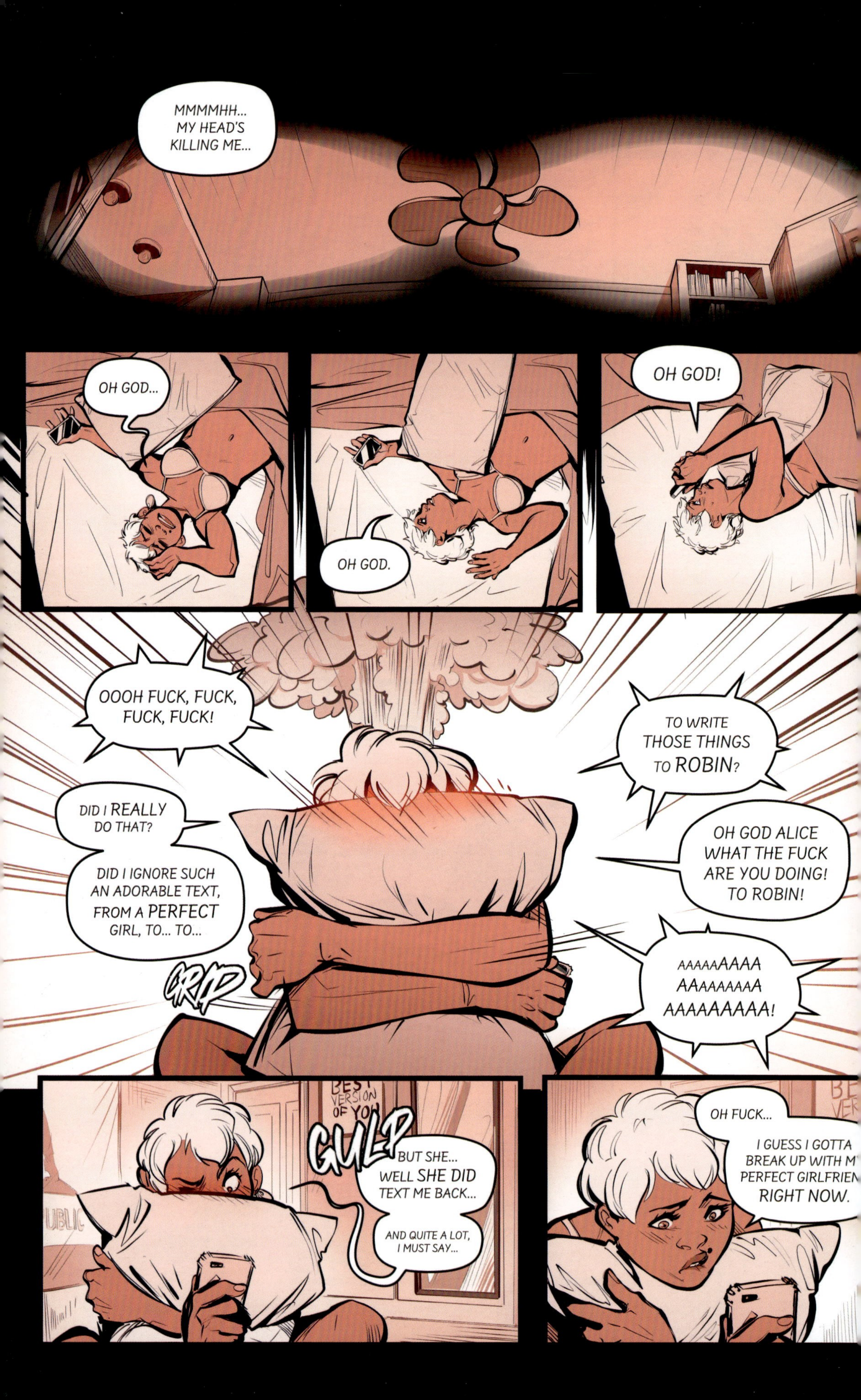
MMMMHH... MY HEAD'S KILLING ME...
OH GOD...
OH GOD.
OH GOD!
OOOH FUCK, FUCK, FUCK, FUCK!
DID I REALLY DO THAT?
DID I IGNORE SUCH AN ADORABLE TEXT, FROM A PERFECT GIRL, TO... TO...
TO WRITE THOSE THINGS TO ROBIN?
OH GOD ALICE WHAT THE FUCK ARE YOU DOING! TO ROBIN!
GRIP
AAAAAAAAA AAAAAAAAA AAAAAAAAA!
BEST VERSION OF YOU
GULP
BUT SHE... WELL SHE DID TEXT ME BACK...
AND QUITE A LOT, I MUST SAY...
OH FUCK...
I GUESS I GOTTA BREAK UP WITH M PERFECT GIRLFRIEN RIGHT NOW.

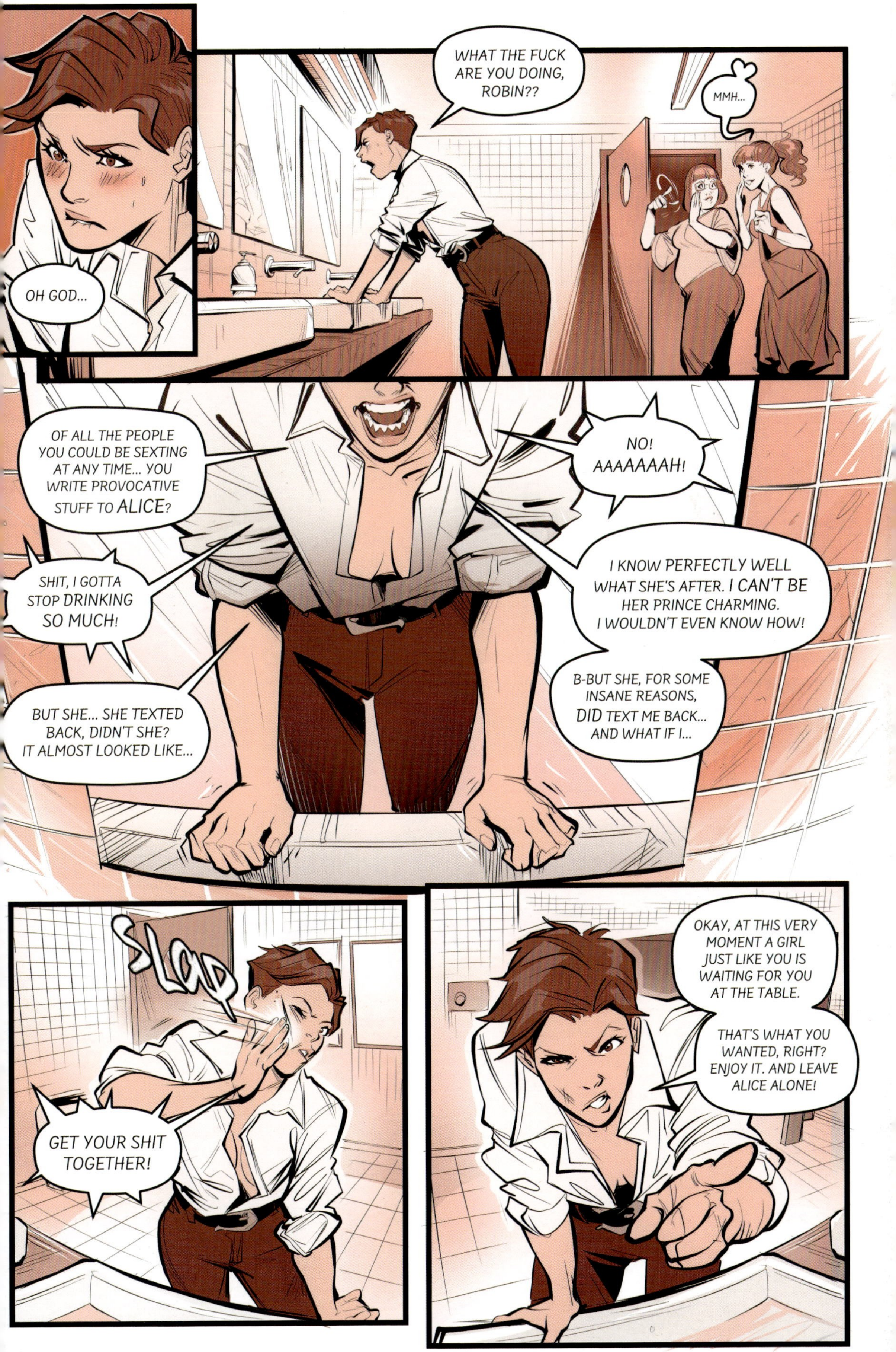

OH GOD...
WHAT THE FUCK ARE YOU DOING, ROBIN??
MMH...
OF ALL THE PEOPLE YOU COULD BE SEXTING AT ANY TIME... YOU WRITE PROVOCATIVE STUFF TO ALICE?
NO! AAAAAAAH!
SHIT, I GOTTA STOP DRINKING SO MUCH!
I KNOW PERFECTLY WELL WHAT SHE'S AFTER. I CAN'T BE HER PRINCE CHARMING. I WOULDN'T EVEN KNOW HOW!
BUT SHE... SHE TEXTED BACK, DIDN'T SHE? IT ALMOST LOOKED LIKE...
B-BUT SHE, FOR SOME INSANE REASONS, DID TEXT ME BACK... AND WHAT IF I...
SLAP
GET YOUR SHIT TOGETHER!
OKAY, AT THIS VERY MOMENT A GIRL JUST LIKE YOU IS WAITING FOR YOU AT THE TABLE.
THAT'S WHAT YOU WANTED, RIGHT? ENJOY IT. AND LEAVE ALICE ALONE!

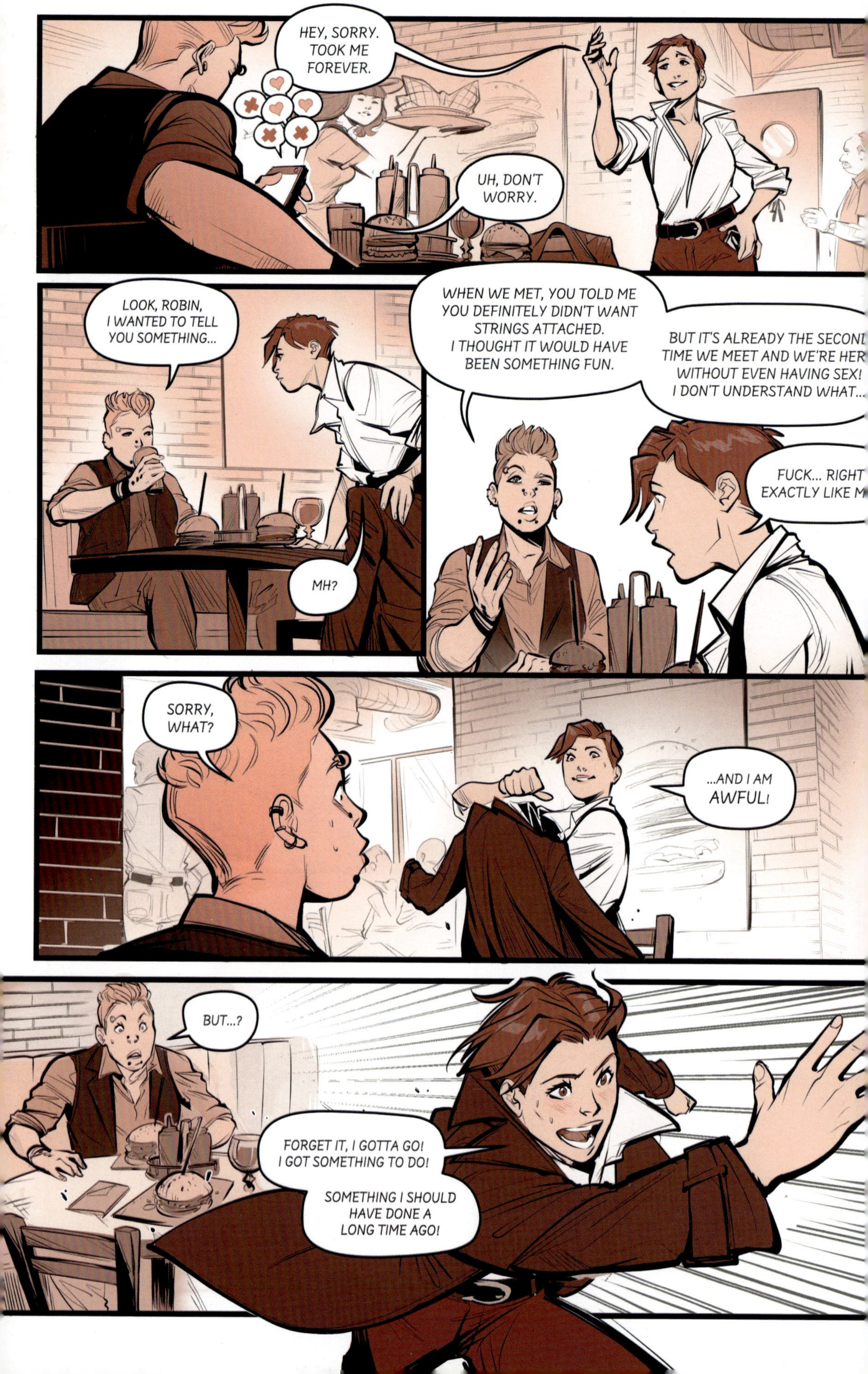
HEY, SORRY. TOOK ME FOREVER.
UH, DON'T WORRY.
LOOK, ROBIN, I WANTED TO TELL YOU SOMETHING...
MH?
WHEN WE MET, YOU TOLD ME YOU DEFINITELY DIDN'T WANT STRINGS ATTACHED. I THOUGHT IT WOULD HAVE BEEN SOMETHING FUN.
BUT IT'S ALREADY THE TIME WE MEET AND WE'RE WITHOUT EVEN HAVING SEX! I DON'T UNDERSTAND WHAT...
FUCK... RIGHT EXACTLY
SORRY, WHAT?
...AND I AM AWFUL!
BUT...?
FORGET IT, I GOTTA GO! I GOT SOMETHING TO DO!
SOMETHING I SHOULD HAVE DONE A LONG TIME AGO!

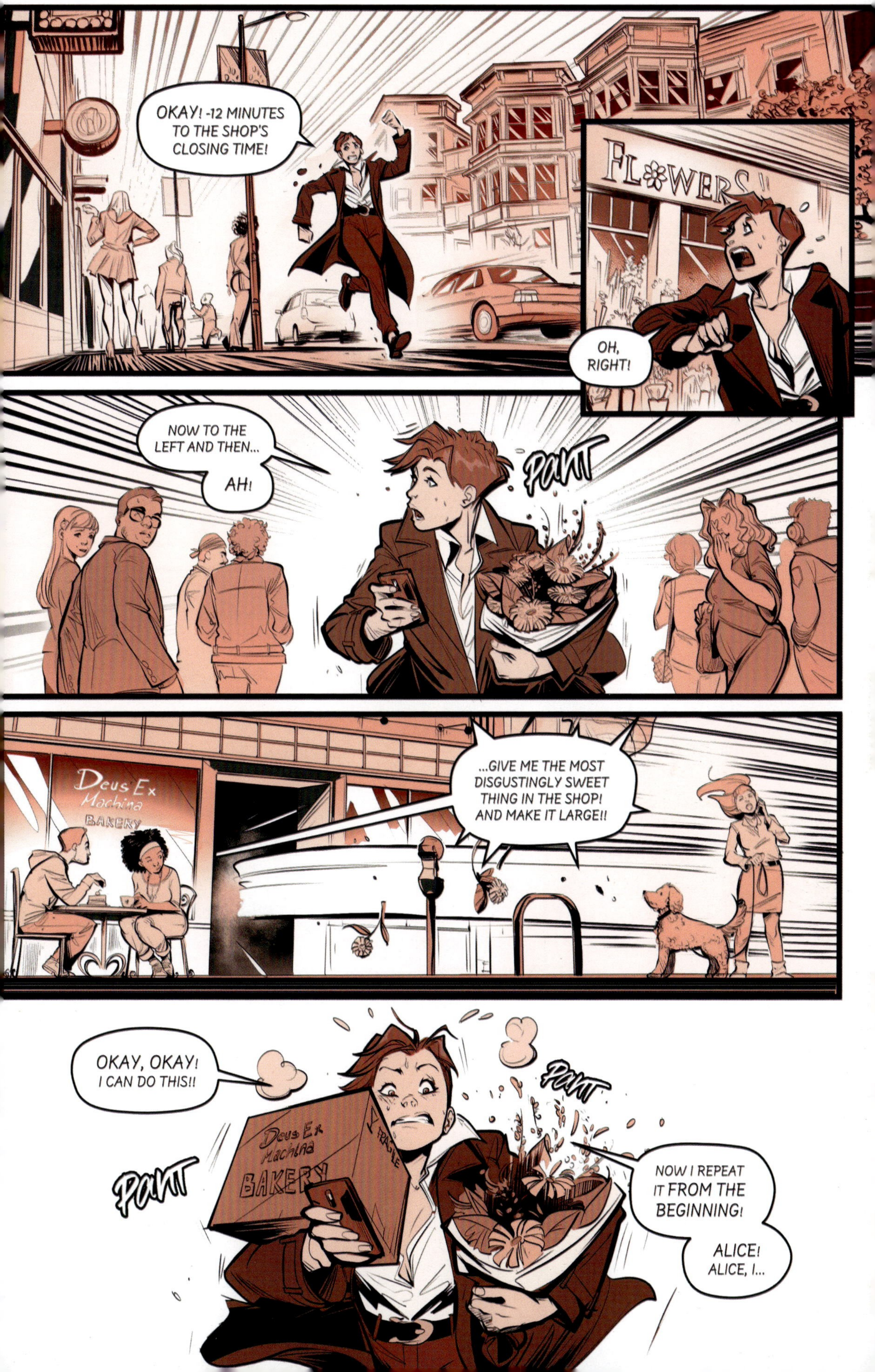
OKAY! -12 MINUTES TO THE SHOP'S CLOSING TIME!
FLOWERS
OH, RIGHT!
NOW TO THE LEFT AND THEN...
AH!
PANT
Deus Ex Machina BAKERY
...GIVE ME THE MOST DISGUSTINGLY SWEET THING IN THE SHOP! AND MAKE IT LARGE!!
OKAY, OKAY! I CAN DO THIS!!
PANT
Deus Ex Machina BAKERY
FRAGILE
PANT
NOW I REPEAT IT FROM THE BEGINNING!
ALICE! ALICE, I...

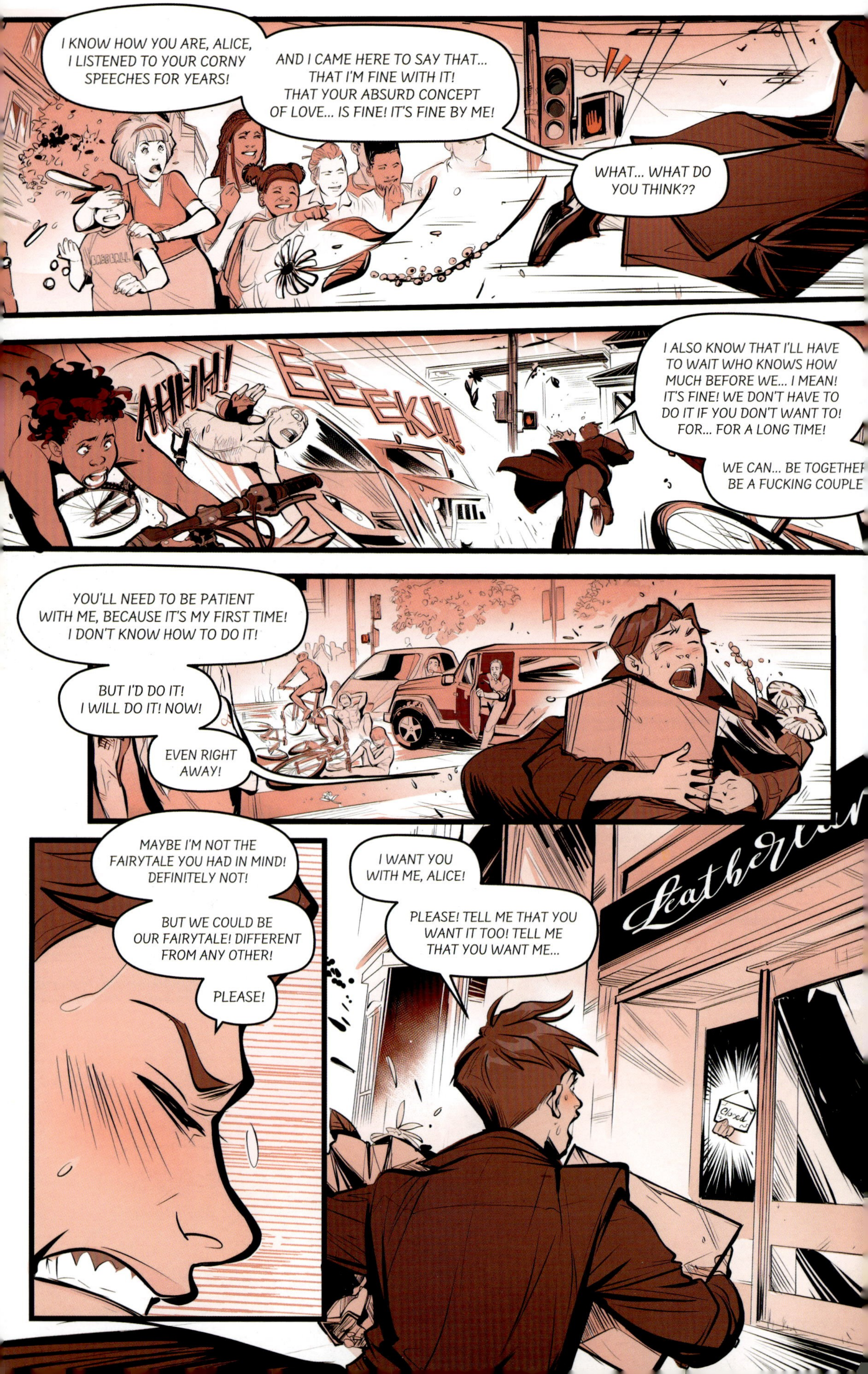
I KNOW HOW YOU ARE, ALICE, I LISTENED TO YOUR CORNY SPEECHES FOR YEARS!
AND I CAME HERE TO SAY THAT... THAT I'M FINE WITH IT! THAT YOUR ABSURD CONCEPT OF LOVE... IS FINE! IT'S FINE BY ME!
WHAT... WHAT DO YOU THINK??
AHHH!
EEEEK!!!
I ALSO KNOW THAT I'LL HAVE TO WAIT WHO KNOWS HOW MUCH BEFORE WE... I MEAN! IT'S FINE! WE DON'T HAVE TO DO IT IF YOU DON'T WANT TO! FOR... FOR A LONG TIME!
WE CAN... BE TOGETHER BE A FUCKING COUPLE
YOU'LL NEED TO BE PATIENT WITH ME, BECAUSE IT'S MY FIRST TIME! I DON'T KNOW HOW TO DO IT!
BUT I'D DO IT! I WILL DO IT! NOW!
EVEN RIGHT AWAY!
MAYBE I'M NOT THE FAIRYTALE YOU HAD IN MIND! DEFINITELY NOT!
BUT WE COULD BE OUR FAIRYTALE! DIFFERENT FROM ANY OTHER!
PLEASE!
I WANT YOU WITH ME, ALICE!
PLEASE! TELL ME THAT YOU WANT IT TOO! TELL ME THAT YOU WANT ME...
Closed

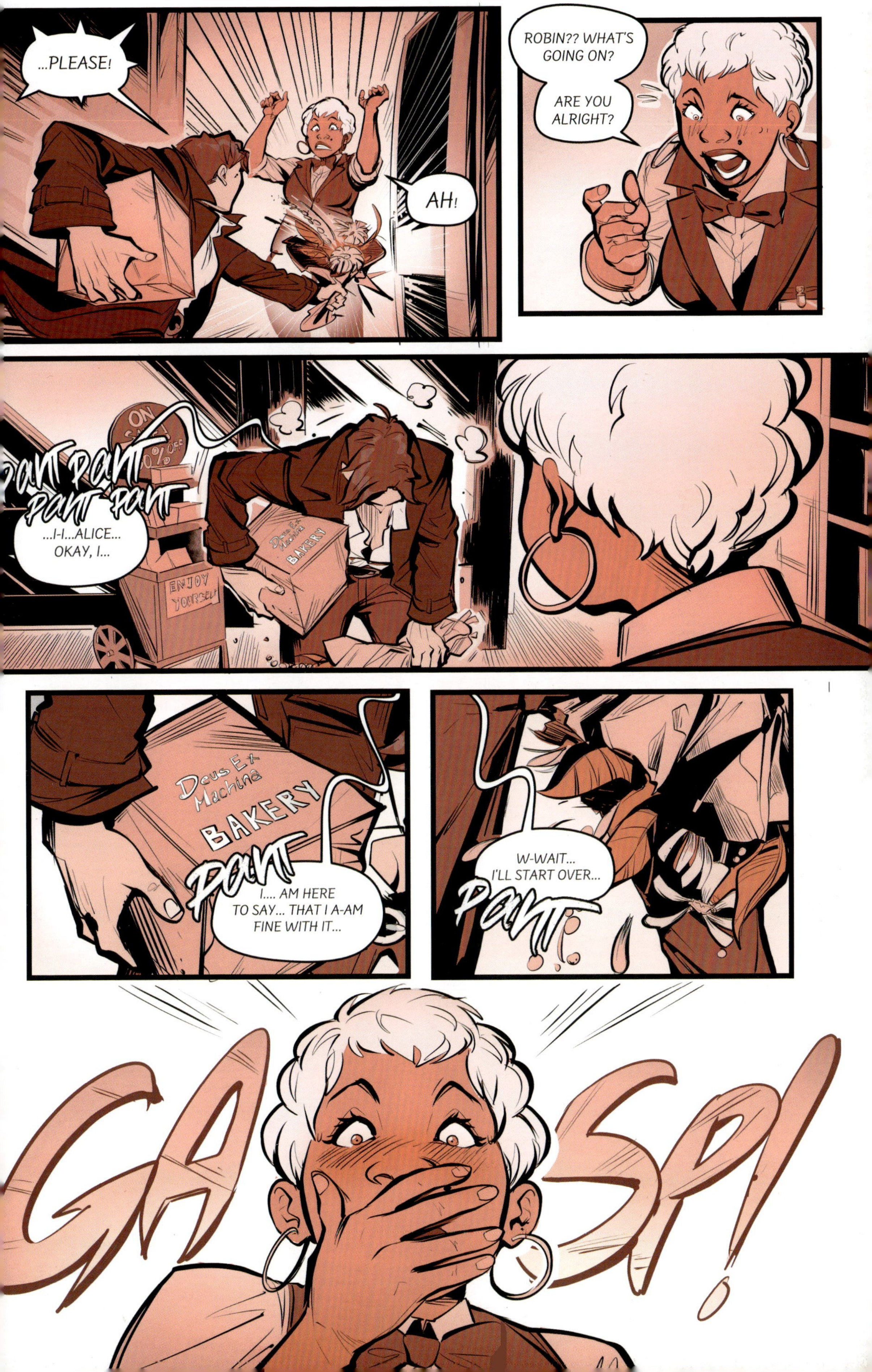
...PLEASE!
AH!
ROBIN?? WHAT'S GOING ON?
ARE YOU ALRIGHT?
ON SALE
ENJOY YOURSELF
PANT PANT PANT PANT
...I-I...ALICE... OKAY, I...
Deus Ex Machina BAKERY
Deus Ex Machina BAKERY
PANT
I.... AM HERE TO SAY... THAT I A-AM FINE WITH IT...
W-WAIT... I'LL START OVER...
PANT
GASP!

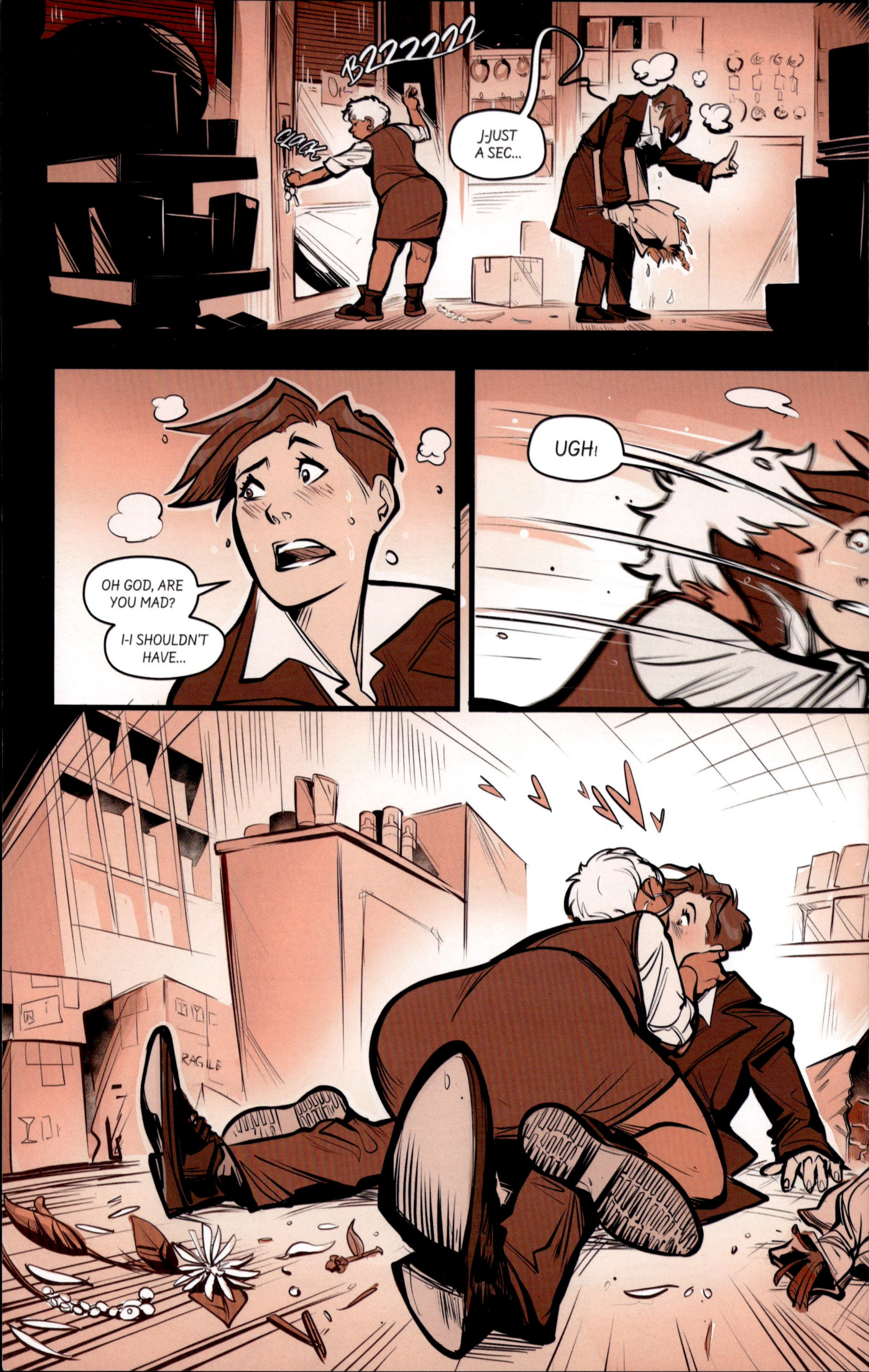
BZZZZZZ
CLACK
J-JUST A SEC...
OH GOD, ARE YOU MAD?
I-I SHOULDN'T HAVE...
UGH!
RAGILE

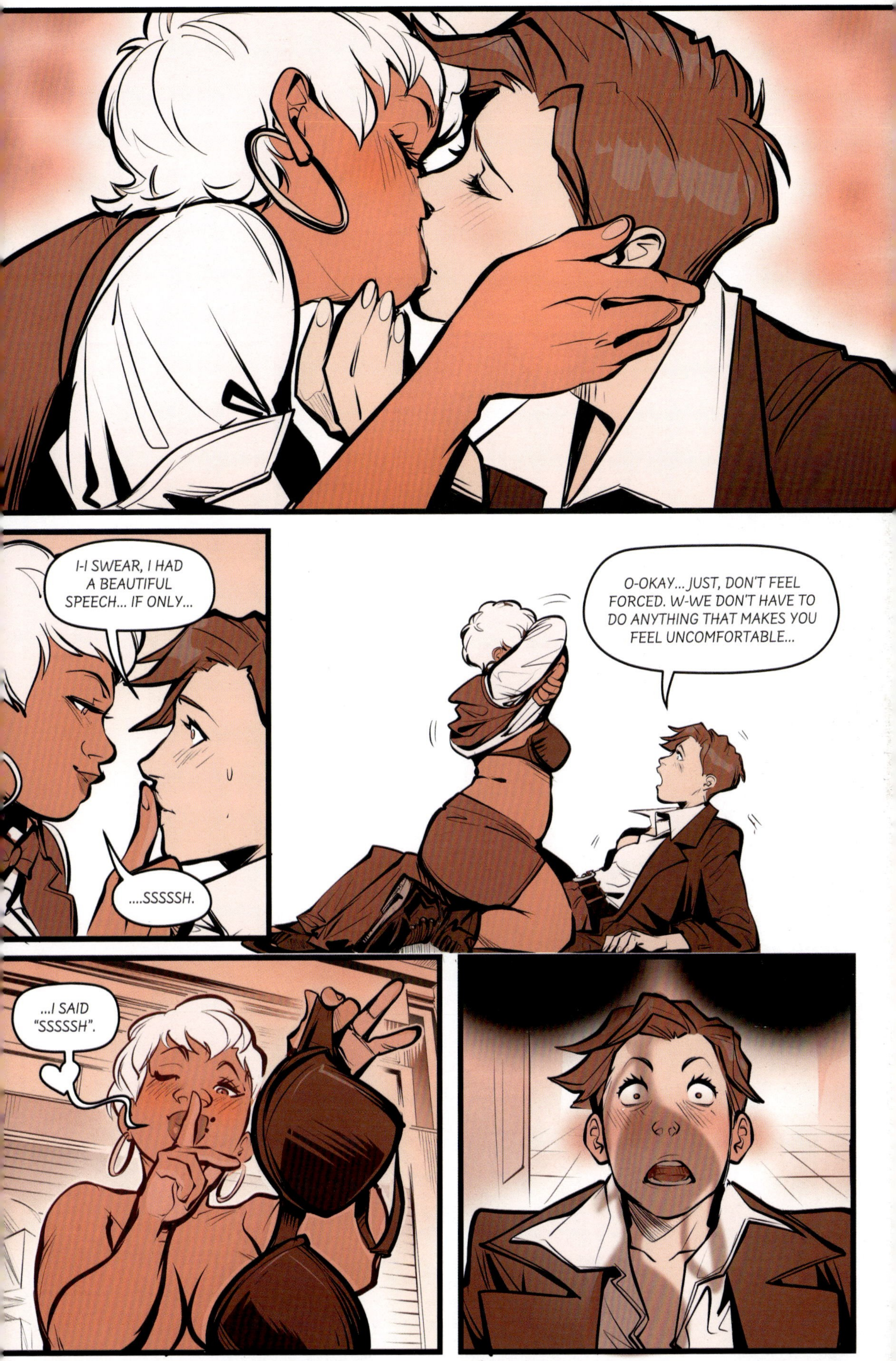
I-I SWEAR, I HAD A BEAUTIFUL SPEECH... IF ONLY...
....SSSSSH.
O-OKAY... JUST, DON'T FEEL FORCED. W-WE DON'T HAVE TO DO ANYTHING THAT MAKES YOU FEEL UNCOMFORTABLE...
...I SAID "SSSSSH".

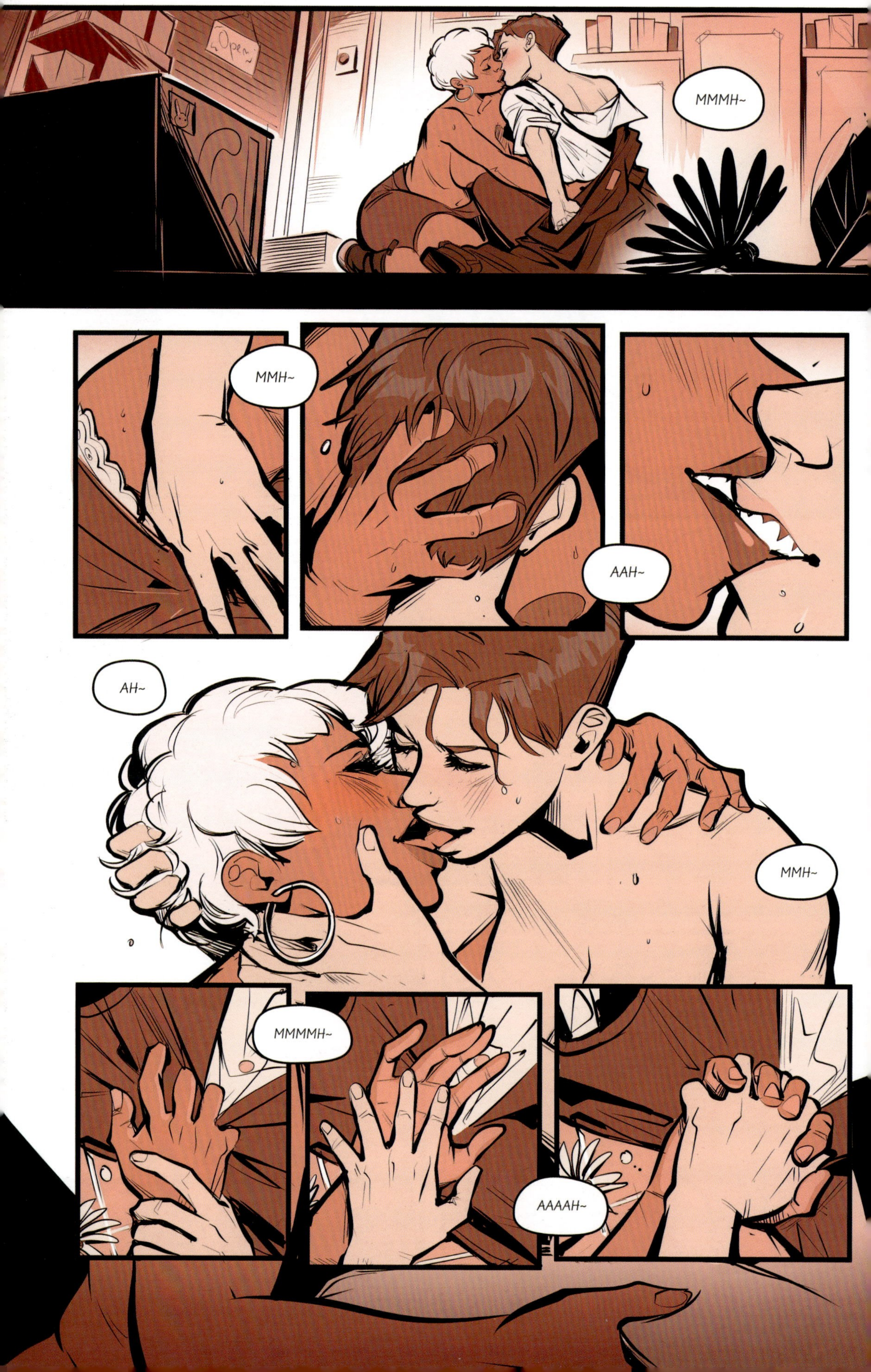
Open
MMMH~
MMH~
AAH~
AH~
MMH~
MMMMH~
AAAAH~

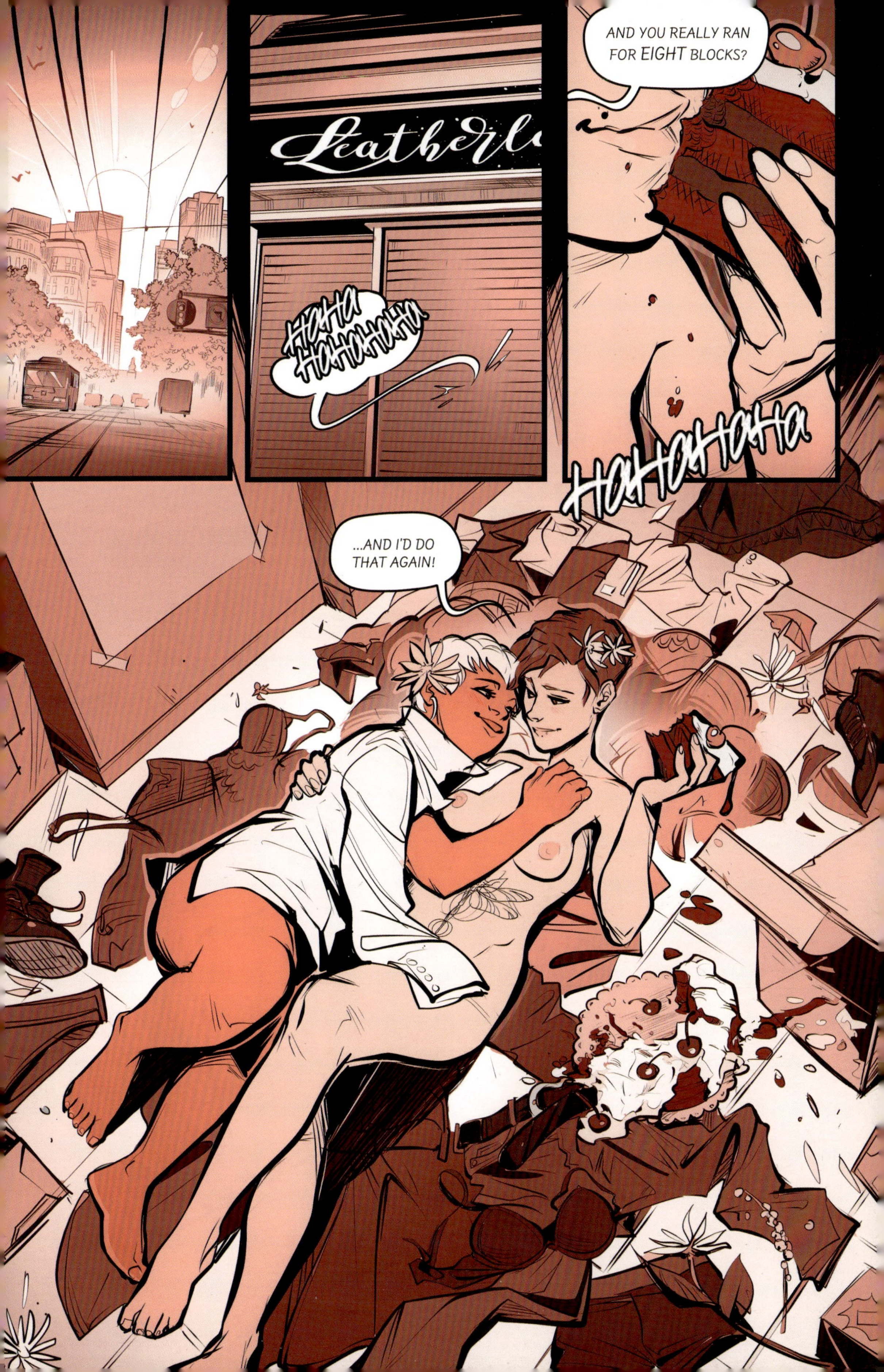

Haha Hahahaha
AND YOU REALLY RAN FOR EIGHT BLOCKS?
Hahahaha
...AND I'D DO THAT AGAIN!

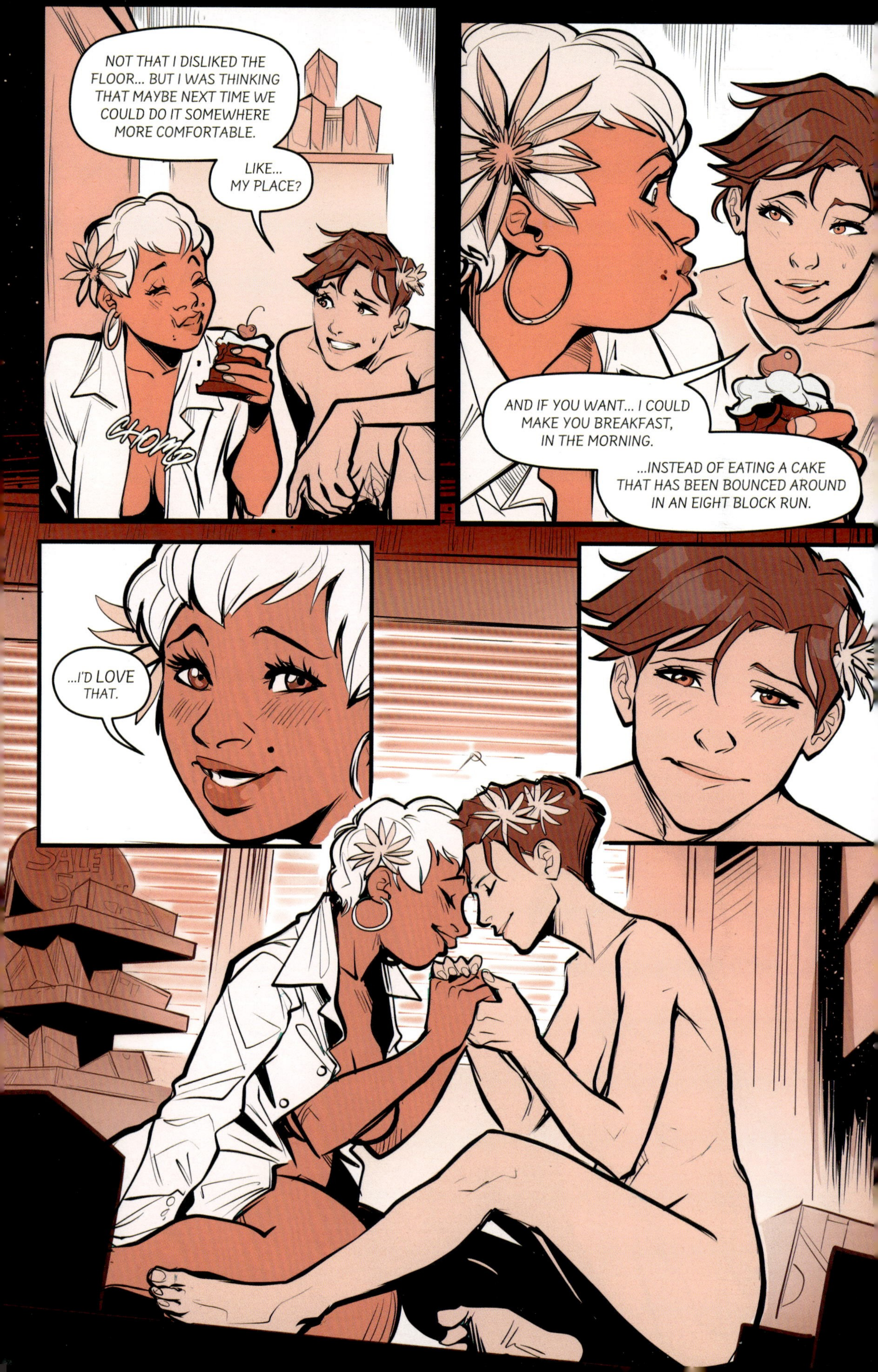
NOT THAT I DISLIKED THE FLOOR... BUT I WAS THINKING THAT MAYBE NEXT TIME WE COULD DO IT SOMEWHERE MORE COMFORTABLE.
LIKE... MY PLACE?
CHOMP
AND IF YOU WANT... I COULD MAKE YOU BREAKFAST, IN THE MORNING.
...INSTEAD OF EATING A CAKE THAT HAS BEEN BOUNCED AROUND IN AN EIGHT BLOCK RUN.
...I'D LOVE THAT.

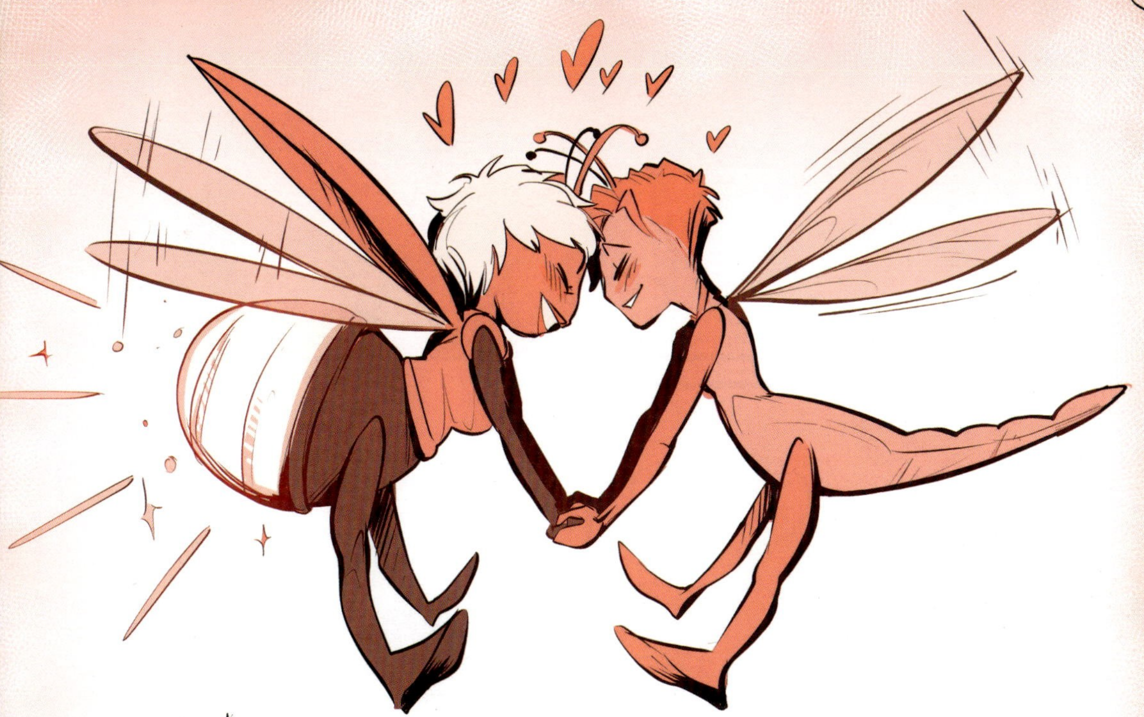

And our firefly discovered that shining again
was easy and so natural that she was astonished.
That there was nothing wrong with her,
she just had to listen to herself more and be able to let go.
She just needed to slowly go back to trusting.
And, obviously, to chase the stars. Not alone anymore, though.

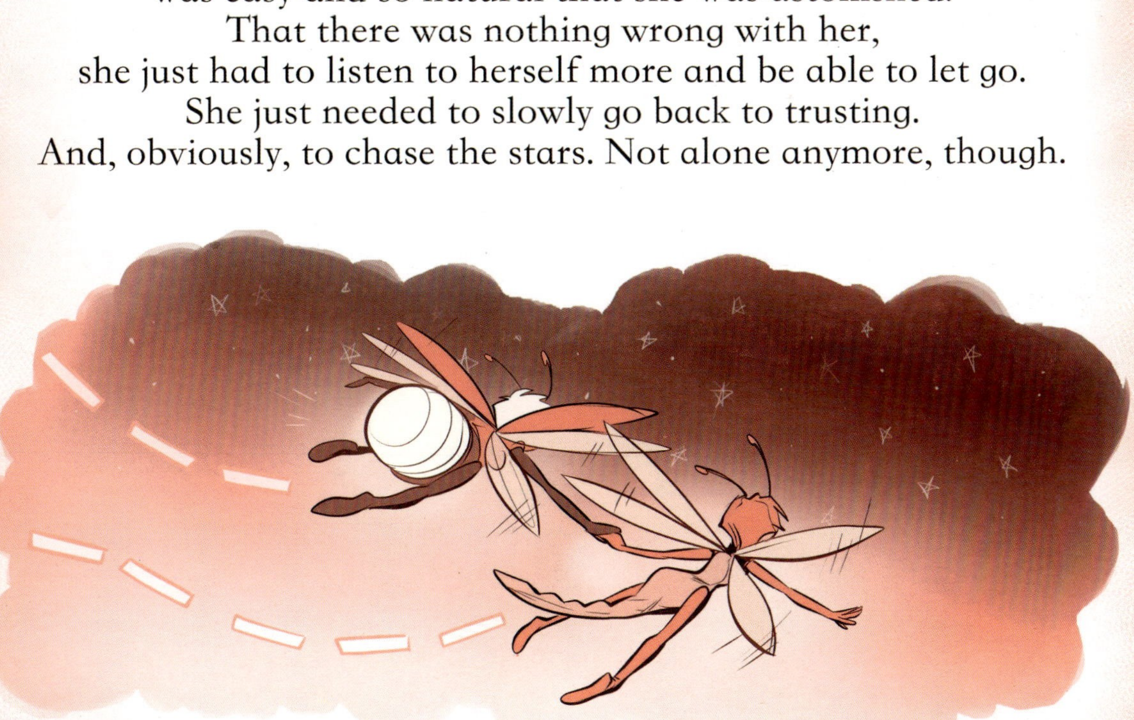

And they lived happily ever after.

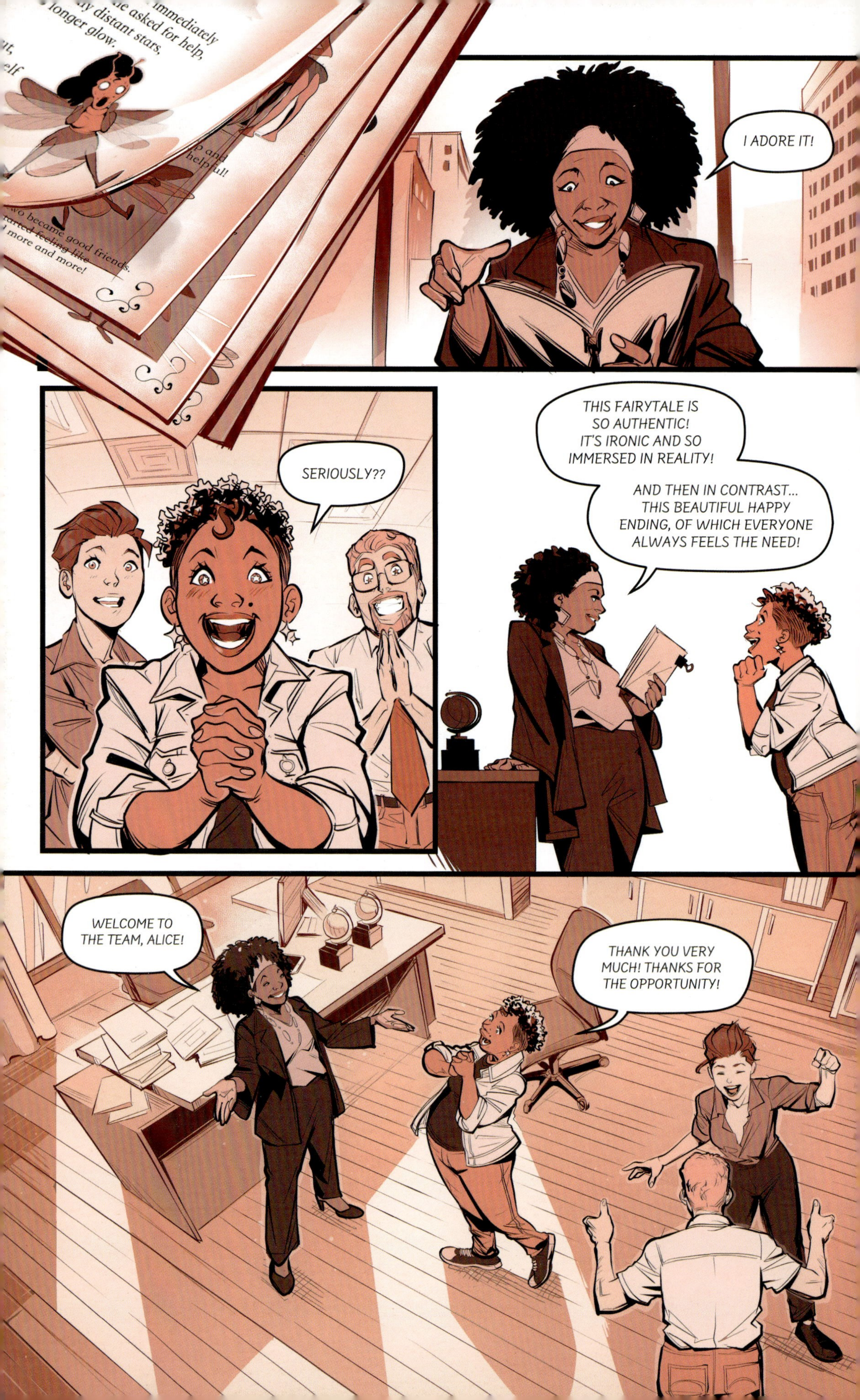
I ADORE IT!
SERIOUSLY??
THIS FAIRYTALE IS SO AUTHENTIC! IT'S IRONIC AND SO IMMERSED IN REALITY!
AND THEN IN CONTRAST... THIS BEAUTIFUL HAPPY ENDING, OF WHICH EVERYONE ALWAYS FEELS THE NEED!
WELCOME TO THE TEAM, ALICE!
THANK YOU VERY MUCH! THANKS FOR THE OPPORTUNITY!

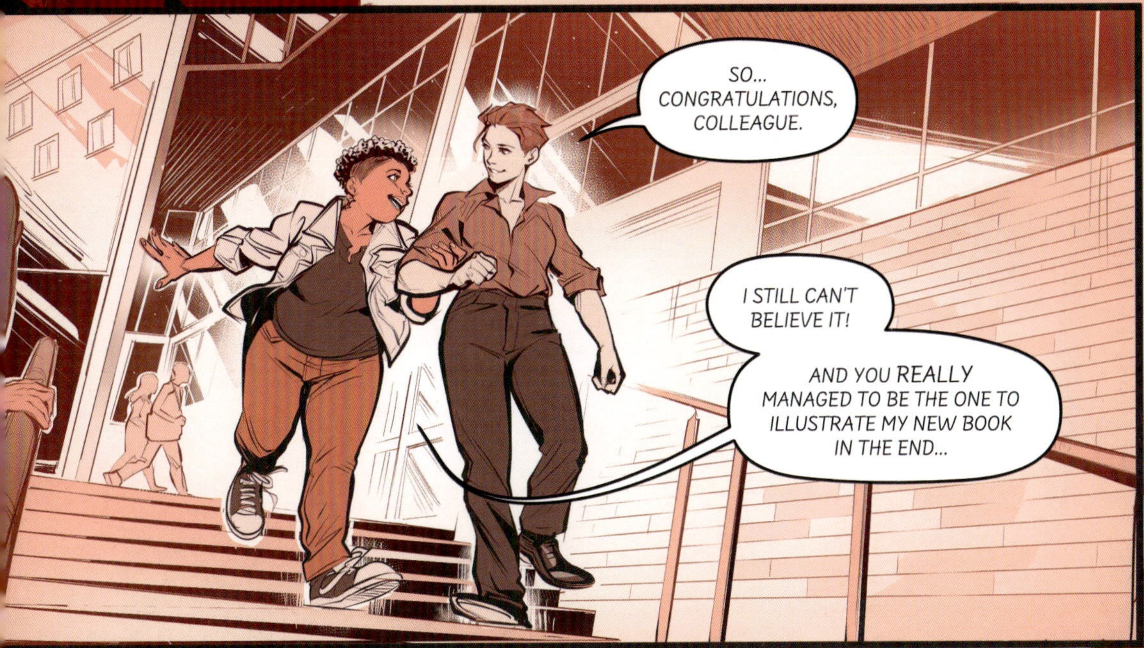
SO... CONGRATULATIONS, COLLEAGUE.
I STILL CAN'T BELIEVE IT!
AND YOU REALLY MANAGED TO BE THE ONE TO ILLUSTRATE MY NEW BOOK IN THE END...

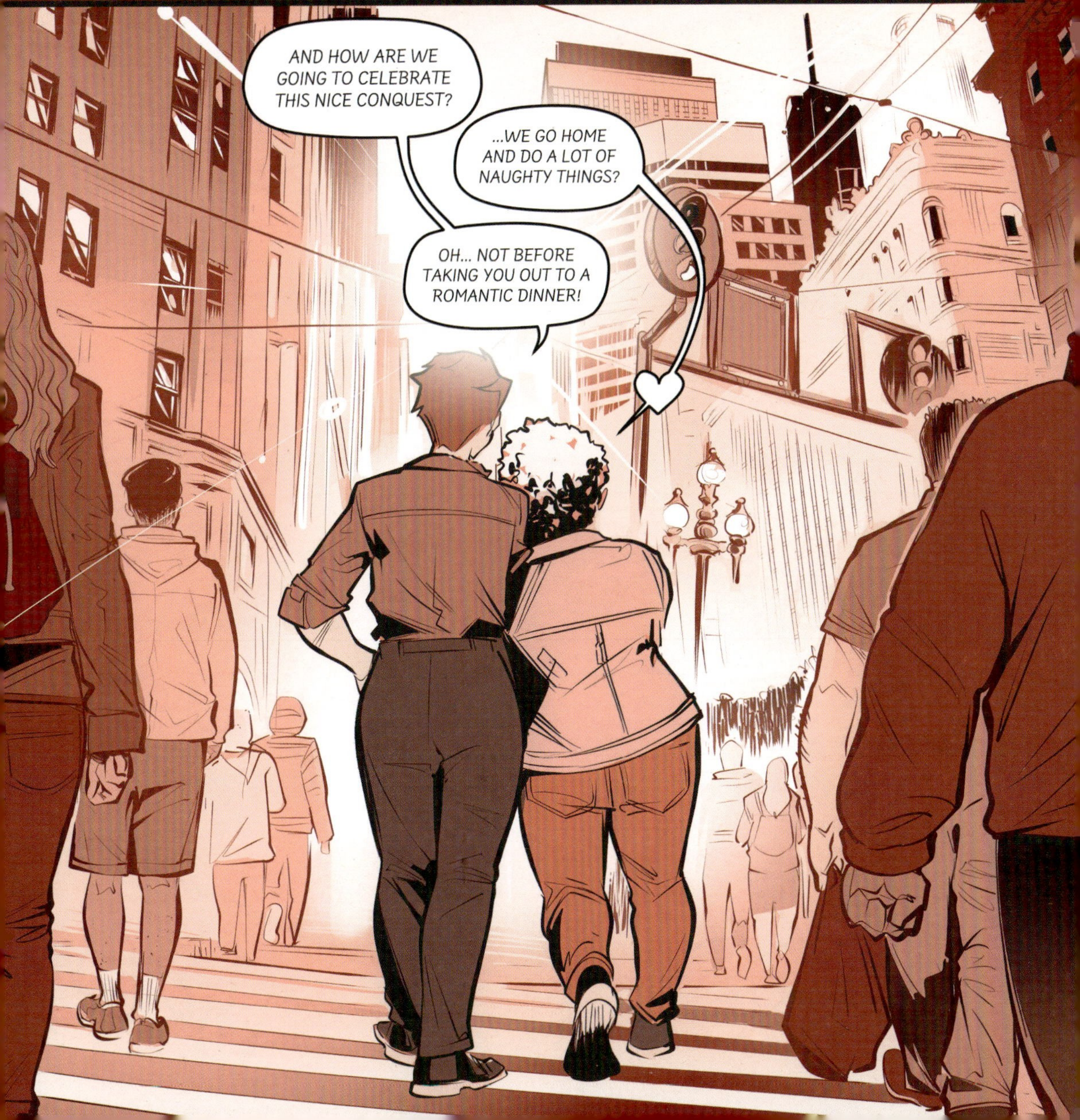
AND HOW ARE WE GOING TO CELEBRATE THIS NICE CONQUEST?
OH... NOT BEFORE TAKING YOU OUT TO A ROMANTIC DINNER!
...WE GO HOME AND DO A LOT OF NAUGHTY THINGS?

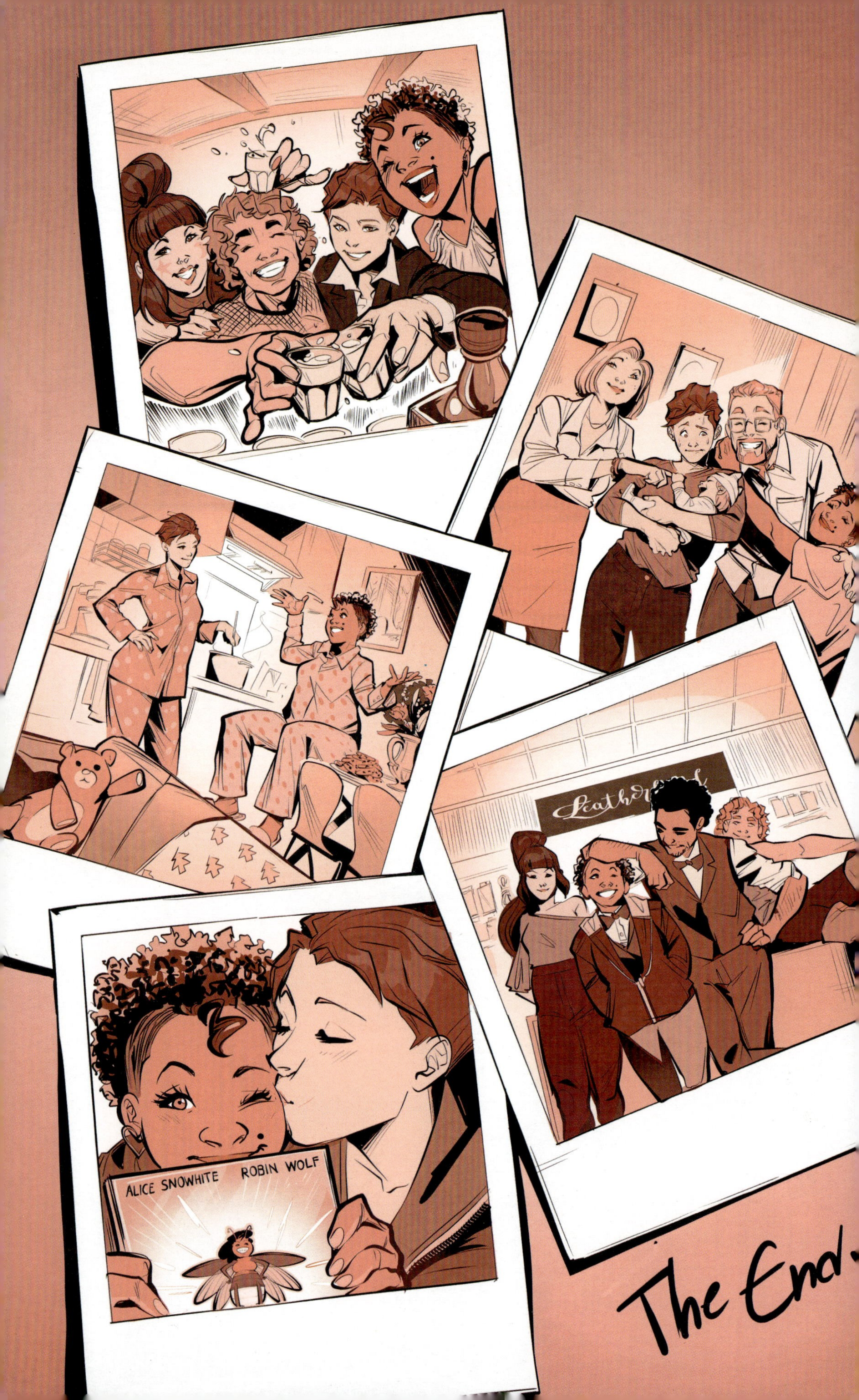
ALICE SNOWHITE
ROBIN WOLF
The End.

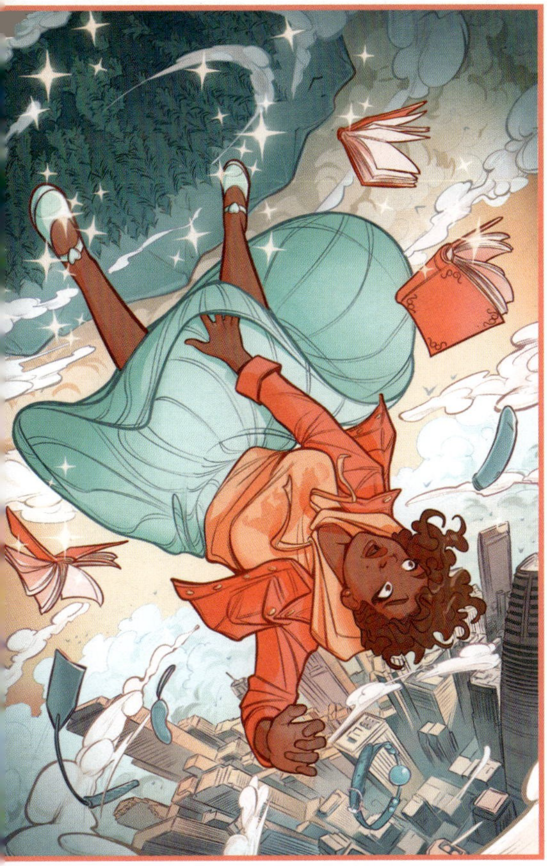

Issue 1 • cover B
Jolanda Zanfardino

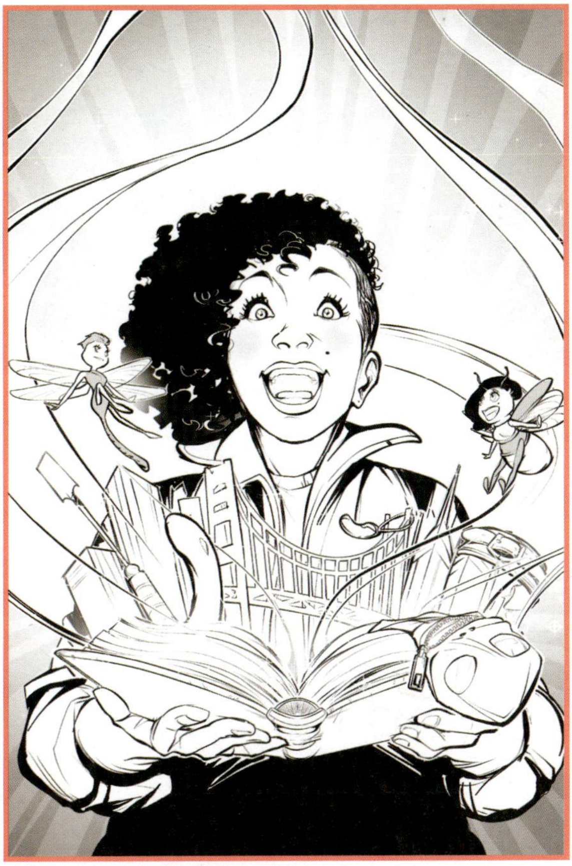

Issue 1 • cover C

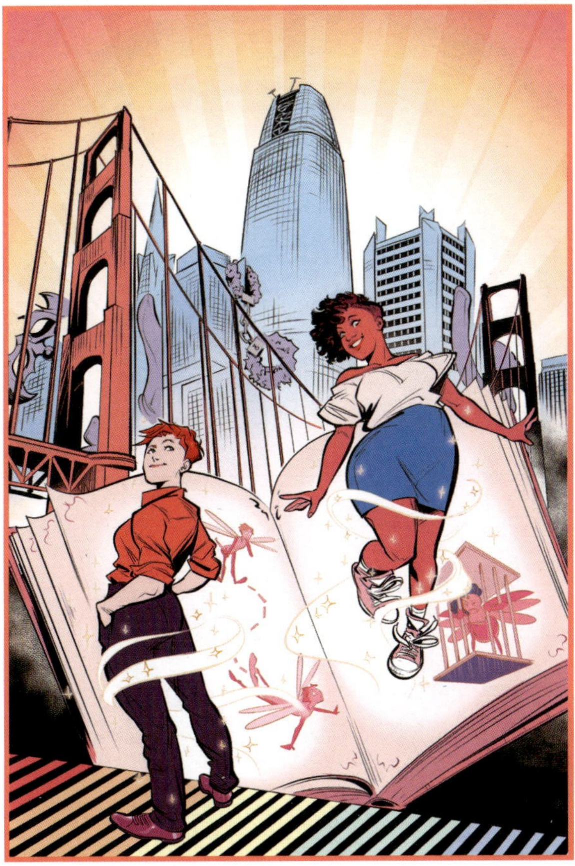

Issue 1 • Second Print

Alice Snowhite

Character sheet

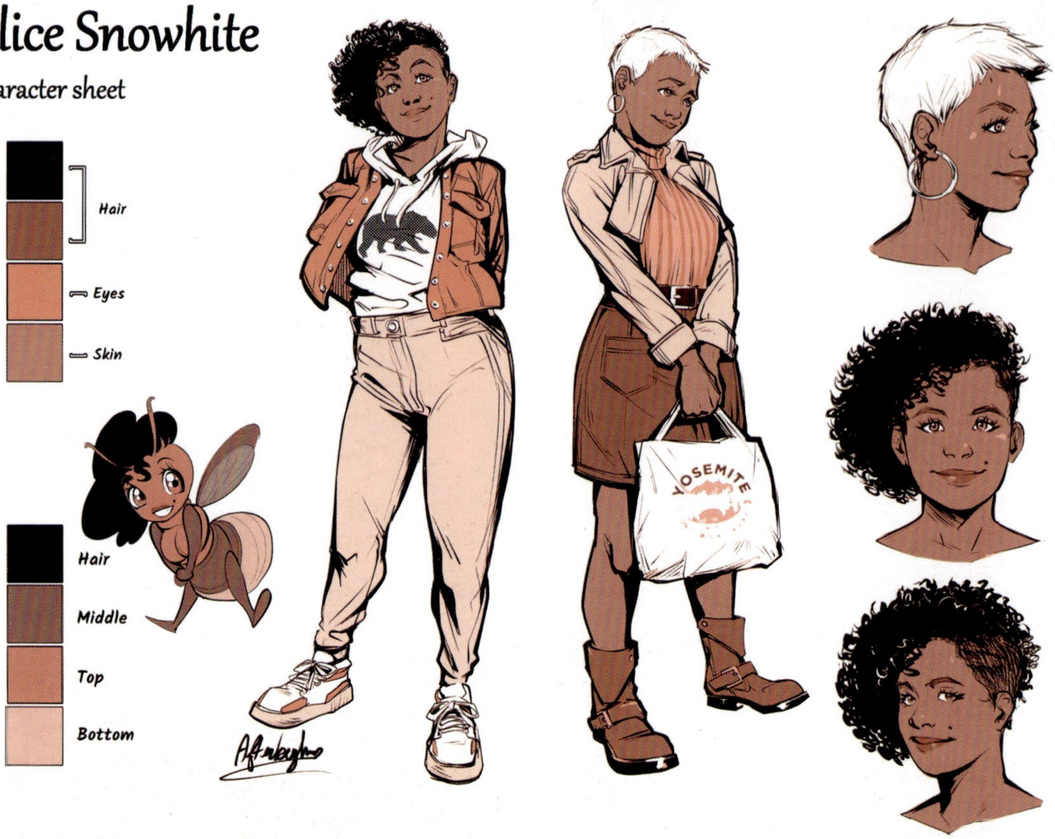
Hair
Eyes
Skin
Hair
Middle
Top
Bottom
YOSEMITE

Robin Wolf

Character sheet

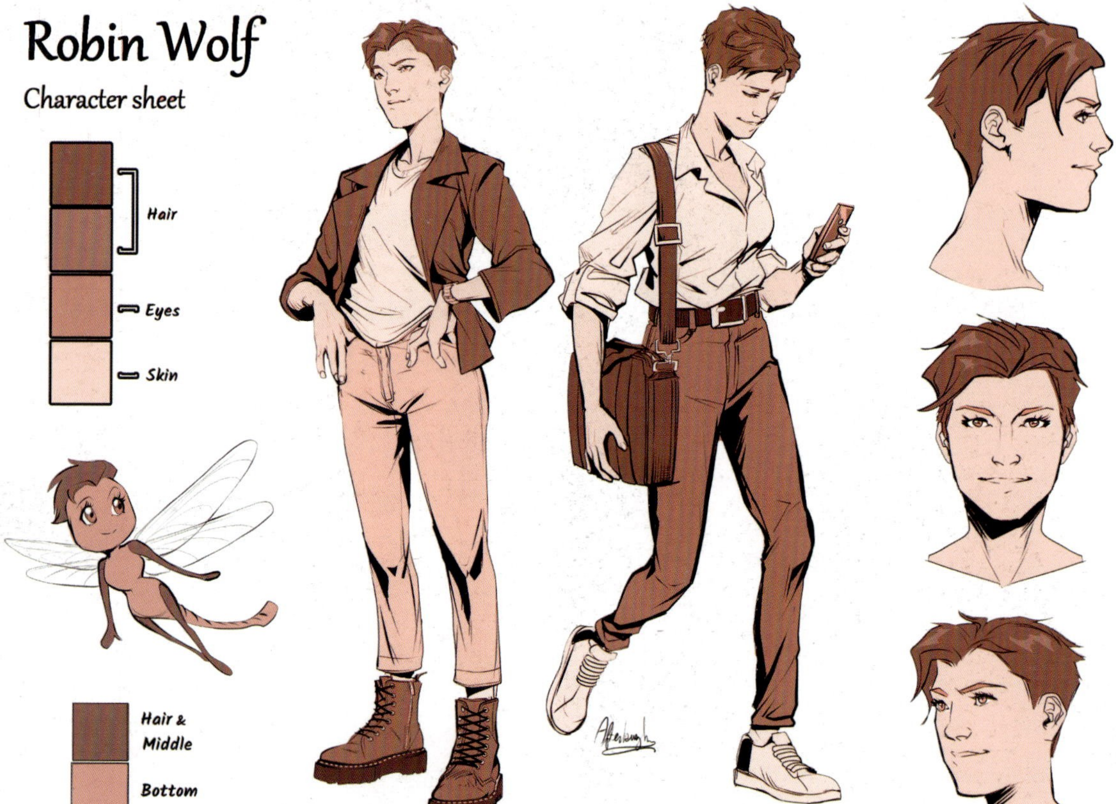
Hair
Eyes
Skin
Hair & Middle
Bottom